In the Garden of Evil . . .

Mr. Moffett was smiling faintly as he walked to the front door, fishing in his pocket for his keys. He'd dosed his beds with a hormonal additive he'd ordered from Dresden, *Azetelia Ziehenstoff*. Perhaps he'd been a little excessive with the statice.

He inserted the key in the lock. "Betsy, are you home?" he called.

The rosebushes trained up the pillars to either side rustled. They gripped his shoulders from behind.

Mr. Moffett shouted. For a moment he thought his daughter was playing a joke. He looked around. The bush to his left extended a tendril toward his elbow. The spray of fresh leaves on the end exaggerated the movement like the popper tip of a bullwhip.

"Hey!"

The main stems were ⸺⸺⸺⸺⸺⸺⸺ layers of cloth and the ⸺⸺⸺⸺⸺⸺⸺⸺⸺⸺ on the tendril prick⸺⸺⸺⸺⸺⸺⸺⸺⸺ arm.

Holding h⸺⸺⸺⸺⸺⸺

The front d⸺⸺⸺⸺⸺⸺⸺⸺⸺⸺⸺ himself toward it, but ⸺⸺⸺⸺⸺⸺⸺⸺⸺⸺ his back. Another tendri⸺⸺⸺⸺⸺⸺ neck. He wriggled out of his coat, all b⸺⸺⸺⸺ arm, and then tore himself free of that also. The lining pulled from his sleeve. There were streaks of blood on his polyester-blend shirt. He fell on the living room floor.

The suitcoat writhed in the air behind him as the roses continued to explore the fabric.

Mr. Moffett was breathing hard. A rose tendril waggled interrogatively toward the doorway. Mr. Moffett kicked the door shut violently.

The living room seemed dark. He looked around to be sure the bank of growlights in the ceiling was turned on. It was, but the datura in the central planter had more than doubled in height since he left in the morning. The dark, bluish-green leaves now wrapped the fixture, permitting only a slaty remnant of the light to wash the room.

—from *"Cannibal Plants from Heck"*
by David Drake

In the Garden of Evil . . .

DANGEROUS

Created By
KEITH LAUMER

VEGETABLES

DANGEROUS VEGETABLES

This is a work of fiction. All the characters and events portrayed in this book are fictional, and any resemblance to real people or incidents is purely coincidental.

A Baen Books Original

Baen Publishing Enterprises
P.O. Box 1403
Riverdale, NY 10471

ISBN: 0-671-57781-6

Cover art by Bob Eggleton

First printing, December 1998

Distributed by Simon & Schuster
1230 Avenue of the Americas
New York, NY 10020

Typeset by Windhaven Press, Auburn, NH
Printed in the United States of America

Contents

CREDITS

Introduction:
Mostly About Keith Laumer

Ben Bova

Those who know of Keith Laumer only from his fiction, or from the admittedly terrible reputation he acquired in the last years of his life, may find it odd to see his name associated with *Dangerous Vegetables*, a title that seems whimsical, perhaps even absurd.

Ah, but you don't know the Keith Laumer that I knew. He had a wicked sense of humor, and delighted in puncturing people's balloons. If you hear a faint ring of Harlan Ellison's *Dangerous Visions* in the title of this marvelous anthology, you hear correctly.

There must be an ancient Chinese proverb that says the more dissimilar two people are, the more alike they are. If there wasn't, there is now. You couldn't picture two men less alike physically or in living style than Harlan and Keith. Harlan is neither tall nor handsome in the Hollywood sense, but he's as intense as a nuclear reactor. Keith looked like an Air Force captain (which he had been) even when he was wearing jeans and a tee shirt. He could have played the lead in any movie about test pilots, but his style was understated, his humor dry rather than pungent.

As Robert Culp once said of Harlan, so could it have been said of Keith: having him for a friend was a test of one's adulthood. Keith was my friend; Harlan still is.

1

And, strangely, Keith and Harlan were friends with each other, but it was like the friendship between Wyatt Earp and Doc Holliday, built on mutual respect and admiration for each other's talents rather than on softer sentiments.

Hence Keith's sly little play on Harlan's title. I can see the grin on his chiselled features as the thought first occurred to him.

Although Keith died while this anthology was still a-borning, Charles Waugh and the indefatigable Martin Greenberg have taken that original idea and turned it into this remarkable collection of science-fiction and fantasy stories. Many of the stories in this book are honored and treasured classics by some of the most revered writers in the field. My personal favorite is Carol Carr's, "Look, You Think You've Got Troubles," with its perfect last line. And new stories are here, also, written especially for this anthology; they will take their places in the field's roll of honor, too.

Keith Laumer died in his Brooksville, Florida, home during the night of 22–23 January 1993, apparently of a stroke suffered while he was asleep. He would have been 68 the following June.

Best-known as the author of the Retief stories and other hard-edged action novels, Keith's work combined tough male characters and sharp social commentary. He was a pretty tough male character, himself, and not averse to dishing out sharp criticisms.

He had been half-crippled by a massive stroke since 1970. I was there when it happened. Keith had invited me to visit him in Brooksville. I flew down from Boston and Keith met me at the Tampa airport, with Gay Haldeman. While he was driving off the airport parking lot he slumped over. We got him to the area VA hospital, where doctors told Gay, Joe Haldeman, and me not to expect him to last the night.

As he was being wheeled into the intensive care ward, his whole left side paralyzed, Keith looked up at me and muttered out of the half of his mouth that was still working, "Make a good chapter in a novel, wouldn't it?" He was a professional writer above everything else, and as stalwart as they come. He not only lived through that harrowing night, he fought back and survived for twenty-two years. And continued to write, despite the growing debilitation of his body.

I first met Keith at one of the Milford Writers' Workshops, back in the 1960s when they were held in the home of Damon Knight and Kate Wilhelm, in Milford, Pennsylvania. A former Air Force captain, Keith immediately came across as a no-nonsense kind of guy, a sturdy good friend with a quiet but very pointed sense of humor. He did not suffer fools gladly. Or at all.

Keith had spent several years in the State Department as a Foreign Service Officer, and this gave him the background for his best-known character, Jame Retief, a broad-shouldered, keen-minded diplomat who is not above using trickery and his two fists to settle problems that have the more conventional diplomats helplessly tied in knots—usually of their own making.

He was an utterly professional writer, the kind who could sit down and write a short story over a weekend specifically aimed at a particular editor. And sell it to that editor. He was a good and loyal friend. The best afternoon I ever spent in my life was once at Milford when Keith, Ted Thomas, Gordy Dickson and I played hooky from the workshop and passed the hours in a local bar, drinking beer and talking. Don't ask me what we talked about; I just remember those hours as golden.

Being the kind of person he was, Keith did not allow his nearly-killing stroke to stop him. For twenty-two years he worked to bring back his physical strength. He was a proud man, and pretty testy even before that calamity hit him. Locked inside a body that had failed him, unable to accept what fate had done to him, in constant pain, Keith became ever more difficult a personality. He literally drove his friends away from him, and he could be a terror in a restaurant over the slightest of reasons.

The last time I saw him was 8 November 1992, my birthday. We met at a Greek restaurant in Tarpon Springs, together with my wife Barbara and fellow writer Rick Wilber.

It took Keith more than five minutes to work his way out of his Cougar. (He had a collection of more than 60 Cougars, which he was painstakingly refinishing. With one good hand.) But once on his feet, albeit leaning heavily on a cane, he flashed that heroic grin that I had known for more than a quarter-century and said:

"I died twenty-two years ago, but I'm still here and I'm going to beat this thing."

In the end, it beat him. It always does. But like the strong, capable men he wrote about, Keith went down fighting to the very last.

So here is the final product of his wit and talent, an anthology of stories that range from the macabre to the hilarious, the kind of stories that Keith himself enjoyed to read. You will enjoy them too, I know.

Ben Bova
Naples, Florida

Ray Bradbury's early tales of fantasy and horror, most of which were collected in Dark Carnival *and* The October Country, *have been endlessly reprinted and are considered milestones in twentieth century American literature. With the publication of* The Martian Chronicles, *his classic compilation of vignettes about man's colonization of Mars, and his futuristic dystopia* Fahrenheit 451, *he became one of the first science fiction writers to cross over from the pulp magazines into the literary mainstream. His novels* Dandelion Wine, Something Wicked This Way Comes, Death is a Lonely Business, A Graveyard for Lunatics, *and* Green Shadows, White Whale, *are lyrical evocations of his experiences as a young writer, laced with elements of fantasy and mystery. His many story collections include* The Illustrated Man, The Golden Apples of the Sun, *and most recently* Quicker Than the Eye *and* Driving Blind.

Boys! Raise Giant Mushrooms in *Your* Cellar!

Ray Bradbury

Hugh Fortnum woke to Saturday's commotions and lay, eyes shut, savoring each in its turn.

Below, bacon in a skillet; Cynthia waking him with fine cookings instead of cries.

Across the hall, Tom actually taking a shower.

Far off in the bumblebee dragonfly light, whose voice was already damning the weather, the time, and

the tides? Mrs. Goodbody? Yes. That Christian giant-
ess, six foot tall with her shoes off, the gardener
extraordinary, the octogenarian dietitian and town
philosopher.

He rose, unhooked the screen and leaned out to hear
her cry, "There! Take *that! This'll* fix you! Hah!"

"Happy Saturday, Mrs. Goodbody!"

The old woman froze in clouds of bug spray pumped
from an immense gun.

"Nonsense!" she shouted. "With these fiends and pests
to watch for?"

"What kind *this* time?" called Fortnum.

"I don't want to shout it to the jaybirds, but"—she
glanced suspiciously around—"what would you say if I
told you I was the first line of defense concerning flying saucers?"

"Fine," replied Fortnum. "There'll be rockets between
the worlds any year now."

"There already *are!*" She pumped, aiming the spray
under the hedge. "There! Take that!"

He pulled his head back in from the fresh day,
somehow not as high-spirited as his first response had
indicated. Poor soul, Mrs. Goodbody. Always the essence
of reason. And now what? Old age?

The doorbell rang.

He grabbed his robe and was half down the stairs
when he heard a voice say, "Special delivery. Fortnum?"
and saw Cynthia turn from the front door, a small packet
in her hand.

"Special-delivery airmail for your son."

Tom was downstairs like a centipede.

"Wow! That must be from the Great Bayou Novelty
Greenhouse!"

"I wish I were as excited about ordinary mail,"
observed Fortnum.

"Ordinary!" Tom ripped the cord and paper wildly.
"Don't you read the back pages of *Popular Mechanics*?
Well, here they are!"

Everyone peered into the small open box.

"Here," said Fortnum, "what are?"

"The Sylvan Glade Jumbo-Giant Guaranteed Growth Raise-Them-in-Your-Cellar-for-Big-Profit Mushrooms!"

"Oh, of course," said Fortnum. "How silly of me."

Cynthia squinted. "Those little teeny bits?"

" 'Fabulous growth in twenty-four hours,' " Tom quoted from memory. " 'Plant them in your cellar . . .' "

Fortnum and wife exchanged glances.

"Well," she admitted, "It's better than frogs and green snakes."

"Sure is!" Tom ran.

"Oh, Tom," said Fortnum lightly.

Tom paused at the cellar door.

"Tom," said his father. "Next time, fourth-class mail would do fine."

"Heck," said Tom. "They must've made a mistake, thought I was some rich company. Airmail special, who can afford that?"

The cellar door slammed.

Fortnum, bemused, scanned the wrapper a moment then dropped it into the wastebasket. On his way to the kitchen, he opened the cellar door.

Tom was already on his knees, digging with a hand rake in the dirt.

He felt his wife beside him, breathing softly, looking down into the cool dimness.

"Those *are* mushrooms, I hope. Not . . . toadstools?"

Fortnum laughed. "Happy harvest, farmer!"

Tom glanced up and waved.

Fortnum shut the door, took his wife's arm and walked her out to the kitchen, feeling fine.

Toward noon, Fortnum was driving toward the nearest market when he saw Roger Willis, a fellow Rotarian and a teacher of biology at the town high school, waving urgently from the sidewalk.

Fortnum pulled his car up and opened the door.

"Hi, Roger, give you a lift?"

Willis responded all too eagerly, jumping in and slamming the door.

"Just the man I want to see. I've put off calling for days. Could you play psychiatrist for five minutes, God help you?"

Fortnum examined his friend for a moment as he drove quietly on.

"God help you, yes. Shoot."

Willis sat back and studied his fingernails. "Let's just drive a moment. There. Okay. Here's what I want to say: Something's wrong with the world."

Fortnum laughed easily. "Hasn't there always been?"

"No, no, I mean . . . something strange—something unseen—is happening."

"Mrs. Goodbody," said Fortnum, half to himself, and stopped.

"Mrs. Goodbody?"

"This morning, gave me a talk on flying saucers."

"No." Willis bit the knuckle of his forefinger nervously. "Nothing like saucers. At least, I don't think. Tell me, what exactly is intuition?"

"The conscious recognition of something that's been subconscious for a long time. But don't quote this amateur psychologist!" He laughed again.

"Good, good!" Willis turned, his face lighting. He readjusted himself in the seat. "That's it! Over a long period, things gather, right? All of a sudden, you have to spit, but you don't remember saliva collecting. Your hands are dirty, but you don't know how they got that way. Dust falls on you everyday and you don't feel it. But when you get enough dust collected up, there it is, you see and name it. That's intuition, as far as I'm concerned. Well, what kind of dust has been falling on me? A few meteors in the sky at night? Funny weather just before dawn? I don't know. Certain colors, smells, the way the house creaks at three in the morning? I don't know. Hair prickling on my arms? All I know is, the damn dust has collected. Quite suddenly I know."

"Yes," said Fortnum, disquieted. "But what is it you know?"

Willis looked at his hands in his lap. "I'm afraid. I'm not afraid. Then I'm afraid again, in the middle of the day. Doctor's checked me. I'm A-one. No family problems. Joe's a fine boy, a good son. Dorothy? She's remarkable. With her I'm not afraid of growing old or dying."

"Lucky man."

"But beyond my luck now. Scared stiff, really, for myself, my family; even right now, for you."

"Me?" said Fortnum.

They had stopped now by an empty lot near the market. There was a moment of great stillness, in which Fortnum turned to survey his friend. Willis' voice had suddenly made him cold.

"I'm afraid for everybody," said Willis. "Your friends, mine, and their friends, on out of sight. Pretty silly, eh?"

Willis opened the door, got out and peered in at Fortnum.

Fortnum felt he had to speak. "Well, what do we do about it?"

Willis looked up at the sun burning blind in the sky. "Be aware," he said slowly. "Watch everything for a few days."

"Everything?"

"We don't use half what God gave us, ten per cent of the time. We ought to hear more, feel more, smell more, taste more. Maybe there's something wrong with the way the wind blows these weeds there in the lot. Maybe it's the sun up on those telephone wires or the cicadas singing in the elm trees. If only we could stop, look, listen, a few days, a few nights, and compare notes. Tell me to shut up then, and I will."

"Good enough," said Fortnum, playing it lighter than he felt. "I'll look around. But how do I know the thing I'm looking for when I see it?"

Willis peered in at him, sincerely. "You'll know. You've

got to know. Or we're done for, all of us," be said quietly.

Fortnum shut the door and didn't know what to say. He felt a flush of embarrassment creeping up his face. Willis sensed this.

"Hugh, do you think I'm . . . off my rocker?"

"Nonsense!" said Fortnum, too quickly. "You're just nervous, is all. You should take a week off."

Willis nodded. "See you Monday night?"

"Any time. Drop around."

"I hope I will, Hugh. I really hope I will."

Then Willis was gone, hurrying across the dry weed-grown lot toward the side entrance of the market.

Watching him go, Fortnum suddenly did not want to move. He discovered that very slowly he was taking deep breaths, weighing the silence. He licked his lips tasting the salt. He looked at his arm on the doorsill, the sunlight burning the golden hairs. In the empty lot the wind moved all alone to itself. He leaned out to look at the sun, which stared back with one massive stunning blow of intense power that made him jerk his head in. He exhaled. Then he laughed out loud. Then he drove away.

The lemonade glass was cool and deliciously sweaty. The ice made music inside the glass, and the lemonade was just sour enough, just sweet enough on his tongue. He sipped, he savored, he tilted back in the wicker rocking chair on the twilight front porch, his eyes closed. The crickets were chirping out on the lawn. Cynthia, knitting across from him on the porch, eyed him curiously; he could feel her attention.

"What are you up to?" she said at last.

"Cynthia," he said, "is your intuition in running order? Is this earthquake weather? Is the land going to sink? Will war be declared? Or is it only that our delphinium will die of the blight?"

"Hold on. Let me feel my bones."

He opened his eyes and watched Cynthia in turn

closing hers and sitting absolutely statue-still, her hands on her knees. Finally she shook her head and smiled.

"No. No war declared. No land sinking. Not even a blight. Why?"

"I've met a lot of doom talkers today. Well, two anyway, and—"

The screen door burst wide. Fortnum's body jerked as if he had been struck. "What—!"

Tom, a gardener's wooden flat in his arms, stepped out on the porch.

"Sorry," he said. "What's wrong, Dad?"

"Nothing." Fortnum stood up, glad to be moving. "Is that the crop?"

Tom moved forward eagerly. "Part of it. Boy, they're doing great. In just seven hours, with lots of water, look how big the darn things are!" He set the flat on the table between his parents.

The crop was indeed plentiful. Hundreds of small grayish-brown mushrooms were sprouting up in the damp soil.

"I'll be damned," said Fortnum, impressed.

Cynthia put out her hand to touch the flat, then took it away uneasily.

"I hate to be a spoilsport, but . . . there's no way for these to be anything else but mushrooms, is there?"

Tom looked as if he had been insulted. "What do you think I'm going to feed you? Poisoned fungoids?"

"That's just it," said Cynthia quickly. "How do you tell them apart?"

"Eat 'em," said Tom. "If you live, they're mushrooms. If you drop dead—*well!*"

He gave a great guffaw, which amused Fortnum but only made his mother wince. She sat back in her chair.

"I—I don't like them," she said.

"Boy, oh, boy." Tom seized the flat angrily. "When are we going to have the next wet-blanket sale in *this* house?"

He shuffled morosely away.

"Tom—" said Fortnum.

"Never mind," said Tom. "Everyone figures they'll be ruined by the boy entrepreneur. To heck with it!"

Fortnum got inside just as Tom heaved the mushrooms, flat and all, down the cellar stairs. He slammed the cellar door and ran out the back door.

Fortnum turned back to his wife, who, stricken, glanced away.

"I'm sorry," she said. "I don't know why, I just *had* to say that to Tom. I—"

The phone rang. Fortnum brought the phone outside on its extension cord.

"Hugh?" It was Dorothy Willis' voice. She sounded suddenly very old and very frightened. "Hugh, Roger isn't there, is he?"

"Dorothy? No."

"He's gone!" said Dorothy. "All his clothes were taken from the closet." She began to cry.

"Dorothy, hold on, I'll be there in a minute."

"You must help, oh, you must. Something's happened to him, I know it," she wailed. "Unless you do something, we'll never see him alive again."

Very slowly he put the receiver back on its hook, her voice weeping inside it. The night crickets quite suddenly were very loud. He felt the hairs, one by one, go up on the back of his neck.

Hair can't do that, he thought. Silly, silly. It can't do that, not in *real* life, it can't!

But, one by slow prickling one, his hair did.

The wire hangers were indeed empty. With a clatter, Fortnum shoved them aside and down along the rod, then turned and looked out of the closet at Dorothy Willis and her son Joe.

"I was just walking by," said Joe, "and saw the closet empty, all Dad's clothes gone!"

"Everything was fine," said Dorothy. "We've had a

wonderful life. I don't understand, I don't, I don't!"
She began to cry again, putting her hands to her
face.

Fortnum stepped out of the closet.

"You didn't hear him leave the house?"

"We were playing catch out front," said Joe. "Dad said
he had to go in for a minute. I went around back. Then
he was gone!"

"He must have packed quickly and walked wherever
he was going, so we wouldn't hear a cab pull up in front
of the house."

They were moving out through the hall now.

"I'll check the train depot and the airport." Fortnum
hesitated. "Dorothy, is there anything in Roger's background—"

"It wasn't insanity took him." She hesitated. "I feel,
somehow, he was kidnapped."

Fortnum shook his head. "It doesn't seem reasonable
he would arrange to pack, walk out of the house and
go meet his abductors."

Dorothy opened the door as if to let the night or the
night wind move down the hall as she turned to stare
back through the rooms, her voice wandering.

"No. Somehow they came into the house. Right in
front of us, they stole him away."

And then: "A terrible thing has happened."

Fortnum stepped out into the night of crickets and
rustling trees. The doom talkers, he thought, talking
their dooms. Mrs. Goodbody, Roger, and now Roger's
wife. Something terrible *has* happened. But what, in
God's name? And how?

He looked from Dorothy to her son. Joe, blinking the
wetness from his eyes, took a long time to turn, walk
along the hall and stop, fingering the knob of the cellar
door.

Fortnum felt his eyelids twitch, his iris flex, as if he
were snapping a picture of something he wanted to
remember.

Joe pulled the cellar door wide, stepped down out of sight, gone. The door tapped shut.

Fortnum opened his mouth to speak, but Dorothy's hand was taking his now, he had to look at her.

"Please," she said. "Find him for me."

He kissed her cheek. "If it's humanly possible."

If it's humanly possible. Good Lord, why had he picked *those* words?

He walked off into the summer night.

A gasp, an exhalation, a gasp, an exhalation, an asthmatic insuck, a vaporing sneeze. Somebody dying in the dark? No.

Just Mrs. Goodbody, unseen beyond the hedge, working late, her hand pump aimed, her bony elbow thrusting. The sick sweet smell of bug spray enveloped Fortnum as he reached his house.

"Mrs. Goodbody? Still at it?"

From the black hedge her voice leaped. "Damn it, yes! Aphids, water bugs, woodworms, and now the *Marasmius oreades*. Lord, it grows fast!"

"What does?"

"The *Marasmius oreades*, of course! It's me against them, and I intend to win! There! There! There!"

He left the hedge, the gasping pump, the wheezing voice, and found his wife waiting for him on the porch almost as if she were going to take up where Dorothy had left off at her door a few minutes ago.

Fortnum was about to speak when a shadow moved inside. There was a creaking noise. A knob rattled.

Tom vanished into the basement.

Fortnum felt as if someone had set off an explosion in his face. He reeled. Everything had the numbed familiarity of those waking dreams where all motions are remembered before they occur, all dialogue known before it falls from the lips.

He found himself staring at the shut basement door. Cynthia took him inside, amused.

"What? Tom? Oh, I relented. The darn mushrooms meant so much to him. Besides, when he threw them into the cellar they did nicely, just lying in the dirt—"

"Did they?" Fortnum heard himself say.

Cynthia took his arm. "What about Roger?"

"He's gone, yes."

"Men, men, men," she said.

"No, you're wrong," he said. "I saw Roger every day the last ten years. When you know a man that well, you can tell how things are at home, whether things are in the oven or the Mixmaster. Death hadn't breathed down his neck yet; he wasn't running scared after his immortal youth, picking peaches in someone else's orchards. No, no, I swear, I'd bet my last dollar on it, Roger—"

The doorbell rang behind him. The delivery boy had come up quietly onto the porch and was standing there with a telegram in his hand.

"Fortnum?"

Cynthia snapped on the hall light as he ripped the envelope open and smoothed it out for reading.

TRAVELING NEW ORLEANS. THIS TELEGRAM POSSIBLE OFF-GUARD MOMENT. YOU MUST REFUSE, REPEAT REFUSE, ALL SPECIAL-DELIVERY PACKAGES. ROGER

Cynthia glanced up from the paper.

"I don't understand. What does he mean?"

But Fortnum was already at the telephone, dialing swiftly, once. "Operator? The police, and hurry!"

At ten-fifteen that night the phone rang for the sixth time during the evening. Fortnum got it and immediately gasped. "Roger! Where are you?"

"Where am I, hell," said Roger lightly, almost amused. "You know very well where I am, you're responsible for this. I should be angry!"

Cynthia, at his nod, had hurried to take the phone

in the kitchen. When he heard the soft click, he went on.

"Roger, I swear I don't know. I got that telegram from you—"

"What telegram?" said Roger jovially. "I sent no telegram. Now of a sudden, the police come pouring onto the south-bound train, pull me off in some jerk-water, and I'm calling you to get them off my neck. Hugh, if this is some joke—"

"But, Roger, you just vanished!"

"On a business trip, if you can call that vanishing. I told Dorothy about this, and Joe."

"This is all very confusing, Roger. You're in no danger? Nobody's blackmailing you, forcing you into this speech?"

"I'm fine, healthy, free and unafraid."

"But, Roger, your premonitions?"

"Poppycock! Now, look, I'm being very good about this, aren't I?"

"Sure, Roger—"

"Then play the good father and give me permission to go. Call Dorothy and tell her I'll be back in five days. How *could* she have forgotten?"

"She did, Roger. See you in five days, then?"

"Five days, I swear."

The voice was indeed winning and warm, the old Roger again. Fortnum shook his head.

"Roger," he said, "this is the craziest day I've ever spent. You're not running off from Dorothy? Good Lord; you can tell *me*."

"I love her with all my heart. Now here's Lieutenant Parker of the Ridgetown police. Goodbye, Hugh."

"Good—"

But the lieutenant was on the line, talking, talking angrily. What had Fortnum meant putting them to this trouble? What was going on? Who did he think he was? Did or didn't he want this so-called friend held or released?

"Released," Fortnum managed to say somewhere along the way, and hung up the phone and imagined he heard a voice call all aboard and the massive thunder of the train leaving the station two hundred miles south in the somehow increasingly dark night.

Cynthia walked very slowly into the parlor.

"I feel so foolish," she said.

"How do you think I feel?"

"Who could have sent that telegram, and why?"

He poured himself some Scotch and stood in the middle of the room looking at it.

"I'm glad Roger is all right," his wife said at last.

"He isn't," said Fortnum.

"But you just said—"

"I said nothing. After all, we couldn't very well drag him off that train and truss him up and send him home, could we, if he insisted he was okay? No. He sent that telegram, but changed his mind after sending it. Why, why, why?" Fortnum paced the room, sipping the drink. "Why warn us against special-delivery packages? The only package we've got this year which fits that description is the one Tom got this morning . . ." His voice trailed off.

Before he could move, Cynthia was at the wastepaper basket taking out the crumpled wrapping paper with the special-delivery stamps on it.

The postmark read: NEW ORLEANS, LA.

Cynthia looked up from it. "New Orleans. Isn't that where Roger is heading right now?"

A doorknob rattled, a door opened and closed in Fortnum's mind. Another doorknob rattled, another door swung wide and then shut. There was a smell of damp earth.

He found his hand dialing the phone. After a long while Dorothy Willis answered at the other end. He could imagine her sitting alone in a house with too many lights on. He talked quietly with her a while, then cleared his throat and said, "Dorothy, look. I know it sounds silly. Did any special-delivery packages arrive at your house the last few days?"

Her voice was faint. "No." Then: "No, wait. Three days ago. But I thought you *knew*! All the boys on the block are going in for it."

Fortnum measured his words carefully.

"Going in for what?"

"But why ask?" she said. "There's nothing wrong with raising mushrooms, is there?"

Fortnum closed his eyes.

"Hugh? Are you still there?" asked Dorothy. "I said there's nothing wrong with—"

"Raising mushrooms?" said Fortnum at last. "No. Nothing wrong. Nothing wrong."

And slowly he put down the phone.

The curtains blew like veils of moonlight. The clock ticked. The after-midnight world flowed into and filled the bedroom. He heard Mrs. Goodbody's clear voice on this morning's air, a million years gone now. He heard Roger putting a cloud over the sun at noon. He heard the police damning him by phone from down state. Then Roger's voice again, with the locomotive thunder hurrying him away and away, fading. And, finally, Mrs. Goodbody's voice behind the hedge:

"Lord, it grows fast!"

"What does?"

"The *Marasmius oreades*!"

He snapped his eyes open. He sat up.

Downstairs, a moment later, he flicked through the Unabridged dictionary.

His forefinger underlined the words:

"*Marasmius oreades*; a mushroom commonly found on lawns in summer and early autumn . . ."

He let the book fall shut.

Outside, in the deep summer night, he lit a cigarette and smoked quietly.

A meteor fell across space, burning itself out quickly. The trees rustled softly.

The front door tapped shut.

Cynthia moved toward him in her robe.

"Can't sleep?"

"Too warm, I guess."

"It's not warm."

"No," he said, feeling his arms. "In fact, it's cold." He sucked on the cigarette twice, then, not looking at her, said, "Cynthia, what if . . ." He snorted and had to stop. "Well, what if Roger was right this morning. Mrs. Goodbody, what if she's right, too? Something terrible is happening. Like, well," —he nodded at the sky and the million stars— "Earth being invaded by things from other worlds, maybe."

"Hugh—"

"No, let me run wild."

"It's quite obvious we're not being invaded, or we'd notice."

"Let's say we've only half noticed, become uneasy about something. What? How could we be invaded? By what means would creatures invade?"

Cynthia looked at the sky and was about to try something when he interrupted.

"No, not meteors or flying saucers, things we can see. What about bacteria? That comes from outer space, too, doesn't it?"

"I read once, yes."

"Spores, seeds, pollens, viruses probably bombard our atmosphere by the billions every second and have done so for millions of years. Right now we're sitting out under an invisible rain. It falls all over the country, the cities, the towns, and right now, our lawn."

"*Our* lawn?"

"*And* Mrs. Goodbody's. But people like her are always pulling weeds, spraying poison, kicking toadstools off their grass. It would be hard for any strange life form to survive in cities. Weather's a problem, too. Best climate might be South: Alabama, Georgia, Louisiana. Back in the damp bayous they could grow to a fine size."

But Cynthia was beginning to laugh now.

"Oh, really, you don't believe, do you, that this Great Bayou or Whatever Greenhouse Novelty Company that sent Tom his package is owned and operated by six-foot-tall mushrooms from another planet?"

"If you put it that way, it sounds funny."

"Funny! It's hilarious." She threw her head back, deliciously.

"Good grief!" he cried, suddenly irritated. "Something's going on! Mrs. Goodbody is rooting out and killing *Marasmius oreades*. What is *Marasmius oreades*? A certain kind of mushroom. Simultaneously, and I suppose *you'll* call it coincidence, by special delivery, what arrives the same day? Mushrooms for Tom! What *else* happens? Roger fears he may soon cease to be! Within hours, he vanishes, then telegraphs us, warning us not to accept what? The special-delivery mushrooms for Tom! Has Roger's son got a similar package in the last few days? He has! Where do the packages come from? New Orleans! And where is Roger going when he vanishes? New Orleans! Do you see, Cynthia, do you see? I wouldn't be upset if all these separate things didn't lock together! Roger, Tom, Joe, mushrooms, Mrs. Goodbody, packages, destinations, everything in one pattern!"

She was watching his face now, quieter, but still amused. "Don't get angry."

"I'm not!" Fortnum almost shouted. And then he simply could not go on. He was afraid that if he did he would find himself shouting with laughter too, and somehow he did not want that. He stared at the surrounding houses up and down the block and thought of the dark cellars and the neighbor boys who read *Popular Mechanics* and sent their money in by the millions to raise the mushrooms hidden away. Just as he, when a boy, had mailed off for chemicals, seeds, turtles, numberless salves and sickish ointments. In how many million American homes tonight were billions of mushrooms rousing up under the ministrations of the innocent.

"Hugh?" His wife was touching his arm now. "Mushrooms, even big ones, can't think, can't move, don't have arms and legs. How could they run a mail-order service and 'take over' the world? Come on, now, let's look at your terrible fiends and monsters!"

She pulled him toward the door. Inside, she headed for the cellar, but he stopped, shaking his head, a foolish smile shaping itself somehow to his mouth. "No, no, I know what we'll find. You win. The whole thing's silly. Roger will be back next week and we'll all get drunk together. Go on up to bed now and I'll drink a glass of warm milk and be with you in a minute."

"That's better!" She kissed him on both cheeks, squeezed him and went away up the stairs.

In the kitchen, he took out a glass, opened the refrigerator, and was pouring the milk when he stopped suddenly.

Near the front of the top shelf was a small yellow dish. It was not the dish that held his attention, however. It was what lay in the dish.

The fresh-cut mushrooms.

He must have stood there for half a minute, his breath frosting the air, before he reached out, took hold of the dish, sniffed it, felt the mushrooms, then at last, carrying the dish, went out into the hall. He looked up the stairs, hearing Cynthia moving about in the bedroom, and was about to call up to her, "Cynthia, did you put *these* in the refrigerator?" Then he stopped. He knew her answer. She had not.

He put the dish of mushrooms on the newel-upright at the bottom of the stairs and stood looking at them. He imagined himself in bed later, looking at the walls, the open windows, watching the moonlight sift patterns on the ceiling. He heard himself saying, Cynthia? And her answering, Yes? And him saying, There *is* a way for mushrooms to grow arms and legs. What? she would say, silly, silly man, what? And he would gather courage against her hilarious reaction and go on, What if a man wandered through the swamp, picked the mushrooms and *ate* them . . . ?

No response from Cynthia.

Once inside the man, would the mushrooms spread through his blood, take over every cell and change the man from a man to a—Martian? Given this theory, would the mushroom *need* its own arms and legs? No, not when it could borrow people, live inside and become them. Roger ate mushrooms given him by his son. Roger became "something else." He kidnapped himself. And in one last flash of sanity, of being himself, he telegraphed us, warning us not to accept the special-delivery mushrooms. The 'Roger' that telephoned later was no longer Roger but a captive of what he had eaten! Doesn't that figure, Cynthia, doesn't it, doesn't it?

No, said the imagined Cynthia, no, it doesn't figure, no, no, no. . . .

There was the faintest whisper, rustle, stir from the cellar. Taking his eyes from the bowl, Fortnum walked to the cellar door and put his ear to it.

"Tom?"

No answer.

"Tom, are you down there?"

No answer.

"Tom?"

After a long while, Tom's voice came up from below. "Yes, Dad?"

"It's after midnight," said Fortnum, fighting to keep his voice from going high. "What are you doing down there?"

No answer.

"I said—"

"Tending to my crop," said the boy at last, his voice cold and faint.

"Well, get the *hell* out of there! You hear me?"

Silence.

"Tom? Listen! Did you put some mushrooms in the refrigerator tonight? If so, why?"

Ten seconds must have ticked by before the boy replied from below, "For you and Mom to eat, of course."

Fortnum heard his heart moving swiftly and had to take three deep breaths before he could go on.

"Tom? You didn't . . . that is, you haven't by any chance eaten some of the mushrooms yourself, *have* you?"

"Funny you ask that," said Tom. "Yes. Tonight. On a sandwich. After supper. Why?"

Fortnum held to the doorknob. Now it was his turn not to answer. He felt his knees beginning to melt and he fought the whole silly senseless fool thing. No reason, he tried to say, but his lips wouldn't move.

"Dad?" called Tom, softly from the cellar. "Come on down." Another pause. "I want you to see the harvest."

Fortnum felt the knob slip in his sweaty hand. The knob rattled. He gasped.

"Dad?" called Tom softly.

Fortnum opened the door.

The cellar was completely black below.

He stretched his hand in toward the light switch.

As if sensing this from somewhere, Tom said, "Don't. Light's bad for the mushrooms."

He took his hand off the switch.

He swallowed. He looked back at the stair leading up to his wife. I suppose, he thought, I should go say goodbye to Cynthia. But why should I think that! Why, in God's name, should I think that at all? No reason, *is* there?

None.

"Tom?" he said, affecting a jaunty air. "Ready or not, here I come!"

And stepping down in darkness, he shut the door.

Fred Saberhagen began writing science fiction in 1961 and shortly thereafter published the first of his Berserker stories. These popular tales of human encounters with interstellar killing machines have spawned the novels Brother Assassin *and* Berserker Planet *and the shared world anthology* Berserker Base. *His multi-volume* Book of Swords *and* Book of Lost Swords *series are imaginative blends of science fiction and fantasy set in a post-apocalyptic universe where science has been forsaken for magic. With the publication of* The Dracula Tape *in 1975, he embarked on an ongoing series of more than 10 novels, including* Dominion, Thorn *and* An Old Friend of the Family, *which feature Count Dracula as their hero.*

Pressure

Fred Saberhagen

The ship had been a human transport once, and it still transported humans, but now they rode like well-cared for cattle on the way to market. Control of their passage and destiny had been vested in the electronic brain and auxiliary devices built into the *New England* after its capture in space by a berserker machine.

Gilberto Klee, latest captive to be thrust aboard, was more frightened than he had ever been before in his young life, and trying not to show it. Why the berserker had kept him alive at all he did not know, and be was afraid to think about it. Like everyone else he had heard the horror stories: Of human brains, still half-alive, built into berserker computers as auxiliary circuits. Of human bodies used in the berserkers' experiments intended to produce convincing artificial men. Of humans kept as test-targets for new berserker death-rays, toxins, ways to drive men mad.

After the raid Gil and the handful of others who had been taken with him—for all they knew, the only survivors of their planet—had been separated and kept in solitary compartments aboard the great machine in space. And now the same berserker devices that had captured him, or others like them, had taken him from his cell and led him to an interior dock aboard the berserker, which was the size of a minor planet; and before they had put him aboard this ship that had been a human transport once, he had time to see the name *New England* on her hull.

Once aboard, he was put into a chamber about twenty paces wide and perhaps fifty long, four or five meters high. Evidently all interior decks and paneling, everything nonessential, had been ripped out. There was left the inner hull, some plumbing, artificial gravity, some light and air at a good level.

There were eight other people in the chamber, standing together and talking among themselves; they fell silent as the machines opened the door and thrust Gil in with them.

"How do," said one man to Gil. The speaker was a thin character who wore some kind of spaceman's uniform that now bagged loosely on his frame. As he spoke, he took a cautious step forward and nodded. Everyone was watching Gil alertly—just in case he should turn out to be violently crazy, Gil supposed. Well, it wasn't the first time in his life he'd been thrown in with a group of prisoners who looked at him like that.

"My name is Rom," the thin guy was saying "Ensign Rom, United Planets Space Force."

"Gilberto Klee."

Everyone relaxed just slightly, seeing that he was at least fairly normal.

"This is Mr. Hudak," said Ensign Rom, indicating another young, once-authoritative man. Then he went on to name the others, but Gil couldn't remember all their names at once. Three of them were women, one of them young enough to make Gil look at her with some interest. Then he saw how she kept half-crouching behind the other people, staring, smiling at nothing, fingers playing unceasingly with her long and unkempt hair.

Mr. Hudak had started to ask Gil questions, his voice gradually taking on the tone used by people-in-charge conducting an examination. In school, Youth Bureau, police station, Resettlement, there was always a certain tone of voice used by the processors when speaking to the processed—though Gil had never put the thought in just those words.

Hudak was asking him: "Were you on another ship or what?" *On* a ship. You were not a spaceman, of course, said the tone of authority now. You were just a boy being processed somewhere; we see that by looking at you. Not that the tone of authority was intentionally nasty. It usually wasn't.

"I was on a planet," said Gil. "Bella Coola."

"My God, they hit that too?"

"They sure hit the part where I was, anyway." Gil hadn't seen anything to make him hopeful about the rest of the planet. At the Resettlement Station where he was they had had just a few minutes warning from the military, and then the radios had gone silent. When the berserker's launch came down, Gil had been out in the fields just watching. There wasn't much the people at the Station could do with the little warning they had been given; already they could see the berserker heat-rays and dust-machines playing over the woods, which was the only concealment they might have run to.

Still, some of the kids had been trying to run when

the silvery, poisonous-looking dart that was the berserker's launch had appeared descending overhead. The Old Man had come tearing out of the compound into the fields on his scooter—maybe to tell his young people to run, maybe to tell them to stand still. It didn't seem to make much difference. The ones who ran were rayed down by the enemy, and the ones who didn't were rounded up. What Gil recalled most clearly about the other kids dying was the look of agony on the Old Man's face—that one face of authority that had never seemed to be looking at Gil from the other side of a glass wall.

When all the survivors of the Station had been herded together in a bunch, standing in a little crowd under the bright sky in the middle of a vine-grown field, the machines singled out the Old Man.

Some of the machines that had landed were in the shape of metal men; some looked more like giant steel ants. "Thus to all life save that which serves the cause of Death," said a twanging metal voice. And a steel hand picked a squash from a vine and held the fruit up and squeezed through so it fell away in broken pulpy halves. And then the same hand, with squash-pulp still clinging to the bright fingers, reached to take the Old Man by the wrist,

The twanging voice said: "You are to some degree in control, of these other life-units. You will now order them to cooperate willingly with us."

The Old Man only shook his head, no. Muttered something.

The bright hand squeezed, slowly.

The Old Man screamed, but did not fall. Neither did he give any order for cooperation. Gil was standing rigid, and silent, but screaming in his own mind for the Old Man to give in, to fall down and pass out, anything to make it stop. . . .

But the Old Man would not fall, or pass out, or give the order that was wanted. Not even when the berserker's big hand came up to clamp around his skull, and the pressure, was once more applied, slowly as before.

"What was on Bella Coola?" Ensign Rom was asking him. "I mean, military?"

"Not much, I guess," said Gil. "I don't know much about military stuff. I was just sort of studying to be a farmer."

"Oh." Rom and Hudak, the two sharp, capable-looking ones among the prisoners, exchanged glances. Maybe they knew the farms on Bella Coola had been just a sort of reform-school setup for tough kids from Earth and other crowded places. Gil told himself he didn't give a damn what anyone thought.

And then he realized that he had always been telling himself that, and now, maybe for the first time, it was the truth.

In a little while the prisoners were fed. A machine brought in a big cake of mottled pink and green stuff, the same tasteless substance Gil had lived on since his capture eight or ten days ago. While he ate he sat off to one side by himself, looking at nothing and listening to the two sharp guys talking to each other in low voices.

Rom was saying: "Look—we're in what was the crew quarters, right?"

"If you say so."

"Right. Now they brought me in through the forward compartment, the control room, and I had a chance to take a quick look around there. And I've paced off the length of this chamber we're in. I tell you I served aboard one of these ships for a year; I know 'em inside out."

"So?"

"Just this—" There came a faint scrape and shudder through the hull when Rom spoke again his low voice was charged with excitement. "Feel that? We're going spaceborne again; the big machine's sending this ship somewhere for some reason. That means we would have a chance if only . . . Listen, the circuitry that makes up the brain that's controlling this ship and keeping us prisoner—it *has* to be spread out along that plastic bulkhead at the forward end of this compartment we're in. On the control room side another plastic slab's been installed, and the circuitry must be sandwiched in between the two."

"How can you know?" Hudak sounded skeptical.

Rom's voice dropped even lower, giving arguments most of which Gil could not hear. " . . . as well protected there against outside attack as anywhere in the ship . . . paced off the distance . . . overhead here, look at the modifications in the power conduits going forward. . . ."

Hudak: "You're right, I guess. Or at least it seems probable. That plastic barrier is all that keeps us from getting at it, then I wonder how thick. . . ."

Gil could see from the corner of his eye that the two sharp guys were trying not to look at what they were talking about; but he was free to stare. The forward end of the big chamber they were in was a blank greenish plastic wall, pierced at the top for some pipes, and at one side by the door through which Gil had been brought in.

"Thick enough, of course. We don't have so much as a screwdriver and we'd probably need a cutting torch or a hydraulic jack—"

Hudak nudged Rom and they fell silent. The door forward had opened and one of the man-sized machines came in.

"Gilberto Klee," it twanged. "Come."

Rom had been right, they were spaceborne again, away from the big berserker. In the forward compartment Gil had a moment to look out before the man-sized machine turned him away from a view of stars and faced him toward a squat console, a thing of eyelike lights and a radiolike speaker, which seemed to crouch before the front of the plastic wall.

"Gilberto Klee," said the console's speaker. "It is my purpose to keep a number of human life-units alive and in good health."

"For a while," Gil thought.

The speaker said: "The standard nutrient on which prisoners are fed is evidently lacking in one or more necessary trace ingredients. In several places where prisoners are being held symptoms of nutritional deficiency have developed, including general debility, loss of sight, loss of teeth." Pause. "Are you aware of my meaning?"

"Yeah, I just don't talk much."

"You Gilberto Klee, are experienced at growing lifeforms to be consumed by human life-units as food. You will begin here in this ship to grow food for yourself and other human life-units."

There was a pause that stretched on. Gil could see the Old Man very plainly and hear him scream.

"Squash would be good," Gil said at last. "I know how to raise it, and there's lots of vitamins and stuff in the kind of squash we had at the Station. But I'd need seeds and soil. . . ."

"A quantity of soil has been provided," said the console. And the man-sized machine picked up and held open a plastic case that was divided into many compartments. "And seeds," the console added. "Which are the ones for squash?"

When Gil was returned to the prison chamber other machines were already busy there with the modifications he had said would be needed. They were adding more overhead lights, and covering most of the deck space with wide deep trays. These trays were set on the transverse girders of the inner hull, revealed by the removal of decking. Under the tray's drainage pipes were being connected, while sprinklers went high overhead. Into the trays the machines were dumping soil they carted from somewhere in the stern of the ship.

Gil gave his fellow prisoners an explanation of what was going on.

"So that's why it took you and some of the other farmers alive," said Hudak. "There must be a lot of different places, where human prisoners are being held and maybe bred for experiments. Lots of healthy animals needed."

"So," said Rom, looking sideways at Gil. "You're going to do what it wants?"

"A guy has to keep himself alive," Gil said, "before he can do anything else."

Rom began in a heated whisper: "Is it better that a berserker's prisoners should be kept—"

But he broke off when one the man-sized machines paused nearby, as if it was watching and listening.

They came to call that machine the Overseer, because from then on it never left the humans, though the other machines departed when the construction job was done. Through the Overseer the berserker-brain controlling the ship informed Gil that the other prisoners were there mainly as a labor pool should he need human help in food growing. Gil thought it over briefly. "I don't need any help—yet. Just leave the people stay here for now, but I'll do the planting."

Spacing the hills and dropping the seeds was easy enough, though the machines had left no aisles between the trays of soil except for a small passage leading to the forward door. The trays farthest forward almost touched the plastic bulkhead, and others were laid edge to edge back to within a few paces of the rear. The machines gave Gil a platform the size of a short surfboard, on which be could sit or lie while hovering a steady fifty centimeters or so above the soil. Hudak said the thing must work by a kind of hole in the artificial gravity field. On the platform was a simple control lever by means of which Gil could cause it to move left or right, forward or back. Almost as soon as the planting was done, he had to start tending his fast-growing vines. The vines had to be twisted to make them grow along the soil in the proper direction, and then there were extra blossoms to be pinched off. A couple of the other prisoners offered to help, despite Rom's scowling at them, but Gil refused the offer. You had to have a knack, he said, and some training, and he did it all himself.

The two sharp guys had little to say to Gil about anything anymore. But they were plainly interested in his surfboard, and one day while the Overseer's back was turned Rom took Gil hurriedly aside. Rom whispered quickly and feverishly, like a man taking what he knows is a crazy chance, fed up enough to take it anyway. "The Overseer doesn't pay much attention to you anymore when you're working, Gil. You could take that platform of yours"—Rom's right hand, extended horizontally, rammed the tips of its fingers into the palm of his vertical left hand into the wall. "If you could only make a little crack in the plastic, a hole big enough to stick a hand through, we'd have some chance. I'd do it but the Overseer won't let anyone but you near the platform—"

Gil's lip curled. "I ain't gonna try nothin' like that."

The thin sickly man was not used to snotty kids talking back to him, and he flared feebly into anger. "You think the berserker's going to take good care of *you*?"

"The machine built the platform, didn't it?" Gil demanded. "Wouldn't give us nothing we could bust through there with. Not if there's anything so important as you think back there."

For a moment Gil thought Rom was going to swing at him, but other people held Rom back. And suddenly the Overseer was no longer standing on the other side of the chamber with its back turned, but right in front of Rom, staring at him with its lenses. A few long, long seconds passed before it was plain that the machine was not going to do anything this time. But maybe its hearing was better than the sharp guys had thought.

"They ain't ripe yet, but we can eat some of 'em

anyway," said Gil a couple of weeks later as he slid off his platform to join the other people in the few square meters of living space left along the chamber's rear bulkhead. Cradled in Gil's arm were half a dozen dull yellowish ovoids. He turned casually to the Overseer and asked: "Got a knife?"

There was a pause. Then the Overseer put out a hand from which a wicked blade extended itself like an extra finger. "I will divide the fruit," it said, and proceeded to do so with great precision.

The little group of prisoners had come crowding around, interest stirring in their dull eyes. They ate greedily the little morsels that the Overseer doled out; anything tasted good after weeks or months of the changeless pink-and-green cake. Rom, after a scarcely perceptible hesitation, joined the others in eating some raw squash. He showed no enjoyment as the others did. It was just that a man had to be healthy he seemed to be thinking, before he could persuade others to get themselves killed, or let themselves sicken and die.

Under the optimum conditions provided by the berserker at Gil's direction, only weeks rather than months were needed for the trays to become filled with broad roundish leaves, spreading above a profusion of thickening ground-hugging vines. Half of the fast-growing fruit were hidden under leaves, while others burgeoned in full light, and a few hung over the edges of the trays, resting their new weight on the girders under the trays or sagging all the way to the deck.

Gil maintained that the time for a proper harvest was still an indefinite number of days away. But each day he now came back to the living area with a single squash to be divided by the Overseer's knife; and each day the fruit he brought was larger.

He was out in the middle of his "fields," lying prone on his platform and staring moodily at a swelling squash when the sound of a sudden commotion back in the living area made him raise himself and turn his head.

The center of the commotion was the Overseer. The machine was hopping into the air again and again as if the brain that controlled it had gone berserker indeed. The Prisoners cried out, scrambling to get away from the Overseer. Then the machine stopped its mad jumping, and stood turning in a slow circle, shivering, the knife-finger on its hand flicking in and out repeatedly.

"Attention, we are entering battle," the Overseer proclaimed suddenly, dead monotone voice turned up to deafening volume. "Under attack. All prisoners are to be—they will all—"

It said more, but at a speed no human ear could follow, gibbering up the frequency scale to end in something like a human scream. The mad girl who never spoke let out a blending yell of terror.

The Overseer tottered and swayed, brandishing its knife. It babbled and twitched—like an old man with steel fingers vising his head. Then it leaned forward, leaned further, and fell on its face, disappearing from Gil's sight below the level of trays and vines, striking the deck with a loud clang.

That clang was echoed, forward, by a cannon-crack of sound. Gil had been keeping himself from looking in that direction but now he turned. The plastic wall had been split across the center third of its extent by a horizontal fissure a couple of meters above the trays.

Gil lay still on his platform, watching cautiously. Ensign Rom came charging across the trays and past him, trampling the crop to hurl himself at the wall. Even cracked, it resisted his onslaught easily, but he kept pounding at it with his fists trying to force his fingers into the tiny crevice. Gil looked back the other way. The Overseer was still down. Hudak was trying the forward door and finding it locked. Then first he, and then the other people, were scrambling over trays to join Rom and help him.

Gil tested his platform's control and found that it no longer worked, though the platform was still aloft. He got up from it, setting foot in soil for the first time in a couple of months; it was a good feeling. Then he lifted the thin metal platform out of its hull and carried it over to where everyone else was already struggling with the wall. "Here," Gil said, "try sticking the corner of this in the crack and pryin'."

It took them several hours of steady effort to make a hole in the wall big enough for Rom to squeeze through. In a minute he was back, crying and shouting, announcing freedom and victory. They were in control of the ship!

When he came back the second time, he was in control of himself as well, and puzzled. "What cracked the wall? There's no other ships around, no fighting—"

He fell silent as he joined Hudak in staring down into the narrow space between the farthest forward tray and the slightly bulged-in section of wall where the strain had come to force the first crack above. Gil had already looked down there into the niches between wall and transverse girder. Those niches were opened up now, displaying their contents—the dull yellowish fruit Gil had guided into place with a pinch and a twist of vine. The fruit had been very small, then, but now they were huge, and cracked gently open with the sudden release of their own internal pressure.

Funny pulpy things that a man could break with a kick, or a steel hand squeeze through like nothing.

"But growth is stubborn, boys," the Old Man said, squinting to read a dial, then piling more weights onto the machine with the growing squash inside it, a machine he'd set up to catch kids' eyes and minds. "Can't take a sudden shock. Slow. But now, look. Three hundred fifty kilograms pressure per square centimeter. All from millions of tiny cells, just growing, all together. Ever see a tree root swell under a concrete walk—?"

It was on Rom's, and Hudak's faces now that they understood. Gil nodded to them once and smiled just faintly to make sure they knew it had been no accident. Then the smile faded from his face as he looked up at the edges of broken plastic, the shattered tracery of what had been a million sandwiched circuits.

"I hope it was slow," Gil said. "I hope it felt the whole thing."

Since his first published story appeared in 1970, Michael Bishop has written some of the most literate and intelligent fantasy and science fiction of the twentieth century. His novels include A Funeral for the Eyes of Fire, *the time travel epic* No Enemy But Time, *the Philip K. Dick homage* The Secret Ascension, *the horror satire* Who Made Stevie Crye, *and* Brittle Innings, *a reworking of the Frankenstein theme as an exploration of personal and cultural identity. His short fiction has been collected in* Blooded on Arachne *and* One Winter in Eden. *He has edited three volumes of the Nebula Awards series.*

Rogue Tomato

Michael Bishop

THE METAMORPHOSIS OF PHILIP K.

When Philip K. awoke, he found that overnight he had grown from a reasonably well shaped, bilaterally symmetrical human being into . . . a rotund and limbless planetary body circling a gigantic gauzy-red star. In fact, by the simple feel, by the total aura projected into the seeds of his consciousness, Philip K. concluded that he was a tomato. A tomato of approximately the same dimensions and mass as the planet Mars. That was it, certainly: a tomato of the hothouse variety. Turning leisurely on a vertical axis tilted seven or eight degrees out of the perpendicular, Philip K. basked in the angry light of the distant red giant. While basking, he had to admit that he was baffled. This had never happened to

39

him before. He was a sober individual not given to tippling or other forms of riotous behavior, and that he should have been summarily turned into a Mars-sized tomato struck him as a brusque and unfair conversion. Why him? And how? "At least," he reflected, "I still know who I am." Even if in the guise of an immense tomato he now whirled around an unfamiliar sun, his consciousness was that of a human being, and still his own. "I am Philip K. and somehow I'm still breathing and there must be a scientific explanation for this" is a fairly accurate summary of the next several hours (an hour being measured, of course, in terms of one twenty-fourth of Philip K.'s own period of rotation) of his thought processes.

AS I LIVE AND BREATHE

Several Philip K.-days passed. The sufferer of metamorphosis discovered that he had an amenable atmosphere, a topological integument (or *crust*, although for the skin of a void-dwelling variety of *Lycopersicon esculentum* the word crust didn't seem altogether appropriate) at least a mile thick, and weather. Inhaling carbon dioxide and exhaling oxygen, Philip K. photosynthesized. Morning dew ran down his tenderest curvatures, and afternoon dew, too. Some of these drops were ocean-sized. Clouds formed over Philip K.'s equatorial girth and unloaded tons and tons of refreshing rains. Winds generated by these meteorological phenomena and his own axial waltzing blew backward and forward, up and down, over his taut ripening skin. It was good to be alive, even in this disturbing morphology. Moreover, unlike that of Plato's oysters, his pleasure was not mindless. Philip K. experienced the wind, the rain, the monumental turning of himself, the internal burgeoning of his juices, the sweetness of breathing, and he *meditated* on all these things. It was too bad that he was uninhabited (this was one of his frequent meditations), so much rich oxygen did he give off. Nor was there much hope of immediate colonization. Human beings would not very soon venture to the stars. Only two years before his metamorphosis Philip K. had been an aerospace worker in Houston, Texas, who had been laid off and then unable to find other employment. In fact, during the last four or five weeks Philip K. had kept himself alive on soup made out of hot water and dollops of ketchup. It was—upon reflection—a positive relief to be a tomato. Philip K. inhaling, exhaling, photosynthesizing, had the pleasurable existential notion that he had cut out the middleman.

THE PLOT THICKENS

Several Philip K.-months went by. As he perturbated about the fiery red giant, he began to fear that his orbit was decaying and that he was falling inevitably, inexorably, into the furnace of his primary, there to be untimely stewed. How large his sun had become. At last, toward the end of his first year as a planetary tomato, Philip K. realized that his orbit wasn't decaying. No, instead, *he* was growing, plumping out, generating the illimitable juiciness of life. However, since his orange-red epidermis contained an utterly continuous layer of optical cells, his "eyes," or The Eye That He Was (depending on how you desire to consider the matter), had deceived him into believing the worst. What bliss to know that he had merely grown to the size of Uranus, thus putting his visual apparatus closer to the sun. Holoscopic vision, despite the manifold advantages it offered (such as the simultaneous apprehension of daylight and dark, 360-degree vigilance, and the comforting illusion of being at the center of the cosmos), could sometimes be a distinct handicap. But though his orbit was not decaying, a danger still existed. How much larger would he grow? Philip K. had no desire to suffer total eclipse in a solar oven.

INTERPERSONAL RELATIONSHIPS

Occasionally Philip K. thought about things other than plunging into his primary or, when this preoccupation faded, the excellence of vegetable life. He thought about The Girl He Had Left Behind (who was approaching menopause and not the sort men appreciatively call a tomato). Actually, The Girl He Had Left Behind had left *him* behind long before he had undergone his own surreal Change of Life. "Ah, Lydia P.," he nevertheless murmured from the innermost fruity core of himself, and then again. "Ah, Lydia P." He forgave The Girl He Had Left Behind her desertion of him, a desertion that had come hard on the heels of the loss of his job. He forgave . . . and indulged in shameless fantasies in which either Lydia P.—in the company of the first interstellar colonists from Earth—landed upon him, or, shrunk to normal size (for a tomato) and levitating above her sleeping face in her cramped Houston apartment, he offered himself to her. *Pomme d'amour*. Philip K. dredged up these words from his mental warehouse of trivia, and was comforted by them. So the French, believing it an aphrodisiac, had called the tomato when it was first imported from South America. *Pomme d'amour*. The apple of love. The fruit of the Tree of Knowledge perhaps. But what meaningful relationship could exist between a flesh-and-blood woman and a Uranus-sized tomato? More and more often Philip K. hallucinated an experience in which interstellar colonist Lydia P. fell to her knees somewhere south of his leafy stem, sank her tiny teeth into his ripe integument, and then cried out with tiny cries at the sheer magnificent taste of him. This vision so disconcerted and titillated Philip K. that for days and days he whirled with no other thought, no other hope, no other desire.

❖   ❖   ❖

ONTOLOGICAL CONSIDERATIONS

When not hallucinating eucharistic fantasies in which his beloved ate and drank of him, Philip K. gave serious thought to the question of his being. "Wherefore a tomato?" was the way he phrased this concern. He could as easily have been a ball bearing, an eightball, a metal globe, a balloon, a Japanese lantern, a spherical piñata, a diving bell. But none of these things respired, none of them lived. Then why not a grape, a cherry, an orange, a cantaloupe, a coconut, a water melon? These were all more or less round; all were sun-worshipers; all grew, all contained the vital juices and the succulent sweetmeats of life. But whoever or whatever had caused this conversion—for Philip K. regarded his change as the result of intelligent intervention rather than of accident or some sort of spontaneous chemical readjustment—had made him none of those admirable fruits. They had made him a tomato. "Wherefore a tomato?" *Pomme d'amour*. The apple of love. The fruit of the Tree of Knowledge. Ah ha! Philip K. in a suppuration of insight, understood that his erophagous fantasies involving Lydia P. had some cunning relevance to his present condition. A plan was being revealed to him, and his manipulators had gone to the trouble of making him believe that the operations of his own consciousness were little by little laying bare this plan. O edifying deception! The key was *pomme d'amour*. He was a tomato rather than something else because the tomato *was* the legendary fruit of the Tree of Knowledge. (Never mind that tomatoes do not grow on trees.) After all, while a human being, Philip K. had had discussions with members of a proliferating North American sect that held that the biblical Eden had in fact been located in the New World. Well, the tomato was indigenous to South America (not too far from these sectarians' pinpointing of Eden, which they argued lay somewhere in the

Ozarks), and he, Philip K., *was* a new world. Although the matter still remained fuzzy, remote, fragmented, he began to feel that he was closing in on the question of his personal ontology. "Wherefore a tomato?" Soon he would certainly know more, he would certainly have his answer.

A BRIEF INTIMATION OF MORTALITY

Well into his second year circling the aloof red giant, Philip K. deduced that his growth had ceased; he had achieved a full-bodied, invigorating ripeness that further rain and sunshine could in no way augment. A new worry beset him. What could he now hope for? Would he bruise and begin to rot away? Would he split, develop viscous scarlike lesions, and die on the invisible vine of his orbit? Surely he had not undergone his metamorphosis for the sake of so ignominious an end. And yet as he whirled on the black velour of outer space, taking in with one circumferential glimpse the entire sky and all it contained (suns, nebulae, galaxies, coal sacks, the inconsequential detritus of the void), Philip K. could think of no other alternative. He was going to rot, that was all there was to it; he was going to rot. Wherefore the fruit of the Tree of Knowledge if only to rot? He considered suicide. He could will the halting of his axial spin; one hemisphere would then blacken and boil, the other would acquire an embroidery of rime and turn to ice all the way to his core. Or he could hold his breath and cease to photosynthesize. Both of these prospects had immensely more appeal to Philip K. than did the prospect of becoming a festering, mephitic mushball. At the height of his natural ripeness then, he juggled various methods of killing himself, as large and as luscious as he was. Thus does our own mortality hasten us to its absolute proof.

THE ADVENT OF THE MYRMIDOPTERANS
(or, The Plot Thickens Again)

Amid these morbid speculations, one fine day-and-night, or night-and-day, the optical cells in Philip K.'s integument relayed to him ("the seeds of consciousness," you see, was something more than a metaphor) the information that now encroaching upon his solar system from every part of the universe was a multitude of metallic-seeming bodies. He saw these bodies. He saw them glinting in the attenuated light of Papa (this being the name Philip K. had given the red giant about which he revolved, since it was both handy and comforting to think in terms of anthropomorphic designations), but so far away were they that he had no real conception of their shape or size. Most of these foreign bodies had moved to well within the distance to Papa's nearest stellar neighbors, three stars forming an equilateral triangle with Papa roughly at the center. At first Phillip K. assumed these invaders to be starships, and he burbled "Lydia P., Lydia P." over and over again—until stricken by the ludicrousness of this behavior. No expeditionary force from Earth would send out so many vessels. From the depths of ubiquitous night the metallic shapes floated toward him, closer and closer, and they flashed either silver or golden in the pale wash of Papa's radiation. When eight or nine Philip K.-days had passed, he could see the invaders well enough to tell something about them. Each body had a pair of curved wings that loomed over its underslung torso/fuselage like sails, sails as big as Earth's biggest skyscrapers. These wings were either silver or gold; they did not flap but instead canted subtly whenever necessary in order to catch and channel into propulsion the rays of the sun. Watching these bright creatures—for they were not artifacts but living entities—waft in on the thin winds of the cosmos was beautiful. Autumn had come to Philip K.'s solar system. Golden and silver, burnished maple and singing chrome.

And from everywhere these great beings came, these god-metal monarchs, their wings filling the globe of the heavens like precious leaves or cascading, beaten coins. "Ah," Philip K. murmured. "Ah . . . Myrmidopterans." This name exploded inside him with the force of resurgent myth: Myrmidon and Lepidoptera combined. And such an unlikely combination did his huge, serene visitors indeed seem to Philip K.

ONSLAUGHT

At last the Myrmidopterans, or the first wave of them, introduced themselves gently into Philip K.'s atmosphere. Now their great silver or gold wings either flapped or, to facilitate soaring, lay outstretched on the updrafts from his unevenly heated surface. Down the Myrmidopterans came. Philip K. felt that metal shavings and gold dust had been rudely flung into The Eye That Was Himself, for these invaders obscured the sky and blotted out even angry, fat Papa—so that it was visible only as a red glow, not as a monumental roundness. Everything was sharp light, reflected splendor, windfall confusion. What was the outcome of this invasion going to be? Philip K. looked up—all around himself—and studied the dropping Myrmidopterans. As the first part of the name he had given them implied, their torso/fuselages resembled the bodies of ants. Fire ants, to be precise. On Earth such ants were capable of inflicting venomous stings, and these alien creatures had mouthparts, vicious mandibles, of gold or silver (always in contrast to the color of their wings). Had they come to devour him? Would he feel pain if they began to eat of him? "No, go away!" he wanted to shout, but could only shudder and unleash a few feeble dermal-quakes in his southern hemisphere. They did not heed these quakes. Down the Myrmidopterans came. Darkness covered Philip K. from pole to pole, for so did Myrmidopterans. And for the first time in his life, as either tomato or man, he was utterly blind.

THE TIRESIAS SYNDROME

Once physically sightless, Philip K. came to feel that his metaphysical and spiritual blinders had fallen away. (Actually, this was an illusion fostered by the subconscious image of the Blind Seer; Tiresias, Oedipus, Homer, and, less certainly, John Milton exemplify good analogs of this archetypal figure. But with Philip K. the *illusion* of new insight overwhelmed and sank his sense of perspective.) In world-wide, self-wide dark he realized that it was his ethical duty to preserve his life, to resist being devoured. "After all," he said to himself, "in this new incarnation, or whatever one ought to term the state of being a tomato, I could prevent universal famine for my own species—that is, if I could somehow materialize in my own solar system within reasonable rocket range of Earth." He envisioned shuttle runs from Earth, mining operations on and below his surface, shipments of his nutritious self (in refrigerator modules) back to the homeworld, and, finally, the glorious distribution of his essence among Earth's malnourished and starving. He would die, of course, from these consistent depredations, but he would have the satisfaction of knowing himself the savior of all humanity. Moreover, like Osiris, Christ, the Green Knight, and other representatives of salvation and/or fertility, he *might* undergo resurrection, especially if someone had the foresight to take graftings home along with his flesh and juice. But these were vain speculations. Philip K. was no prophet, blind or otherwise, and the Myrmidopterans, inconsiderately, had begun to eat of him. "Ah, Lydia P.," he burbled at the first simultaneous, regimented bites. "Ah, humanity."

NOT AS AN ADDICT
(or, The Salivas of Ecstasy)

And so Philip K. was eaten. The Myrmidopterans, their wings overlapping all over his planet-sized body,

feasted. Daintily they devoured him. And . . . painlessly.
In fact, with growing wonder Philip K. realized that their
bites, their gnawings, their mandibles' grim machinations,
injected into him not venom but a saliva that fed volts
and volts of current into his vestigial (from the period
of his humanity) pleasure centers. God, it was not to
be believed! The pleasure he derived from their steady
chowing-down had nothing to do with any pleasure he
had experienced on Earth. It partook of neither the
animal nor the vegetable, of neither the rational nor the
irrational. Take note: Philip K could think about how
good he felt without in any way diminishing the effect
of the Myrmidopterans' ecstasy-inducing chomps. Then,
too soon; they stopped—after trimming off only a few
hundred meters of his orange-red skin (a process
requiring an entire Philip K.-month, by the way, though
because of his blindness he was unable to determine
how long it had taken). But as soon as his eaters had
flown back into the emptiness of space, permitting him
brief glimpses of Papa, a few stars, and the ant-moths'
heftier bodies, another wave of Myrmidopterans moved
in from the void, set down on his ravaged surface, and
began feeding with even greater relish, greater dispatch.
This continued for years and years, the two waves of
Myrmidopteran's alternating, until Philip K. was once
more a tomato little bigger than Mars, albeit a sloppy
and moth-eaten tomato. What cared he? Time no longer
meant anything to him, no more than did the fear of
death. If he were to die, it would be at the will of
creatures whose metal wings he worshipped, whose jaws
he welcomed, whose very spit he craved—not as an
addict craves, but instead as the devout communicant
desires the wine and the wafer. Therefore, though
decades passed, Philip K. let them go.

SOMEWHERE OVER THE SPACE/TIME BOW

Where did the Myrmidopterans come from? Who

were they? These were questions that Philip K pon-
dered even in the midst of his ineffable bliss. As he
was eaten, his consciousness grew sharper, more aware,
almost uncanny in its extrapolations. And he found an
answer . . . for the first question, at least. The Myrmidopterans came from beyond the figurative horizon of
the universe, from over the ultimate curvature where
space bent back on itself. Philip K. understood that
a paradox was involved here, perhaps even an obfus-
cation which words, numbers, and ideograms could
never resolve into an explanation commensurate with
the lucid reality. Never mind. The Myrmidopterans had
seemed to approach Philip K. from every direction,
from every conceivable point in the plenum. This fact
was significant. It symbolized the creature's customary
independence of the space/time continuum to which
our physical universe belongs. "Yes," Philip K. admitted to himself, "they operate in the physical universe,
they even have physical demands to meet—as demonstrated by their devouring of me. But they belong
to the . . . Outer Demesnes of Creation, a nonplace
where they have an ethereal existence that this continuum (into which they must occasionally venture)
always debases." How did Philip K. know? He knew.
The Myrmidopterans ate; therefore, he knew.

MOVING DAY

Then they stopped feeding altogether. One wave of
the creatures lifted from his torn body, pulled themselves
effortlessly out of his gravitational influence, and dis-
persed to the . . . well, the uttermost bounds of night.
Golden and silver, silver and golden—until Philip K.
could no longer see them. How quickly they vanished,
more quickly than he would have believed possible.
There, then gone. Of the second wave of Myrmidopterans, which he then expected to descend, only
twelve remained, hovering at various points over him

in outer space. He saw them clearly, for his optical cells, he understood, were now continuous with his whole being, not merely with his long-since-devoured original surface—a benefit owing to his guests' miraculous saliva and their concern for his slow initiation into The Mystery. These twelve archangels began canting their wings in such a way that they maneuvered him Philip K., out of his orbit around the angrily expanding Papa. "Papa's going to collapse," he told himself, "he's going to go through a series of collapses, all of them so sudden as to be almost simultaneous." (Again, Philip K. knew; he simply knew.) As they moved him farther and farther out, by an arcane technology whose secret he had a dim intuition of, the Myrmidopterans used their great wings to reflect the giant's warming rays on every inch of his surface. They were not going to let him be exploded, neither were they going to let him freeze. In more than one sense of the word, Philip K. was moved. But what would these desperation tactics avail them? If Papa went nova, finally exploded, and threw out the slaglike elements manufactured in its one-hundred-billion-degree furnace, none of them would escape, neither he nor the twelve guardian spirits maneuvering him ever outward. Had he been preserved from rotting and his flesh restored like Osiris' (for Philip K. was whole again, though still approximately Mars-sized) only to be flash-vaporized or, surviving that, blown to purée by Papa's extruded shrapnel? No. The Myrmidopterans would not permit it, assuredly they would not.

THE NOVA EXPRESS

Papa blew. But just before Philip K.'s old and in many ways beloved primary bombarded him and his escorts with either deadly radiation or deadly debris, the Myrmidopterans glided free of him and positioned themselves in a halolike ring above his northern pole (the one with the stem). Then they canted their wings and with the refracted energy of both the raging solar wind and their own spirits pushed Philip K. into an invisible slot in space. Before disappearing into it completely, however, he looked back and saw the twelve archangels spread wide their blinding wings and . . . *wink out* of existence. In our physical universe, at least. Then Philip K. himself was in another continuum, another reality, and could feel himself failing through it like a great Newtonian *pomme d'amour*. Immediately after the winking out of the twelve Myrmidopterans, Papa blew; and Philip K., even in the new reality, was being propelled in part by the colossal concussion resulting from that event. He had hitched, with considerable assistance, a ride on the Nova Express. But where to, he wondered, and why?

SPECIAL EFFECTS ARE DO-IT-YOURSELF UNDERTAKINGS

In transit between the solar system of his defunct red giant and wherever he now happened to be going, Philip K. watched—among other things—the colors stream past. Colors, lights, elongated stars; fiery smells, burning gong-sounds, ripplings of water, sheets of sensuous time. This catalogue makes no sense, or very little sense, expressed in linguistic terms; therefore, imagine any nonverbal experience that involves those senses whereby sense may indeed be made of this catalogue. Light shows, Moog music, and cinematic special effects are good starting places. Do not ask me to be more specific, even though I could; allusion to other works, other media, is at best a risky business, and you will do well to exercise your own imaginative powers in conjuring up a mental picture of the transfinite reality through which Philip K. plunged. Call it the avenue beyond a stargate. Call it the interior of a chronosynclastic infundibulum. Call it the enigmatic subjective well that one may enter via a black hole. Call it sub-, para-, warp-, anti-, counter-, or even id-space.

Many do. The nomenclature, however, will fail to do justice to the transfinite reality itself, the one in which Philip K. discovered that he comprehended The Mystery that the Myrmidopterans had intended him as a tomato, to comprehend *in toto*. For as he fell, or was propelled, or simply remained stationary while the new Continuum roared vehemently by, he bathed in the same ineffable pleasure he had felt during the many dining-ins of the gold and silver ant-moths. At the same time, he came to understand (1) the identity of these beings, (2) his destination, (3) the nature of his mission, and (4) the glorious and terrible meaning of his bizarre metamorphosis. All became truly clear to him, everything. And this time his enlightenment was not an illusion, not a metaphysical red herring like the Tiresias Syndrome. For, you see, Philip K. had evolved beyond self, beyond illusion, beyond the bonds of space/time—beyond everything, in fact, but his roguish giant-tomatohood.

HOW THE MANDALA TURNED
(or, What Philip K. Learned)

Although one ought to keep in mind that his learning process began with the first feast of the ant-moths, this is what Philip K. discovered in transit between two realities: It was not by eating of the fruit of the Tree of Knowledge that one put on the omniscience and the subtle ecstasy of gods, but instead by *becoming* the fruit itself—in the form of a sentient, evolving world—and then by *being eaten* by the seraphically winged, beatifically silver, messianically golden Myrmidopterans. They, of course, were the incarnate (so to speak) messengers of the universe's supreme godhead. By being consumed, one was saved, apotheosized, and lifted to the omega point of man's evolutionary development. This was the fate of humankind, and he, Philip K., only a short time before—on an absolute, extrauniversal scale—an insignificant man of few talents and small means, had been chosen by the Myrmidopterans to reveal to the struggling masses of his own species their ineluctable destiny. Philip K. was again profoundly moved, the heavens sang about him with reverberant hosannas, all of creation seemed to open up for him like a blood-crimson bud. Filled with bright awe, then, and his own stingingly sweet ichor, Philip K. popped back into our physical universe in the immediate vicinity of Earth (incidentally capturing the moon away from its rightful owner). Then he sat in the skies of an astonished North America just as if he had always been there. Millions died as a result of the tidal upheavals he unfortunately wrought, but this was all in the evolutionary Game Plan of the supreme godhead, and Philip K. felt exultation rather than remorse. (He did wonder briefly if Houston had been swamped and Lydia P. drowned.) He was a rogue tomato, yes, but no portent of doom. He was the messenger of the New Annunciation, and he had come to apprise his people of it. Floating three hundred fifty thousand miles from Earth, he had no idea how he would deliver this message, the news that the mandala of ignorance, knowledge, and ultimate perception was about to complete its first round. No idea at all. Not any. None.

CODA

But, as the saying goes, he would think of something.

John Taine is the well-known pseudonym of mathematician Eric Temple Bell (1883–1960), who began writing science fiction in the 1920s and whose work forms an important bridge between the early scientific romance and pulp science fiction. His novels The Iron Star, The Crystal Horde, *and* Seeds of Life *explore the themes of evolution and mutation and are memorable for their vast scope and sense of cataclysmic doom.* The Greatest Adventure, The Purple Sapphire *and his time travel tale* The Time Stream *were collected as* Three Science Fiction Novels. *Most of his fiction runs to novel length but two of his novellas have been collected as* The Cosmic Geoids and One Other.

The Ultimate Catalyst

John Taine

The Dictator shoved his plate aside with a petulant gesture. The plate, like the rest of the official banquet service, was solid gold with the Dictator's monogram, K. I.—Kadir Imperator, or Emperor Kadir—embossed in a design of machine guns round the edge. And, like every other plate on the long banquet table, Kadir's was piled high with a colorful assortment of raw fruits.

This was the dessert. The guests had just finished the main course, a huge plateful apiece of steamed vegetables. For an appetizer they had tried to enjoy an iced tumblerful of mixed fruit juices.

There had been nothing else at the feast but fruit juice, steamed vegetables, and raw fruit. Such a meal might have sustained a scholarly vegetarian, but for soldiers of a domineering race it was about as satisfying as a bucketful of cold water.

"Vegetables and fruit," Kadir complained. "Always vegetables and fruit. Why can't we get some red beef with blood in it for a change? I'm sick of vegetables. And I hate fruit. Blood and iron—that's what we need."

The guests stopped eating and eyed the Dictator apprehensively. They recognized the first symptoms of an imperial rage. Always when Kadir was about to explode and lose control of his evil temper, he had a preliminary attack of the blues, usually over some trifle.

They sat silently waiting for the storm to break, not daring to eat while their Leader abstained.

Presently a middle-aged man, halfway down the table on Kadir's right, calmly selected a banana, skinned it, and took a bite. Kadir watched the daring man in amazed silence. The last of the banana was about to disappear when the Dictator found his voice.

"Americano!" he bellowed like an outraged bull. "Mister Beetle!"

"*Doctor Beetle*, if you don't mind, Senhor Kadir," the offender corrected. "So long as every other white man in Amazonia insists on being addressed by his title, I insist on being addressed by mine. It's genuine, too. Don't forget that."

"Beetle!" The Dictator began roaring again.

But Beetle quietly cut him short. " 'Doctor' Beetle please. I insist."

Purple in the face, Kadir subsided. He had forgotten what he intended to say. Beetle chose a juicy papaya for himself and a huge, greenish plum for his daughter, who sat on his left. Ignoring Kadir's impotent rage, Beetle addressed him, as if there had been no unpleasantness. Of all the company, Beetle was the one man with nerve enough to face the Dictator as an equal.

"You say we need blood and iron," he began. "Do you mean that literally?" the scientist said slowly.

"How else should I mean it?" Kadir blustered, glowering at Beetle. "I always say what I mean. I am no theorist. I am a man of action, not words!"

"All right, all right," Beetle soothed him. "But I thought perhaps your 'blood and iron' was like old Bismarck's—blood and sabres. Since you mean just ordinary blood, like the blood in a raw beefsteak, and iron not hammered into sabres, I think Amazonia can supply all we need or want."

"But beef, red beef—" Kadir expostulated.

"I'm coming to that in a moment." Beetle turned to his daughter. "Consuelo, how did you like that greenbeefo?"

"That what?" Consuelo asked in genuine astonishment. Although as her father's laboratory assistant she had learned to expect only the unexpected from him, each new creation of his filled her with childlike wonderment and joy. Every new biological creation her father made demanded a new scientific name. But, instead of manufacturing new scientific names out of Latin and Greek, as many reputable biologists do, Beetle used English, with an occasional lapse into Portuguese, the commonest language of Amazonia. He had even tried to have his daughter baptized Buglette, as the correct technical term of the immature female offspring of a Beetle. But his wife, a Portuguese lady of irreproachable family, had objected, and the infant was named Consuelo.

"I asked how you liked the greenbeefo," Beetle repeated. "That seedless green plum you just ate."

"Oh, so that's what you call it." Consuelo considered carefully, like a good scientist, before passing judgment on the delicacy. "Frankly, I didn't like it a little bit. It smelt like underdone pork. There was a distinct flavor of raw blood. And it all had a rather slithery wet taste, if you get what I mean."

"I get you exactly," Beetle exclaimed. "An excellent description." He turned to Kadir. "There! You see we've already done it."

"Done what?" Kadir asked suspiciously.

"Try a greenbeefo and see."

Somewhat doubtfully, Kadir selected one of the huge greenish plums from the golden platter beside him, and slowly ate it. Etiquette demanded that the guests follow their Leader's example.

While they were eating the greenbeefos, Beetle watched their faces. The women of the party seemed to find the juicy flesh of the plums unpalatable. Yet they kept on eating and several, after finishing one, reached for another.

The men ate greedily. Kadir himself disposed of the four greenbeefos on his platter and hungrily looked about for more. His neighbors on either side, after a grudging look at their own diminishing supplies, offered him two of theirs. Without a word of thanks. Kadir devoured the offerings.

As Beetle sat calmly watching their greed, he had difficulty in keeping his face impassive and not betraying his disgust. Yet these people were starving for flesh. Possibly they were to be pardoned for looking more like hungry animals than representatives of the conquering race at their first taste in two years of something that smelt like flesh and blood.

All their lives, until the disaster which had quarantined them in Amazonia, these people had been voracious eaters of flesh in all its forms from poultry to pork. Now they could get nothing of the sort.

The dense forests and jungles of Amazonia harbored only a multitude of insects, poisonous reptiles, gaudy birds, spotted cats, and occasional colonies of small monkeys. The cats and the monkeys eluded capture on a large scale, and after a few half-hearted attempts at trapping, Kadir's hardy followers had abandoned the forests to the snakes and the stinging insects.

The chocolate-colored waters of the great river skirting Amazonia on the north swarmed with fish, but they were inedible. Even the natives could not stomach the pulpy flesh of these bloated mud-suckers. It tasted like the water of the river, a foul soup of decomposed vegetation and rotting wood. Nothing remained for Kadir and his heroic followers to eat but the tropical fruits and vegetables.

Luckily for the invaders, the original white settlers from the United States had cleared enough of the jungle and forest to make intensive agriculture possible. When Kadir arrived, all of these settlers, with the exception of Beetle and his daughter, had fled. Beetle remained, partly on his own initiative, partly because Kadir insisted that he stay and "carry on" against the snakes. The others traded Kadir their gold mines in exchange for their lives.

The luscious greenbeefos had disappeared. Beetle suppressed a smile as he noted the flushed and happy faces of the guests. He remembered the parting words of the last of the mining engineers.

"So long, Beetle. You're a brave man and may be able to handle Kadir. If you do, we'll be back. Use your head, and make a monkey of this dictating brute. Remember, we're counting on you."

Beetle had promised to keep his friends in mind. "Give me three years. If you don't see me again by then, shed a tear and forget me."

"*Senhorina Beetle!*" It was Kadir roaring again. The surfeit of greenbeefos restored his old bluster.

"Yes?" Consuelo replied politely.

"I know now why your cheeks are always so red," Kadir shouted.

For a moment neither Consuelo nor her father got the drift of Kadir's accusation. They understood just as Kadir started to enlighten them.

"You and your traitorous father are eating while we starve."

Beetle kept his head. His conscience was clear, so far as the greenbeefos were concerned, and he could say truthfully that they were not the secret of Consuelo's rosy cheeks and his own robust health. He quickly forestalled his daughter's reply.

"The meat-fruit, as you call it, is not responsible for Consuelo's complexion. Hard work as my assistant keeps her fit. As for the greenbeefos, this is the first time anyone but myself has tasted one. You saw how my daughter reacted. Only a great actress could have feigned such inexperienced distaste. My daughter is a biological chemist, not an actress."

Kadir was still suspicious. "Then why did you not share these meatfruits with us before?"

"For a very simple reason. I created them by hybridization only a year ago, and the first crop of my fifty experimental plants ripened this week. As I picked the ripe fruit, I put it aside for this banquet. I thought it would be a welcome treat after two years of vegetables and fruit. And," Beetle continued, warming to his invention, "I imagined a taste of beef—even if it is only green beef, 'greenbeefo'—would be a very suitable way of celebrating the second anniversary of the New Freedom in Amazonia."

The scientist's sarcasm anent the "new freedom" was lost upon Kadir, nor did Kadir remark the secret bitterness in Beetle's eyes. What an inferior human being a dictator was, the scientist thought! What stupidity, what brutality! So long as a single one remained—and Kadir was the last—the Earth could not be clean.

"Have you any more?" Kadir demanded.

"Sorry. That's all for the present. But I'll have tons in a month or less. You see," he explained, "I'm using hydroponics to increase production and hasten ripening."

Kadir looked puzzled but interested. Confessing that he was merely a simple soldier, ignorant of science, he deigned to ask for particulars. Beetle was only too glad to oblige.

"It all began a year ago. You remember asking me when you took over the country to stay and go on with my work at the antivenin laboratory? Well, I did. But what was I to do with all the snake venom we collected? There was no way of getting it out of the country now that the rest of the continent has quarantined us. We can't send anything down the river, our only way out to civilization—"

"Yes, yes," Kadir interrupted impatiently. "You need not remind anyone here that the mountains and the jungles are the strongest allies of our enemies. What has all this to do with the meat-fruit?"

"Everything. Not being able to export any venom, I went on with my research in biochemistry. I saw how you people were starving for flesh, and I decided to help you out. You had slaughtered and eaten all the horses at the antivenin laboratory within a month of your arrival. There was nothing left, for this is not a cattle country, and it never will be. There was nothing to do but try chemistry. I already had the greenhouses left by the engineers. They used to grow tomatoes and cucumbers before you came."

"So you made these meat-fruits chemically?"

Beetle repressed a smile at the Dictator's scientific innocence.

"Not exactly. But really it was almost as simple. There was nothing startlingly new about my idea. To see how simple it was, ask yourself what are the main differences between the higher forms of plant life and the lower forms of animal life.

"Both are living things. But the plants cannot move about from place to place at will, whereas, the animals can. A plant is, literally, 'rooted to the spot.'

"There are apparent exceptions, of course, like water hyacinths, yeast spores, and others that are transported by water or the atmosphere, but they do not transport themselves as the living animal does. Animals have a 'dimension' of freedom that plants do not have."

"But the beef—"

"In a moment. I mentioned the difference between the freedoms of plants and animals because I anticipate that it will be of the utmost importance in the experiments I am now doing. However, this freedom was not, as you have guessed, responsible for the greenbeefos. It was another, less profound, difference between plants and animals that suggested the 'meat-fruits.'"

Kadir seemed to suspect Beetle of hidden and unflattering meanings, with all this talk of freedom in a country dedicated to the "New Freedom" of Kadir's dictatorship. But he could do nothing about it, so he merely nodded as if he understood.

"Plants and animals," Beetle continued, "both have a 'blood' of a sort. The most important constituents in the 'blood' of both differ principally in the metals combined chemically in each.

"The 'blood' of a plant contains chlorophyll. The blood of an animal contains haemoglobin. Chemically, chlorophyll and haemoglobin are strangely alike. The metal in chlorophyll is magnesium; in haemoglobin, it is iron.

"Well, it occurred to chemists that if the magnesium could be 'replaced' chemically by iron, the chlorophyll could be converted into haemoglobin! And similarly for the other way about: replace the iron in haemoglobin by magnesium, and get chlorophyll!

"Of course it is not all as simple or as complete as I have made it sound. Between haemoglobin and chlorophyll is a long chain of intermediate compounds. Many of them have been formed in the laboratory, and they are definite links in the chain from plant blood to animal blood."

"I see," Kadir exclaimed, his face aglow with enthusiasm at the prospect of unlimited beef from green vegetables. He leaned over the table to question Beetle.

"It is the blood that gives flesh its appetizing taste and nourishing strength. You have succeeded in changing the plant blood to animal blood?"

Beetle did not contradict him. In fact, he evaded the question.

"I expect," he confided, "to have tons of greenbeefos

in a month, and thereafter a constant supply as great as you will need. Tray-culture—hydroponics—will enable us to grow hundreds of tons in a space no larger than this banquet hall."

The "banquet hall" was only a ramshackle dining room that had been used by the miners before Kadir arrived. Nevertheless, it could be called anything that suited the Dictator's ambition

"Fortunately," Beetle continued, "the necessary chemicals for tray culture are abundant in Amazonia. My native staff has been extracting them on a large scale for the past four months and we will have ample for our needs."

"Why don't you grow the greenbeefos in the open ground?" one of Kadir's officers inquired a trifle suspiciously.

"Too inefficient. By feeding the plants only the chemicals they need directly, we can increase production several hundredfold and cut down the time between successive crops to a few weeks. By properly spacing the propagation of the plants, we can have a constant supply. The seasons cut no figure."

They seemed satisfied, and discussion of the glorious future in store for Amazonia became general and animated. Presently Beetle and Consuelo asked the Dictator's permission to retire. They had work to do at the laboratory.

"Hydroponics?" Kadir inquired jovially. Beetle nodded, and they bowed themselves out of the banquet hall.

Consuelo withheld her attack until they were safe from possible eavesdroppers.

"Kadir is a lout," she began, "but that is no excuse for your filling him up with a lot of impossible rubbish."

"But it *isn't* impossible, and it *isn't* rubbish," Beetle protested "You know as well as I do—"

"Of course I know about the work on chlorophyll and haemoglobin. But you didn't make those filthy green plums taste like raw pork by changing the chlorophyll of the plants, into haemoglobin or anything like it. How did you do it, by the way?"

"Listen Buglette. If I tell you, it will only make you sick. You ate one, you know."

"I would rather be sick than ignorant. Go on, you may as well tell me."

"Very well. It's a long story, but I'll cut it short. Amazonia is the last refuge of the last important dictator on earth. When Kadir's own people came to their senses a little over two years ago and kicked him out, he and his top men and their women came over here with their 'new freedom.' But the people of this continent didn't want Kadir's brand of freedom. Of course a few thousand crackpots in the larger cities welcomed him and his gang as their 'liberators,' but for once in history the mass of the people knew what they did not want. They combined forces and chased Kadir and his cronies up here.

"I never have been able to see why they did not exterminate Kadir and company as they would any other pests. But the presidents of the United Republics agreed that to do so would only be using dictatorial tactics, the very thing they had united to fight. So they let Kadir and his crew live—more or less—in strict quarantine. The temporary loss of a few rich gold mines was a small price to pay, they said, for world security against dictatorships.

"So here we are, prisoners in the last plague spot of civilization. And here is Kadir. He can dictate to his heart's content, but he can't start another war. He is as powerless as Napoleon was on his island.

"Well, when the last of our boys left, I promised to keep them in mind. And you heard my promise to help Kadir out. I am going to keep that promise, if it costs me my last snake."

They had reached the laboratory. Juan, the night nurse for the reptiles, was going his rounds.

"Everything all right, Juan?" Beetle asked cordially.

He liked the phlegmatic Portuguese who always did his job with a minimum of talk. Consuelo, for her part, heartily disliked the man and distrusted him profoundly. She had long suspected him of being a stool-pigeon for Kadir.

"Yes, Dr. Beetle. Good night."

"Good night, Juan."

When Juan had departed, Consuelo returned to her attack.

"You haven't told me yet how you made these things taste like raw pork."

She strolled over to the tank by the north window where a luxuriant greenbeefo, like an overdeveloped tomato vine, grew rankly up its trellis to the ceiling. About half a dozen of the huge greenish "plums" still hung on the vine.

Consuelo plucked one and was thoughtfully sampling its quality.

"This one tastes all right," she said. "What did you do to the others?"

"Since you really want to know, I'll tell you. I took a hypodermic needle and shot them full of snake blood. My pet constrictor had enough juice in him to do the whole job without discomfort to himself or danger to his health."

Consuelo hurled her half-eaten fruit at her father's head, but missed. She stood wiping her lips with the back of her hand.

"So you can't change the chlorophyll in a growing plant into anything like haemoglobin? You almost had me believing you could."

"I never said I could. Nor can anybody else, so far as I know. But it made a good story to tell Kadir."

"But why?"

"If you care to analyze one of these greenbeefos in your spare time, you will find their magnesium content extraordinarily high. That is not accident, as you will discover if you analyze the chemicals in the tanks. I shall be satisfied if I can get Kadir and his friends to gorge themselves on greenbeefos when the new crop comes in. Now, did I sell Kadir the greenbeefo diet, or didn't I? You saw how they all fell for it. And they will keep on falling as long as the supply of snake blood holds out."

"There's certainly no scarcity of snakes in this charming country," Consuelo remarked. "I'm going to get the taste of one of them out of my mouth right now. Then you can tell me what you want me to do in this new culture of greenbeefos you've gone in for."

So father and daughter passed their days under the last dictatorship. Beetle announced that in another week the lush crop of greenbeefos would be ripe. Kadir proclaimed the following Thursday "Festal Thursday" as the feast day inaugurating "the reign of plenty" in Amazonia.

As a special favor, Beetle had requested Kadir to forbid any sightseeing or other interference with his work.

Kadir had readily agreed, and for three weeks Beetle had worked twenty hours a day, preparing the coming banquet with his own hands.

"You keep out of this," he had ordered Consuelo. "If there is any dirty work to be done, I'll do it myself. Your job is to keep the staff busy as usual, and see that nobody steals any of the fruit. I have given strict orders that nobody is to taste a greenbeefo till next Thursday, and Kadir has issued a proclamation to that effect. So if you catch anyone thieving, report to me at once."

The work of the native staff consisted in catching snakes. The workers could see but little sense in their job as they knew that no venom was being exported. Moreover the eccentric Doctor Beetle had urged them to bring in every reptile they found, harmless as well as poisonous, and he was constantly riding them to bestir themselves and collect more.

More extraordinary still, he insisted every morning

that they carry away the preceding day's catch and dump it in the river. The discarded snakes, they noticed, seemed half dead. Even the naturally most vicious put up no fight when they were taken from the pens.

Between ten and eleven every morning Beetle absented himself from the laboratory, and forbade anyone to accompany him. When Consuelo asked him what he had in the small black satchel he carried with him on these mysterious trips, he replied briefly:

"A snake. I'm going to turn the poor brute loose."

And once, to prove his assertion, he opened the satchel and showed her the torpid snake.

"I must get some exercise, and I need to be alone," he explained, "or my nerves will snap. Please don't pester me."

She had not pestered him, although she doubted his explanation. Left alone for an hour, she methodically continued her daily inspection of the plants till her father returned, when she had her lunch and he resumed his private business.

On the Tuesday before Kadir's Festal Thursday, Consuelo did not see her father leave for his walk, as she was already busy with her inspection when he left. He had been gone about forty minutes when she discovered the first evidence of treachery.

The foliage of one vine had obviously been disturbed since the last inspection. Seeking the cause, Consuelo found that two of the ripening fruits had been carefully removed from their stems. Further search disclosed the theft of three dozen in all. Not more than two had been stolen from any plant.

Suspecting Juan, whom she had always distrusted, Consuelo hastened back to her father's laboratory to await his return and report. There she was met with an unpleasant surprise.

She opened the door to find Kadir seated at Beetle's desk, his face heavy with anger and suspicion.

"Where is your father?"

"I don't know."

"Come, come. I have made women talk before this when they were inclined to be obstinate. Where is he?"

"Again I tell you I don't know. He always takes his exercise at this time, and he goes alone. Besides," she flashed, "what business is it of yours where he is?"

"As to that," Kadir replied carelessly, "everything in Amazonia is my business."

"My father and I are not citizens—or subjects—of Amazonia."

"No. But your own country is several thousand miles away Senhorina Beetle. In case of impertinent questions I can always report—with regrets, of course—that you both died by one of the accidents so common in Amazonia. Of snakebite, for instance."

"I see. But may I ask the reason for this sudden outburst?"

"So you have decided to talk? You will do as well as your father, perhaps better."

His eyes roved to one of the wire pens.

In it were half a dozen small red snakes.

"What do you need those for, now that you are no longer exporting venom?"

"Nothing much. Just pets, I suppose."

"Pets? Rather an unusual kind of pet, I should say." His face suddenly contorted in fear and rage. "Why is your father injecting snake blood into the unripe meat-fruit?" he shouted.

Consuelo kept her head. "Who told you that absurdity?"

"Answer me!" he bellowed.

"How can I? If your question is nonsense, how can anybody answer it?"

"So you refuse. I know a way to make you talk. Unlock that pen."

"I haven't the key. My father trusts nobody but himself with the keys to the pens."

"No? Well, this will do." He picked up a heavy ruler and lurched over to the pen. In a few moments he had sprung the lock.

"Now you answer my question or I force your arm into that pen. When your father returns I shall tell him that someone had broken the lock, and that you had evidently been trying to repair it when you got bitten. He will have to believe me. You will be capable of speech for just about three minutes after one of those red beauties strike. Once more, why did your father inject snake blood into the green meatfruits?"

"And once more I repeat that you are asking nonsensical questions. Don't you dare—"

But he did dare. Ripping the sleeve of her smock from her arm, he gripped her bare wrist in his huge fist and began dragging her toward the pen. Her frantic resistance was no match for his brutal strength. Instinctively she resorted to the only defense left her. She let out a yell that must have carried half a mile.

Startled in spite of himself, Kadir paused, but only for an instant. She yelled again.

This time Kadir did not pause. Her hand was already in the pen when the door burst open. Punctual as usual, Beetle had returned exactly at eleven o'clock to resume his daily routine.

The black satchel dropped from his hand.

"What the hell—" A well-aimed laboratory stool finished the sentence. It caught the Dictator squarely in the chest. Consuelo fell with him, but quickly disengaged herself and stood panting.

"You crazy fool," Beetle spat at the prostrate man. "What do you think you are doing? Don't you know that those snakes are the deadliest of the whole lot?"

Kadir got to his feet without replying and sat down heavily on Beetle's desk. Beetle stood eyeing him in disgust.

"Come on, let's have it. What were you trying to do to my daughter?"

"Make her talk," Kadir muttered thickly. "She wouldn't—"

"Oh, she wouldn't talk. I get it, Consuelo! You keep out of this. I'll take care of our friend. Now, Kadir, just what did you want her to talk about?"

Still dazed, Kadir blurted out the truth.

"Why are you injecting snake blood into the unripe meat-fruit?"

Beetle eyed him curiously. With great deliberation he placed a chair in front of the Dictator and sat down.

"Let us get this straight. You ask why I am injecting snake blood into the greenbeefos. Who told you I was?"

"Juan. He brought three dozen of the unripe fruit to show me."

"To show you what?" Beetle asked in deadly calm. Had that fool Juan brains enough to look for the puncture-marks made by the hypodermic needle?

"To show me that you are poisoning the fruit."

"And did he show you?"

"How should I know? He was still alive when I came over here I forced him to eat all three dozen."

"You had to use force?"

"Naturally. Juan said the snake blood would poison him."

"Which just shows how ignorant Juan is." Beetle sighed his relief. "Snake blood is about as poisonous as cow's milk."

"Why are you injecting—"

"You believed what that ignorant fool told you? He must have been drinking again and seeing things. I've warned him before. This time he goes. That is, if he hasn't come to his senses and gone already of his own free will."

"Gone? But where could he go from here?"

"Into the forest, or the jungle," Beetle answered indifferently. "He might even try to drape his worthless hide over a raft of rotten logs and float down the river. Anyhow, he will disappear after having made such a fool of himself. Take my word for it, we shan't see Juan again in a month of Sundays."

"On the contrary," Kadir retorted with a crafty smile, "I think we shall see him again in a very few minutes." He glanced at the clock. It showed ten minutes past eleven. "I have been here a little over half an hour. Juan promised to meet me here. He found it rather difficult to walk after his meal. When he comes, we can go into the question of those injections more fully."

For an instant Beetle looked startled, but quickly recovered his composure.

"I suppose as you say, Juan is slow because he has three dozen of those unripe greenbeefos under his belt. In fact I shouldn't wonder if he were feeling rather unwell at this very moment."

"So there is a poison in the fruits?" Kadir snapped.

"A poison? Rubbish! How would you or anyone feel if you had been forced to eat three dozen enormous green apples, to say nothing of unripe greenbeefos? I'll stake my reputation against yours that Juan is hiding in the forest and being very sick right now. And I'll bet anything you like that nobody ever sees him again. By the way, do you know which road he was to follow you by? The one through the clearing, or the cut-off through the forest?"

"I told him to take the cut-off, so as to get here quicker."

"Fine. Let's go and meet him—only we shan't. As for what I saw when I opened that door, I'll forget it if you will. I know Consuelo has already forgotten it. We are all quarantined here together in Amazonia, and there's no sense in harboring grudges. We've got to live together."

Relieved at being able to save his face, Kadir responded with a generous promise.

"If we fail to find Juan, I will admit that you are right, and that Juan has been drinking."

"Nothing could be fairer. Come on, let's go."

Their way to the Dictator's "palace"—formerly the

residence of the superintendent of the gold mines—lay through the tropical forest.

The road was already beginning to choke up in the gloomier stretches with a rank web of trailing plants feeling their way to the trees on either side, to swarm up their trunks and ultimately choke the life out of them. Kadir's followers, soldiers all and new to the tropics, were letting nature take its course. Another two years of incompetence would see the painstaking labor of the American engineers smothered in rank jungle.

Frequently the three were compelled to abandon the road and follow more open trails through the forest till they again emerged on the road. Dazzling patches of yellow sunlight all but blinded them temporarily as they crossed the occasional barren spots that seem to blight all tropical forests like a leprosy. Coming out suddenly into one of these blinding patches, Kadir, who happened to be leading, let out a curdling oath and halted as if he had been shot.

"What's the matter?" Consuelo asked breathlessly, hurrying to overtake him. Blinded by the glare she could not see what had stopped the Dictator.

"I stepped on it." Kadir's voice was hoarse with disgust and fear.

"Stepped on what?" Beetle demanded. "I can't see in this infernal light. Was it a snake?"

"I don't know," Kadir began hoarsely. "It moved under my foot. Ugh! I see it now. Look."

They peered at the spot Kadir indicated, but could see nothing. Then, as their eyes became accustomed to the glare, they saw the thing that Kadir had stepped on.

A foul red fungus, as thick as a man's arm and over a yard long, lay directly in the Dictator's path.

"A bladder full of blood and soft flesh," Kadir muttered, shaking with fright and revulsion. "And I stepped on it."

"Rot!" Beetle exclaimed contemptuously, but there was a bitter glint in his eyes. "Pull yourself together, man. That's nothing but a fungus. If there's a drop of blood in it, I'll eat the whole thing."

"But it moved," Kadir expostulated.

"Nonsense. You stepped on it, and naturally it gave beneath your weight. Come on. You will never find Juan at this rate."

But Kadir refused to budge. Fascinated by the disgusting object at his feet, the Dictator stood staring down at it with fear and loathing in every line of his face.

Then, as if to prove the truth of his assertion, the thing did move, slowly, like a wounded eel. But, unlike an eel, it did not move in the direction of its length. It began to roll slowly over.

Beetle squatted, the better to follow the strange motion. If it was not the first time he had seen such a freak of nature, he succeeded in giving a very good imitation of a scientist observing a novel and totally unexpected phenomenon. Consuelo joined her father in his researches. Kadir remained standing

"Is it going to roll completely over?" Consuelo asked with evident interest.

"I think not," Beetle hazarded. "In fact, I'll bet three to one it only gets halfway over. There—I told you so. Look, Kadir, your fungus is rooted to the spot, just like any other plant."

In spite of himself, Kadir stooped down and looked. As the fungus reached the halfway mark in its attempted roll, it shuddered along its entire length and seemed to tug at the decayed vegetation. But shuddering and tugging got it nowhere. A thick band of fleshy rootlets, like coarse green hair, held it firmly to the ground. The sight of that futile struggle to move like a fully conscious thing was too much for Kadir's nerves.

"I am going to kill it," he muttered, leaping to his feet.

"How?" Beetle asked with a trace of contempt. "Fire is the only thing I know of to put a mess like that out of its misery—if it is in misery. For all I know, it may enjoy life. You can't kill it by smashing it or chopping it into mincemeat. Quite the contrary, in fact. Every piece of it will start a new fungus, and instead of one helpless blob rooted to the spot, you will have a whole colony. Better leave it alone, Kadir, to get what it can out of existence in its own way. Why must men like you always be killing something?"

"It is hideous and—"

"And you are afraid of it? How would you like someone to treat you as you propose treating this harmless fungus?"

"If I were like that," Kadir burst out, "I should want somebody to put a torch to me."

"What if nobody knew that was what you wanted? Or if nobody cared? You have done some pretty foul things to a great many people in your time, I believe."

"But never anything like this!"

"Of course not. Nobody has ever done anything like this to anybody. So you didn't know how. What were you trying to do to my daughter an hour ago?"

"We agreed to forget all that," Consuelo reminded him sharply.

"Sorry. My mistake. I apologize, Kadir. As a matter of scientific interest, this fungus is not at all uncommon."

"I never saw one like it before," Consuelo objected.

"That is only because you don't go walking in the forest as I do," he reminded her. "Just to prove I'm right, I'll undertake to find a dozen rolling fungi within a hundred yards of here. What do you say?"

Before they could protest, he was hustling them out of the blinding glare into a black tunnel of the forest. Beetle seemed to know where he was going, for it was certain that his eyes were as dazed as theirs.

"Follow closely when you find your eyes," he called. "I'll go ahead. Look out for snakes. Ah, here's the first beauty! Blue and magenta, not red like Kadir's friend.

Don't be prejudiced by its shape. Its color is all the beauty this poor thing has."

If anything, the shapeless mass of opalescent fungus blocking their path was more repulsive than the monstrosity that had stopped Kadir. This one was enormous, fully a yard in breadth and over five feet long. It lay sprawled over the rotting trunk of a fallen tree like a decomposing squid.

Yet, as Beetle insisted, its color was beautiful with an unnatural beauty. However, neither Consuelo nor Kadir could overcome their nausea at their living death. They fled precipitately back to the patch of sunlight. The fleshy magenta roots of the thing, straining impotently at the decaying wood which nourished them, were too suggestive of helpless suffering for endurance. Beetle followed at his leisure, chuckling to himself. His amusement drew a sharp reprimand from Consuelo.

"How can you be amused? That thing was in misery."

"Aren't we all?" he retorted lightly, and for the first time in her life Consuelo doubted the goodness of her father's heart.

They found no trace of Juan. By the time they reached the Dictator's palace, Kadir was ready to agree to anything. He was a badly frightened man.

"You were right," he admitted to Beetle. "Juan was lying, and has cleared out. I apologize."

"No need to apologize," Beetle reassured him cordially. "I knew Juan was lying."

"Please honor me by staying to lunch," Kadir begged. "You cannot? Then I shall go and lie down."

They left him to recover his nerve, and walked back to the laboratory by the long road, not through the forest. They had gone over halfway before either spoke. When Beetle broke the long silence, he was more serious than Consuelo ever remembered his having been.

"Have you ever noticed," he began, "what arrant cowards all brutal men are?" She made no reply, and he continued, "Take Kadir, for instance. He and his gang have tortured and killed thousands. You saw how that harmless fungus upset him. Frightened half to death of nothing."

"Are you sure it was nothing?"

He gave her a strange look, and she walked rapidly ahead. "Wait," he called, slightly out of breath.

Breaking into a trot, he overtook her.

"I have something to say that I want you to remember. If anything should ever happen to me—I'm always handling those poisonous snakes—I want you to do at once what I tell you now. You can trust Felipe."

Felipe was the Portuguese foreman of the native workers.

"Go to him and tell him you are ready. He will understand. I prepared for this two years ago, when Kadir moved in. Before they left, the engineers built a navigable raft. Felipe knows where it is hidden. It is fully provisioned. A crew of six native river men is ready to put off at a moment's notice. They will be under Felipe's orders. The journey down the river will be long and dangerous, but with that crew you will make it. Anyhow, you will not be turned back by the quarantine officers when you do sight civilization. There is a flag with the provisions. Hoist it when you see any signs of civilization, and you will not be blown out of the water. That's all."

"Why are you telling me this now?"

"Because dictators never take their own medicine before they make someone else taste it for them."

"What do you mean?" she asked in sudden panic.

"Only that I suspect Kadir of planning to give me a dose of his peculiar brand of medicine the moment he is through with me. When he and his crew find out how to propagate the greenbeefos, I may be bitten by a snake. He was trying something like that on you, wasn't he?"

She gave him a long doubtful look. "Perhaps," she

admitted. She was sure that there was more in his mind than he had told her.

They entered the laboratory and went about their business without another word. To recover lost time, Consuelo worked later than usual. Her task was the preparation of the liquid made up by Beetle's formula, in which the greenbeefos were grown.

She was just adding a minute trace of chloride of gold to the last batch when a timid rap on the door of the chemical laboratory startled her unreasonably. She had been worrying about her father.

"Come in," she called.

Felipe entered. The sight of his serious face gave her a sickening shock. What had happened? Felipe was carrying the familiar black satchel which Beetle always took with him on his solitary walks in the forest.

"What is it?" she stammered.

For answer Felipe opened his free hand and showed her a cheap watch. It was tarnished greenish blue with what looked like dried fungus.

"Juan's," he said. "When Juan did not report for work this afternoon, I went to look for him."

"And you found his watch? Where?"

"On the cut-off through the forest."

"Did you find anything else?"

"Nothing belonging to Juan."

"But you found something else?"

"Yes. I had never seen anything like them before." He placed the satchel on the table and opened it.

"Look. Dozens like that one, all colors, in the forest. Doctor Beetle forgot to empty his bag when he went into the forest this morning."

She stared in speechless horror at the swollen monstrosity filling the satchel. The thing was like the one that Kadir had stepped on except that it was not red but blue and magenta. The obvious explanation flashed through her mind, and she struggled to convince herself that it was true.

"You are mistaken," she said slowly. "Doctor Beetle threw the snake away as usual and brought this specimen back to study."

Felipe shook his head.

"No, Senhorina Beetle. As I always do when the Doctor comes back from his walk, I laid out everything ready for tomorrow. The snake was in the bag at twelve o'clock this morning. He came back at his regular time. I was busy then, and did not get to his laboratory till noon. The bag had been dropped by the door. I opened it, to see if everything was all right. The snake was still there. All its underside had turned to hard blue jelly. The back was still a snake's back, covered with scales. The head had turned green, but it was still a snake's head. I took the bag into my room and watched the snake till I went to look for Juan. The snake turned into this. I thought I should tell you."

"Thank you, Felipe. It is all right; just one of my father's scientific experiments. I understand. Goodnight, and thank you again for telling me. Please don't tell anyone else. Throw that thing away and put the bag in its usual place."

Left to herself, Consuelo tried not to credit her reason and the evidence of her senses. The inconsequential remarks her father had dropped in the past two years, added to the remark of today that dictators were never the first to take their own medicine, stole into her memory to cause her acute uneasiness.

What was the meaning of this new technique of his, the addition of a slight trace of chloride of gold to the solution? He had talked excitedly of some organic compound of gold being the catalyst he had sought for months to speed up the chemical change in the ripening fruit.

"What might have taken months the old way," he had exclaimed, "can now be done in hours. I've got it at last!"

What, exactly, had he got? He had not confided in her. All he asked of her was to see that the exact amount of chloride of gold which he prescribed was added to the solutions. Everything she remembered now fitted into its sinister place in one sombre pattern.

"This must be stopped," she thought.

It must be stopped, yes. But how?

The next day the banquet took place.

"Festal Thursday" slipped into the past, as the long shadows crept over the banquet tables—crude boards on trestles—spread in the open air. For one happy, gluttonous hour the bearers of the "New Freedom" to a benighted continent had stuffed themselves with a food that looked like green fruit but tasted like raw pork. Now they were replete and somewhat dazed.

A few were furtively mopping the perspiration from their foreheads, and all were beginning to show the sickly pallor of the gourmand who had overestimated his capacity for food. The eyes of some were beginning to "wander" strangely. These obviously unhappy guests appeared to be slightly drunk.

Kadir's speech eulogizing Beetle and his work was unexpectedly short. The Dictator's famous gift for oratory seemed to desert him, and he sat down somewhat suddenly, as if he were feeling unwell. Beetle rose to reply.

"Senhor Kadir! Guests and bearers to Amazonia of the New Freedom, I salute you! In the name of a freedom you have never known, I salute you, as the gladiators of ancient Rome saluted their tyrant before marching into the arena where they were to be butchered for his entertainment."

Their eyes stared up at him, only half-seeing. What was he saying? It all sounded like the beginning of a dream.

"With my own hands I prepared your feast, and my hands alone spread the banquet tables with the meat-fruits you have eaten. Only one human being here has eaten the fruit as nature made it, and not as I remade it. My daughter has not eaten what you have eaten. The cold, wet taste of the snake blood which you have mistaken for the flavor of swine-flesh, and which you have enjoyed, would have nauseated her. So I gave her uncontaminated fruit for her share of our feast."

Kadir and Consuelo were on their feet together, Kadir cursing incoherently, Consuelo speechless with fear. What insane thing had her father done? Had he too eaten of— But he must have, else Kadir would not have touched the fruit!

Beetle's voice rose above the Dictator's, shouting him down.

"Yes, you were right when you accused me of injecting snake blood into the fruit. Juan did not lie to you. But the snake blood is not what is making you begin to feel like a vegetable. I injected the blood into the fruit only to delude all you fools into mistaking it for flesh. I anticipated months of feeding before I could make of you what should be made of you.

"A month ago I was relying on the slow processes of nature to destroy you with my help. Light alone, that regulates the chemistry of the growing plant and to a lesser degree the chemistry of animals, would have done what must be done to rid Amazonia and the world of the threat of your New Freedom, and to make you expiate your brutal past.

"But light would have taken months to bring about the necessary *replacement of the iron in your blood by magnesium.* It would have been a slow transformation— almost, I might say, a lingering death. By feeding you greenbeefo I could keep your bodies full at all times with magnesium in chemically available form to replace every atom of iron in your blood!

"Under the slow action of photosynthesis—the chemical transformations induced by exposure to light—you would have suffered a lingering illness. You would not have died. No! You would have lived, but not as animals. Perhaps not even as degenerated vegetables, but as some new form of life between plant and the animal. You might even have retained your memories.

"But I have spared you this—so far as I can prophesy. You will live, but you will not remember—much. Instead of walking forward like human beings, you will roll. That will be your memory.

"Three weeks ago I discovered the organic catalyst to hasten the replacement of the iron in your blood by magnesium and thus to change your animal blood to plant blood, chlorophyll. The catalyst is merely a chemical compound which accelerates chemical reactions without itself being changed.

"By injecting a minute trace of chloride of gold into the fruits, I—and the living plant—produced the necessary catalyst. I have not yet had time to analyze it and determine its exact composition. Nor do I expect to have time. For I have, perforce, taken the same medicine that I prescribed for you!

"Not so much, but enough. I shall remain a thinking animal a little longer than the rest of you. That is the only unfair advantage I have taken. Before the sun sets we shall all have ceased to be human beings, or even animals."

Consuelo was tugging frantically at his arm, but he brushed her aside. He spoke to her in hurried jerks as if racing against time.

"I did not lie to you when I told you I could not change the chlorophyll in a living plant into haemoglobin. Nobody has done that. But did I ever say I could not change the haemoglobin in a living animal into chlorophyll? If I have not done that, I have done something very close to it. Look at Kadir, and see for yourself. Let go my arm—I must finish."

Wrenching himself free, he began shouting against time.

"Kadir! I salute you. Raise your right hand and return the salute."

Kadir's right hand was resting on the bare boards of the table. If he understood what Beetle said, he refused to salute. But possibly understanding was already beyond him. The blood seemed to have ebbed from the blue flesh, and the coarse hairs on the back of the hand had lengthened perceptibly even while Beetle was demanding a salute.

"Rooted to the spot, Kadir! You are taking root already. And so are the rest of you. Try to stand up like human beings! Kadir! Do you hear me? Remember that blue fungus we saw in the forest? I have good reason for believing that was your friend Juan. In less than an hour you and I and all these fools will be exactly like him, except that some of us will be blue, others green, and still others red—like the thing you stepped on.

"It rolled. Remember, Kadir? That red abomination was one of my pet fungus snakes—shot full of salts of magnesium and the catalyst I extracted from the fruits. A triumph of science. I am the greatest biochemist that ever lived! But I shan't roll farther than the rest of you. We shall all roll together—or try to. 'Merrily we roll along, roll along'—I can see already you are going to be a blue and magenta mess like your friend Juan."

Beetle laughed harshly and bared his right arm. "I'm going to be red, like the thing you stepped on, Kadir. But I've stepped on the lot of you!"

He collapsed across the table and lay still. No sane human being could have stayed to witness the end. Half mad herself, Consuelo ran from the place of living death.

"Felipe, Felipe! Boards, wood—bring dry boards, quick, quick! Tear down the buildings and pile them up over the tables. Get all the men, get them all!"

Four hours later she was racing down the river through the night with Felipe and his crew. Only once did she glance back. The flames which she herself had kindled flapped against the black sky.

British writer John Christopher is best known for his 1956 novel No Blade of Grass, *a prescient ecodisaster story which studied the devastating impact of a natural phenomenon on human civilization. His novels* The World in Winter, A Wrinkle in the Skin, The Year of the Comet, *and* Pendulum *are cautionary tales of survival in blighted futures, and* The Possessors *an alien invasion story that combines elements of horror and science fiction. Since 1967, he has concentrated on writing fantasy and science fiction for young adult readers.*

Manna

John Christopher

It drifted down through the early morning air of North America. It was heavier than air, but not very much heavier. In color it was a pinky white, with the texture of a honeycomb, and the size of individual fragments ranged from a few inches to some feet in diameter. It had a smell that was tantalizing and strange and almost irresistible.

George Dell Parker, head janitor of a large office building in Boston, was probably the first to encounter it. At any rate, he put in the earliest report. He had once had journalistic ambitions, and he still made a few dollars a year by passing on such information that came his way as was newsworthy. He carried the fragment in his hand, when he went downstairs to telephone the *Monitor*.

83

The operator knew him. "City Desk," George said. "Yes, sir! I'll connect you with Mr. Lomax."

He was put on to the cub room. He had expected that. The reporter who took the call was tired and bored; there had been just enough doing during the night to keep from getting more than an hour's sleep.

"O.K." he said, "I'm listening."

George said: "There's some notably peculiar stuff floating down out of the sky, Mr. Lomax. I got a hunk of it right here beside the telephone. You want I should tell you all about it?"

"Public health," Lomax said. "Try it on them. So the smog is killing us all by inches, it still isn't a story. Not in Boston it isn't."

"This is no smog." George looked down from the telephone at the piece of the substance that lay, white with a pinky glow, against the battered yellow surface of his old desk. The smell of it pricked his nostrils. "This sure enough no smog, Mr. Lomax. And it's big. This piece is maybe four inches across."

"Blown up from a garbage can, maybe."

"There's hardly any wind. I was up on the roof and I saw this piece coming down from the west, falling at an angle of about forty-five degrees. It near enough hit me, and went on to smack against the chimney stack. I went over and picked it up, of course. It's not from any garbage can, Mr. Lomax. I guess I know as much about trash cans as anyone. It's kind of delicate looking, a sort of pearly mushroom color. I never saw anything like it. Smells powerful, too."

Lomax was beginning to make jottings on his pad. It was a story. An inch, maybe two inches. What does it smell of? Unpleasant?"

"No. It's a good smell, Mr. Lomax. Makes you want to put your teeth right into it. I never met it before, but it's good."

"Then put your teeth in it, George. What are, you waiting for? What's it taste like?"

"I don t know what it is, Mr. Lomax. It may be anything—poison."

"George, it's a hard drag trying to turn you into a reporter. We'll look after your widow."

"Haven't got a wife, Mr. Lomax."

"Then get those shiny teeth stuck in."

George lifted the piece up. Holding it under his nose, he could not believe that it could be poisonous. The smell was delicious. He broke off a corner and nibbled at it. The taste, like the smell, was something completely new. And it was completely satisfying.

Lomax said. "Well? You chewing yet?"

"It melts right away in your mouth Mr. Lomax. You know what it is? It's manna. Manna, Mr. Lomax."

"Manna? That I don't get."

Lomax's failure to grasp a Biblical allusion neither surprised nor dismayed George. He explained it carefully.

"Like the Lord sent down to the Israelites, Mr. Lomax. The manna in the desert. That kind of manna." He was continuing to eat while he talked. "It sure has a heavenly taste, and it came right down out of the sky."

Yes, Lomax reflected. A story. "Manna from Heaven," he said, more to himself than to George. Three inches, perhaps even more. He heard George say: "That's right, Mr. Lomax," and awoke to the immediate needs of the situation.

"Bring that manna in to me, George. Take a taxi."

There was a slight pause. George said: "I guess . . . I guess I've eaten it, Mr. Lomax. It kind of slipped down."

"Why, you fool, man!"

"I'm sorry, Mr. Lomax. It tasted so good."

"George," Lomax said bitterly, "don't go and get married for the next two or three hours. That widow's pension is out—right out."

"I'll go look on the roof. Maybe I'll find another piece."

"Don't bother," Lomax said. "Just don't bother."

Lomax put down the telephone as the cub room door opened. One of the night drivers came in.

"What do you make of this, Luke? Two or three hunks of it in the yard." He held his hand up, showing a piece of manna, a couple of inches square. "Smells good, too."

The first fall was light, and concentrated on Boston. There were other light falls during the next week. Geographically the distribution was impartial; New Delhi made the second report closely followed by Edinburgh, Stockholm, Melbourne and Buenos Aires. By that time the manna had been thoroughly analyzed. It had a highly complex organic structure, and no noxious properties as far as was known. At the same time, people were strongly advised against eating the manna until further tests, necessarily of long duration, had been made.

The tests of long duration were simply the investigation of the effects of manna on laboratory animals. The publication of the results of the preliminary analysis of manna was incomplete; that part of the analysts' report which remarked, with some astonishment, on the fact that manna contained high protein, high carbohydrate, essential fats and, as far as could be judged, all the essential vitamins, was circulated only to the governments of other nations, with the suggestion that it would be good policy to suppress this news until the tests on animals had put it in better perspective.

In the second week after the first fall, news from Moscow made it certain that the falls were planet-wide. The Russian report said much the same as the American one had and expressed the same caution.

Manna was front-page news.

The question of its point of origin naturally provoked the main interest. In the first week, a moderately well known biologist allowed his astonishment to overcome his caution and described the substance as "unearthly." It was enough to start a riot of speculation. After a day

vegetable matter, almost decomposed . . . total fall of 500 tons estimated."

Rustus Hereford looked up. "That's a sample. There's a lot more. Now, I'm not interested in Fort's conjectures about the falls; I don't suppose that you are, either. What is interesting is that the falls came, and then stopped. I think we can assume the same will be true of the present fall of manna."

Von Eckers, the sales director, asked him: "What's your plan, Rustus?"

"Stockpile it. Buy up whatever we can. We can say we're buying it for research purposes, and to a certain extent it will be true, though the lab people don't think much of the chances of duplicating it. Then put it in the deep freeze. When manna has stopped dropping and the Government report has told people how the mice thrived on it, we shall have a nice little luxury product on ice. Caviar will be out."

Gavin objected: "It looks like a long chance. The stuff may stop falling tomorrow—today. Is it worth our while to undertake an operation of this scale for a profit that may be no more than a few dollars?"

"I'll always go after a few dollars if there's a chance in a thousand of them leading me to a million. What do we lose?"

He had his way; he was used to doing so. In three months' time he reported the acquisition of more extensive deep freezer space for the manna and the entry of some belated rivals into the field. Six months later again, he addressed another board meeting.

"At present count, gentlemen," he said, this company has in stock approximately fifteen thousand cubic feet of manna. Once the manna stops falling, I estimate this as worth not much short of fifteen million dollars in luxury food. The first frozen manna has been sampled and shows no signs of deterioration. The Government report on manna will be issued tomorrow morning. It confirms the first reports of the food's edibility and nutritive content, and advises that it can be consumed without any fear of bad effects, providing, of course, that it has not been contaminated on the ground."

"The only trouble," Gavin said, "is that it hasn't stopped falling."

"Not yet But it must eventually. Some of the falls Fort catalogued ran for months, but they all ended. We only have to sit tight."

Gavin's nephew, Peter Gavin, asked: "What's the latest official theory about the stuff, anyway?"

Rustus Hereford shook his head. "None official. The view that strikes most people as the most plausible is that something—nuclear fusion tests, maybe or just Mother Nature—has triggered off a fungus mutation. But nobody can suggest where except that it should be somewhere pretty high, to account for the wind distribution—probably several high places . . . the Andes, the Himalayas—that sort of setting. Biologically it's difficult to see how this wind distribution business fits in—the manna that does fall has no spores that they can recognize and it certainly doesn't start manna colonies. Maybe there's a complex involving barometric pressure, hours of sunlight, and so on, which triggers off spore production when met. They don't know."

Gavin, looked up slowly. "If that theory is true, there is no reason to expect the falls to stop. Rather you could expect them to increase."

Rustus Hereford nodded. "Yeah."

"Well?"

Rustus Hereford smiled. "I'm waiting for them to turn up one manna source. Just one. Don't think they haven't been looking—in the Andes and the Himalayas and even here in the Rockies."

Gavin said: "In that case, where does the stuff come from? From outer space? Someone suggests that in the Herald-Tribune today—that the planet, the solar system, might be passing through a cloud of it. Is that your view?"

Rustus Hereford said. "If that were what was happening, do you know what we would be collecting? Cinders! There have been cinder falls, but the manna I've tasted doesn't give the impression."

"Then you think . . . ?"

"I don't think anything, except in terms of profit and loss. When the falls stop, we've got a fortune in our lockers."

Von Eckers said: "When." There was something in his voice that focused their attention on him. He said apologetically: "I've been, looking out of the window."

They followed his gaze. It was like a snowstorm, with incredibly large flakes. The sky was thick with it, drifting down on a sharp north-east wind. Gavin, who had a fad about fresh air, had opened some of the windows at the beginning of the meeting, to augment the air conditioning. While they watched, a flake of manna curled in on a vagrant draught of air and eddied down. Before their dumbfounded eyes, it came to rest on the table around which they were sitting.

Young Peter Gavin said uneasily: "Just think—if it doesn't stop . . ." He laughed at the thought, but his laugh wasn't happy. "If it goes on falling, in greater and greater quantities—and that Government reports says it's O.K. to eat—what if people get to eating it? It's free. It's free and it tastes wonderful and the Government says it's full of vitamins. Who's going to buy our stuff? And what's all the manna in our deep freezes worth if it keeps on coming down like this?"

Rustus Hereford picked up the piece that had come in. It wasn't very big. He looked at it for a moment, and then put it in his mouth. After he had swallowed it, he said:

"If it does—I don't know what will happen, but I know one thing that won't." They looked at him. "We won't starve."

In various countries there had been lobbying by food

interests against the publication of official reports
approving the food value of manna, but in every case
they had lost. No government that has to appeal to an
electorate with general adult franchise dared lift a finger
against the cry for cheap food, and this food was free.
The food interests settled back into resignation at the
prospect of decreased profits and possible losses, until
one of two things happened—the manna stopped falling
or people got tired of the taste.

The unfortunate result was that neither thing happened. In fact, the manna fell more and more heavily
and more and more universally, and far from getting
tired of the taste, people who had eaten it became increasingly reluctant to eat anything else. The cry was,
in fact, raised that manna incorporated some kind of
drug that produced addiction, but tests fail to bear out
the claim. Human guinea-pigs were found to live on
non-manna diets after varying periods of manna-only
diets; they reported no physical or psychological ill
effects, but they were very glad to go back to manna
when the tests were over.

Three years after the first fall, manna was dropping
in sufficient quantity to feed the world. Rustus Hereford,
who, on the failure of Ambrosia, Inc. two years earlier,
had been invited into a State Department post, was
present at a meeting in which an official Government
attitude towards manna was finally hammered out. He
heard the President say:

"We don't know where it comes from, and we don't
know what it is. All right, gentlemen, all right! It's a
fungus structure, and you guess some isolated high
mountain sources, but the fact remains that no one has
managed to identify a source. Your guess strikes me as
being about as near the truth as that of a certain
gentleman with religious views who has gone on record
as explaining that we are in a spiritual wilderness. It may
be a good guess, but it gets us no place.

"The question we are faced with, primarily, is the

problem of manna in relation to the feeding habits of this nation. A month ago the last food marketing concern went out of business. The farmers have been living on relief for over eighteen months, and those of them who are any good are doing their damndest to get into some other kind of work—for they can see no future in their own.

"The Government's first concern was as to the edibility of manna. We have checked that, and triple checked it: The fifteenth generation descendants of the mice that were first fed on manna are frisking around in the pink of physical condition. There's some suggestion that they may be a little better at mouse IQ tests, too, but statistically it's only just significant, and we needn't bother about that. The point is that manna is good for you.

"The Government's second concern, apart from its natural concern at the disruption in national life caused by manna becoming the staple diet, must be to secure against something that could precipitate the worst disaster in history—the end of the falls of manna. Fortunately that security can be achieved. Manna stores, with no loss of quality, in deep freeze containers. We already have extensive deep-freeze storage, and we are in the process of multiplying that capacity a hundredfold. In addition we are planning to maintain adequate seed stocks of all pre-manna foodstuffs. We aim to have at least two years' supply of manna in hand. Should the falls cease, we can be back onto a normal agricultural economy in less than half that time."

The President paused. He picked up a fragment of manna from the tray in front of him and nibbled it thoughtfully.

"Well, gentlemen," he inquired, "any questions?"

Rustus Hereford sat behind his grade A desk and looked at the man Cafferty had just brought in. He was a little man, and although his face was deeply wrinkled, Rustus did not guess him to be more than forty. He sat,

not quite at his ease, in the visitor's chair. Rustus leaned
forward.

"Cigarette?"

The man took one. "Thanks."

Rustus checked the dossier that had been completed
in the outer office. He looked up again.

"Your name's Thomas Herbert—Herbert's your family
name, that right?" The man nodded. "You know why
you've been brought in?"

Thomas Herbert shook his head. "They didn't tell
me."

"I'll tell you. I'm interested in you. You run a farming
group in Maine. I want to know why."

"There's nothing against it?"

"Nothing. It's a free country. You can walk right out
of that door, and pause on the way to tell me to go to
hell. But I'd like to know. I may as well tell you that
this is not an official inquiry at all. It's a personal one.
I'm very interested in manna and in peoples' reactions
to it. When it first started dropping I made an error
of judgment about the stuff. I lost a lot of money—my
own and other peoples'."

Herbert looked at him curiously. "I guess the source
of your information about what I do must have told you
the kind of people I have up at my place. Cranks. What
makes you interested in cranks?"

"Cranks . . ." Rustus said thoughtfully. "Working in
the fields when you don't have to, building up stocks
of agricultural equipment and machines—I guess cranks
do those kind of things. But some other things seem
funny. I hear you've got a good technical and scientific
library—books and, microfilms—up at that place?"

"Pretty good."

"I also hear that you've got a deep-freeze unit up
there, and that you've got it stocked with, of all things,
manna. Could that be right?"

"It could."

"Then the crank label doesn't fit."

"It may not fit, but it suits us well enough."

"Look," Rustus said. "What are you doing? You've got a theory about manna. What is it? I want to know for my own peace of mind, and if it's any good at all I'll get from behind this desk and join you. If you'll have me, I will."

Herbert said slowly. "No, cranks doesn't fit. But uneasy people would do. My friends up there are all uneasy people. They don't trust manna, and they do trust me. I didn't have to sell any of them any theories or ideas to get them there, or to keep them there. I'm sorry, Mr. Secretary, but I'm not looking particularly for converts. I've got nothing to tell you."

"If there had been nothing," Rustus said, "—really nothing, then you'd have told me something. That's true, isn't it? There is something. You have got a theory, and a purpose?"

Herbert looked at him. "I'll give you that. But that's all I give you. I've got a theory, all right, and a purpose, but I don't even think of them in my own mind if I can help it and I never expect to make a friend close enough for me to share it with. Those who take me, take me on trust."

Rustus grinned wrily, "Take it or leave it—that, right? You win. I'm uneasy myself. My resignation goes in today I can be with you in a month, on the dot. Will you take me?"

"We'll take you."

Within a year, Rustus had taken almost entire charge of the administration of the colony. Thomas Herbert was glad to pass the handling over to him, and to stay himself in the background. The two men got on well together. Herbert did no more than throw out a suggestion from time to time; when he did it was acted on with alacrity by Rustus. And in between those times, Rustus exercised his tireless energy on keeping things ticking over quietly and evenly. The small group increased in size, but slowly.

A year after Rustus joined there, were forty-one of them an increase of seven. There were sixteen married couples, and nine children.

Late one afternoon, Rustus backed the bulldozer away from a bank he had been tearing down, and saw Herbert sitting on the stump of a tree nearby. Herbert called and Rustus climbed down.

"You look hot, Rusty. I brought a jar of beer along."

Rustus drank deeply. He wiped the sweat from his face with his forearm. "Thanks, Tom. I was thirsty, all right."

He sat down beside Herbert. Herbert nodded towards the western horizon.

"Fine old sunset."

The sky was green and gold, heaped up with indigo clouds. High in the air there were golden flecks; flecks that drifted down towards the waiting earth.

"Good manna shower tonight."

Herbert lit his pipe and began drawing on it. "Spoils the view to my way of looking."

"It goes on and on." Rustus looked at him. "I wish I knew what the hell we were waiting for."

Herbert did not say anything for a moment. When he did, it was to the accompaniment of a jerk of his pipe towards the bulldozer.

"Don't like the sound of that engine. I should get Hank to have a look at it in the morning, before you take it out again."

Rustus grinned. The conversation had been turned like this before. He said:

"You've done a few different things in your time, Tom."

Herbert watched the smoke curl up from his pipe. "I guess so. Grade-school teacher, travelling salesman, garage mechanic, window cleaner, dog catcher, rat killer . . . I never seemed to find the job to settle down in. Maybe this is it." He glanced sardonically at Rustus.

"Having knocked around so much, I'm happy enough.

'Come day, go day, God send Sunday,' as my old man used to say."

Rustus said: "I figure it's a good philosophy at that."

"Depends whether you've got a restless nature. You have, Rusty. How'd you like a trip to the big town?"

"More books?"

Herbert nodded. "And some instruments. Can you go tomorrow? Hank can be stripping the dozer."

Rustus had not been away from the settlement since his first arrival, apart from one early trip to Sanford. He looked at New York with interest. There didn't seem to be any great change in the place; the people were still breaking their necks to get from one block to the next, and if one missed the pungent smell of the small hash-joints, the gasoline fumes made up for that. He collected together the hooks and instruments Herbert had asked for, and left the next morning for what he now thought of as home.

Herbert checked through the stuff. He nodded at last. "That's O.K." His look went up to Rustus. "How was it, Rusty? Didn't get too home-sick for the bright lights?"

Rustus shook his head decisively. "Nothing like that."

"Applejack?" Herbert asked. He poured from the stone jar into two glasses. The two were sitting in Herbert's cabin, on wooden chairs beside a wooden table. There was an oil lamp hanging from the ceiling, because the generator had gone on the blink.

Rustus took the drink. He raised his glass. "Here's to us—the uneasy people."

Herbert nodded. "I'll join you."

Rustus said: "I'm still not asking you what's in your mind, Tom. But I'm going to tell you what I've been thinking it was. I've been thinking that maybe, someone, somehow, was sending the manna deliberately. And that the intention was to sap folks morale. You know the principle: hand-out makes for bums. Someone was trying to turn the West—the world, maybe—into a bunch of loafers. In the end civilization would just curl up and die. It didn't seem too fantastic a notion to me; I was trained in big business.

"But that's not the way things are coming out, Tom. New York is turning on its spindle just as fast as ever. People aren't any different. They eat manna, and they eat nothing else but manna, but outside of that they aren't changed at all."

He waited for Herbert to say something. There was silence for a moment. Then Herbert said:

"I'm glad you got that McGuire book. It was never published in this country, and the London edition has been out of print for ten years. But it's a very useful book."

Rustus said quietly: "I'm still not to be trusted. Is that it, Tom?"

Herbert said: "Trust doesn't come into this, Rusty. Maybe . . . Look, Rusty. What's in my mind is too crazy to talk about. I told you before you came that this outfit operates on a crazy hunch. I don't want to keep you if you want to go. Go and eat manna and live a normal life, if that's the way you'd rather have it. I'd be sorry as hell to see you go, for more than one reason. But if you've started being uneasy about me and not about the rest of the world, then I don't see how you can stay."

Their eyes met and held. Rustus said: "You're the boss, Tom."

It was three or four mouths later that Hank reported the auto wreck. The road between Sanford and Springvale ran fairly close to the settlement; it was not an especially busy road, especially now, at the beginning of winter. The auto was a six-seater convertible, and it had its nose in the ditch.

Hank said: "I don't know how he came to kill hisself. Paint's no more than scratched."

Herbert said: "He's dead?"

"Dead right enough. Face twisted real nasty."

Herbert said: "Where is he? His voice was grim. "I'd like you to come along, too, Rusty."

They got the driver out of the car. He was a man about forty and his dead face was contorted in an agonized grimace of pain. Herbert looked at him for a moment.

"Heart failure?" Hank suggested. "Scared hisself to death?"

Herbert said: "Bury him, Hank. Rusty and I will take a run into Sanford. Think this car will run?"

"Don't see why not."

While Hank was checking the car's engine, Herbert said to Rusty: "How's your stomach? If it's not too good, you'd better stay here."

Rustus still did not know what Herbert was driving at, but in a way his curiosity had soured. He said briefly: "Good enough I guess."

They met death on the way in to town—death sprawled in a hundred different attitudes of agony and despair. In the town itself, the sidewalks were thick with bodies, as though the dying had come crowding out for air. Herbert stopped the car when it could be seen that the road itself was impassible, just a little way ahead.

The words almost choking him, Rustus said: "O.K. You can tell me now, I guess. The manna? But I don't get it. It was all right. They checked it and triple checked it!"

Herbert said: "The reason I wouldn't tell you, Rusty . . . when I first had the idea, I tried to tell people. That was in the early days. They thought I was mad—mad in a nasty way. One time it was touch and go whether I was certified. After that, I didn't tell anybody."

Rustus said: "But it was good. You even put some in deep freeze up at the settlement."

"Then it was good. The idea . . . I got it from one of the jobs I used to do. There it was good at first. You could have checked it anyway. You get their confidence first with the good stuff. Then the stuff is . . . slightly different."

Rustus stared at the heaped parade of corpses. "The stuff . . . ?" he echoed.

Herbert spoke the word softly. *"Bait!* That's the way you kill rats. Rats are cunning devils. You can't just put poison down and expect them to take it. You've got to feed them up first."

"My God! Who . . . the Russians?"

Herbert shook his head. "I wouldn't like to see Moscow right now."

"Then . . ."

Herbert looked up, into the pale blue wintry sky. "We haven't met them yet. I guess we will eventually. They may just have killed to wipe out a future danger, but it's more likely they want our planet."

"From outer space? But it was proved the manna wouldn't hold together in that kind of fall . . . it would fry, too."

Herbert said wearily: "That's easy enough. It isn't hard to work out a container that will dissolve—burn maybe— at the right height, and release the contents for a short drop."

Rustus looked up at the sky himself, and back to the tumbled bodies.

"The swine!"

"Swine, all right."

Despair was heavy on him. "And they've won."

Herbert began backing the car. "Not yet they haven't."

"What can a group like ours do?"

"Organize. There will be others who've missed the poison. People sick maybe, or just fasting. We'll find them, or they will find us. When our rat-killing friends drop down . . ."

"We don't know anything about them—what weapons they may have."

"Two things we know—they preferred *not* to risk a straight fight, and they're poisoners. I've got another hunch, Rusty. I've got a hunch that when they come they're going to be over-confident. They may expect some of the rats to be alive, but they won't expect them to be in fighting trim."

"No, by God!" Rustus said. "They won't."

Bentley Little is one of the best-known writers to have emerged from the horror small press. He received the Horror Writers of America's Bram Stoker Award for his first novel, The Revelation, *and has written many other highly praised dark fantasy novels, including* The Summoning, The Mailman, Dark Dominion, The Night School, University *and* The Ignored. *Under the pseudonym Philip Emmons, he published the crime novel* Death Instinct. *His quirky, offbeat shorter fiction has appeared in* Cemetery Dance, The Horror Show, *and the* Borderlands *anthologies, and the best of it has been collected in* Murmerous Haunts.

The Potato

Bentley Little

The farmer stared down at the . . . thing . . . which lay at his feet. It was a potato. No doubt about that. It had been connected to an ordinary potato plant, and it had the irregular contours of a tuber. But that was where the resemblance to an ordinary potato ended. For the thing at his feet was white and gelatinous, well over three feet long. It pulsed rhythmically, and when he touched it tentatively with his shovel, it seemed to shrink back, withdrawing in upon itself.

A living potato.

It was an unnatural sight, wrong somehow, and his first thought was that he should destroy it, chop it up with his shovel, run it over with the tractor. Nature did not usually let such abominations survive, and he knew that he would be doing the right thing in destroying it. Such an aberration was obviously not meant to be. But he took no action. Instead he stared down at the potato, unable to move, hypnotized almost, watching the even ebb and flow of its pulsations, fascinated by its methodical movement. It made no noise, showed no sign of having a mind, but he could not help feeling that the thing was conscious, that it was watching him as he watched it, that, in some strange way, it even knew what he was thinking.

The farmer forced himself to look up from the hole and stared across his field. There were still several more rows to be dug, and there was weeding and watering to do, but he could not seem to rouse in himself any of his usual responsibility or sense of duty. He should be working at this moment—his time was structured very specifically, and even a slight glitch could throw off his schedule for a week—but he knew that he was not going to return to his ordinary chores for the rest of the day. They were no longer important to him. Their value had diminished, their necessity had become moot. Those things could wait.

He looked again at the potato. He had here something spectacular. This was something he could show at the fair. Like the giant steer he had seen last year, or the two-headed lamb that had been exhibited a few years back. He shook his head. He had never had anything worth showing at the fair, had not even had any vegetables or livestock worth entering in competition. Now, all of a sudden, he had an item worthy of its own booth. A genuine star attraction.

But the fair was not for another four months.

Hell, he thought. He could set up his own exhibit here. Put a little fence around the potato and charge people to look at it. Maybe he'd invite Jack Phelps, Jim Lowry and some of his closest friends to see it first. Then they'd spread the word, and pretty soon people from miles around would be flocking to see his find.

The potato pulsed in its hole, white flesh quivering rhythmically, sending shivers of dirt falling around it. The farmer wiped a band of sweat from his forehead with a handkerchief, and he realized that he no longer felt repulsed by the sight before him.

He felt proud of it.

The farmer awoke from an unremembered dream, retaining nothing but the sense of loss he had experienced within the dream's reality. Though it was only three o'clock, halfway between midnight and dawn, he knew he would not be able to fall back asleep, and he got out of bed, slipping into his Levi's. He went into the kitchen, poured himself some stale orange juice from the refrigerator, and stood by the screen door, staring out across the field toward the spot where he'd unearthed the living potato. Moonlight shone down upon the field, creating strange shadows, giving the land a new topography. Although he could not see the potato from this vantage point, he could imagine how it looked in the moonlight, and he shivered, thinking of the cold pulsing gelatinous flesh.

He should have killed it, he thought. He should have stabbed it with the shovel, chopped it into bits, gone over it with the plow.

He finished his orange juice, placing the empty glass on the counter next to the door. He couldn't go back to sleep, and he didn't feel like watching TV, so he stared out at the field, listening to the silence. It was moments like these, when he wasn't working, wasn't eating, wasn't sleeping, when his body wasn't occupied with something else, that he felt Murial's absence the most acutely. It was always there—a dull ache that wouldn't go away—but when he was by himself like this, with nothing to do, he felt the true breadth and depth of his loneliness, felt the futility and pointlessness of his existence.

The despair building within him, he walked outside onto the porch. The wooden boards were cold and rough on his bare feet. He found himself, unthinkingly, walking down the porch steps, past the front yard, into the field. Here, the blackness of night was tempered into a bluish purple by the moon, and he had no trouble seeing where he was going.

He walked, almost instinctively, to the spot where the living potato lay in the dirt. He had, in the afternoon, gingerly moved it out of the hole, with the help of Jack Phelps, burying the hole, and had gathered together the materials for a box to be placed around it. The potato had felt cold and slimy and greasy, and both of them had washed their hands immediately afterward, scrubbing hard with Lava. Now the boards lay in scattered disarray in the dirt, like something that had been torn apart rather than something which had not yet been built.

He looked down at the bluish-white form, pulsing slowly and evenly, and the despair he had felt, the loneliness, left him, dissipating outward in an almost physical way. He stood rooted in place, too stunned to move, wondering at the change that had come instantly over him. In the darkness of night, the potato appeared phosphorescent, and it seemed to him somehow magical. Once again, he was glad he had not destroyed his discovery, and he felt good that other people would be able to see and experience the strange phenomenon. He stood there for awhile, not thinking, not doing anything, and then he went back to the house, stepping slowly and carefully over rocks and weeds this time. He knew that he would have no trouble falling asleep.

In the morning it had moved. He did not know how it had moved—it had no arms or legs or other means of locomotion—but it was now definitely closer to the house. It was also bigger. Whereas yesterday it had been on the south side of his assembled boards, it was now well to the north, and it had increased its size by half. He was not sure he would be able to lift it now, even with Jack's help.

He stared at the potato for awhile, looking for some sort of trail in the dirt, some sign that the potato had moved itself, but he saw nothing.

He went into the barn to get his tools.

He had finished the box and gate for the potato, putting it in place, well before seven o'clock. It was eight o'clock before the first carload of people arrived. He was in the living room, making signs to post on telephone poles around town and on the highway, when a station wagon pulled into the drive. He walked onto the porch and squinted against the sun.

"This where y'got that monster tater?" a man called out. Several people laughed.

"This is it," the farmer said. "It's a buck a head to see it, though."

"A buck?" The man got out of the car. He looked vaguely familiar, but the farmer didn't know his name. "Jim Lowry said it was fifty cents."

"Nope." The farmer turned as if to go in the house.

"We'll still see it, though," the man said. "We came all this way, we might as well see what it's about."

The farmer smiled. He came off the porch, took a dollar each from the man, his brother and three women, and led them out to the field. He should have come up with some kind of pitch, he thought, some sort of story to tell, like they did with that steer at the fair. He didn't want to just take the people's money, let them look at the potato and leave. He didn't want them to feel cheated, but he couldn't think of anything to say.

He opened the top of the box, swinging open the gate, and explained in a stilted, halting manner how he had found the potato. He might as well have saved his breath. None of the customers gave a damn about what he was saying. They didn't even pay any attention to him. They simply stared at the huge potato in awe, struck dumb by this marvel of nature. For that's how he referred to it. It was no longer an abomination, it was a marvel. A marvel of nature. A miracle. And the people treated it as such.

Two more cars pulled up soon after, and the farmer left the first group staring while he collected money from the newcomers.

After that, he stayed in the drive, collecting money as people arrived, pointing them in the right direction and allowing them to stay as long as they wanted. Customers came and went with regularity, but the spot next to the box was crowded all day, and by the time he hung a "Closed" sign on the gate before dark, he had over a hundred dollars in his pocket.

He went out to the field, repositioned the box, closed the gate, and retreated into the house.

It had been a profitable day.

Whispers. Low moans. Barely audible sounds of despair so forlorn that they brought upon him a deep dark depression, a loneliness so complete that he wept like a baby in his bed, staining the pillows with his tears.

He stood up after awhile and wandered around the house. Every room seemed cheap and shabby, the wasted effort of a wasted life, and he fell into his chair before the TV, filled with utter hopelessness, lacking the energy to do anything but stare into the darkness.

In the morning, everything was fine. In the festive, almost carnival-like atmosphere of his exhibition, he felt rejuvenated, almost happy. Farmers who had not been out of their overalls in ten years showed up in their Sunday best, families in tow. Little Jimmy Hardsworth's lemonade stand, set up by the road at the head of the drive, was doing a thriving business, and there were more than a few repeat customers from the day before.

The strange sounds of the night before, the dark emotions, receded into the distance of memory.

He was kept busy all morning, taking money, talking to people with questions. The police came by with a town official, warning him that if this went on another day he would have to buy a business license, but he let them look at the potato and they were quiet after that. There was a lull around noon, and he left his spot near the head of the drive and walked across the field to the small crowd gathered around the potato. Many of his crops had been trampled, he noticed. His rows had been flattened by scores of spectator feet. He'd have to take a day off tomorrow and take care of the farm before it went completely to hell.

Take a day off.

It was strange how he'd come to think of the exhibition as his work, of his farm as merely an annoyance he had to contend with. His former devotion to duty was gone, as were his plans for the farm.

He looked down at the potato. It had changed. It was bigger than it had been before, more misshapen. Had it looked like this the last time he'd seen it? He hadn't noticed. The potato was still pulsing, and its white skin looked shiny and slimy. He remembered the way it had felt when he'd lifted it, and he unconsciously wiped his hands on his jeans.

Why was it that he felt either repulsed or exhilarated when he was around the potato?

"It's sum'in, ain't it?" the man next to him said.

The farmer nodded. "Yeah, it is."

He could not sleep that night. He lay in bed, staring up at the cracks in the ceiling, listening to the silence of the farm. It was some time before he noticed that it was not silence he was hearing—there was a strange high-pitched keening sound riding upon the low breeze which fluttered the curtains.

He sat up in bed, back flat against the headboard. It was an unearthly sound, unlike anything he had ever heard, and he listened carefully. The noise rose and fell in even cadences, in a rhythm not unlike that of the pulsations of the potato. He turned his head to look out the window. He thought he could see a rounded object in the field, bluish white in the moonlight, and he remembered that he could not see it at all the night before.

It was getting closer.

He shivered, and he closed his eyes against the fear.

But the high-pitched whines were soothing, comforting, and they lulled him gently to sleep.

When he awoke, he went outside before showering or eating breakfast, walking out to the field. Was it closer to the house? He couldn't be sure. But he remembered the keening sounds of the night before, and a field of goosebumps popped up on his arms. The potato definitely looked more misshapen than it had before, its boundaries more irregular. If it was closer, he thought, so was the box he had built around it. Everything had been moved.

But that wasn't possible.

He walked back to the house, ate, showered, dressed and went to the foot of the drive where he put up a chain between the two flanking trees and hung a sign which read: "Closed for the Day." There were chores to be done, crops to water, animals to be fed, work to be completed.

But he did none of these things. He sat alone on a small bucket, next to the potato, staring at it, hypnotized by its pulsations, as the sun rose slowly to its peak, then dipped into the west.

Murial was lying beside him, not moving, not talking, not even touching him, but he could feel her warm body next to his and it felt right and good. He was happy, and he reached over and laid a hand on her breast. "Murial," he said. "I love you."

And then he knew it was a dream, even though he was still in it, because he had never said those words to her, not in the entire thirty-three years they had been married. It was not that he had not loved her, it was that he didn't know how to tell her. The dream faded into reality, the room around him growing dark and cold, the bed growing large and cold. He was left with only a memory of that momentary happiness, a memory which taunted him and tortured him and made the reality of the present seem lonelier and emptier than even he had thought it could seem.

Something had happened to him recently. Depression had graduated to despair, and the tentative peace he had made with his life had all but vanished. The utter hopelessness which had been gradually pressing in on him since Murial's death had enveloped him, and he no longer had the strength to fight it.

His mind sought out the potato, though he lacked even the energy to look out the window to where it lay in the field. He thought of its strangely shifting form, of its white slimy skin, of its even pulsations, and he realized that just thinking of the object made him feel a little better.

What was it?

That was the question he had been asking himself ever since he'd found the potato. He wasn't stupid. He knew it wasn't a normal tuber. But neither did he believe that it was a monster or a being from outer space or some other such movie nonsense.

He didn't know what it was, but he knew that it had been affecting his life ever since he'd discovered it, and he was almost certain that it had been responsible for the emotional roller coaster he'd been riding the past few days.

He pushed aside the covers and stood up, looking out the window toward the field. Residual bad feelings fled from him, and he could almost see them flying toward the potato as if they were tangible, being absorbed by that slimy white skin. The potato offered no warmth, but it was a vacuum for the cold. He received no good feelings from it, but it seemed to absorb his negative feelings, leaving him free from depression, hopelessness, despair.

He stared out the window and thought he saw

something moving out in the field, blue in the light of the moon.

The box was still in the field, but the potato was lying on the gravel in front of the house. In the open, freed from the box, freed from shoots and other encumbrances, it had an almost oval shape, and its pulsing movements were quicker, more lively.

The farmer stared at the potato unsure of what to do. Somewhere in the back of his mind, he had been half-hoping that the potato would die, that his life would return to normal. He enjoyed the celebrity, but the potato scared him.

He should have killed it the first day.

Now he knew that he would not be able to do it, no matter what happened.

"Hey!" Jack Phelps came around the side of the house from the back. "You open today? I saw some potential customers driving back and forth along the road, waiting."

The farmer nodded tiredly. "I'm open."

Jack invited him to dinner, and the farmer accepted. It had been a long time since he'd had a real meal, a meal cooked by a woman, and it sounded good. He also felt that he could use some company tonight.

But none of the talk was about crops or weather or neighbors the way it used to be. The only thing Jack and Myra wanted to talk about was the potato. The farmer tried to steer the conversation in another direction, but he soon gave it up, and they talked about the strange object. Myra called it a creature from hell, and though Jack tried to laugh it off and turn it into a joke, he did not disagree with her.

When he returned from the Phelps' it was after midnight. The farmer pulled into the dirt yard in front of the house and cut the headlights, turning off the ignition. With the lights off, the house was little more than a dark hulking shape blocking out a portion of the starlit sky. He sat unmoving, hearing nothing save the

ticking of the pickup's engine as it cooled. He stared
at the dark house for a few moments longer, then got
out of the pickup and clomped up the porch steps,
walking through the open door into the house.

The open door?

There was a trail of dirt on the floor, winding in a
meandering arc through the living room into the hall,
but he hardly noticed it. He was filled with an unfamiliar
emotion, an almost pleasant feeling he had not experienced since Murial died. He did not bother to turn on
the house lights but went into the dark bathroom,
washed his face, brushed his teeth and got into his
pajamas.

The potato was waiting in his bed.

He had known it would be there, and he felt neither
panic nor exhilaration. There was only a calm acceptance.
In the dark, the blanketed form looked almost like
Murial, and he saw two lumps protruding upward which
looked remarkably like breasts.

He got into bed and pulled the other half of the
blanket over himself, snuggling close to the potato. The
pulsations of the object mirrored the beating of his own
heart.

He put his arms around the potato. "I love you," he
said.

He hugged the potato tighter, crawling on top of it,
and as his arms and legs sunk into the soft slimy flesh,
he realized that the potato was not cold at all.

David Drake has been one of the most visible presences in horror, fantasy and science fiction for the last two decades. He is the author of the multi-volume Hammer's Slammers *series, a saga of intergalactic mercenary warfare, and co-editor of* The Fleet *shared-world anthologies of military science fiction. In 1991, he wrote* The Jungle, *a sequel to Henry Kuttner and C. L. Moore's classic tale of human civilization on Venus, "Clash by Night." His fantasy volume* Vettius and His Friends *collects his stories of a legionnaire confronting marvels and monsters at the twilight of Roman civilization, and his collection* From the Heart of Darkness *features his groundbreaking tales of contemporary horror fiction, many with a Vietnam setting.*

Cannibal Plants from Heck

David Drake

Betsy Moffett stood beside her father in the gravel driveway, judging the house with-nine-year-old eyes. Behind them the real estate agent rummaged in the trunk of her BMW.

It wasn't a large house: one story and forty feet wide by twenty-four deep. There were only two of them now, so that was all right. The three dogwood trees in front had gnarled, low-branching trunks four to six inches in diameter. Betsy had never before been close to a tree she thought she could climb.

In back were a rusty swing set and a length of old telephone pole. The bare, trampled soil around the pole showed that it once had mounted a net and backboard. A new set couldn't cost *very* much, and Betsy had a birthday coming in July.

The agent found what she wanted, a thin cap reading UNDER CONTRACT in blue letters on white. She walked over to the realty company's white-on-blue sign, careful because of the soil's March squishiness, and clipped the cap into place to hide FOR SALE.

There were children playing down the street. Betsy couldn't see them from where she stood, but voices rose and fell in shrill enthusiasm.

The other houses in the subdivision were pretty much like this one. Some had brick facades, some had decks; but none of them were very large, and Mr. Moffett's four-year-old Ford fit in much better than the agent's sparkling BMW. The agent had mentioned the well and septic tank in a hurried voice quite different from that in which she described the house as *so cute, a little jewelbox!*

A horse-drawn wagon turned the corner at the end of the block and plodded down the street. The driver was a shabby-looking black man; a large dog walked beside the horse with its head down. Betsy had never seen a real horse-drawn wagon before. She was surprised to notice that it had rubber tires like a car instead of the wooden wheels like the ones on TV.

Neighborhood dogs barked. Several kids appeared on fluorescent bicycles and swooped around the wagon. The driver waved to them.

The agent returned to the Moffetts. For a moment as she glanced toward the wagon her face had been without expression, but the professional smile returned an instant later. "Charles," she said, extending her hand to Betsy's father, "I'm sure you'll be *very* happy here. Let me know when you've decided on the lender and we'll set up the closing."

She shook hands firmly. Her fingernails were the same shade as the cuffs and collar of the blouse she wore beneath the jacket of her gray suit.

"And, Betsy," the agent added as she took Betsy's hand in turn, "you're going to have a wonderful time, too. Look at all the children to play with!"

The bicycles now lay on their sides in the front yard of a house three doors down. A group had coalesced there to chalk markers on the concrete driveway. The kids ranged from older than Betsy to an infant whose elder brother pushed the stroller.

"I'll be talking to you soon!" the agent said brightly as she got into her car. The BMW's door thunked with a dull finality.

The black man guided his horse to the side of the road, out of the way. The agent backed with verve, then chirped her tires as she took off toward town.

Mr. Moffett put an arm around Betsy's shoulders. "This is my chance to garden," he said. He gestured with the glossy catalogs in his other hand. Those on top read White Flower Farm and Thompson & Morgan, but there were several more in the sheaf.

"Your mother would never let me garden, you know," Mr. Moffett went on, surveying the yard with his eyes. "She ridiculed the whole idea. Well, I'm going to prove how wrong she was."

"Whoa, Bobo," murmured the black man.

The Moffetts turned. The wagon halted directly in front of the house. It was full of live plants. Instead of pots, the root balls were wrapped in burlap. Most of the plants were in flower, and the blooms were gorgeous.

"Dad, can I play with the horse?" Betsy asked as she skipped toward the animal without waiting for what might have been a negative answer.

"The mule, missie," the driver said. "Bobo's a mule, and just the stubbornest mule there ever was—"

He winked toward Mr. Moffett.

"—but he's on company manners right this moment."

Bobo eyed Betsy over the traces. The mule's head was huge, but he looked friendly in a solemn, reserved fashion.

"That's Harbie," the black man said, nodding toward the dog who sniffed the mailbox post meaningfully, "and I'm Jake."

"Can I touch Bobo?" Betsy asked, her hand half extended.

"You surely can, missie," Jake said. To Betsy's father he went on, "Might I interest you in some plants, sir? A new house ought to have flowers around it, don't you think?"

Betsy rubbed the white blaze on the mule's forehead. One of Bobo's long ears twitched and caressed her wrist. Harbie trotted over, sat at Betsy's feet, and raised a paw for attention.

"Well, I'm going to be gardening, yes," Mr. Moffett said. He waved the catalogs. "But I'll be getting my stock only from the best nurseries I—what *are* these plants? I don't think I recognize any of them."

"They's flowers, sir," Jake said. Betsy couldn't tell how old he was. Older than her father, anyway. "I grows them because they's pretty, is all. I've got bushes up to the house, if you'd like something bigger."

"No, I . . ." Mr. Moffett said. He glanced doubtfully at his catalogs, then back to the wagonload of plants. "Are those Hemerocallis so early?"

"There's daylilies, yessir," Jake agreed. "The tall ones, there, and they's some smaller ones around back as would make a nice bed along the street here."

Harbie rolled over on her back and kicked her legs in the air. Her weight pinned Betsy's right toes warmly. Betsy squatted to rub the dog's belly. The mule snorted.

"Those are eight feet *tall*," Mr. Moffett said, staring at the dark green stems from which brilliant red flowers spread.

"Yessir," Jake agreed. "But they's short ones, too. Would you like something for the new house, then?"

Mr. Moffett looked again at the catalogs. To Betsy, the illustrated plants seemed dim and uninteresting compared to the variegated richness in the back of the wagon.

"No thank you," Mr. Moffett said abruptly. "I prefer to trust certified species. Betsy, come along. We need to get back to the apartment."

He reached decisively for her hand. Harbie rolled to her feet and wagged her tail as Betsy straightened.

"Good day to you, then, sir," Jake said. He touched his cap and clucked to his mule.

Mr. Moffett didn't get into the car immediately after all. Instead, he continued to watch the wagon clopping down the street.

"What an odd man," he said.

The lustrous flowers nodded from the back of the wagon.

When Betsy ran up at the head of a delegation of five children, Mr. Moffett was loading a cart with washed stone from the pile the truck had deposited at the end of the driveway.

It was a clear day; even at ten in the morning the June sun was hot. Mr. Moffett nonetheless wore his new gardening apron. The pockets glittered with tools: clippers, hedge trimmers, a planting dibble, and a set of cast-aluminum trowels with a matching spading fork.

"Dad!" Betsy cried. "Stepan's mom says we can take the backboard off their garage and bring it over to our pole so it can be regulation height!"

The rest of the children waited behind Betsy, viewing with interest the work Mr. Moffett had already done in the yard. Except for the driveway itself and a narrow walk, the area between the house and the street was now a flowerbed. Irises, tulips, and the daylilies which Mr. Moffett always called Hemerocallis predominated, but there many more bulb plants that Betsy didn't recognize. Perhaps some of them would have been familiar under other names, but as Acidanthia, Zantedeschia, and similar sounds they could have been tribes of the Amazon.

The climbable dogwoods were gone, chain-sawed off

flush with the ground. Near where they stood, Mr. Moffett had planted what he called Cornus Alba Elegantissima—which looked like dogwoods to Betsy, only very spindly. The saplings had to be guyed in three directions to hold them straight.

"Pole?" Mr. Moffett said. He looked doubtfully at the group of children.

Betsy glanced over her shoulder to make sure the other children were staying in the driveway as she'd warned them to do so that they didn't threaten the plantings. Everybody was fine.

Jake and his wagon clopped down the street. Harbie walked ahead of Bobo with head up, stepping in a sprightly fashion. Jake raised his cap in salute when he saw Betsy.

Mr. Moffett noticed the wagon also. "Does that man live around here?" he asked with an edge in his voice. His eyes were on Stepan, the only black in the present group.

"No, sir," Stepan said, holding himself stiff. "But my mom, she buys his flowers sometimes."

"We buy flowers, too!" said Muriel, who was only six.

"You know the pole, Dad," said Betsy, determined to get the discussion back on course. "In the back yard. The people who lived here before took the backboard when they moved, but Stepan's mom says we can move theirs and have it regulation height!"

"Oh, that pole," Mr. Moffett said. He rubbed his forehead with the back of his hand, looking serious. "Ah."

The car was parked in the street because the driveway was full of gardening supplies. Besides the peanut-sized washed stone for drainage at the bottom of pots and flower beds, there were pallets of bagged topsoil and other bags marked ORGANIC PEAT MOSS—but with a stenciled cow to indicate the real contents more delicately than DRIED COW FLOP would have done.

Mr. Moffett had said he would carry the temporary

excess to the metal storage shed he'd built at the back of the property, but he hadn't gotten around to it yet. The five-horsepower rototiller that had dug the front lawn into flowerbeds was in the shed already, parked beside the powerful chipper/shredder that had ground up all but the lower trunks of the dogwood trees with an amazing amount of racket.

Betsy was a little concerned that her father hadn't bought a lawn mower among all the other new equipment. She was afraid he decided that there wouldn't be any lawn left when he was done with the yard.

"We can get it right now, Dad," Betsy pressed. "You don't have to help. The bolts are still up in the pole, and we can borrow Lee's father's ladder. You can go on digging."

"I'm sorry darling," Mr. Moffett said. He sounded at least uncomfortable it not exactly sorry. "*That* pole is part of my plan for the garden. I'm going—I'm preparing right now—to plant Ipomoea around it. So that the vines can climb properly."

"Whoa, Bobo," Jake muttered out in the street.

Betsy glanced sideways so that she didn't have to look at her father for the moment he wouldn't meet her eyes anyway. He never did at times like these.

Roses twined up the wrought iron posts which supported the rain-shield over the front door. The window to Betsy's bedroom was a green blur from the potted fern which Mr. Moffett had hung there to catch the natural light.

"Good day, sir," Jake called. "I guess you're going to raises some tomatoes."

Harbie snuffled the back of Betsy's knees. Betsy turned quickly and bent to pet the dog. Harbie's tail waggled enthusiastically, whopping all the children as they crowded around her.

"No sir, I don't intend to raise vegetables," Mr. Moffett said stiffly. "I'm concentrating on flowers and flowering shrubs, so if you're selling tomato plants—"

"Not me, sir," Jake said with a chuckle. "But if you don't plan to raise tomatoes—"

He nodded toward the bags of "organic peat moss."

"—then did you tell the cows?"

"Can we get the backboard, now?" Muriel demanded.

"Yeah, what did he say?" Stepan said.

Mr. Moffett grunted angrily. "I don't care to buy any of your plants," he said. "Good day."

"You said," Jake said from the seat of his wagon, "that you were going to plant morning glories around the pole in the back, sir. I've got some fine morning glories here myself."

"I'm quite satisfied with my Purpurea Splendens, thank you," Mr. Moffett said, taking a brightly colored seed packet from an apron pocket. "They have a delicate lavender—"

He stopped. Even the children gaped at the size of the trumpet-shaped blooms Jake held up for approval. They were pure white and at least eight inches across.

Mr. Moffett swallowed. "Lavender picotee, I was saying," he concluded weakly.

"If you want purple edges, sir," Jake said agreeably as he leaned farther back into the loaded wagon, "then I got them, too."

The flower he raised on a vine trailing back into the mass of root balls and foliage was ten inches in diameter. As Jake had said, the edges of the broad bell were faintly lavender.

Mr. Moffett stared at the picture on the seed packet in his hand. "No," he said. He sounded angry. It seemed to Betsy that her father was afraid to look directly at the black man's obviously superior bloom.

"No!" Mr. Moffett repeated. "I prefer a certified product, thank you. Now if you all will leave me alone, I have a great deal of work to do."

Mr. Moffett lifted the handles of his cart and began wheeling it around the side of the house. He had only a part load of gravel, and that was unbalanced.

Harbie had been lying on her back so that the children could rub her belly. She rolled to her feet and trotted to the wagon.

"Good day, then, sir," Jake called. He bowed in his seat to the children. "And good day to you, sirs and missies."

Bobo clopped forward again without a formal order from his driver.

"Let's go back to Stepan's and choose up sides," Betsy said.

"I don't get it," said Stepan, looking in the direction Mr. Moffett had taken around the house. "What's your dad mean certified? He could see the flowers, couldn't he? They're *real*."

"I don't know what real means any more," Betsy answered morosely. She broke into a run to get out of the yard—her father's yard—quickly.

The school bus stopped half a block up from the Moffetts' house. There were still hours of daylight left on an early September afternoon. Todd ran past Betsy calling, "Come on! We're all going to meet at Stepan's when we change clothes!"

Betsy waved, but she didn't much feel like playing. With every step toward home she felt less like playing, or starting the leaf collection for science class, or doing anything at all.

The front yard was dug up again. Betsy's father had removed the bulbs for storage through the winter, then tilled the beds and worked in compost. The rototiller waited beside the house with a blanket over it, ready to finish the job under the yard light above the porch as soon as Mr. Moffett got home.

Because the front yard looked so much like a construction site, Betsy picked her way past bushes to the side door. The hydrangeas were done blooming now, but during their season her father had gotten sprays of pink, white and blue flowers in the same bed by careful liming to lower the soil acidity at one end.

Mr. Moffett was always careful. He didn't even own a grass-whip for edging, because the spinning fishline wasn't precise enough. He used hedge trimmers and his trowels instead.

Betsy's father was always careful with his gardening.

Hollies grew along the side of the house, flanking the doorway two and two. There were three China Girls and a China Boy that Mr. Moffett said wouldn't form berries but were necessary anyway. The holly leaves were sharp. They crowded the concrete pad in front of the door.

Shrubs concealed the back yard. The top of what had been the swing set was just visible above the forsythias. The bars were now festooned with baskets holding fuchsias and campanula. Betsy didn't suppose those plants would spend the winter outdoors, but she was afraid to ask her father what he planned to do with them.

Betsy unlocked the door and went into the kitchen. She dropped her jacket on a chair and opened a can of ravioli to warm for a snack in the microwave while she changed clothes.

Three large bird-of-paradise plants grew from a pot in front of the window beside the refrigerator. A pothos sprawled from the tray beneath the sink window and across most of the back wall. The growlight in the ceiling flooded down on them as well as on the cycads and baobab on the kitchen table.

Betsy visualized the baobab spurting up to the size its ancestors grew to on the African plains—seventy feet tall, with a huge water-filled trunk. The house would disintegrate, and the Moffetts would have to move back to an apartment where Betsy's father couldn't garden any more.

Oh, well.

Betsy changed her school clothes for worn jeans and a sweatshirt in her room. She had to turn the overhead light on to see, because the basket-hung fern covered the window almost completely. At least the light fixture held a regular bulb. Her father had given up on another growlight when Betsy began to cry.

A free-standing hanger rail holding skirts and blouses filled the space between the bed and the wall. The closet had been converted to shelves to store bulbs through the winter. Betsy's father had given her a choice. She could have kept the closet, but then her sweaters and underwear would have gone into cardboard boxes while her dresser provided for the bulbs.

Sighing, Betsy went back to the kitchen. The pothos tickled her neck with a pointed leaf as she got a soda out of the refrigerator. She dumped the ravioli on a plate and carried the snack out through the living room to the front door.

The box in the center of the living room holding the datura was four feet square. It would have made the room seem claustrophobically small even without the other plants filling the corners and shelves on all the walls.

Betsy sat down on the front steps and ate her ravioli bleakly. She could hear the other children playing down the street, but she was too depressed to go join them.

"Whoa, Bobo," a voice said.

Betsy's eyes focused. Though she'd been looking toward the street, there was nothing in her mind but dull green thoughts. Now she saw that Jake had halted his heavily-laden wagon in front of the Moffetts' driveway. "Oh!" she called. "Hi, Jake!"

As always before when Betsy had seen him, Jake was carrying a new assortment of plants. This time many of them were completely covered in what looked like blankets and old bedsheets.

Harbie ran to Betsy and began licking her hands. The dog didn't try to get the last three ravioli until Betsy put the plate down on the step and walked out to the wagon.

"Good afternoon, missie," Jake said, tipping his hat. "Might I trouble you for a bucket of water for Bobo?"

It was funny: even in Betsy's present mood, the flowers and bushes in the wagon had a cheerful look to them. Most of the blooms were bigger and brighter than anything Betsy's father had managed to grow, but the difference was greater than that.

"Sure," Betsy said, starting toward the shed where she knew her father kept galvanized buckets of various sizes. Then she stopped and turned around again. "Jake," she said. "Would you like a soda?"

"I surely would," the black man said. "But let me pay for it, missie. It's better that I do if anybody should ask."

Betsy still wasn't sure about Jake's age. His face was unwrinkled and his mustache was dark, but sometimes she got the feeling he was—old. Very old.

"I—" Betsy said. "Jake, come in the house with me."

Bobo snorted. Jake shook his head firmly. "No, missie," he said. "That I will *not* do, nossir."

Betsy squeezed her eyes to keep from crying. "Will you look in through all the windows at least?" she begged. "You know about plants. I want you to see the house. And the yard!"

Jake got down from the wagon seat, moving with the deliberation of a big cat rather than an old man. He walked to the front window, careful not to step on the low bushes planted along the front of the house. "Pretty enough bog rosemaries," he said. "A bit on the puny side, though."

"My dad calls them andromeda," Betsy said.

"To tell the truth," Jake murmured, "I thought he might."

Betsy darted inside, ready to move anything that prevented Jake from getting a clear view of the environment in which she lived. He walked to her window after gazing seriously into the living room. Betsy opened the closet doors and swung the fern out of the way so that he could look in.

The spare bedroom had become a hothouse with

multiple banks of growlights. Betsy couldn't get to the orchid-shrouded window, but the mass of variegated green Jake could glimpse was sufficient to give him the picture. Her father's bedroom was almost as packed, though the plants lowering over the dresser and single bed weren't as temperature sensitive.

The bathroom window was above head height. Jake could see the begonias in the hanging basket, but the tubbed water lily that turned the shower/bath into a cramped shower was concealed. She could tell him about it, but it was such a drop in the bucket that she didn't suppose she'd bother.

While Jake peered through one kitchen window, then the other, Betsy flicked her way past the pothos and got another soda. She met Jake again at the side door, where he was fingering the leaves of the China Boy holly. His lips smiled slightly, but his eyes were a cold brown Betsy hadn't seen before.

"Jake," she said, "I can't stand this. What am I going to do?"

Jake sipped the soda, looking over the top of the can as he surveyed the back yard. At last he lowered the can and handed it back to Betsy, empty, without looking at her.

"You know," he said, "ever'body ought to have plants in their life, missie. But they oughtn't to be your life . . . and sure you oughtn't to make them somebody else's life besides."

"But what am I going to *do*, Jake?"

Jake suddenly beamed at her. "Come along with me to the wagon, missie," he said. He waved her ahead of him. Harbie led them up the congested path, barking cheerfully.

"It seems to me," Jake resumed as he pulled a shovel and a narrow spade from the bed of his wagon, "that since your father likes plants so all fired much, we ought to give him some more plants."

He handed the tools to Betsy and reached back for

one of the larger plants—one completely covered by a stained wool blanket that had originally been olive drab.

Betsy thought about her savings passbook with the—small—amount of her aunt's Christmas gift in it. "Ah . . ." she said. "How much will this cost? Because—"

Jake looked down. For a moment, he seemed as old as the Earth itself, but he was smiling.

"I'll barter the plants to you, missie," he said. "For one Pepsi Cola. And a smile."

Betsy gave him a broad, glowing smile.

The sky was still bright when Mr. Moffett pulled up in the street, but the ground was a pattern of shadows and muted colors that made the headlights necessary for safety. He'd be able to get the last of the front beds turned, but the remainder of the evening would be spent inside with the orchids.

The air had a slight nip to it. Warm days weren't over yet, but the nights were getting cool. He'd have to bring in all the half-hardy plants within the month. Locating them indoors would require planning.

Children called to one another down the street as Mr. Moffett followed the walk to his front door. A basketball whopped a backboard, though there didn't seem to be enough light to play. He wondered if Betsy was among the group.

Something caught at Mr. Moffett's legs. He'd built the walk of round, pebble-finished concrete pavers, bordered on either side by statice. The flowers were finished growing, but the papery blooms remained on the stems like so many attractive, dried-flower displays.

They should have finished growing. In fact, the plants at the head of the walk seemed to have spread inward during the day. They were sticking to his knees.

Mr. Moffett detached himself carefully. He couldn't afford to replace the trousers of this suit, not with the bulb order he was preparing for next spring.

The small earth-toned flowers even clung to his hands. Statice didn't have stickers, so it must be dried bud casings that gripped him.

Mr. Moffett was smiling faintly as he walked to the front door, fishing in his pocket for his keys. He'd dosed his beds with a hormonal additive he'd ordered from Dresden, *Azetelia Ziehenstoff*. Perhaps he'd been a little excessive with the statice.

He inserted the key in the lock. "Betsy, are you home?" he called.

The rosebushes trained up the pillars to either side rustled. They gripped his shoulders from behind.

Mr. Moffett shouted. For a moment he thought his daughter was playing a joke. He looked around. The bush to his left extended a tendril toward his elbow. The spray of fresh leaves on the end exaggerated the movement like the popper tip of a bullwhip.

"Hey!"

The main stems were biting through multiple layers of cloth and the skin of his shoulders. Lesser thorns on the tendril pricked him as well, almost encircling his arm. Holding him.

The front door was unlatched. Mr. Moffett hurled himself toward it, but he couldn't break the thorns' grip on his back. Another tendril slid dryly across his neck. He wriggled out of his coat, all but the left arm, and then tore himself free of that also. The lining pulled from his sleeve. There were streaks of blood on his polyester-blend shirt. He fell on the living room floor.

The suitcoat writhed in the air behind him as the roses continued to explore the fabric.

Mr. Moffett was breathing hard. A rose tendril waggled interrogatively toward the doorway. Mr. Moffett kicked the door shut violently.

The living room seemed dark. He looked around to be sure the bank of growlights in the ceiling was turned on. It was, but the datura in the central planter had more than doubled in height since he left in the morning. The dark, bluish-green leaves now wrapped the fixture, permitting only a slaty remnant of the light to wash the room.

The plant whispered. The flowers, white and the size of a human head, rotated toward the man on the floor. They were deadly poison, like all parts of the datura. Stamens quivered in the throats of the trumpet shaped blooms as if they were so many yellow tongues.

Mr. Moffett got up quickly and walked to the kitchen. His right pants leg flapped loose. He hadn't noticed it being torn while he struggled with the rose.

He was sweating. He wasn't a drinker, but there was a bottle of Old Crow in the cabinet behind the oatmeal. This was the time to get it down

The kitchen . . . The kitchen wasn't right. The bird-of-paradise plants made a thin buzzing noise, and their flowers trembled. They didn't look the way they—

Mr. Moffett had put his hand on the kitchen table without being aware of the fact in his concentration on the birds-of-paradise. Pain worse than he ever recalled feeling lanced up his arm.

The dwarf baobab had swung down a branch. There were spikes in the bottom of every one of the tiny leaves. They stabbed deeply through the back of Mr. Moffett's hand.

He screamed and hurled himself sideways. He collided with the refrigerator. The back of his hand looked as though he'd been using it as a pull-toy for a score of insufficiently-socialized cats. He was spattering blood all over the kitchen.

Something dropped around his neck. The pothos was trying to strangle him. The thin, green-white vine was no match for the hysterical strength with which Mr. Moffett tore its stem and leaves to shreds.

The buzzing was louder. He glanced up. The orange bird-of-paradise flowers lifted off their stems. They hovered for a moment, looking and sounding like the largest hornets in the world. They started toward Mr. Moffett.

Crying uncontrollably, Mr. Moffett threw open the side door and jumped clear of the kitchen. He might have been all right if he'd continued running, but he paused to slam the panel against the oncoming birds-of-paradise.

The holly bushes were waiting.

Until the side door banged, Betsy waited in the back yard with the hedge trimmers in her hands. Jake had told her not to move until her father came outside again and shouted. The blood-curdling shriek an instant after the door closed was her signal.

She ran around the corner. The China Girl to the right of the door had her father in a full, prickly embrace. Mr. Moffett had taken off his coat, and his tie was twisted back behind him.

The China Boy on the other side bent sideways. The two bushes on the ends of the border were shivering in frustration that they hadn't been planted close enough to join in the attack.

"I'll help you, daddy!" Betsy shrilled. She thrust the hedge trimmers toward a branch clutching her father's left shoulder. She clamped down with all her strength.

The holly's woody core resisted the blades. Betsy twisted, worrying at the limb when she couldn't shear it.

The branch parted at last. Those leaves' grip on her father weakened, but he was still held by a dozen other limbs. A branch was twisting toward him from the rear of the bush to replace the severed one, and branches reached for Betsy as well.

The tips of China Boy's limbs bent gracefully toward Mr. Moffett's face.

"Betsy, get out of here!" Mr. Moffett cried. He pushed away jagged leaves that threatened his eyes, but more poised to engulf his head from all directions. "Run away! Run away!"

An air-cooled engine fired up nearby with a ringing clatter. Doors banged shut as neighbors came out to see what the shouting was about. By the time anybody could tell in the twilight, it would be too late.

Betsy hacked at a twig, severing it cleanly. She was crying. It wasn't supposed to be like this! She closed the trimmer on another branch, this one thicker than her thumb. The blades wouldn't cut. She tugged and twisted and bawled.

"Darling, get away!" her father cried.

Something grabbed the cuff of her jeans. She ignored it. China Boy unfolded a limb toward her face. The kinked branch was amazingly long when it straightened to its full length. The touch on her cuff was now a spiky, circular grip that held her like a shackle.

Harbie curved through the air and caught the China Boy branch in teeth that were amazingly long and white. The dog's weight slapped the spray of jagged leaves away from Betsy's face an instant before the big jaws crushed through and severed the branch completely.

Jake came around the front corner, guiding the big rototiller. The spinning bolo tines chewed into the end China Girl. The engine labored, then roared with triumph as the blades ground free and forward again.

The holly gripping Mr. Moffett shuddered as the rototiller slammed it, shredding roots and main stem together. The limb Betsy hacked at finally parted.

All the holly branches relaxed with the suddenness of a string snapping. Mr. Moffett fell free.

"Watch yourselves, Sir and missie!" Jake shouted over the racket of the rototiller's exhaust. The tines sparked as Jake drove over the concrete pad outside the door and into the recoiling China Boy.

Betsy sat down abruptly on the gravel. Her knees suddenly wouldn't lock. Her father crawled over to her.

Harbie, wagging her tail furiously, began to lick Betsy's face. Beside the house, the rototiller bellowed as it devoured the fourth holly.

The morning was overcast, but it wasn't raining. Mr. Moffett wore his overcoat, leather gloves, and the motorcycle helmet he'd borrowed from Ricky Tilden at the head of the block. He picked up the last of the plants, a geranium.

Pink flowers gummed Mr. Moffett's gloves harmlessly as he flung the plant into the intake of the roaring chipper/shredder. The machine didn't react to the minuscule load.

Mr. Moffett reached down and shut off the spark. As the powerful hammermill spun down slowly against the inertia of its flywheel, he stripped off his gloves and then removed the helmet.

Betsy and Jake took their hands away from their ears. Harbie, who'd been lying under the wagon, got up and walked over to the humans again. The chipper/shredder had made an incredible amount of noise.

A long trail of wood chips and chopped foliage led up the drive to the machine. Rather than clear away the piles of debris that spewed out through the grating in the bottom, Mr. Moffett had simply rolled the chipper/shredder backward to each new concentration of vegetation to process.

"There!" Mr. Moffett said. He took off the overcoat. The heavy fabric was stained and even torn in a few places.

The yard had been converted to raw dirt and chewed-up vegetation.

"You've got ever' thing turned up, sir," Jake said as the last ringing chatter of the chipper/shredder died away. "And you know, a yard ought to have *some* plants in it—"

"No," Mr. Moffett said with absolute finality. "It should not."

He looked around him. "I may pave it. Though I suppose grass would be all right. Or maybe gravel . . ."

Betsy ran over to her father and hugged him. His face was scratched and blood seeped through the thin cotton gloves he'd worn under the leather pair, but he hadn't been seriously injured in the previous evening's events.

"I think," Mr. Moffett said as he squeezed his daughter's shoulders, "that I'm going to get a dog. My wife would never let me have a dog. I've always regretted that."

"Is that so, sir?" Jake said with enthusiasm. "Why, you know, Harbie here's going to have a litter just next month. She likes kids, Harbie does, and I reckon her puppies'd like them, too."

"Oh, Dad, could we?" Betsy asked. "Could we have one of Harbie's puppies?"

"Harbie's puppies?" her father said in puzzlement. "Well, I don't think . . ."

He looked at Jake. "Your Harbie is a *mongrel*, isn't she?"

Jake smiled. "Harbie's a dog, sir," he said. "A good dog, though she has her ways like we all do."

Harbie dropped over onto her back with an audible thump and kicked her legs in the air. Jake rubbed her belly with his fingertips. Harbie's dugs were beginning to protrude from pregnancy hormones and the pressure of the puppies beneath.

"That's very well, I'm sure," Mr. Moffett said in a voice that gave the lie to his words. "But I'm thinking of something pedigreed. A Bernese Mountain Dog, I believe."

Jake nodded. "I reckon you know your own mind, sir," he said as he walked back to his wagon.

"I'm going to shower, darling," Mr. Moffett said to Betsy. "Would you carry the helmet back to Mr. Tilden for me?"

"Yes, daddy," Betsy said to her father's back.

"Get on, Bobo," Jake murmured.

Betsy looked at the wagon. Bobo glanced over the traces and winked at her. Harbie barked cheerfully and winked.

And Jake, turning on the wagon seat, winked also. His smile was as bright as the summer sun.

Known as "the speed merchant of the pulps," Arthur J. Burks wrote millions of words for the horror, mystery, adventure, romance and science fiction magazines in the first half of the twentieth century. Although most of his weird fiction appeared in Horror Stories, Terror Tales, Dime Mystery, *and other shudder pulps, he also contributed to the distinguished fantasy magazines* Unknown, Strange Tales, *and* Weird Tales *which published his highly regarded stories of magic and mystery set in Santo Domingo. His best short fiction was collected in* Black Medicine. *His other books include the compilation* Look Behind You *and the novels* The Casket, The Great Amen *and* The Great Mirror.

BLACK HARVEST OF MORAINE

ARTHUR J. BURKS

I: THE HATED DRAW

I had been afraid of that particular field since I could remember. It was a mounded promontory where two whispering draws met. It looked like a monstrous brazen bosom spangled with pebbles of many colors, all of them round and smooth with age. My uncle's farmhouse sat in the side of the draw, perhaps seventy feet below the surface of the field, but sufficiently above the draw's floor to escape sudden inundation. I hated the draw, called Toler Draw, and the nameless other draws that came

137

into it from the east, but both fascinated me so that when I visited my uncle I could not be satisfied without venturing onto the pebbly bosom of the shoulders of the high field and down into the secondary draw.

"A draw," out West, is a deep ravine or gully.

I was fifteen years old when my fear of the field between the two draws came to a head because I could see my ancient fear in the faces of the other harvest hands. I watched Charles Norman, my uncle, who acted as separator tender of the combined harvester. He stood atop the combined harvester and stared moodily out across the half section of wheat we were about to harvest, *if* he gave the word. On the lefthand side of the separator, on his little platform, the sack sewer, a Norwegian, sat on his little box under the twin spouts and watched Charles Norman. He had tried his best to talk Charles out of harvesting this half section. Apparently he had failed, but he had done his best.

Lonnie Keel, fourteen, tended the header. He had affixed a seat to the railing above the open maw of the cylinders at the inner end of the header; he sat on it now, hands engaged in the spokes of the wheel, watching me. I could see he was afraid, too, but excited as only an ambitious youngster can get.

I had tended header the two previous harvests, but now I drove the whole shebang, thirty-two head of horses and mules, five teams of six animals each with two leaders. The separator was run by a distillate engine set just behind the teams, at the base of the slanting ladder that led up to the dizzy seat where the driver, myself, Cappy Payne, tried to still the hammering of his heart.

Even yet Charles Norman had not decided for sure. There was danger in the high wheat, nobody knew just how great or varied. Then, the crew was untried, even to the horses and mules. Only the oldest animals had worked ahead of the clamoring engine. I felt it took courage to try to handle the thirty-two animals with only two lines attached to the leaders.

"Well," said Charles Norman, "hang onto the jug-heads, we're getting under way!"

I faced the front. Charles Norman, a man of forty or so, climbed down to the distillate engine, cranked it. My horses and mules almost jumped through their collars when the engine broke into raucous song and the hidden machinery of the combined harvester began its roaring. Out of the harvester rose the dust left from last year's last work in the fields, to form a brown cloud about the ponderous machinery.

"Steady, Kate! Hold it, Jerry!" I spoke softly to my leaders, one a sensitive horse mare, the other a steady old mule who had been combined harvester leader since my uncle first owned one of the roaring monsters. I had handled all these animals on other farm equipment, so they knew my voice. I managed to keep them steady.

The blades of the leader were tapping at the first of the wheat in the field, folding them back onto the canvas of the conveyor. Even this gentle hammering, for the wooden blades were intended only to keep wheat stalks from bending away under the reaper and being lost behind the machine, emphasized the thing all of us feared: for out of those few heads came the bronze, slick-looking, sooty smut which had turned the old field into a horror.

We all stared at the field as Norman climbed back onto the separator. As far as we could see the heads of wheat which should have gone fifty bushels to the acre, should have been white and firm under the hulls, were a sullen black that threatened to burst from the heads in an ebon inundation.

None of us had ever seen a field so smutted.

"Charlie," John Cavick, the sack sewer had said, "the best thing you can do with that field, for the good of the neighbors if not for yourself, is set it afire! You won't save ten bushels to the acre, and you'll scatter smut from Hades to breakfast!"

"Even ten bushels will keep me out of the red," said Norman. "I've got to take the risk. Of course, if you're afraid to tackle it, maybe I can hire someone else in Waterville."

"I'll do any work anywhere anybody else will," said Cavick, but he kept right after Uncle Charles to the moment I actually started pushing those thirty-two head of animals around the huge field.

There was a weirdness about the field we all recognized. It was surrounded by vast fields of neighbors, and on the north, across the main road, was another half section belonging to Norman, too. No other field in the county suffered smut! How did it happen that this one field alone should be so ridden with it? And why should an aura of *waiting*, of *threat*, of psychic terror, hang over this one particular field? I confess my own terrors went back further than those of Cavick, Lonnie, Uncle Charles or anyone else. I kept remembering from childhood, my secret adventures into the two draws, around the mounded bosom of the high field. I remembered badgers drumming into the holes among the sagebrush along the wash at the bottom of the subsidiary draw. I had flushed skulking coyotes, jackrabbits, cottontails, and almost scared myself to death when an occasional sagehen whirred out of hiding in some area of eerie silence. I had heard old tales of strange walkers among the brush, tales told around late supper tables for the sole purpose of scaring kids of the dark.

Charles Norman, atop the separator, hesitated again. I was looking back at him. I held a small rock in my hand. Above the roaring of the engine a man couldn't hear himself think. Charles Norman nodded to me. He had made his final decision. The die was cast.

"Kate! Jerry!" I heaved the rock out ahead of my leaders, careful not to hit either of them. The mules and horses hit their tugs. The huge combined harvester began to move. I had to hold back the animals to keep them from traveling too fast to catch the grain. It was almost as if they, too, feared the field and were running away from it. But for them, as far as I know, it was the motor they feared, and the fact that they could not seem to outrun it.

Almost instantly the harvester and everybody on it, including myself perched out there atop that ladder far in advance of the main body of the machine, including the horses and mules, disappeared into a black-bronze pall, a towering smut cloud that was utterly terrifying. The header, an eighteen-foot "cut," which meant that it cut a swath eighteen feet wide if I held the team so that the header cut its entire width— a driving trick I made up my mind I could manage—laid the smutted wheat back on the drapers, the reapers cut off the stalks, the drapers bore the fallen wheat up the short feed into the body of the machine where the threshing took place. Out of the main body of the machine straw fell into a trip behind the separator, where the header tender, with a long rope attached to his railing, dumped it at intervals in piles behind us. The wheat, separated from the stalks and fanned of chaff, poured into the sacks on Cavick's platform, to be sewn, slid into the carrier beside him, which slanted down to within a few inches of the ground, and tripped when there were six sacks.

Separate from the harvester was the sack-buck, a husky man with a team and a flat-bed wagon, who hauled the sacks to central piling areas.

Nobody aboard the harvester saw the sack-buck, Karl Orme, while the harvester moved, because we could not see out of the pall of smut. That cloud, as smut burst from the wheat inside the harvester, belched out of every nook and cranny. Some of the spores burst on hitting the drapers, some when touched by the fanning blades, some burst on the first contact.

The rising smut cloud, which followed us like Nemesis because there was no wind, was worse than any dust

storm I had ever witnessed. Looking back and down to
the right it was all I could do to see the inner end of
the header, to know whether I was cutting too wide a
swath and missing some, or using less than I should of
the "cut." I could just see. But up ahead, when I tried
to see my laboring animals, I could scarcely see Kate
and Jerry, my leaders. The horses and mules, even those
directly under me, which included the first twelve
animals, six abreast, were vague shadowy phantoms in
the sooty pall.

I could make out the back of Cavick as he worked
like some imp out of hell there on his little platform,
fighting the sack-jigger from which poured a stream that
would have been wheaten gold if it had not been for
the smut. Even with all the fanning, vast amounts of
smut went into the wheat sacks. Cavick had turned black
and hideous within a few minutes. He had a bright red
bandanna about his neck; it became black-bronze in no
time. Atop the harvester Lonnie and Uncle Charles were
black gnomes in the cloud, and when Uncle Charles
walked back to the rear of the separator to study his
mazes of wheels, sprockets, belts and pullies, he mingled
so closely with the cloud that I could not see him unless
he moved an arm suddenly.

I leaned back and looked up. The sun itself was a
blur through the horror. Horror? That's what I said. True
or not, there was a terror about smut. Most farmers believed that it could be ignited, that it might at any time
explode, if there were enough of it, by spontaneous
combustion. No farmer would allow his hands to smoke
where there was even the vaguest hint of smut, and
every last one of us, before coming to the field, had
supposedly ditched his matches at the farmhouse. I could
just imagine what it would be like even if the smut did
no more than take *fire*. It expanded outward, that thick
cloud, to hold us within its heart and travel along with
us around the field, clockwise. A series of swaths had

already been cut around the field, some weeks earlier, with a binder. Good hay had been the result, and this was another one of the fear-provoking facts about this particular field. There had been no evidence of smut in the *hay*!

The smut had apparently come full into being between a night and a morning!

Horses, mules and farm hands, especially in harvest time, become accustomed to choking dust. I had driven for hours in clouds of ordinary dust as thick as this without much discomfort, though a doctor would have thrown up his hands and uttered all sorts of dire things. I hadn't even coughed. Mules and horses coughed occasionally, but it never seemed to be anything that a good long drink of water at noon and night would not arrange.

Now, though, before I even reached the first corner and started the ponderous swinging of that team— there'd have been fifty-six head if Uncle Charles hadn't "modernized" by attaching the engine to run the separator—everyone on the separator was coughing. Lonnie sounded as if he had whooping cough; deep, rasping, tearing coughs burst from apparently the very bottom of his lungs. Cavick coughed as if he was swearing. Uncle Charles coughed like a consumptive, as if he would spit blood any instant. I coughed as if I were young again and lost, and sobbing.

But the worst was the coughing of the mules and horses. Men can help themselves. They can stop work. Animals are slaves and must obey their owners and masters. Thirty-two head of mules and horses then, about half of each, struggled grimly through the sooty pall and coughed, deep and drumming, out of their very guts.

I made the first turn. The cloud went with us! It should have gone straight ahead, mind you; why should the *cloud* have turned the corner? I wondered if anybody noticed it but me.

✧   ✧   ✧

There were tiny draws in the great field. When we slid down into one I could reach out to right and left and touch the backs of my rearmost animals. When we rose out of the ditch I leaped at the sky like hay on the end of a pitchfork, legs hooked around the jacobstaff to keep from being thrown. These ditches and steep hillsides were why Uncle Charles did not use tractors to pull the harvester in this particular field—mules and horses could manage better.

By the time we reached the second corner of the huge half section, with all its wheat covered knolls, deep pitches, steep hillsides where the leveler had to be worked like crazy to keep the monster from overturning, I was conscious of something new in the cloud of smut: in some eerie fashion it was *in tune with the chugging of the motor and the drumming of machinery in the guts of the separator, with the low murderous growling of the cylinders especially*. These cylinders now, for the benefit of the mechanically minded, were not the cylinders of the engine; they were the two sets of opposing concave and convex metal "teeth" just behind the short feed from the drapers, through which the wheat passed—the heads to be ripped asunder by the teeth to separate the roughest wheat from the straw. I had known of men to go through those cylinders, come out in fingertip-sized pieces behind the separator.

There was, as I've indicated, an eternal murderous growl about those cylinders when the separator was in gear that made me afraid for the header tender, Lonnie. I'd had that job for two years myself, and always the cylinders had seemed to me to be too close under me for comfort. A bit of dizziness, a fall, and the machine couldn't be thrown out of gear fast enough to keep a man out of the metal teeth.

But why should I fear that now? Because of the sound I *felt* in the sooty cloud—keeping time with the roaring of the cylinders!

The cloud stayed with us as we traveled the far side, slow, ponderous, noisy, every living thing of us coughing his guts out, and started back on the fourth side, which paralleled the subsidiary draw that had always held such terror for me as a child. The side of the draw was steep. I had plowed and seeded it myself, plowing and seeding down as far as I could, to where the streambed was just too steep for anything but a goat—where only sagebrush and rye grass grew. Down there I knew was the perpendicular wash with badger holes in the banks, and big mounds on the streambed. Down there was land that to me, even at fifteen, was terror-land.

You see, I had always, from earliest memories of visits to Uncle Charles' place, been conscious that the entire high field resembled a monstrous grave-mound! It was a feeling I could not escape, of which I could not rid myself. If my feeling had any basis in fact— and I doubted it too much, ever to mention it to anyone—*what was buried under it and how far back did it date?*

As we fought our way back to the starting corner, around that gargantuan bosom, or grave mound, I had the strangest feeling that the deep freshet-bed, into which I could not see because of the borders of sagebrush and rye grass, was a-crawl with something. Badgers? Coyotes? Sagehens? Rabbits? What else had I ever seen or heard, in the sandy hot wash? Nothing, save in imagination. But in imagination there had been Indian bones, stalking warriors out of elder time—and things man no longer remembered or had heard about, dating back and back and back.

This part of the Big Bend country of the Columbia River was the tag-end of the Great Moraine, almost the exact line on which the Ice Age from the north died, began slowly retreating back to the Arctic.

Why I should remember that in that high field of strangely smutted grain I had no idea, then.

Uncle Charles signaled for a halt at the starting spot. The mules and horses, black with sweat all over their bodies, sweat into which the smut was worked like boring maggots stood and coughed horribly. We all coughed.

The smut cloud did not move on, as it seemed it should. It just stayed there as we stayed, a dome of ebony glisten over and around us. There was a whiteness about the mouths, eyes and nostrils of men and beast. Our hair and lashes were beaded with smut. Our lungs were afire with it. It tasted bitter as lye on our parched tongues.

I expected Uncle Charles to call it quits, but he was a stubborn man. He signaled for the second round.

II: EBON EXODUS

The same stubbornness, suddenly, was in all of us. We refused to be beaten. How could any of us, simple farm people, have realized *what made us stubborn?* We were just people, descended from pioneer stock, who wouldn't allow a little thing like smut to which all farmers were occasionally accustomed, to keep us from the harvest. The world was hungry, must be fed, and feeding the world gave us money for luxuries. That was the simple truth of it.

It wouldn't have made any difference, I realize now, if Uncle Charles had given orders to knock off, had decided to let the field rot, for once we had rounded the field we were *committed*. The damage, which we could not even guess at then, was already done.

I'll never know how we got around that second time. It's a long drag around a half section. At first, if you can make three "rounds" without leaving half the wheat, in half a day, you're doing all right. We made three rounds and that smut cloud never left us. The coughing was hideous. Lonnie especially felt it. He bent double as he coughed. He had had whooping cough that winter, I knew, and his lungs had been weakened by it.

The cloud had expanded and deepened unbelievably. I felt that every spore we had released from the wheat had joined the cloud. I felt that the rhythm I had sensed in the cloud was faster, should have been an audible sound to everybody on the separator, but everybody was too hard at work, too busy coughing, to pay any attention.

We were coming around the shoulder where the two draws merged when the first catastrophe happened—and I was to remember with horror that I had so often thought of this very possibility. *Had I made it happen?*

I heard a scream and whirled on my high perch to see Lonnie Keel fall upon the drapers, bounce, grab for the sides of the feed, ride the canvas into the maw of the machine. He screamed all the way in, until the cylinder teeth got him. His screaming made the mules and horses unmanageable for a full minute, and though Uncle Charles hurried to throw the machinery out of gear, there was no use. Lonnie Keel was doomed from the moment he fell.

And yet, he should have been able to grab the sides of the feed, haul himself out. He had tried, but as I thought of it later it seemed to me that his hands were *snatched* back, the clutching fingers *prevented* from pulling the boy out, saving his life. But of course every farmer knows how to compare hindsight with foresight. I was always one to do a lot of imagining.

The animals wouldn't stop until we made that last corner. Uncle Charles and Cavick were both off the separator, running back behind it. No doubting what they would find—the tiny bloody pieces of Lonnie Keel!

I swung the horses and mules to a halt finally. I fastened the two lines to the whip-stock in the rock box, climbed down and killed the distillate-burning engine. Then, sick, coughing, my fear a tangible thing now, I raced back to Uncle Charles and Cavick.

They were bending over something in the stubble.

I bent down, too. I got even sicker. There wasn't enough left of any part of Lonnie Keel to wad a shotgun! And yet, attached to some of the smallest bits were shreds and patches of his shirt, overalls and shoes!

We three were very close together.

"God!" said Uncle Charles. "Go ahead, Cavick, say you told me so! But that don't explain what made the kid fall! There was no reason. I saw him go, and it looked as if he was *pulled* off his seat, *thrown* into the cylinders!"

"I couldn't see," said Cavick, "there's too much machinery between me and the header tender—and the smut's too thick anyway!"

We moved back from the combined harvester, the three of us, and noted the pieces of Lonnie Keel, but I think I was the first to notice the real horror of what was just now really starting.

I was staring at a lump of flesh when it seemed to *move*. Then I realized that it wasn't a tiny piece of *Lonnie* that was moving, but something else that was moving *onto* the crimson flesh! It didn't take two shakes to figure out what it was. The smut was alive! It was a tiny glistening army. It crawled onto those pieces of flesh, covered them from sight, *fed upon them!*

Uncle Charles cried out. John Cavick swore savagely. There was nothing we could do for Lonnie, but even so the next move seemed cruel—at *first*. We heard one of the horses scream like a woman in pain. We all three straightened, whirled to look. Several of the horses and mules were down on their bellies in their harness, threshing, coughing—and now several of them followed suit of the first one and screamed. It isn't often, thank God, that a farmer hears a horse scream; usually only when the animal is dying in a fire.

"Get them out!" yelled Uncle Charles. "Get them out of the smut, down to the troughs!"

We didn't forget Lonnie, mind you, nor ourselves. I

realized that I was more or less burning up myself, with something more than the heat. A steadily increasing inward pressure was all over my body, and its warmth, too, was increasing.

Uncle Charles didn't ordinarily help with the draft animals, but he did this time. Lonnie usually handled eight head, while Cavick and I took twelve each; but Lonnie wouldn't be doing that kind of work ever again. Uncle Charles had to.

The animals were half crazy but they knew us, knew we were trying to save them, so they stood, fretting a little but not so much, until we had all the tugs unfastened and folded back inside the back-bands.

I mounted Kate. Uncle Charles mounted one of the others, Cavick a third. The rest were apportioned among us, held together by their halter chains. I gave the word to Kate when the rest signaled they were ready.

My twelve head of animals, as if at a signal, broke into a dead run from a standing start. It almost threw me. But behind us the rest came on just as fast, as if invisible whips had suddenly been laid upon the backs of every last one!

My twelve headed for the gate and the main road. I did not try to hold them in. It would have been no use. I yelled ahead for the chore-man we had left in the barnyard to have the yard gate open. I could see it start swinging inward as we started down the steep rocky grade into the draw. Our galloping had thunder in it, and danger. If one horse or mule even stumbled we would have a murderous pile-up.

I looked back once. Cavick and Uncle Charles were clinging to their riding animals for dear life. I expected somehow to find the smut cloud still with us, but it had halted, rather oddly I thought, partly in and partly outside the field gate. The cloud reached fully a thousand feet into the air and seemed to hover over the entire field.

I thought, as we swung crazily into the gate like

chariots taking a dangerous turn, that the smut cloud, on whose sides the sun shone as on the back of a smoothly curried horse, was beginning to sink down upon the field. I saw Karl Orme, the sack-buck, come racing through the gate, standing spread-legged in his flatbed sack wagon, his horses apparently crazy with fear. I saw him fight the lines, turn and face the field from which all of its had just escaped. ,Yes even then I used the word, "escaped!" Then Karl Orme did an odd thing, though I didn't see all of it because I had things of my own to do. He jumped from his wagon, lashed his animals into a dead run, and moved slowly back, afoot, to the gate in which the smut cloud seemed to hesitate. It was afterward I remembered that slow, queer return.

Then I lost Karl Orme behind the barn as my animals reached the huge circular galvanized tank in the barnyard, so big that all of Uncle Charles' animals could drink from it at once. I flung myself from Kate's back as Cavick and Uncle Charles swung their animals in against the tank, too.

Uncle Charles yelled at Cavick and me while he himself ran awkwardly toward the blacksmith shop where he kept tools, hoses, odds and ends always needed around a farm.

"Into the tank, both of you!" Uncle Charles yelled. "Get your clothes off! I'll be right back!"

Odd, but I had been wanting to fling myself into the tank. The water in it was about three and a half feet deep. The horses and mules pushed their nostrils clear under. I saw all their eyes bulged. There were lines of white about them.

Aunt Claudia and my two gal cousins came running from the house to ask silly questions just as Uncle Charles came from the shop with a length of hose. He yelled at his wife and daughters:

"Get back away from us! Don't stop for anything,

but go on past the house to the next neighbor's. Stay by the telephone there. I'll let you know what to do! *Run!*"

Naturally they thought Uncle Charles was crazy, and I thought so, too, but they turned and fled as their forebears must have fled from charging Indians. Women and girls can run when they're scared.

Uncle Charles flung himself into the tank with Cavick and me.

Cavick and I had both dived in, going under, much to the amazement of the horses and mules. Then, standing, we stripped off our clothes, and began to wash our hair, bathe our bodies. Uncle Charles followed suit, but his first thought was of the animals. He affixed one end of the hose to the faucet, turned it on full, and began spraying the horses and mules. The water had plenty of pressure and the stream was strong, but each animal seemed to realize at once that again their best interests were being taken care of.

While he worked on himself Uncle Charles handed the hose to me. I worked on the animals, too. I watched the smut which had covered them vanish into the longer hair under their bellies. I washed that off, too. Karl Orme's team reached the tank, hauling back to stop the wagon as if Orme had still been in it.

I washed them off, too, then John Cavick took a crack at it. Still there were no explanations of anything.

Soon Karl Orme, hatless, his legs pumping like those of a college sprinter, came through the gate, pushed past the animals and flung himself into the trough. Was all this crazy, even a little humorous? Not if you remembered Lonnie Keel and the creeping smut spores which had started devouring his remnants.

Karl Orme stood in the tank, began ripping off his clothes. I noticed that Uncle Charles, standing there in the tank from which now rose the odor of smut, stared up the rounded mound of the drawside at his smutted field. Over the field hung a tremendous black cloud, into which shot tongues of flame. Uncle Charles whirled on Karl Orme.

"What happened, Karl?" He choked. "You were the last out of the field. Did it just take fire?"

"No, Charlie," said Orme grimly, "I took the law into my own hands. Your stubbornness might cost lives. I saw Lonnie Keel tumble, read sign when you went back to look. The rest was just common sense. I dashed out of the field, freed the horses, turned back and took the greatest chance I ever hope to take. *I threw a match into the cloud!*"

"How dared you do such a thing?" demanded Uncle Charles hoarsely. "You're a hired hand! You've set fire to a half section of wheat. My loss will run into thousands—"

"And how many lives?" said Karl Orme softly. "Listen, Charlie, while I tell you something. I picked up those smutty sacks that John here sewed and dropped. There smut in all of them I had piled maybe a hundred in one area, when what do you suppose happened?"

"How would I know?" said Uncle Charles sulkily.

"The sacks began bursting their seams!" said Karl Orme. "They just exploded like over-inflated toy balloons, *and the smut began creeping out, to spread on the ground!* I knew if I didn't take steps your stubbornness would return us all to the field of smut, and no telling what might happen!"

"And now," said Uncle Charles hoarsely, "you've completely released the *things* in the wheat."

"*Things?*" said Karl Orme. "What are you talking about. I've burned out that half section, or will have within an hour. The smut won't spread to neighboring fields. The fire—"

"Fire won't do anything to *this*," said Uncle Charles. "It will just complete, a lot faster, the exodus of the—"

What he was going to say I didn't know then, couldn't even guess, for all four of us noticed the same thing at the same time. We had washed from ourselves the smut which had been driving us crazy. We had drunk deeply to wash the stuff out of our gullets. The smut had lain, a thin film, atop the water in the tank. Now we all saw that the stuff had drawn together atop the water, moved slowly to the sides of the tank where it became a thick brown mass. And that mass began crawling up the side of the tank to escape! The horses and mules saw it, snorted, backed away.

We couldn't find a thing to say. We moved to the side of the tank, watching that stuff—and as if it watched us also, and were afraid of being captured, *it gathered speed like some shapeless spider, slid over the rim of the tank, dropped to the ground beyond!* We heard it, and the sound had a kind of jeer in it, strike the ground.

We put our hands on the sides and looked down— just as the smut we had washed off the animals gathered in one place, joined that which had come out of the tank! The mass of smut was dark bronze. It formed a circular smudge, the center of which began to rise perceptibly.

As we stared, our months hanging open, the smut-mass doubled in size, doubled again!

"John!" yelled Uncle Charles. "Get a stick of dynamite out of the shed. Cap it, fuse it, bring it here fast!"

It didn't look silly, not now, to see a naked man racing to the blacksmith shop. The mules and horses—as Karl Orme unhitched his two—retreated to a far corner of the barn yard. Orme started for the gate; he, too, was naked. Soon, we hoped, we could get to the house, get into fresh clothes.

John Cavick came running back. He raced to the house to get matches. He had cut the fuse awfully short. The smut-mass was now five feet across, still roughly circular. Then it was ten feet across. Then Cavick was back, and all of us ducked into the water as the stick of dynamite was dropped into the mass.

After the explosion we looked out. The smut-mass was nowhere to be seen. Even then I felt I could hear queer jeering laughter in the very air.

Cavick swore again. Uncle Charles began to pray. I felt like it myself. Not much explanation was needed. Scores of circular smut-masses suddenly sprang into being in the barnyard, and as far in all directions as we could see. That dynamite had blown the mass into tiny bits. But already each bit had grown, expanded, until we could see it.

As each of us noted this, each circular smut-smudge *jumped* in size, its center rose like the crown of a hat, a *peon's* hat, pointed!

"The telephone!" said Uncle Charles, almost moaning. "We've got to have help! And clothes!"

Uncle Charles was an old man as he crawled out of the tank, started a dripping run for the house. As we ran we watched the smut-masses *jumping, spreading, growing,* all around us—and I for one wondered if even we started now, and ran faster and faster, we could ever again escape them.

"Look!" said Karl Orme, as he turned at the door to look back the way we had come.

There was now no smoke, no fire, on the high field. There was no smut cloud. But a fringe of bronze extended all along the edge of the field we could see— and as I looked the fringe crept noticeably down the mounded side of the hill where the two draws met!

III: HOPELESS STRUGGLE

By noon of the next day it seemed to me there had never been a time when we hadn't been fighting the smut. We still called it "smut" because that had been the manner of its appearance, but none of us really believed that's what it was—not anymore. An agricultural expert from Port Orchard flew in the next morning after Uncle Charles appealed for help by telephone. He put some of the "smut" under his microscope.

"It's not kernel, covered or naked smut," he said. "It's not *tilletia tritici* or *levis*. It's not *Ustilago tritici* or *Urocystis tritici*. In fact, Norman, it's not smut at all! I don't know what it is!"

The horror surrounding the death of Lonnie Keel had long since become a minor thing. Too much else had happened since. In the first place, firing the smut had released every bit of it simultaneously from the wheat by destroying the wheat around it. Fire seemed to have no other effect on the stuff.

First, the smut-masses we had washed off ourselves and the horses and mules had widened, spread, grown upward, to meet the brown-black fringe which seemed to be overflowing from the high field. That smut, creeping down the bosom of the field like molasses running down outside the neck of a jug was a hellish thing to watch.

Birds, animals, everything in the area, became aware of the creeping horror. Grass on the hillside disappeared, devoured by the stuff. By the next morning, after Uncle Charles had told Aunt Claudia and the cousins to bed down with neighbors, they'd be in the battle line soon enough, hundreds of men and women were helping to fight the smut.

The entire field, which I had seen from an airplane—one of a dozen that constantly circled above the area of spreading spores—was blanketed with the stuff. Moreover, the center of the field was now easily two hundred feet in height. The stuff had moved inexorably out in all directions. Charles Norman's own wheat on the north was being devoured. Some of the men who fought the creeping smut insisted they could hear the stuff *chew*, as if the smut were animal and equipped with a myriad of infinitesimal mandibles. Every kind of fire fighting equipment was on the job that was within reach. Flame-throwers from the nearest army base had been tried. Everything had been hurled into that mess except an atom bomb. It was bent on reaching in all directions, we were all sure, but it would travel slower if we fought it and didn't deliberately spread it.

The smut-mass advanced without the slightest harm into the hottest tongues of flame from the flame throwers which had wrought such havoc among Japs and Germans in World War Two.

Brave men faced the slowly advancing horde with clubs, rifles, wet sacks. They sprayed it with water, with kerosene, gasoline. They fought themselves to a standstill, but the stuff seemed invincible. When the fighters against the growing smut-mass thought they had found the answer, the whole mass shuddered, and extended itself in all directions.

Casualties were somewhat high. A dozen men, daring too greatly, had come in contact with the smut and vanished into it, utterly possessed and destroyed by it, as Lonnie Keel had been.

I think every conceivable kind of machine was turned loose on that growing. rising, spreading mass. X-rays, some special secret rays used by the army and navy the exact nature of which I was not informed, were turned on the stuff—and without effect.

The smut-mass did not seem to devour inanimate things—for hours, that second day, we could see the shape of the combined harvester through the growing mass right where we had left it on the rounded bosom of the hill.

"The smut," said our agricultural expert, and scientists of more kinds than I knew or can remember agreed with him, "is an entity or a vast community of entities. If we don't solve the secret there is no way of telling how far the stuff may go. But where did it come from?"

"It came out of the wheat," my Uncle explained. But when he made it clear and neighbors backed him up, that only his field, in all the thousands of acres held by him and his neighbors, had been possessed by the blight, science admitted it had come to a dead end.

"It has to come from somewhere," said Doctor Larsen, the man whom the government entrusted with the secret rays that had been used without effect on our smut-mass. "I can't escape the feeling that in the sudden appearance and spread of this 'smut' there is clear evidence of *intent!*"

Up until I heard that I would not have spoken my thoughts for anything in the world. I'm ordinarily a bit shy. But now I offered my own two cents worth.

"Not only intention," I said, "but scientific implementation of it."

Larsen whirled on me. "I've been thinking the same thing, kid!" he said. "Just what are you driving at?"

"The field," I said, somewhat breathlessly "lies in the general line of the ancient ice fields which came down, ages ago, from the north. The draws have been dug by ice action and seepage from glaciers. That's what my geology teacher said in high school last term, anyway. If there were intelligent life in the land before the ice came down, what happened to it?"

Tired men, resting for a few minutes from fighting the creeping mass, heard me and snorted.

"Cocky kid!" said someone. "Probably write poetry when he grows up, like his utterly useless old man!"

"Do any of you gentlemen," said Larsen, "have any idea about these secret rays I've been using to fight against your smut?"

They shook their heads.

"Then," Larsen continued, "there may be other things ye also wot not of! Go ahead, kid, what's on your mind?"

"I've always felt that the high field was part of some huge grave mound, just because of the shape of it. I've thought since I was little that strange things might be buried in it. Now I wonder what may be a crazy thing—"

"Let us judge what's crazy and what isn't," said

Larsen. "Every pathfinder has been crazy in the eyes of his contemporaries. Go on."

"I think there's something under the hill deep down," I said "I think it's been there for thousands, maybe millions of years, dormant, resting. Now it has readied out. It is life, whatever life it was that ice destroyed, or forced to flee. The intelligence locked under the hill set a trap for us—the smut! We stepped into it and got caught. It reached up somehow from down under, manifested itself as smut."

"You talk as if this isn't new to you," said Larsen, interrupting. "Why isn't it?"

"I've always felt something in the draws, Toler Draw and Norman Draw, the one coming into it from the east," I hurried on. People were close to me now, listening, and I had help from an unexpected quarter.

"I always hated what the kid calls Norman Draw, myself," said Herb Slasser, Uncle Charles' neighbor to the west. "I used to go in there, twenty years ago, before Norman broke the land around it, to get myself a sagehen. *I always felt like running out!* I know there can't be anything in there bigger than badgers or coyotes, yet I finally got so I wouldn't go in there for a sagehen if I was starving!"

"I used to feel," I said, "as if there was someone behind me, who always ducked out of sight when I whirled to look. I always thought I'd run into something hideous around the next turn ahead. I never did, but I always knew why—*it kept just out of sight!*"

"What nonsense!" said the army colonel who commanded the flame throwing equipment and operators. "What can a yokel who has something like second sight tell us that will help combat this stuff?"

A group of people was standing now on the side of the draw opposite where we had left the combine. The draw itself was filled with the smut mass to within a few feet of our level. There was danger, and we all knew it, that it would surge up and out and swallow us all, but the danger was so constant, so commonplace now we almost ignored it.

"Certainly what he suggests," said Larsen, "can't accomplish less than we have! We've tried now to destroy this creeping stuff with every vibration controlled or operated by man—sound waves, electric currents, X-rays, gamma rays, even cosmic—"

Nobody could think of a destructive implement or technique that hadn't been tried on the smut-mass. As we talked there the sooty, shining, ebony-stir stuff in Toler Draw lurched, came within a few feet of our bodies. We stepped back. I stooped again to look. Tentacles so small, so tenuous as to be almost invisible, were reaching out at us through the interstices of the soil on which we stood! And others were coming upward through the soil. I was right, I had to be right—the source of the danger was somewhere underground, maybe far underground.

Larsen more or less had charge of the sector in which we fought the smut-mass. He put his head together with the heads of the plane crews trying to probe the cloud with radar and sonar, trying to get some picture of just what it might be.

"Can you find out for me," he asked, "whether there are any caverns hereabouts?"

Not until the next day, when three Sprengnether earthquake seismographs were set up at the apices of a triangle several miles on each side, with the high field in the triangle's center, was this question answered. Then they did something they called "seismic prospecting for head waves," carried out under Larsen's supervision— he seemed to know everything about everything—and the seismologists all agreed that there were caverns under the high field, not very far down, either!

No sooner had the word passed than half of Uncle Charles' neighbors said they had always known it. They had walked over the field years before and distinctly heard hollow sounds below! No local yokel was going to get ahead of the oldtimers, even if they had to lie a little.

Even my uncle said there had been times when he had felt hollow vibrations come up through the combined harvester and other heavy machinery. He could. also remember times when mules and horses had shied, while working the high field, away from underfoot sounds!

But just what did it matter one way or the other? The entire mounded hill was now deeply buried under a sooty, glistening mass several hundred feet deep all over it! There wasn't a chance of any kind of penetrating the hill into a cavern that might be occupied—*by what was such a cavern likely to be occupied?*

When somebody thought to ask that question a dreadful silence settled over everybody, a silence so deep you could hear the little chewing mouths of the smut.

"Find a way or not," some farmer put it in words, "you wouldn't get me even *trying* to get into it for all the gold in the world!"

"There must be some kind of material," I averred, not feeling as smart and cocky as I must have sounded to the others, "in which men can move into and down under the smut-mass. It apparently doesn't eat metal, plastic, things like that."

"But if there happens to be joints, anywhere at all, through which the stuff can reach your body," said Larsen, "you're just the more firmly trapped in something. You have some idea like a diving suit of steel, or plastic, or something, maybe?"

"Yes, sir, and I'll help get into those caverns if somebody will go along, with lights, weapons, and whatever scientists think we need!" I wished I hadn't said that, even before I started, but a kid sometimes gets too big for his britches and keeps right on getting too big when he knows he is.

Larsen started working by telephone on the Navy at Bremerton. Yes, they could furnish water-tight suits, but would they be smut-tight? And how, if the suits worked, would we penetrate the scores of feet of soil, shale, clay and solid rock which intervened between the covering smut and the caverns in which, I think everybody now believed the smut originated, or from which it was directed?

We did some gambling on a wild theory: those entities down under had sought sanctuary from the Ice Age. Therefore they were averse to ice. We could establish a bridgehead on the surface of the ground from which we could operate, if we could freeze the area and keep back the smut at the right pot. That's a little obscure, but for the time being there's no help for it. And I've said it was a wild gamble on a wilder theory—every bit of which might be utterly wrong. We had tried dropping dry ice on the smut-mass and it had had no more effect than fire, rays, explosions, or anything else we had tried.

The three seismologists gave me a thrill, believe me, when I heard them say that the cavern was nearest the surface at a spot deep in the Norman Draw! They made a map for us, covered with what they called "micro-seisms," which meant nothing at all to me, but Larsen could read without trouble. I was perfectly sure, at this point, that I must have sensed the presence of that cavern when I first sneaked into Norman Draw when I was about six years old.

We were about twenty in number when we finally dared the smut-mass in our air-conditioned diving suits. I was allowed to go along because I knew Norman Draw, badger-hole by badger-hole, better even than Uncle Charles knew it. Besides, Aunt Claudia wouldn't let Uncle Charles even *offer* to go.

I held my breath when the twenty of us, looking like something out of other worlds, put our feet into the smut-mass, walked into it as we would have walked into a lake.

Gradually the stuff crawled up our bodies as we walked down into Toler Draw. I couldn't feel anything getting in, but horror rose up to my heart from my feet as the smut-mass rose and rose and finally covered the eye-pieces of my helmet.

Then I had to lead the way, fumbling with my feet, while behind me all the others clung to a rope which kept us from losing one another, perhaps forever.

IV: SANCTUARY OF THE AGES

I could see nothing through the eyepieces but stygian darkness. But I knew the draws as I did not know the palms of my own hands. There were sandy stream-beds in each of them. I walked down the west side of Toler Draw, my unseen companions following me. There were times when I waited for the man immediately behind me to come up, bump into me. I had a horror of being lost from the others, of being alone on the deepening bottom of the smut. It would have been dreadful. As it was, it was bad enough. It did not seem to me that there was any more weight on us as we went down into night-darkness but there must have been some. I came to the steep sides of the first draw, which led away southeastward. I dropped down into it, with a sudden sickening feeling that there might no longer be a bottom; a thought that vanished when my heavy feet struck and sank leadenly into the sand. I turned right. I felt rather than heard my helpers drop into the wash behind me.

Now I moved to the east side of the wash, held out my hand against the dirt bank, moved along, guiding myself with my hand. As nearly as I could tell there was no material resistance to our advance. We strode through the smut far easier than if it had been water; as easily as if it had been the darkness to which I likened it. I sensed opposition; the same sort of opposition, only many times stronger, one knows exists in a parent or teacher who opposes what one wishes, but says nothing about it—just sulks and opposes!

It must have taken an hour to reach the place where Norman Draw merged with Toler Draw. My left hand found it. I turned into it, memories of old terrors flooding back. Here at this place I had often stood for what seemed hours, mustering up courage to travel into Norman Draw.

I had that same reluctance now, multiplied by the years since I had been a six year old. But I set out. I had fixed in my mind, from the microseism, just where we would face the rounded breast of the hill which we could no longer see, might never see again if we did not conquer the smut, and I held steadily on the tiring course until we reached it—and I visualized it in mind from old memory. It was in the area where badgers multiplied through the years, where literally scores of their burrows led back into the side of the hill, where mounds covered areas of fifty feet per burrow.

I faced the side of the hill, stood very still. The others came up and I knew they formed to my right and left, by the way the segments of rope pulled against the back of my diving suit.

Out of those holes, I was sure—smut was pouring like water from a big hose under high pressure! That was just a feeling I had, based on sensitivity, and a steady pushing against my body from head to heels.

I tapped the man next to me on my right. We had a fairly good set of prearranged signals. This man had a fire drill, a new government contraption which would eat into almost any metal known as it would eat through air itself. He walked ahead and now I clung to his belt. There was no sound, but he touched me with his elbow when he started using his fire drill. And then the ground ahead of my feet became level and I knew we had started into a stope made by the fire drill.

I extended hands from shoulders. The cut into the

hill was about four feet wide, plenty. And soon I had to stand on tiptoe to reach the roof. We ate back under the hill, back under the high field, almost as fast as we could walk. I felt that we had hit the microseism location right on the nose. I tapped again when my feet told me we were in the rock. Almost instantly we slanted downward at a thirty-degree angle. Where we now were we were safe from cave-ins for the moment.

When I estimated that we were perhaps four hundred feet down and five hundred feet back under the hill, I signaled for our lights expert to come forward with his equipment. Mind now, the blazing hell from the fire drill had not been felt by any of us, nor had any of us seen the flames. Nor had we felt the heat along the shaft where much of the stone must have been close to molten.

But when we stopped abysmal cold began to seep through our thick diving suits! One second and they were almost unbearably hot for their own sakes; then the coldness came in and two terrific emotions rose in me at the same time: fear and excitement.

I knew the others felt it also because we closed in to touch one another and both the fear and excitement were communicated through our contacting hands. Also, we all wished to go on and on.

My fire-drill man traveled more slowly. My lights expert had tried to pierce the gloom with his lights with utterly no effect whatever. Now, suddenly, my fire-drill man stopped, tapped me again. He stood, his tapping indicated, inside the cavern! He fumbled forward and I had a chance to marvel at the miracle of mathematics; we had struck the cavern at its base level!

The cold was even more intense. I took the lead now, feeling my way with my feet, not wishing to step into a bottomless pit. I still moved with that effortlessness by which we had made progress through the smut outside. And on a sudden hunch I moved toward the feeling of greatest cold. If the smut-entities were averse to cold, if we entered areas where it was great enough we would be free of them! So I reasoned, if a fifteen-year-old can pride himself on reasoning.

When I began to stiffen with the cold I came up solid against the acme of cold. I ran my hand over a smooth surface. My hands seemed to freeze against it. I signaled for my lights man. He came forward, switched on his light magic—and for the first time since dropping into the smut-mass we could see! I could see, there in the blackness, all of my companions. They looked like something out of Inferno and no mistake. But when we looked around us and saw into what we had come, nothing human, or made by humans, could ever again look anything but commonplace! How does one describe something with which one has nothing to compare?

First, the cavern was vast. I knew, all of us knew how it had been formed. Ice from those ancient glaciers had, by glacier action, been wrapped up in dirt, rock, sand, and all the drippings and dregs of the great moraine; the dirt and rock had been churned, crushed, piled hill on hill, until a world of ice was encased in a world of cataclysmic earth. Then, after ages, the ice outside had receded and the dirt and rocks, miles deep all around, had preserved the ice within, like some unbelievable pig-in-a-blanket.

But what had been preserved in the ice itself?

I knew, all of us knew, that the churning I have referred to, the piling of dirt on dirt, rock on rock, hill on hill, to encase the world of ice, *had been deliberate!* We all knew it because our minds had been prepared for it. We knew it before there was any proof. The black face of ice that had been ages old when Lemuria sank beneath the Pacific, stared out at us with baleful eyes. Oh, I know how ice twinkles and stares when it reflects light, but this was different. The "eyes" were so close together, yet each one distinct, and the balefulness so unmistakable, that I began to shiver with something that was not entirely the cold.

We were surrounded by ice. The cavern in which we stood must have been twenty acres in extent. The ice ceiling was a hundred feet overhead. In spite of the cold some sort of melting was taking place in this cavern, slowly, surely, enlarging it.

The floor underfoot was a-crawl! Water, black water, dripped from the roof, seeped endlessly from the entire surrounding wall. Maybe it came out of the floor, too. But on the floor itself, it *moved and grew!*

I knew we stood in one of the birth places, maybe the only one of the smut! The others knew it with me. We stared at one another through our eye-pieces now. The other faces were all reddish in the reflected light, strange, fearful. The stuff on the floor was not ice, but it had just been ice, and it was colder than any ice we knew on the surface. The coldness crept up our feet into our bodies. It had an added coldness, as profound as absolute zero.

I noticed an outward flow from the center of the mass on the floor. I realized that on the floor of this great mysterious cavern the drippings from roof and walls, the seepage, formed in a kind of reserve poll—and then spread slowly, inexorably outward in all directions! I knew what happened after that. Somehow it slid out under the ice, worked its way down into unfrozen soil—then moved up through the interstices of rocks, however solid, up into the clay, the sand, the gravel, then, by capillarity, the soil itself—into the roots of wheat, up to the heads where it appeared as smut!

But why this particular manifestation? How had *selection* been made? The choosing of just one particular field, *all* of it, but no more, indicated what Larsen had suggested: intention. But what was the entity or entities that intended?

Were we standing even now inside some laboratory of a far-off forgotten day? The ice was alive, I was sure, frozen solid through the centuries, against set time of wakening! But what was the entity? The frozen part that we regarded as ice? Or the separate portions of it we had first regarded as smut spores or *sori* until Larsen said it was not smut?

I signaled our fire-drill man to use his apparatus on the material on the cavern floor. He blazed his flames upon it. The whole cavern, in the light, looked like some unbelievable hell. But the effect of the fire on the mass was astounding. There was instantly faster movement! The stuff on the floor, without diminishing, began to move faster in all directions, out under the ice, as if the fire gave it new life. I saw, and Larsen saw, and signaled me with his fingers against my suit, that the fire caused the material on the cavern floor to increase. Each "spore," it appeared, divided when touched by the flame, reproducing like the amoeba, by division.

Quickly my man played the flame all around the cavern wall—and before he could turn it off the moving mass on the floor, which had been no higher than our knees, rose to our shoulders! The flame, melting the ice, had released the smut and so quickly that it had almost flooded the cavern. And we had no way, down here, to reverse the process. But the flames were quickly turned off—*in spite of a sudden mental message that came to my mind—and I heard later to the minds of all the others—as if the entire ice face were pleading for more and more of the releasing flame!*

I signaled for the fire-drill man to concentrate on a stope cut straight into the ice wall.

He asked by signal if it should be about the same size as that by which we had penetrated the hillside. I nodded. He adjusted his light, played it against the ice face at a spot selected by Larsen.

The flames ate their way in, but it wasn't water that came out of the shaft behind us—it was a steady stream of smut! Our "ice" then, was not ice at all, but the material we had called "smut" frozen solid. And it was sentient. It knew who and what we were. It had known for all the ages of historic man. It communicated with us telepathically somehow! *It?* *They?* How could we tell? The material was immortal, that was clear—as any cellular thing that reproduces by halving itself is immortal.

We deliberately drove back into the ice face until we came to solid rock! We must have gone in a mile behind the face of the "ice." I think we all realized that we were thus traveling into the very heart of some antediluvian monster of which no record had previously come down to man in the rocks. This monster, whatever it was, was a community in itself. It was one as a community, one in each of its tiny separate entities—each of which became two at will, to add to the strength and size of the community.

A chill coursed through me as I remembered that man himself is a community—of nobody really knows how many billions of cells. This community could be some weird progenitor of man himself, easily. Else how could twenty of us—nineteen of us scientists including the greatest, Larsen—have been so sure of telepathic communication from It-Them to our brains?

The Thing welcomed the breath of the flame which released it. The dripping from the flame, from the heart of the pack, seemed almost to sing as it flowed back past us, under our feet, to the cavern, there to flow outward and upward to add to the mass which grew upon the high field, spreading in all directions across Central Washington.

I could just imagine the people on the surface now, noting the increased activity of the smut-mass, wondering what dreadful things were happening to us. We were releasing more of the materials from the elder world, but we did not see how it could be helped. We had to have some idea of this or be utterly defeated at bringing it under control.

But if the ice closed in around us, back there in that tunnel, and our fire-drill suddenly went out of condition! We must all have thought of that at once, for no sooner had realization come than we started backtracking. We could be trapped anywhere between here and the surface! And on the surface the traps were just as thickly set! There was no doubting the danger to us, to our people above, to all the neighboring counties, to the nation, for all we knew.

Nothing could destroy this entity or community of entities; but cold, if sufficiently intense, could immobilize It-Them. Cold was our answer. As we fled back through the tunnel into the great cavern I felt as if the entire pack, with millions of tiny voices, were shrieking silently after me:

"Set me free! Set me free! I will serve you always! You, too, shall be immortal!"

But there was a very human element of stupidity in It-Them, also. For if it had any consideration at all for creatures that were mortal it would certainly not have slain Lonnie Keel and the dozen other human beings the smut-mass had devoured on the surface-and then had any idea that we would listen favorably to It-Them's appeal for release! But the appeal was made. It fled after us, begging, beseeching, promising that immortality which it so plainly knew.

I did not care for its immortality, however, nor just then did my co-workers. For It-Them's immortality had kept it locked underground, like some monstrous black Prometheus chained, for ages mankind could scarcely count. Was immortality worth such restrictions?

I knew then the solution to the smut-mass, a solution that was only temporary, that must be kept active the end of man's life on earth if black Prometheus were to remain chained and thus deterred from possessing the globe.

Engineers who had worked on Grand Coulee Dam were among my nineteen coworkers and I felt sure the idea would have occurred to them also—they had used it on the east bank of the Columbia where briefly, it flowed into the north. It would work here in Norman

Draw and Toler Draw. It had to, or who could say how
far the doom we had released from the old moraine,
in the high field above it, would eventually extend?

V: SUCH BITTER COLD

We had one very obvious and highly dangerous duty
to perform before we returned to the surface. Doing
it would release more and more of the queer black hell-
harvest, but if we didn't find out the truth it wouldn't
matter much how little or extensively we freed the smut.
In a short time it would possess the world anyway,
limited, I supposed, only by the food it would need while
"alive," while not frozen into immobility. Our duty was
to find out something of the limits of the underground
smut field, to check against later efforts of our seismologists.

So we started just inside the cavern, where the tunnel
by which we had entered it from the surface was
running almost full of the smut, and made a tunnel
against the solid rock, behind the "ice" to see whether
there were branching caverns—to find out, in short,
whether this cavern was the only pocket of It-Them, or
whether it might not be that all the land under what
had once been fields of ancient ice, from side to side
of the continent, was inhabited by It-Them! The stuff
might never be released within the lifetime of man. It
might be released everywhere simultaneously, by tomorrow morning! We must be prepared. It was our duty
to take risks.

So behind the eating flames which released more and
more of the ebon horror, we followed the rock face
around the inside of the cavern. We learned that there
were scores of branching tunnels and caverns, each one
tightly packed with the black ice!

Some sort of message, some sort of mapping job must
be done to assist the seismologists. I was the only one
of those twenty who could return to the surface with

any chance of finding my way back. So I went out alone, sick with fear, to the surface. There I procured three sticks of dynamite, fused, capped, spoke briefly to the seismologists, did not take time to explain, and returned to my co-workers in the cavern.

In the cavern we took fresh risks, risks that one or all of us might be crushed by the falling in of the cavern roof. We set off one of the sticks of dynamite at each of three most widely separated points in the cavern. These little explosions, shaking the earth, would reach each seismograph on the surface and write its wave-record thereon. Those who knew how to read the jigglings would know, then, how far the explosion waves of each of the three had traveled to each seismograph, through what media it had traveled—whether rock, clay, sand, gravel or ice!—and a complete map could be made of the dwelling places of It-Them, across all the vast North American Moraine! Thus only could the world protect itself against what we had first known as smut.

Well, then we came out, and I waited, as a youngster should, for science itself to provide what seemed to me to be the only answer. Here it is: During the building of the Grand Coulee Dam, millions of tons of material poured into the hole where the engineers were trying to build an abutment. The material came from the hill on the eastern bank of the river. It could not be removed as fast as it slid into the pit.

So engineers had simply driven pipes into the mountainside, attached them to a special refrigeration plant—and frozen the mountain solid! Here, however, we must freeze the hill solid and keep it thus frozen through the ages. If ever alertness relaxed we were done!

I waited for somebody, probably Larsen, to say what we should do, after we came out of that cavern, reported to our people, to newspaper reporters and thus to the world, what we had found. Our seismologists were already studying the records of our three cavern-explosions.

Toler Draw and Norman Draw were both filled with smut when we came out. The stuff had pushed its fighters back more than five miles in all directions during the time we were down there in the cavern.

When we had done, I waited, and Larsen, grinning at me, said: "I suppose you know the answer, kid?"

I felt shy about the whole thing. "Grand Coulee Dam," I offered, "but *you* know; it's better, coming from you!"

Well, then Larsen told them, and before that same day was ended scores of gallant engineers had gone down into the smut, down into Toler and Norman Draws, to turn the high field and all the land under it, into a gargantuan refrigerator capable of delivering nearly absolute zero cold.

It was easy to tell when they began making cold, for the smut ceased its advance. Then it began to retreat! Its retreat was faster even than its outward charge had been from the moment we began releasing it with the combined harvester, then with the fire Karl Orme had set in the wheat, then with our fire-drill in the cavern.

But not all the ebon horror got back into the cavern-sanctuary before the hillside-refrigerator was completely efficient and operative. A field of it, varying in thickness from inches to feet, covered the high field like a cooling lava flow—a constant threat, a constant reminder, to those who knew.

Scientists often stopped along the road past my Uncle's place, to take note of the ebon blanket over the now useless high field. Invariably they said to Uncle Charles, somewhat loftily:

"Volcanic action here, ages ago! That's black basalt!"

Uncle Charles always widened his eyes as with great surprise.

"I wonder," he invariably answered. "what makes it so cold you can't cross it without freezing?"

They always had some learned explanation. Everybody always had explanations for everything. Only the army of seismologists which planted its seismographs across the North American Moraine offered no explanations of their work. They knew the truth would certainly be laughed to scorn.

Jack Sharkey's first published science fiction story appeared in Fantastic *in 1959. Between 1959 and 1965, he established a reputation as a writer of well-constructed, often amusing fantasy and science fiction in* Playboy, The Magazine of Fantasy and Science Fiction, Amazing, *and* Galaxy, *the latter of which published several of his stories of space zoologist Jerry Norcriss. His novels include the dystopic* Ultimatum in 2050 A.D., *the superman tale* The Secret Martians, *and the light fantasy* It's Magic, You Dope!

No Harm Done

Jack Sharkey

The boy was a good-looking youth, with shiny—if over-long—blond hair, and bright white teeth. But his eyes were cloudy with the emptiness that lay behind them, and the blue circles of their irises hinted at no more mental activity than do the opaque black dots on a rag doll. He sat with vacuous docility upon the small metal stool the guards had provided, and let his arms dangle limp as broken clothesline at his sides, not even crossing them in his lap. He had been led to the chair, told to sit, and left there. If he were not told to arise, he would remain there until the dissolution of his muscle cells following death by starvation caused him to topple from his low perch.

"Total schizophrenia," said Dr. Manton. "For all practical purposes, he is ambulant—when instructed to move, of course—vegetable."

"How terrible," said Lisa, albeit perfunctorily. Lisa Nugent, for all her lovely twenty seven years, was a trained psychologist, and rarely allowed emotion to take her mind from its well-ordered paths of analysis. To be unfeeling was heartless—but to become emotional about a patient was pointless.

"Yes, it's intolerable," nodded Dr. Jeff Manton, keeping his mind strictly on Lisa's scientific qualifications, and deliberately blocking out any other information sent to his brain by his alert senses. The warmth of her smile, the flash of sunlight in her auburn hair, the companionable lilt she could not keep out of her "on-duty" voice—all these were observed, noted, and filed for future reference. At the moment, nothing must go wrong with their capacity for observation of the patient. Emotion had a way of befuddling even the most dedicated minds.

"But why out here?" Lisa said suddenly, returning the conversation to a prior topic. "I should think conditions would be easier to control in the lab."

"Simply because," said Jeff, patting the small metal camera-like device on its rigid tripod, "I as yet have no experimental knowledge of the range of my machine. It may simply be absorbed by the plaster in the walls, back inside the sanatarium. Then again, it may penetrate, likely or not, even the steel beams of the building, with roentgenic ease. There are too many other people in the building, Li—Dr. Nugent. Until I can be certain just what effect the rays have upon a human brain, I dare not use it any place where there might be leakage, possible synaptic damage."

"I understand," said Lisa, nodding after a brief smile at his near-slip with her name. "You assume the earth will absorb any rays that pass beyond this boy's brain, and render them—if not harmless—at least beyond the contamination point with another human being."

"Precisely," said Jeff Manton, moving the tripod a short distance closer to the seated boy. "Now, I want you to assist me in watching him, and if you note in him any change—either in his expression or posture— tell me at once. Then we can turn off the machine and test him for results. For positive results, at any rate."

Lisa could not repress a slight tremor. The trouble with schizophrenia in its most advanced stage was the inability of contacting the patient. The boy, although readily capable of executing simple commands, could not be counted on to aid Dr. Manton or herself in even the most basic test of his mental abilities. If the machine made him any worse—there would hardly be a way for them to discover it. If better—then new hope was born for others similarly afflicted.

"Steady, now," said Jeff, turning the tiny knob at the side of the metal box a quarter turn. "Keep your eye on him. I'm going to turn it on."

Lisa felt the sweat prickling along her back as Jeff flicked the toggle switch atop the box. Her eyes began to burn, and she realized she wasn't even blinking as she locked her gaze upon the figure of the boy through whose brain was now coursing a ray of relatively unknown effect. Rabbits and rats and monkeys in the lab were one thing. This, now, was a human being. Whether the effect upon him would be similar to that of the ray upon test animals (scientifically driven crazy before exposure) remained to be seen.

"Anything?" muttered Jeff, sighting anxiously along the side of the box. "Anything at all?"

"He—no. He just sits there, Doctor. So far as I call see, there is no appreciable effect." She sighed resignedly. "He doesn't even flicker a muscle."

"Damn," said Jeff. He kept his finger lightly atop the sun-glinting toggle switch. "I'm going to give it one more minute before I give up. This thing should be vitalizing his brain by now!"

"But he's not even—" Lisa began, discouraged.

"Keep your eyes on him, damn it!" snapped Jeff,

catching the turn of her head from the corner of his eye. "This *must* work! We daren't miss the least sign that it has!"

Man and woman stood side by side in the hot light of the afternoon sun, staring, staring at the immobile form of the patient, the patient whose disrupted mind they were attempting to reunite into an intelligent whole . . .

My name, he thought. Funny, I should know my own name. I've heard it often enough . . . It's . . . Is it—is it Garret? That sounds like it, but—I can't seem to recall . . .

He thought about the man who tended and took care of him. He had called him by name, hadn't he? And it was most certainly Garret. Yes, of course it was Garret . . . Or was it Curt?

His mind, like badly exposed film, refused to give him an accurate sensation from any of his senses. All he got for strenuous mental gymnastics was vague, blurry reception and muddled thought. And yet, there was a warm sensation that had never been in his mind before—before what? Try as he might, he could not recall anything coherent before this moment in time. Just vague feelings of being alive, and simply growing up . . .

The warmth of the sun was beginning to penetrate. He could feel it, coursing down upon him, soaking into him, revitalizing him . . . But it was unlike this other warmth, this *penetrating* warmth, that tingled through his mind. With the awareness of the sunlight came a slow awareness of shades of light, then of color, then of figures. And, for the first time, he made a strong effort—and *looked*.

He saw the man and woman standing in the sunlight a few feet from himself, saw the harsh glitter of that sunlight upon the strange object on three legs that rested on the ground before them. He tried to speak to them, but something restrained him.

If I can move . . . If I can just move a little bit, he
realized, they'll see me, and they'll know I'm alive and
well and aware.

He tried. He tried desperately to move. His body felt
rigid, imprisoned. Just a little frantic, he thought of
blinking at them, of moving his eyes toward them for
sharp definite focus, so that they would *know* . . .

Nothing happened.

I'm paralyzed! he thought for a terrifying moment.
Then—no, I'm just not used to directing myself. I
haven't the necessary coordination or experience, that
must be it. Take it easy, now. Slow and easy. Don't panic.

He strained desperately, and felt just the slightest hint
of movement. Had they seen? he wondered. He was
certain he had moved. What was the matter with the
two of them?!

He watched them there in the sunlight, this man and
woman who stood so intensely still, the man's hand upon
that metallic thing on three legs. Then he knew that that
thing was the source of the warmth in his mind. It had
brought him to awareness.

But what *good* is it! his mind screamed. To be alive
and aware, and unable to let them know it! The coldly
frantic feeling was growing within him, now, taking hold
of his brain with the frightening fingers of raw panic.

"Look!" he cried out, then knew with crushing despair
that the word had gone no farther than his brain. *Please,*
he begged silently, *see me here, see that I am alive, that
I am not what I was!*

Desperately he strove to rise, felt the strange sensation
of bondage that restrained his body, fought it . . . and
won. It hurt. The sensation was unbearable. Yet he had
moved. Perhaps only the quarter part of an inch, but he
had moved. The woman—had she seen?

Then he saw the man straighten up, heave his
shoulders in a great sigh, and cut off the machine with
a finger-flick. The tingling warmth died within his brain,

and for an icy moment, he expected to plunge back to semicomatose nothingness. But, after a giddy scintilla of dizziness, his mind remained strong and intelligent and alive.

Ignoring the blaze of pain that racked his entire being, he tensed himself, pushed, with strangled cries bursting inside his brain at the self-torture, and made himself move another quarter of an inch.

Did they see? Did they? Did they know? Would they free his mind, and leave his body imprisoned to his innermost pleas for release?

No, he thought, giddy with joy. They . . . they're coming nearer!

"It's no use, Lisa," said Jeff, looking down upon the motionless figure on the stool. "The machine is a flop. Rabbits and lesser creatures, fine, but for the mind of man, no use at all."

"I'm sorry, Jeff," said Lisa, knowing that his calling her by her first name meant that work was done for that day. "Maybe with some adjustments—"

"Yeah," he grunted bitterly, as two white-jacketed guards led the boy to his cell, *"maybe!"*

"At least," said Lisa, taking him gently by the arm, "he's no worse off. The experiment just didn't work out, that's all. But there's no harm done, at rate."

"Nope. I suppose you're right," Jeff said bitterly, reaching to lift the stool from its patch of sunlight. Then, with a brief surge of anger at the futility he felt, he lashed out with his foot and kicked the green parsleylike top clean off a carrot that jutted just a bit higher than its fellows in the garden bed behind the stool. "No harm done," he muttered angrily, and went back with Lisa toward the sanatarium.

While a silent, agony-filled voice behind him kept shrieking, over and over, *My eyes! He kicked out my eyes! I'm blind! Help me! Help me!"*

Mildred Johnson was one of the many new writers to publish in the legendary pulp magazine Weird Tales *in its final years. She showed a talent for short fiction, and her weird fantasy legacy is limited to two stories that appeared in the magazine in 1950: "The Mirror," a tale of the horrors that arise from a family inheritance, and "The Cactus," an uncommon blend of supernatural horror and science fiction.*

The Cactus

Mildred Johnson

The package came by first-class mail. It was from Edith's old friend in Los Angeles, Abby Burden. She opened it with interest, picked out some cotton wadding, a bulky letter, more cotton wadding. That was apparently all, but since nobody, not even Abby, would package a letter so tenderly, she reinspected the cotton and found a small prickly object. The explanation was undoubtedly in the letter.

It was written, as usual, on thin paper, typewritten with hand interlineations and annotations crawling about the pages and into the margins, and Edith had to turn it upside down and endways and trail sentences for sheets before capturing the sense. It dealt with the Burdens' trip to Mexico, but not until the end did it divulge the mystery of the enclosure.

"And now about the cutting," Abby wrote. "I may as well tell you Robert is against my sending it to you. He thinks I'm very silly. Let me tell you about it, though:

"I picked it up in an out-of-the-way, God-forsaken spot about a hundred miles from Chihuahua, where we had a flat tire. It was desert country, ninety in the shade—though there was no shade—and there was poor Robert faced with the prospect of changing a tire. I offered to help but he said the best way for me to help him would be to keep quiet for a while. You know how cranky a man can get under those conditions. The car was like an oven so I took a little walk around to look at the vegetation, such as it was, but there seemed to be nothing for hundreds of miles but sage and scrub and sand, and heat rising and shimmering all about. And then, a short distance away, I seemed to see a kind of fog, an overhanging mist. I thought it was an optical illusion—because whoever heard of a fog in the desert?—but, since it wasn't far away, I walked over to it. And as I approached it I smelled the sweetest, sourest, muskiest odor I've ever known. Suddenly the ground dipped and I was looking at a strange and lovely thing. Do you remember the meteor crater in Arizona? What I saw there was the same thing, much smaller, of course. It was a scoop in the earth, like a great dimple, and it was filled with cactus growths, marvelous, unearthly, beautiful—eight, nine, ten feet tall—gray-green giants stretching their twisted arms to the sky. There were hundreds of them, some of them already blooming with dark red flowers. It was the latter that gave off the strange, sweet smell.

"Edith—actually I felt as if I were on another planet, and what with the heavy perfume and the heat, my head swam. But finally I pulled myself together and rushed back to Robert to beg him to come and see what I had found, and ask him to cut me a slip of one of those weird plants. But his reaction was most peculiar. You know how sensible Robert usually is, but for some private reason he took a dislike to the whole area and became very difficult about getting a cutting for me. He said he wouldn't want a thing like that. He said they looked like goats and smelled like them too. He was positively silly. He said there was something about the little valley and the phalanxes of tortured shapes that gave him the creeps. But finally he gave in and cut me a tiny piece from the nearest plant. He scratched himself doing so and that didn't make him any happier. The spikes on the stem are rather tricky, you'll notice.

"As soon as I got it home I planted it. Edith, it's the finest specimen I've ever seen and grows like—I was going to say like a weed but it's faster than that. In a week I had to transplant it to a larger plant pot.

"Robert is still angry about it, though, and that's why he thinks I'm crazy to send you a cutting of it. But knowing your fondness for cacti, I had to share my discovery with you."

Edith folded up the letter and inspected the little cutting, holding it in her palm. It was no more than an inch in length, brown and shriveled, and so lifeless she doubted that it would grow at all. However, she would give it a chance. She found a small pot, pressed it in, watered it and set it on the shelf with her other cactus plants. "If you're going to be a giant cactus," she said, "you've a long way to go, little friend."

On examination the next morning, she was pleased to see that apparently its grip on life was secure. Watering it on the following Monday with the rest of her cactus collection she decided the infant was going to be a prodigy, for not only had it changed its wizened brown covering for one of healthy green but had straightened up and grown fully two inches. Its shape was somewhat comical: with the fat, spinous stem and the two little horns sprouting from the top, it resembled a rampant tomato caterpillar. Edith wrote to Abby that afternoon thanking her for the little plant.

Six weeks afterward, by the end of May, it was no longer little. In fact it had outstripped all the other cacti on the shelf. Now fifteen inches tall, it had been transplanted to a large urn and, in Edith's mind, was being groomed for a star appearance at the horticultural show in the autumn. Her friends admired it and, at club meetings, inquired about its health as they would about a child's.

When Mrs. Ferguson, her next door neighbor, viewed it, however, she asked the question: "When's it supposed to stop growing?"

"Well," laughed Edith, "my friend who sent it to me said they were eight, nine, and ten feet tall—the ones she saw growing in Mexico, but I don't imagine it will grow so much. I haven't a container large enough for it, for one thing."

"And your porch roof isn't high enough." Leaning over and tentatively feeling the two parallel spikes at the head of the plant, she added, "Not that it couldn't bore a hole right through if it wanted to with these things. They're like daggers."

Her remark prompted Edith to ask Abby how the parent was getting along, and she heard, with slight dismay, that it too was hyperexpansive, already two feet high and showing no signs of stopping. When it outgrew the house, wrote Abby, she had plans for it in the yard, but Edith thought grimly: when it outgrows my house it outgrows me. Goodbye, cactus, in that case.

It blossomed early in June with flowers of a peculiar liverish color. Though she never would have admitted it publicly, Edith thought them unattractive, almost repellent. They were almost like sores, she thought. And their odor was pungent enough to cause comment, the baker's delivery man asking if gas was escaping, the meter reader wanting to know if she had something burning in the oven. But her handy man, Mr. Krakaur, who came on Mondays to put out trash cans, mow the lawn, and so on, and who was the local philosopher on the side, stated frankly that it "stank." "Stinks like a goat," he said.

"Mr. Krakaur, how can you say that?" Laughing she recalled what Robert Burden had said about it.

"And it looks like one too," Mr. Krakaur went on, shifting his cud reflectively. "Got horns and everything. Looks like a sick goat with boils."

But in two weeks the blooms were gone. Most of the smell went with them, although it lingered unaccountably in various portions of the house far away from the porch, in closets, in her bedroom, and seemed to be contained in air pockets for often, usually at night, she would smell it strong and musky, but in the next second lose it. It was as if the cactus itself had passed her open door. She smiled at her fancy, but was surprised to hear from Abby that Robert Burden had the same idea, although he was carrying it to ridiculous extremes, averring, for instance, that he had caught a glimpse of the cactus floating along in its own emanations like a jellyfish in an ocean current. Abby wrote that if he thought that frightening her would make her dispose of the cactus he was mistaken. He was being very stupid and unreasonable, she said. He was even threatening to warn Edith about the danger— "So if you hear a lot of nonsense from him you'll know what it's about."

She was not going to allow herself to be influenced by such palpable friction in the Burden household, Edith thought, but just the same, after reading Abby's letter, she went to the porch and took a good look at her cactus. It *was* a grotesque thing, she admitted, a frame on which mental aberrations could easily be hung. Cruciform in shape, its upraised "arms" were terminated in spiked nodules, like taloned fingers; the forward-sweeping horns were truly formidable; and the withered flowers at the "head" were arranged to suggest an evil face, a demonic, leering, loathsome face.

In sudden revulsion she decided she must destroy it but then, remembering her promise to exhibit it at the flower show and the admiration and interest of her friends, canceled the impulse by laughing herself out of it. "You're not going to pay any attention to Robert

Burden's crazy notions, are you?" she asked herself, reminding herself in addition that she had always thought him neurotic. He sounded positively psychotic now.

But that night she dreamed about the cactus. It seemed that she was in bed and, awakened by a slipping, slithering sound from the hall, got up to investigate. In a shaft of moonlight there sat a tiny animal, like a chipmunk, all agleam with silver light, dainty and pretty, and she was about to approach it when suddenly Ted appeared. He looked young and slim, the way he had been when they were married, but his face was grave. Laying a hand on her shoulder, he shook his head as if to restrain her, but she paid no attention and walked towards the little animal clucking softly. But, as she reached it and was crouching to it, it began to swell and grow and in a second had become the cactus, writhing with vile delight, its malevolent face close to hers, its long arms pinioning hers to her sides in sickening embrace. She screamed for Ted but he had gone. He had left her.

Choking, heart beating wildly, she awoke and lay shaking in terror. Oriented at last, she looked towards the door, and it was as if a hand clutched her heart for the area in the hall was bathed, it seemed, in a deep, oily fog, like a swamp miasma, behind which something gray and green was stirring. She sat up, stared hard, cautiously reached for the bedlamp and quickly turned it on. There was nothing.

There was nothing but moonshine and sinister groupings of shadows and her own heavy breathing.

In the sensible light of day she marveled and was ashamed of the mantle of fear she was weaving for herself out of odds and ends of suggestions, fancied resemblances, and nightmares—she, Edith Porter, middle-aged, matter-of-fact, a professed scoffer at all superstition. Was she going to allow an odor, a shape, and a bad dream to push her into unreason? And as

for Robert Burden's vaporings, for all she knew he might
be joking.

She would take hold of herself firmly and, in the
meantime, try to rid the house of the meandering gamy
stench.

It was nine o'clock on the following Sunday evening.
Having spent the day riding in the country with the
Fergusons, Edith was finishing reading the newspaper
and was beginning to yawn with delicious weariness and
plan early retirement when the telephone rang.

It was a girl's voice, blurred with crying, sharpened
by hysteria, and Edith could not recognize it.

"Mrs. Porter? This is Nancy, Nancy Winnick, the
Burdens' daughter."

"Oh, yes, Nancy—how are you? Is anything the
matter?" Edith's mind skipped about frantically for an
explanation.

The girl was apparently trying to control herself. At
last she said. "The most horrible thing happened this
morning. Dad's dead!"

"Oh, no! How—how did it happen?" She felt herself
turning cold with shock.

"I don't know the whole story because Mother is half
out of her mind and she's given it to us in bits and
pieces. She's resting now under a sedative, but all
afternoon she's kept begging me to call you and let you
know. It's about that cactus she gave you. She wants you
to destroy it, because she says—" Here Nancy burst into
sobs and was a few seconds recovering herself. "She says
it killed him. She knows it killed him deliberately, and
it's all her fault. She's afraid something will happen to
you too and she'll have two deaths on her conscience."

"But how? How did it kill him?"

"This morning Mother finally agreed that he could
get rid of it. You know what controversy there's been
about it. Mother said she wrote you about it, how Dad
hated it so and Mother was set on keeping it. Well, this
morning they had it out, it seems, and she told him to

go ahead and destroy it if he felt so strongly about it. He didn't wait a minute. He took it out to the rubbish can—it grew to an enormous size, you know—and threw it on top of the rubbish, pot and all and then—" Nancy started whimpering again. "I don't know what made him do it, except that he wanted to get rid of it quickly and couldn't wait for the trash collection, but he set it afire and stood there watching it burn. Mother said she shouted to him from the window, but he seemed fascinated by the sight of the flames traveling up it, and then all of a sudden it broke in the middle and the top half flew at him, all ablaze, and landed on him—and it clung to him—he couldn't tear it off—it was all over his face and head—"

"Oh—how horrible—how terrible!" Edith broke down then and wept with Nancy, who at length completed the story:

"When my husband and I arrived we found Mother in a faint, and when she came to she just screamed and screamed; and then my husband went out into the yard, but he wouldn't let us see Dad. He himself was sick because his face and head were all—they took him away to be cremated. We thought that was best."

Lenitive words, condolences—what good were they now? And Edith could not say them; she was too shocked.

After hanging up she sat frozen, staring ahead; then she rose quickly, strode to the porch, lifted down the cactus from the shelf, and, grasping the horns as one would the ears of a rabbit, tore it up by the roots. From the gaping hole there rose the fetid odor so concentrated and powerful that she choked and coughed, but her anger gave her courage and, without looking at the plant in her hand, holding it far off, she ran down cellar and threw it into the trash barrel. She returned for the pot and carried it down too, set it on top of the barrel, took a hammer and smashed it.

She was still panting when she sat at her desk in the

living room to write to Abby all the sympathy she had been unable to express on the telephone and her hand shook so much she had to rest before beginning.

A hand touched her shoulder, gentle but firm—a warning hand; it rested there; she felt the pressure of the fingers. Slowly she unveiled her eyes. All about her was a mist pouring in ever-thickening clouds from the area behind her and obscuring the light, and a foul stink wafted to her nostrils, but she could not move: in that growing fetor, that dankness, that accrescence of vileness, she sat still. The hand pressed hard, and, coming to her senses, she half-turned her head. On the wall, just behind her head, was the shadow of horns.

She lurched to her feet, tore open the casement and flung herself into the darkness, landing on her hands and knees in the soft earth of a flower bed, scrambling to her feet and hurling herself forward across the field separating her house from the Fergusons'. She stumbled, fell, clambered up, ran on and at last reached the back door and pounded on it. When it was opened to her she fell in and pressed against the wall.

Mrs. Ferguson was staring at her, plump, red-faced, round-eyed. "What's wrong?" Edith could not answer.

"Harry!" Mrs. Ferguson called. "Come here!"

Ferguson appeared and together they led Edith to a chair. "Somebody trying to break into your house?" he asked.

"I don't know," she gasped. "I don't know. I've just had a terrible fright."

She sipped the glass of water they gave her, her teeth chattering against the rim.

"Call the police, Harry!" urged Mrs. Ferguson as Edith Porter sat frightened.

Edith raised a protesting hand. The police to rout something from another universe, another stratum of existence; the law to command the supernatural? "Don't call the police," she said, setting the glass on the table and sighing.

"But if there's a prowler around—"

"There's no prowler, I'm sure. I imagined it." She looked at these solid sane people and wondered if it were true. Perhaps she had dreamed it all. Nevertheless she could not return to the house. It was difficult to confess her fear of staying alone, but she had to do it. They said they understood, offered their guest room, but were puzzled. Ferguson went over and locked up and brought her keys back as directed.

When Mr. Krakaur put in an appearance on the street the next morning she joined him and walked with him.

"What you doing out so early, Mrs. Porter?" he asked.

"Last night I had a kind of brainstorm. I had a notion something—someone was breaking in, and so I ran over to the Fergusons and there I stayed. You know how we women get nervous at times."

"At times?" cackled Mr. Krakaur who fancied himself something of a misogynist. "I'd say all the time."

She was in no mood for badinage. Trying to be casual, she said, "I wonder if you'd be good enough to put out the trash barrel right away. I want to straighten up the cellar."

Standing fearfully in the kitchen, not daring to go down the cellar stairs but filled with curiosity she heard him open the outer doors and come back for the barrel. She was not too surprised, though, when he called from the foot of the stairs: "Mrs. Porter, what happened to your cactus?"

"I broke it," she said from the door.

"Did it fall off the shelf?"

"Yes." If one waited others would always provide the answers.

Without realizing it she had moved to the head of the stairs and was peering over the rail just as he was picking up from the floor one of the pieces of the plant pot. Her heart leaped. It could not be coincidence this time, nor a dream. That every piece of the pot had remained in the barrel and none had fallen out she was positive. The sickness of terror rolled over her.

"It don't look too bad," he was saying. "All you got to do is put it in another pot. I think it'll grow just as good."

"No," she said.

"Okay. You're the boss."

She must go away and rest, cleanse her brain of this viscid horror that kept her trembling, made her afraid to go to bed, had her staring hard at shadows, sniffing the air, starting and glancing over her shoulder. She was sure now that the hand on her shoulder had been Ted's and that only her enormous danger had enabled him to get through to her. But it was over; the peril was gone; and perhaps a summer in Maine, at the little hotel in Winter Harbor where she and Ted had spent their honeymoon would eradicate its immediate effects.

When she took one of her keys over to Mrs. Ferguson the latter expressed approval of her decision. "To tell you the truth Harry and I have been worried about you. It's so easy to go into a nervous breakdown, you know." She gave some instances of friends who had slipped into them. She would step in once a week and water the plants and see that everything was all right, she promised. "That was too bad about your big cactus," she said then. "Krakaur told me it fell off the shelf. And after you set such store by it too. But that's the way it is: it's always the things we like the most that get smashed."

It was September when Edith returned. Riding in the taxi from the station, listening to the church clock bong eleven in the clear air, she felt calm, able to pick up her life where she had abandoned it on that Sunday evening in June. It seemed far away now. The peaceful summer, the new friends, the fresh stimuli, they had helped her forget. And she was not afraid. Never again would she be completely sure of herself and of the order of existence, for something strange and unearthly had touched her she knew, but she was not afraid. There was good to surmount evil, a tender hand to warn her of its approach.

The driver set her trunk in the hall, took his money, thanked her for the tip and left, closing the door behind him. And now she was alone; but everything was in its place, familiar and dear and homey: the grand-mother's clock tick-tocking in the corner (Mrs. Ferguson hadn't forgotten to wind it, then), the Meissen figurines, a man and woman, in their perpetual saraband on the table, the Regency mirror reflecting a portion of the living room and beyond it the porch with its greenery of plants. She released the breath she had been holding, smiled, walked to the mirror and took off her hat. Then she felt it, the hand on her shoulder.

"This is ridiculous!" she said aloud. "Now I'm sure I dreamed the whole thing!" The pressure was renewed and she wheeled about and shouted, "It's gone, don't you know that?" In hysterical triumph she ran to the porch and turned on the light. "See?" she cried, standing in the middle and sweeping her arm around. "It's gone, I tell you. It's gone!"

But, on the wall, she saw the outline of its horns and, simultaneously, smelled its sickly odor. Her cry was guttural. With hands stretched out protectively, mouth squared in fear, she stepped backwards, crashed into a hard object, turned, and in the last second of consciousness saw the cactus teetering and falling. . . .

"But I feel responsible. I feel that it's my fault." Mrs. Ferguson had said it over and over. She would never be done saying it nor forget the sight which had met her eyes when, seeing the light, she had gone over to welcome Edith home. Again she explained. "I knew she was fond of that cactus and when I found it growing with the rubber plant I was so pleased. I didn't tell her. I wanted to surprise her. And so I planted it in a pot of its own and it grew even faster than the other one. I should have let her know, though—shouldn't I?"

"It was an accident," Harry Ferguson said patiently. "You're not to blame. Anybody would have done the same in the same circumstances. It was an accident, that's all."

"But it would never have happened if I hadn't done it. Oh, God, when I walked in and saw her lying there with those spikes in her throat—"

Carol Carr's amusing tales of cultural clashes between humans and extraterrestrials were highlights of Damon Knight's Orbit *series and other anthologies of original fantasy and science fiction published in the 1960s and '70s. She was married to renowned author and editor Terry Carr and collaborated with him on the short story "Some are Born Cats." Her short fiction has appeared in* Omni *and been reprinted in* Best Stores from Orbit, Wandering Stars, Creatures from Beyond, *and* Into the Unknown.

Look, You Think You've Got Troubles

Carol Carr

To tell you the truth, in the old days we would have sat shivah for the whole week. My so-called daughter gets married, my own flesh and blood, and not only he doesn't look Jewish, he's not even human.

"Papa," she says to me, two seconds after I refuse to speak to her again in my entire life, "if you know him you'll love him, I promise." So what can I answer— the truth, like I always tell her: "If I know him I'll vomit, that's how he affects me. I can help it? He makes me want to throw up on him."

With silk gloves you have to handle the girl, just like her mother. I tell her what I feel, from the heart, and right away her face collapses into a hundred cracks and water from the Atlantic Ocean makes a soggy mess out of her paper sheath. And that's how I remember her after six months—standing in front of me, sopping wet from the tears and making me feel like a monster—me—when all the time it's her you-should-excuse-the-expression husband who's the monster.

After she's gone to live with him (New Horizon Village, Crag City, Mars), I try to tell myself it's not me who has to—how can I put it?—deal with him intimately; if she can stand it, why should I complain? It's not like I need somebody to carry on the business; my business is to enjoy myself in my retirement. But who can enjoy? Sadie doesn't leave me alone for a minute. She calls me a criminal, a worthless no-good with gallstones for a heart.

"Hector, where's your brains?" she says, having finally given up on my emotions. I can't answer her. I just lost my daughter, I should worry about my brains too? I'm silent as the grave. I can't eat a thing. I'm empty—drained. It's as though I'm waiting for something to happen but I don't know what. I sit in a chair that folds me up like a bee in a flower and rocks me to sleep with electronic rhythms when I feel like sleeping, but who can sleep? I look at my wife and I see Lady Macbeth. Once I caught her whistling as she pushed the button for her bath. I fixed her with a look like an icicle tipped with arsenic.

"What are you so happy about? Thinking of your grandchildren with the twelve toes?"

She doesn't flinch. An iron woman.

When I close my eyes, which is rarely, I see our daughter when she was fourteen years old, with skin just beginning to go pimply and no expression yet on her face. I see her walking up to Sadie and asking her what she should do with her life now she's filling out, and my darling Sadie, my life's mate, telling her why not marry a freak; you got to be a beauty to find a man here, but on Mars you shouldn't know from so many fish. "I knew I could count on you, Mama," she says, and goes ahead and marries a plant with legs.

Things go on like this—impossible—for months. I lose twenty pounds, my nerves, three teeth and I'm on the verge of losing Sadie, when one day the mailchute goes ding-doing and it's a letter from my late daughter. I take it by the tips of two fingers and bring it in to where my wife is punching ingredients for the gravy I won't eat tonight.

"It's a communication from one of your relatives."

"Oh-o-oh." My wife makes a grab for it, meanwhile punching CREAM-TOMATO-SAUCE-BEEF-DRIPPINGS. No wonder I have no appetite.

"I'll give it to you on one condition only," I tell her, holding it out of her trembling reach. "Take it into the bedroom and read it to yourself. Don't even move your lips for once; I don't want to know. If she's God forbid dead, I'll send him a sympathy card."

Sadie has a variety of expressions but the one thing they have common is they all wish me misfortune in my present and future life.

While she's reading the letter I find suddenly I have nothing to do. The magazines I read already. Breakfast I ate (like a bird). I'm all dressed to go out if I feel like, but there's nothing outside I don't have inside. Frankly, I don't feel like myself—I'm nervous. I say a lot of things I don't really intend and now maybe this letter comes to tell me I've got to pay for my meanness. Maybe she got sick up there; God knows what they eat, the kind of water they drink, the creatures they run around with. Not wanting to think about it too much, I go over to my chair and turn it on to brisk massage. It doesn't take long till I'm dreaming (fitfully).

I'm someplace surrounded by sand, sitting in a baby's crib and bouncing a diapered kangaroo on my knee. It gurgles up at me and calls me grandpa and I don't know what I should do. I don't want to hurt its feelings, but if I'm a grandpa to a kangaroo, I want no part of it; I only want it should go away. I pull out a dime from my

pocket and put it into its pouch. The pouch is full of
tiny insects which bite my fingers. I wake up in a sweat.

"Sadie! Are you reading, or rearranging the sentences?
Bring it in here and I'll see what she wants. If it's a
divorce, I know a lawyer."

Sadie comes into the room with her I-told-you-so
waddle and gives me a small wet kiss on the cheek—
a gold star for acting like a mensch. So I start to read
it in a loud monotone so she shouldn't get the impression I give a damn:

"Dear Daddy, I'm sorry for not writing sooner. I
suppose I wanted to give you a chance to simmer down
first." (Ingrate! Does the sun simmer down?) "I know
it would have been inconvenient for you to come to the
wedding, but Mor and I hoped you would maybe send
us a letter just to let us know you're okay and still love
me, in spite of everything."

Right at this point I feel a hot sigh followed by a short
but wrenching moan.

"Sadie, get away from my neck. I'm warning you . . ."

Her eyes are going flick-a-fleck over my shoulder,
from the piece of paper I'm holding to my face, back
to the page, flick-a-fleck, flick-a-fleck.

"All right, already," she shoo-shoos me. "I read it, I
know what's in it. Now it's your turn to see what kind
of a lousy father you turned out to be." And she waddles
back into the bedroom, shutting the door extra careful,
like she's handling a piece of snow-white velvet.

When I'm certain she's gone, I sit myself down on
the slab of woven dental floss my wife calls a couch and
press a button on the arm that reads SEMI-CL.: FELDMAN
To FRIML. The music starts to slither out from the
speaker under my left armpit. The right speaker is dead
and buried, and the long narrow one at the base years
ago got drowned from the dog, who to this day hasn't
learned to control himself when he hears "Desert Song."

This time I'm lucky; it's a piece by Feldman that
comes on. I continue to read, calmed by the music.

"I might as well get to the point, Papa, because for all I know you're so mad you tore up this letter without even reading it. The point is that Mor and I are going to have a baby. Please, please don't throw this into the disintegrator. It's due in July, which gives you over three months to plan the trip up here. We have a lovely house, with a guest room that you and Mama can stay in for as long as you want."

I have to stop here to interject a couple of questions, since my daughter never had a head for logic and it's my strong point.

First of all, if she were in front of me in person right now I would ask right off what means "Mor and I are going to have a baby." Which? Or both? The second thing is, when she refers to it as "it" is she being literal or just uncertain? And just one more thing and then I'm through for good: Just how lovely can a guest room be that has all the air piped in and you can't even see the sky or take a walk on the grass because there is no grass, only simulated this and substituted that?

All the above notwithstanding, I continue to read:

"By the way, Papa, there's something I'm not sure you understand. Mor, you may or may not know, is as human as you and me, in all the important ways—and frankly a bit more intelligent."

I put down the letter for a minute just to give the goose-bumps a chance to fly out of my stomach ulcers before I go on with her love and best and kisses and hopes for seeing us soon, Lorinda.

I don't know how she manages it, but the second I'm finished, Sadie is out of the bedroom and breathing hard.

"Well, do I start packing or do I start packing? And when I start packing, do I pack for us or do I pack for me?"

"Never. I should die three thousand deaths, each one with a worse prognosis."

It's a shame a company like Interplanetary Aviation

can't afford, with the fares they charge, to give you a comfortable seat. Don't ask how I ever got there in the first place. Ask my wife—she's the one with the mouth. First of all, they only allow you three pounds of luggage, which if you're only bringing clothes is plenty, but we had a few gifts with us. We were only planning to stay a few days and to sublet the house was Sadie's idea, not mine.

The whole trip was supposed to take a month, each way. This is reason Sadie thought it was impractical to stay for the weekend and then go home, which was the condition on which I'd agreed to go.

But now that we're on our way, I decide I might as well relax. I close my eyes and try to think of what the first meeting will be like.

"How." I put up my right band in a gesture of friendship and trust. I reach into my pocket and offer him beads.

But even in my mind he looks at me blank, his naked pink antennas waving in the breeze like a worm's underwear. Then I realize there isn't any breeze where we're going. So they stop waving and wilt.

I look around in my mind. We're alone, the two of us, in the middle of a vast plain, me in my business suit and him in his green skin. The scene looks familiar like something I had experienced, or read about. . . . "We'll meet at Philippi," I think, and stab him with my sword.

Only then am I able to catch a few winks.

The month goes by. When I begin to think I'll never remember how to use a fork, the loudspeaker is turned on and I hear this very smooth, modulated voice, the tranquilized tones of a psychiatrist sucking glycerine, telling us it's just about over, and we should expect a slight jolt upon landing.

That slight jolt starts my life going so fast I'm missing all the good parts. But finally the ship is still and all you can hear are the wheezes and sighs of the engines— the sounds remind me of Sadie when she's winding down from a good argument. I look around. Everybody is very white. Sadie's five fingers are around my upper arm like a tourniquet.

"We're here," I tell her. "Do I get a hacksaw or can you manage it yourself?"

"Oh, my goodness." She loosens her grip. She really looks a mess—completely pale, not blinking, not even nagging.

I take her by the arm and steer her into customs. All the time I feel that she's a big piece of unwilling luggage I'm smuggling in. There's no cooperation at all in her feet and her eyes are going every which way.

"Sadie, shape up!"

"If you had a little more curiosity about the world you'd be a better person," she says tolerantly.

While we're waiting to be processed by a creature in a suit like ours who surprises me by talking English, I sneak a quick look around.

It's funny. If I didn't know where we are I'd think we're in the back yard. The ground stretches out pure green, and it's only from the leaflet they give you in the ship to keep your mind off the panic that I know it's 100 percent Acrispan we're looking at, not grass. The air we're getting smells good, too, like fresh-cut flowers, but not too sweet.

By the time I've had a good look and a breathe, what's-its-name is handing us back our passports with a button that says to keep Mars beautiful don't litter.

I won't tell you about the troubles we had getting to the house, or the misunderstanding about the tip, because to be honest I wasn't paying attention. But we do manage to make it to the right door, and considering that the visit was a surprise, I didn't really expect they would meet us at the airport. My daughter must have been peeking, though, because she's in front of us even before we have a chance to knock.

"Mother!" she says, looking very round in the stomach. She hugs and kisses Sadie, who starts bawling. Five minutes later, when they're out of the clinch, Lorinda turns to me, a little nervous.

You can say a lot of things about me, but basically I'm a warm person, and we're about to be guests in this house, even if she is a stranger to me. I shake her hand.

"Is he home, or is he out in the back yard, growing new leaves?"

Her face (or what I can see of it through the climate adapter) crumbles a little at the chin line, but she straightens it out and puts her hand on my shoulder.

"Mor had to go out, Daddy—something important came up—but he should be back in an hour or so. Come on, let's go inside."

Actually there's nothing too crazy about the house, or even interesting. It has walls, a floor and a roof, I'm glad to see, even a few relaxer chairs, and after the trip we just had, I sit down and relax. I notice my daughter is having a little trouble looking me straight in the face, which is only as it should be, and it isn't long before she and Sadie are discussing pregnancy, gravitational exercise, labor, hospitals, formulas and sleep-taught toilet training. When I'm starting to feel that I'm getting overeducated, I decide to go into the kitchen and make myself a bite to eat. I could have asked them for a little something but I don't want to interfere with their first conversation. Sadie has all engines going and is interrupting four times a sentence, which is exactly the kind of game they always had back home—my daughter's goal is to say one complete thought out loud. If Sadie doesn't spring back with a non sequitur, Lorinda wins that round. A full-fledged knockout with Sadie still champion is when my daughter can't get a sentence in for a week. Sometimes I can understand why she went to Mars.

Anyway, while they're at the height of their simultaneous monologues, I go quietly off to the kitchen to see what I can dig up. (Ripe parts of Mor, wrapped in plastic? Does he really regenerate, I wonder. Does Lorinda fully understand how he works, or one day will she make an asparagus omelet out of one of his appendages, only to learn that's the part that doesn't grow back? "Oh, I'm so sorry," she says. "Can you ever forgive me?")

The refrigerator, though obsolete on Earth, is well stocked—fruits of a sort, steaks, it seems, small chicken-type things that might be stunted pigeons. There's a bowl of a brownish, creamy mess—I can't even bring myself to smell it. Who's hungry, anyway, I think. The rumbling in my stomach is the symptom of a father's love turning sour.

I wander into the bedroom. There's a large portrait of Mor hanging on the wall—or maybe his ancestor. Is it true that instead of hearts, Martians have a large avocado pit? There's a rumor on Earth that when Martians get old they start to turn brown at the edges, like lettuce.

There's an object on the floor and I bend down and pick it up. A piece of material—at home I would have thought it was a man's handkerchief. Maybe it is a handkerchief. Maybe they have colds like us. They catch a germ, the sap rises to combat the infection, and they have to blow their stamens. I open up a drawer to put the piece of material in (I like to be neat), but when I close it, something gets stuck. Another thing I can't recognize. It's small, round and either concave or convex, depending on how you look at it. It's made of something black and shiny. A cloth bowl? What would a vegetable be doing with a cloth bowl? Some questions are too deep for me, but what I don't know I eventually find out—and not by asking, either.

I go back to the living room.

"Did you find anything to eat?" Lorinda asks. "Or would you like me to fix—"

"Don't even get up," Sadie says quickly. "I can find my way around any kitchen, I don't care whose."

"I'm not hungry. It was a terrible trip. I thought I'd never wake up from it in one piece. By the way, I heard a good riddle on the ship. What's round and black, either concave or convex, depending on how you look at it, and made out of a shiny material?"

Lorinda blushed. "A skullcap? But that's not funny."

"So who needs funny? Riddles have to be a laugh a minute all of a sudden? You think Oedipus giggled all the way home from seeing the Sphinx?"

"Look, Daddy, I think there's something I should tell you."

"I think there are all sorts of things you should tell me."

"No, I mean about Mor."

"Who do you think I mean, the grocery boy? You elope with a cucumber from outer space and you want I should be satisfied because he's human in all the important ways? What's important—that he sneezes and hiccups? If you tell me he snores, I should be ecstatic? Maybe he sneezes when he's happy and hiccups when he's making love and snores because it helps him think better. Does that make him human?"

"Daddy, *please*."

"Okay, not another word." Actually I'm starting to feel quite guilty. What if she has a miscarriage right on the spot? A man like me doesn't blithely torture a pregnant woman, even if she does happen to be his daughter. "What's so important it can't wait till later?"

"Nothing, I guess. Would you like some chopped liver? I just made some fresh."

"What?"

"Chopped liver—you know, chopped liver."

Oh yes, the ugly mess in the refrigerator. "You made it, that stuff in the bowl?"

"Sure. Daddy, there's something I really have to tell you."

She never does get to tell me, though, because her husband walks in, bold as brass.

I won't even begin to tell you what he looks like. Let me just say he's a good dream cooked up by Mary

Shelley. I won't go into it, but if it gives you a small idea, I'll say that his head is shaped like an acorn on top of a stalk of broccoli. Enormous blue eyes, green skin and no hair at all except for a small blue round area on top of his head. His ears are adorable. Remember Dumbo the Elephant? Only a little smaller—I never exaggerate, even for effect. And he looks boneless, like a filet.

My wife, God bless her, I don't have to worry about; she's a gem in a crisis. One look at her son-in-law and she faints dead away. If I didn't know her better, if I wasn't absolutely certain that her simple mind contained no guile, I would have sworn she did it on purpose, to give everybody something to fuss about. Before we know what's happening, we're all in a tight, frantic conversation about what's the best way to bring her around. But while my daughter and her husband are in the bathroom looking for some deadly chemical, Sadie opens both eyes at once and stares up at me from the floor.

"What did I miss?"

"You didn't miss anything—you were only unconscious for fifteen seconds. It was a cat nap, not a coma."

"Say hello, Hector. Say hello to him or so help me I'll close my eyes for good."

"I'm very glad to meet you, Mr. Trumbnick," he says. I'm grateful that he's sparing me the humiliation of making the first gesture, but I pretend I don't see the stalk he's holding out.

"Smutual," I say.

"I beg your pardon?"

"Smutual. How are you? You look better than your pictures." He does, too. Even though his skin is green, it looks like the real thing up close. But his top lip sort of vibrates when he talks, and I can hardly bear to look at him except sideways.

"I hear you had some business this afternoon. My daughter never did tell me what your line is, uh, Morton."

"Daddy, his name is Mor. Why don't you call him Mor?"

"Because I prefer Morton. When we know each other better I'll call him something less formal. Don't rush me, Lorinda; I'm still getting adjusted to the chopped liver."

My son-in-law chuckles and his top lip really goes crazy. "Oh, were you surprised? Imported meats aren't a rarity here, you know. Just the other day one of my clients was telling me about an all-Earth meal he had at home."

"Your client?" Sadie asks. "You wouldn't happen to be a lawyer?" (My wife amazes me with her instant familiarity. She could live with a tyrannosaurus in perfect harmony. First she faints, and while she's out cold everything in her head that was strange becomes ordinary and she wakes up a new woman.)

"No, Mrs. Trumbnick. I'm a—"

"—rabbi, of course," she finishes. "I knew it. The minute Hector found that skullcap. I knew it. Him and his riddles. A skullcap is a skullcap and nobody not Jewish would dare wear one—not even a Martian." She bites her lip but recovers like a pro. "I'll bet you were out on a Bar Mitzvah—right?"

"No, as a matter of fact—"

"—a Bris. I knew it."

She's rubbing her hands together and beaming at him. "A Bris, how nice. But why didn't you tell, Lorinda? Why would you keep such a thing a secret?"

Lorinda comes over to me and kisses me on the cheek, and I wish she wouldn't because I'm feeling myself go soft and I don't want to show it.

"Mor isn't just a rabbi, Daddy. He converted because of me and then found there was a demand among the colonists. But he's never given up his own beliefs, and part of his job is to minister to the Kopchopees who camp outside the village. That's where he was earlier, conducting a Kochopee menopausal rite."

"A what?"

"Look, to each his own," says my wife with the open mind. But me, I want facts, and this is getting more bizarre by the minute.

"Kopchopee. He's a Kopchopee priest to his own race and a rabbi to ours, and that's how he makes his living? You don't feel there's a contradiction between the two, Morton?"

"That's right. They both pray to a strong silent god, in different ways of course. The way my race worships, for instance—"

"Listen, it takes all kinds," says Sadie.

"And the baby, whatever it turns out to be—will it be a Choptapi or a Jew?"

"Jew, schmoo," Sadie says with a wave of dismissal. "All of a sudden it's Hector the Pious—such a megilla out of a molehill." She turns away from me and addresses herself to the others, like I've just become invisible. "He hasn't seen the inside of a synagogue since we got married—what a rain that night—and now he can't take his shoes off in a house until he knows its race, color and creed." With a face full of fury, she brings me back into her sight. "Nudnick, what's got into you?"

I stand up straight to preserve my dignity. "If you'll excuse me, my things are getting wrinkled in the suitcase."

Sitting on my bed (with my shoes on), I must admit I'm feeling a little different. Not that Sadie made me change my mind. Far from it; for many years now her voice is the white sound that lets me think my own thoughts. But what I'm realizing more and more is that in a situation like this a girl needs her father, and what kind of a man is it who can't sacrifice his personal feelings for his only daughter? When she was going out with Herbie the Hemopheliac and came home crying it had to end because she was afraid to touch him, he might bleed, didn't I say pack your things, we're going to Grossingers Venuis for three weeks? When my twin brother Max went into kitchen sinks, who was it that helped him out at only four percent? Always, I stood ready to help my family. And if Lorinda ever needed me, it's now when she's pregnant by some religious maniac. Okay—he makes me retch, so I'll talk to him with a tissue over my mouth. After all, in a world that's getting smaller all the time, it's people like me who have to be bigger to make up for it, no?

I go back to the living room and extend my hand to my son-in-law the cauliflower. (Feh.)

Irwin Sonenfield's "The Pure Essence" takes a humorous look at the mystery of human perception and the view of the artist. A native of Green Bay, Wisconsin, this is his first published story.

The Pure Essence

Irwin Sonenfield

The reason I'm writing this down is because then people are more likely to pay attention. When I try to tell Mr. Feinstein something, he says, "Not now Sammy, I'm busy." But if you write something, people will figure it must be worthwhile or else why would you take all the trouble?

Besides not listening to me, there are two things that bug me about Mr. Feinstein, the man who owns the delicatessen where I work. First, he calls me Sammy. My whole life I tried to get my mother to quit calling me Sammy, and now, finally, she's stopped. But not Mr. Feinstein. The other thing is that Feinstein isn't really his name. You could say he's going around under false intentions. But he told me once, who buys delicatessen from someone named Reilly?

But this isn't what I'm writing about. My biggest problem as a writer, Mrs. Popless used to say, was that I don't stick to the point. I keep regressing, she said in a writing class I took last year, when I was a senior in High School. At that time I didn't really expect to be a writer. I took the class because it was the only thing open when I had study hall. And I knew it had to be

better than study hall. But Mrs. Popless, the teacher,
thought I could learn to write real good if I would only
apply myself. I wasn't sure what she meant by applying
myself. It made me think of smearing on lineament after
a basketball game. I guess I'm applying myself now. And
like she always said, I'm writing about a true experience
that really happened.

It never would of happened if Mr. Feinstein didn't
make me do deliveries. (I'll go on calling him Mr.
Feinstein. I wonder if Mrs. Reilly calls him that.) At first
I complained because, when I took the job, he didn't
say anything about deliveries. After all, I'm a High
School graduate with a diploma and have to think about
learning a business. You can't learn anything from making
deliveries. At least I used to think so. Now I know
different.

It's like when I got into Mrs. Popless's class, I didn't
know I was going to be a writer. To be honest with you,
I don't know everything yet about writing, because I still
have a few problems with details. But when you get to
be a famous writer, all you need is to have an idea and
the publisher fixes up the mistakes and adds a few
commas and semi commas. That's what publishers are
for.

So when I told Mr. Feinstein, when I took the job
I didn't know I had to make deliveries, he said, "When
you came I told you I would teach you the business
inside and out. This is the out part."

Really, there weren't so many deliveries—a couple old
ladies who didn't like to carry packages and Mr. Brassic
who worked at home and wanted us to bring him salami
sandwiches sometimes, so he wouldn't be interrupted.

I remember thinking at first that Brassic was a funny
name. I decided he must be a Hungarian or a Turk or
something. But at the time, I didn't know how funny
this guy really was.

The first time I brought him his salami sandwiches,
I noticed the smell as soon as I was on the stairs of

his old two-family house. Inside the apartment, the smell was even stronger. I could of written there was a terrible stink, but Mrs. Popless always said not to use words like that, because people would think you didn't know any better. She really hated bad language. It was a good thing she didn't hear some of the things the kids said. Especially the things they said about her. There was a poem someone made up.

> Mrs. Popless
> Went out topless
> Darling fair lass
> Kiss my . . .

Well, I don't have to write down everything they said, because it's not very nice and besides it's a regression. This lady was about ninety years old and you would think they could have a little respect.

Anyhow, the stink, or I could say the stench that perforated my olefactory nostrils, I could tell was partly turpentine and partly I don't know what. And there was Mr. Brassic standing in his blue jeans and T-shirt, paint all over him, with a long brush in his hand. So I knew right away he was a painter.

"Hello kid," he said. "Put the sandwiches down. What's your name?"

"My name is Sam," I said, like I was underlining the words, so he wouldn't make a mistake.

"Okay Sam, stand next to me and look at this painting."

It was a big painting, bigger than the door to Mr. Feinstein's meat locker. I looked at it but I didn't know what to say. So I said, "Mr. Brassic, I didn't take art class because I took writing instead."

He looked at me very serious. "You don't need art class to look at a painting. In fact you're better off without it. Just react. What do you see?"

I saw a whole lot of lines and circles and squiggles in different colors, so I told him.

"Yes, but what does it make you feel?" he asked. "Do you feel the energy, the rhythm? Does it make you think of your girl friend? Do you have a girl friend?"

"Sure I have. Cindy."

"Does it make you want her right now, right here?"

"Of course not. She's working right now. She's a waitress at the Super Sanitary Homecooking Cafe."

"Doesn't looking at this painting make you want to . . . you know . . . with Cindy?"

I got what he was talking about, but I was embarrassed. A grown man shouldn't talk that way to a kid. So I said, "Cindy is a nice girl and she's very ambitious. She says we're both learning the food game so some day we'll have a place of our own." I was purposely invading his question because what I did with Cindy was none of his business. I could tell he was disappointed with me because he suddenly sat down like he was tired. I noticed he had a big smear of green paint right in the middle of his bald head. And when I say bald, I mean he had no hair. It was a fat, round head, like a vegetable with a face.

"All right," he said, "what don't you like about the painting?"

"I didn't say I don't like it. I do like it. It's got a lot of color."

"You think it's exciting?"

"Sure. Only I don't know what it's a picture of."

"I knew it didn't communicate," he said. "You see, it's a picture of my inner self, my unconscious."

"Then why should it make me think of Cindy?"

"Because the sight of a naked soul should be stimulating. You have to add the rest from your own experience."

"Then all those lines and squiggles aren't really anything in particular?"

"They are whatever they make you think of."

"But there are so many of them, I can't think of so much at once."

Then he was quiet and a funny look came over his face. Finally he said, "I think you've got a point. Maybe it's too intense, too overwhelming.""

When I got back to the store, Mr. Feinstein said, "Where you been so long? We had a hundred customers I had to wait on myself."

"Mr. Brassic wanted to talk to me."

"He pays for salami, not conversation. What does he have to talk about with a kid?"

"Painting."

"Look, are you learning the deli business or the painting business?"

I figured there wasn't any use trying to tell him about Mr. Brassic. I don't think Mr. Feinstein ever graduated from high school, so he didn't know about some of the modern ideas, like self-expression. Not that I was an expert, but I liked Mr. Brassic. At least he thought something I said made sense. Up till then, nobody but Mrs. Popless thought my ideas were worth anything.

A few days later, when Mr. Brassic called for salami, I even looked forward to going. When I got in the door, I saw he had a new painting. Not that it was so different. It still had circles and squiggles. But there were less of them.

"Well Sam," Mr. Brassic said, "I took your advice. I simplified it. What do you think?"

"I like it," I said. I felt I had to agree with my own advice. Besides, I did kind of like it, now that I was almost getting used to it.

"But look at it carefully. Especially at the lower right corner. What do you see there?"

I looked where he was pointing, but I didn't see much. Just a round, pale green thing, about three inches across.

"Do you see it?" he asked.

"Sure."

"But what do you see? What does it make you think of?"

"It's a cabbage," I said.

That gave him something to think about. "A cabbage?" He was thinking it over. "Well, maybe it is something like a cabbage. But it's more than a cabbage. It's a cabbage with a face. Don't you see it?"

"Maybe I do." I wasn't sure I did, but I didn't want to argue with him.

"And whose face is it?" he asked.

"I give up."

"Doesn't it remind you of anyone? Say someone in this room."

There were only two of us in the room and I knew it wasn't me. "It's your face."

He really was pleased with me. "That's right," he said. "That's exactly right. You're a smart kid."

I didn't want to seem too conceited, so I said, "Well, anyone could see it."

"Do you think so? But I'll tell you the really funny thing about that face. I don't remember painting it. I must have done it unconsciously. Or maybe . . ." here he gave me a strange look . . . "maybe it painted itself."

"Oh come on, Mr. Brassic."

He could see that things were getting a little too weird for me, because he said, I'm not saying that's what really happened. I just said maybe. All I know is that when I got up this morning, there it was."

"You could of forgot that you painted it."

"Could I forget painting such a wonderful thing? It's not only a face . . . it's not only my face—even if it does look a little like a cabbage—it's the eyes. Did you notice the eyes?"

"Sure it has eyes."

"But those eyes look at me. They follow me around the room. They even seem to know what I'm thinking."

I decided it was time to get out, before Mr. Brassic became violent or unranged or something. So I said, like

I was joking, "Well if they can tell what I'm thinking, they know I have to get back to the store or Mr. Feinstein will be sore. He's probably had a hundred customers."

Sure enough, Mr. Feinstein had had a hundred customers. "What do you and Mr. Brassic do all that time," he asked me.

"We talk about art."

"What kind of art? Scenery?"

"Right now," I said, "he's very interested in a picture of a cabbage. He keeps talking about this cabbage."

"He keeps talking about a cabbage? Maybe he's got . . . what is it called when someone talks about the same thing all the time?"

"It's called a concession." I don't like to flaunt my education in front of Mr. Feinstein. It might make him feel bad. But sometimes you have to do that with older people.

"Sure, a concession," he said like he knew the word all along.

I think it was about then I got the idea of writing this down in the form of a true story. How often do you meet a real character like Mr. Brassic? Not very often I can tell you, and that's probably a good thing. If you kept meeting nuts all the time, you would begin thinking they were normal and you were crazy.

I thought I might sell the story to a magazine and, after a while, it's possible I could become a famous writer, which might be even better than the food game. I might get the story in an art magazine, if there is such a thing, because Mr. Brassic could be very well known in the art business.

When I told this to Cindy, she thought Mr. Brassic was probably a famous artist. She said she heard of a man who became very important because he painted pictures of soup cans.

"Why did he want to do that?" I asked her.

"Because no one else ever thought of it. It was his own personal idea. And before you knew it, these soup cans were a smash hit, like in a top ten among pictures."

So when Mr. Brassic called for his salami sandwiches a few days later, I was anxious to go and add to my material for the story. Mrs. Popless used to say that a writer was always looking for true experiences, although sometimes he had to pretend that his characters weren't anybody living or dead because he might get sued or be in big trouble.

What do you suppose I found when I got there? A new painting. And what was on it? Four big cabbages right in the middle of the picture. And that's all.

"What do you think, Sam?" Mr. Brassic asked.

"I think you got the cabbages down real good, Mr. Brassic."

"They're all me, Sam. Different parts of my personality. I think I'm getting a genuine expression of myself."

"Do you think people are going to want to see you expressing yourself so much?"

"That's the beauty of it," he said. "People will see themselves in it. And when those eyes follow them around, it will be like a personal encounter with themselves, which should make them feel a lot better."

"But what if they just see cabbages?"

"Yes, that's a problem. I think I'm on the right track, Sam. But I haven't found the pure essence of the thing yet. Maybe the next time you see me."

I didn't really understand what he was talking about so I looked up the word "essence." It took a while because I had to figure out how it was spelled. At first I thought it might have something to do with delicatessens. But that didn't make sense because usually they don't sell cabbage in a deli. I finally found the word in a dictionary, but it didn't help. When I told Cindy I was trying to find the pure essence of my story, she got mad. She thought I was showing off.

Mr. Brassic didn't phone for his salami for about a week. I was beginning to worry he wasn't going to find whatever he was looking for. I let myself in the door because we were old friends now. But I didn't see him in the room.

"Is that you, Sam?" He was calling from the bathroom.

"Sure it's me."

"Look at the canvas," he said.

It was a big canvas. And what was on it? Nothing. That's right, absolutely nothing. Bald as Mr. Brassic's head.

"The problem," he shouted from the bathroom, "was that I was trying to force people to see through my eyes. People should be able to see freely, without the painter controlling their vision. They must be able to create from their own imaginations. The painter's task is to avoid distracting them with irrelevant directions."

"Suppose they don't see anything," I asked.

"Then that's their own fault. They can't blame the painter for that."

"You think you've got the essence now, Mr. Brassic?"

He was coming into the room when he asked, "What do you see, Sam?"

When I saw him I wanted to run out the door. Instead, I just stood there and said, "I see a cabbage." But I wasn't looking at the canvas.

Okay, I know what you're thinking. You think this crazy writer is going to tell you that Mr. Brassic's head had turned into a cabbage. Well, you're wrong. I'm not going to tell you any such thing. Even if it was true, I would refuse to write it down, because you wouldn't believe it. Why should I tell you something you won't believe, even if I swore and crossed my heart? Although, like Mrs. Popless used to say, truth is stronger than fiction.

Absolutely, I guarantee there wasn't anything wrong with Mr. Brassic's head, at least nothing that wasn't wrong before. Because I don't want you to think this is some kind of fairy tale where people turn into frogs or bugs or whatever.

I was starting to leave when Mr. Brassic said, "I'm glad you see my idea."

"Sure I see it. I see it fine."

"And by the way, Sam . . ."

"What?"

"The next time I call for you to bring something up . . ."

"The next time . . . ?" I was trying to get out the door.

"Change the order to corned beef."

Al Sarrantonio's writing covers a wide range of territory that includes horror, mystery, western, and science fiction. His short tales of horror, which have appeared in Whispers, The Horror Show, and the Shadows anthologies, helped to define contemporary dark fantasy. His novels include The Worms, Campbell Wood, October, House Haunted, and the science fiction werewolf story Moonbane. He has served as an officer of the Horror Writers of America and co-edited the anthology 100 Hair-Raising Little Horror Stories.

Pumpkin Head

Al Sarrantonio

An orange and black afternoon.

Outside, under baring but still-robust trees, leaves tapped across sidewalks, a thousand fingernails drawn down a thousand dry blackboards.

Inside, a party beginning.

Ghouls loped up and down aisles between desks, shouting "Boo!" at one another. Crepe paper, crinkly and the colors of Halloween, crisscrossed over blackboards covered with mad and frightful doodlings in red and green chalk: snakes, rats, witches on broomsticks. Windowpanes were filled with cutout black cats and ghosts with no eyes and giant O's for mouths.

A fat jack-o'-lantern, flickering orange behind its mouth and eyes and giving off spicy fumes, glared down from Ms. Grinby's desk.

Ms. Grinby, young, bright, and filled with enthusiasm,

219

left the room to chase an errant goblin-child, and one blackboard witch was hastily labeled "Teacher." Ms. Grinby, bearing her captive, returned, saw her caricature, and smiled. "All right, who did this?" she asked, not expecting an answer and not getting one. She tried to look rueful. "Never mind, but I think you know I don't really look like that. Except maybe today." She produced a witch's peaked hat from her drawer and put it on with a flourish.

Laughter.

"Ah!" said Ms. Grinby, happy.

The party began.

Little bags were handed out, orange and white with freshly twisted tops and filled with orange and white candy corn.

Candy corn disappeared into pink little mouths.

There was much yelling, and the singing of Halloween songs with Ms. Grinby at the piano, and a game of "Pin the Tail on the Black Cat." And then a ghost story, passed from child to child, one sentence each:

"It was a dark and rainy night—"

"—and . . . Peter had to come out of the storm—"

"—and he stopped at the only house on the road—"

"—and no one seemed to be home—"

"—because the house was empty and haunted—"

The story stopped dead at the last seat of the first row.

All eyes focused back on that corner.

The new child.

"Raylee," asked Ms. Grinby gently, "aren't you going to continue the story with us?"

Raylee, new in class that day—the quiet one, the shy one with black bangs and big eyes always looking down—sat with her small, grayish hands folded, her dark brown eyes straight ahead like a rabbit caught in a headlight beam.

"Raylee?"

Raylee's thin pale hands shook.

Ms. Grinby got up quickly and went down the aisle, setting her hand lightly on the girl's shoulder.

"Raylee is just shy," she said, smiling down at the unmoving top of the girl's head. She knelt down to face-level, noticing two round fat beads of water at the corners of the girl's eyes. Her hands were clenched hard.

"Don't you want to join in with the rest of us?" Ms. Grinby whispered, a kindly look washing over her face. Empathy welled up in her. "Wouldn't you like to make friends with everyone here?"

Nothing. She stared straight ahead, the bag of candy, still neatly wrapped and twisted, resting on the varnished and dented desk top before her.

"She's a faggot!"

This from Judy Linthrop, one of the four Linthrop girls, aged six through eleven, and sometimes trouble.

"Now, Judy—" began Ms. Grinby.

"Faggot!" from Roger Mapleton.

"A *faggot!*"

Peter Pakinski, Randy Feffer, Jane Campbell.

All eyes on Raylee for reaction.

"A pale little faggot!"

"That's enough!" said Ms. Grinby, angry, and there was instant silence; the game had gone too far.

"Raylee," she said softly. Her young heart went out to this girl; she longed to scream at her, "Don't be shy! There's no reason. The hurt isn't real, I know, I know!" Images of Ms. Grinby's own childhood, her awful loneliness, came back to her, and with them a lump to her throat.

I know, I know!

"Raylee," she said, her voice a whisper in the party room, "don't you want to join in?

Silence.

"Raylee—"

"I know a story of my own."

Ms. Grinby nearly gasped with the sound of the girl's voice, it came so suddenly. Her upturned, sad little face

abruptly came to life, took on color, became real. There
was an earnestness in those eyes, which looked out from
the girl's haunted, shy darkness to her and carried her
voice with them.

"I'll tell a story of my own if you'll let me."

Ms. Grinby almost clapped her hands. "Of course!"
she said. "Class"—looking about her at the other child-
faces: some interested, some smirking, some holding
back with comments and jeers, seeking an opening, a
place to be heard— "Raylee is going to tell us a story.
A Halloween story?" she asked, bending back down
toward the girl, and when Raylee nodded yes she
straightened and smiled and preceded her to the front
of the room.

Ms. Grinby sat down on her stool behind her desk.

Raylee stood silent for a moment, before all the eyes
and the almost jeers and the smirks, under the crepe
paper and cardboard monsters and goblins.

Her eyes were on the floor, and then she suddenly
realized that she had taken her bag of candy with her,
and stood alone clutching it before them all. Ms. Grinby
saw it too, and before Raylee began to shuffle her feet
and stand with embarrassment or run from the room,
the teacher stood and said, "Here, why don't you let
me hold that for you until you're finished?"

She took it from the girl's sweaty hand and sat down
again.

Raylee stood silent, eyes downcast.

Ms. Grinby prepared to get up, to save her again.

"This story," Raylee began suddenly, startling the
teacher into settling back into her chair, "is a scary one.
It's about a little boy named Pumpkin Head."

Ms. Grinby sucked in her breath; there were some
whisperings from the class, which she quieted with a
stare.

"Pumpkin Head," Raylee went on, her voice small
and low but clear and steady, "was very lonely. He had
no friends. He was not a bad boy, and he liked to play,

but no one would play with him because of the way he looked.

"He was called Pumpkin Head because his head was too big for his body. It had grown too fast for the rest of him, and was soft and large. He only had a little patch of hair, on the top of his head, and the skin on all of his head was soft and fat. You could almost pull it out into folds. His eyes, nose, and mouth were practically lost in all the fat on his face.

"Someone said Pumpkin Head looked that way because his father had worked at an atomic plant and had been in an accident before Pumpkin head was born. But this wasn't his fault, and even his parents, though they loved him, were afraid of him because of the way he looked. When he stared into a mirror he was almost afraid of himself. At times he wanted to rip at his face with his fingers, or cut it with a knife, or hide it by wearing a bag over it with writing on it that said, 'I am me, I am normal just like you under here.' At times he felt so bad he wanted to bash his head against a wall, or go to the train tracks and let a train run over it."

Raylee paused, and Ms. Grinby almost stopped her, but noting the utter silence of the class, and Raylee's absorption with her story, she held her tongue.

"Finally, Pumpkin Head became so lonely that he decided to do anything he could to get a friend. He talked to everyone in his class, one by one, as nicely as he could, but no one would go near him. He tried again, but still no one would go near him. Then he finally stopped trying.

"One day he began to cry in class, right in the middle of a history lesson. No one, not even the teacher, could make him stop. The tears ran down Pumpkin Head's face, in furrows like on the hard furrows of a pumpkin. The teacher had to call his mother and father to come and get him, and even they had trouble taking him away because he sat in his chair with his hands tight around his seat and cried and cried. There didn't seem to be enough tears in Pumpkin Head's head for all his crying, and some of his classmates wondered if his pumpkin head was filled with water. But finally his parents brought him home and put him in his room, and there he stayed for three days, crying.

"After those three days passed, Pumpkin Head came out of his room. His tears had dried. He smiled through the ugly folds of skin on his face, and said that he wouldn't cry anymore and that he would like to go back to school. His mother and father wondered if he was really all right, but secretly, Pumpkin Head knew, they sighed with relief because having him around all the time made them nervous. Some of their friends would not come to see them when Pumpkin Head was in the house.

"Pumpkin Head went back to school that morning, smiling. He swung his lunch pail in his hand, his head held high. His teacher and his classmates were very surprised to see him back, and everyone left him alone for a while.

"But then, in the middle of the second period, one of the boys in the class threw a piece of paper at Pumpkin Head, and then another. Someone hissed that his head was like a pumpkin, and that he had better plant it before Halloween. 'And on Halloween we'll break open his pumpkin head!' someone else yelled out.

"Pumpkin Head sat in his seat and carefully brought his lunch box up to his desk. He opened it quietly. Inside was his sandwich, made in a hurry by his mother, and an apple and a bag of cookies. He took these out, and also the thermos filled with milk, and set them on the desk. He closed the lunch pail and snapped shut the lid.

"Pumpkin Head stood and walked to the front of the room, carrying his lunch pail in his hand. He walked to the door and closed it, and then walked calmly to the teacher's desk, turning toward the class. He opened his lunch box.

" 'My lunch and dinner,' he said, 'my dinner and breakfast.'

"He took out a sharp kitchen knife from his lunch pail.

"Everyone in the classroom began to scream.

"They took Pumpkin Head away after that, and they put him in a place—"

Ms. Grinby abruptly stepped from behind her desk.

"That's all we have time for, Raylee," she interrupted gently, trying to smile. Inside she wanted to scream over the loneliness of this child. "That was a very scary story. Where did you get it from?"

There was silence in the classroom,

Raylee's eyes were back on the floor. "I made it up," she said in a whisper.

To make up something like that, Ms. Grinby thought. *I know, I know!*

She patted the little girl on her back. "Here's your candy; you can sit down now." The girl returned to her seat quickly, eyes averted.

All eyes were on her.

And then something that made Ms. Grinby's heart leap:

"Neat story!" said Randy Feffer.

"Neat!"

"Wow!"

Roger Mapleton, Jane Campbell.

As she sat down, Raylee was trembling but smiling shyly.

"Neat story!"

A bell rang somewhere.

"Can it be that time already?" Ms. Grinby looked at the full-moon—faced wall clock. "Why, it is! Time to go home. I hope everyone had a nice party—and remember! Don't eat too much candy!"

A small hand waved anxiously at her from the center of the room.

"Yes, Cleo?"

Cleo, red-freckled face and blue eyes, stood up. "Can I please tell the class, Ms. Grinby, that I'm having a party tonight, and that I can invite everyone in the class?"

Ms. Grinby smiled. "You may, Cleo, but there doesn't seem to be much left to tell, does there?"

"Well," said Cleo, smiling at Raylee, "only that everyone's invited."

Raylee smiled back and looked quickly away.

Books and candy bags were crumpled together, and all ran out under crepe paper, cats, and ghouls, under the watchful eyes of the jack-o'-lantern, into darkening afternoon.

A black and orange night.

Here came a black cat walking on two legs; there two percale sheet ghosts trailing paper bags with handles; here again a miniature man from outer space. The wind was up; leaves whipped along the serpentine sidewalk like racing cars. There was an apple-crisp smell in the air, an icicle-down-your-spine, here-comes-winter chill. Pumpkins everywhere, and a half harvest moon playing coyly with wisps of high shadowy clouds. A thousand dull yellow night-lights winked through breezy trees on a thousand festooned porches. A constant ringing of doorbells, the wash of goblin traffic: they traveled in twos, threes, or fours, these monsters, held together by Halloween gravity. Groups passed other groups, just coming up, or coming down, stairs, made faces, and said "Boo!" There were a million "Boo!" greetings this night.

On one particular porch in all that thousand, goblins went up the steps but did not come down again. The door opened a crack, then wider, and groups of ghosts, wizards, and spooks, instead of waiting patiently for a toss in a bag and then turning away, slipped through into the house and disappeared from the night. Disappeared into another night.

Through the hallway and kitchen and down another set of stairs to the cellar. A cellar transformed. A cellar of hell, this cellar—charcoal-pit black with eerie dim red lanterns glowing out of odd corners and cracks. An Edgar Allan Poe cellar—and there hung his portrait over the apple-bobbing tub, raven-bedecked and with a cracked grin under those dark-pool eyes and that ponderous brow. This was his cellar, to be sure, a Masque-of-the-Red-Death cellar.

And here were the Poe people; miniature versions of his evil creatures: enough hideous beasts to fill page after page, and all shrunk down to child size. Devils galore, with papier-mâché masks, and hooves and tails of red rope, each with a crimson fork on the end; a gaggle of poke-hole ghosts; a mechanical cardboard man; two wolfmen; four vampires with wax teeth; one mummy; one ten-tentacled sea beast; three Frankenstein monsters; one Bride of same; and one monster of indefinite shape and design, something like a jellyfish made of plastic bags.

And Raylee.

Raylee came last; was last to slip silently and trembling through the portal of the yellow front door; was last to slip even more silently down the creaking cellar steps to the Poe cellar below. She came cat-silent and cautious, holding her breath—was indeed dressed cat-like, in a whiskered mask, black tights, and black rope tail, all black to mix silently with the black basement.

No one saw her come in; only the black-beetle eyes of Poe over the apple tub noted her arrival.

The apple tub was well in use by now, a host of devils, ghosts, and Frankensteins clamoring around it and eagerly awaiting a turn at its game under Poe's watchful eyes.

"I got one!" shouted one red devil, triumphantly pulling a glossy apple from his mouth; no devil mask here, but a red-painted face, red and dripping from the tub's water. It was Peter, one of the taunting boys in Raylee's class.

Raylee hung back in the shadows.

"I got one!" shouted a Frankenstein monster.

"And me!" from his Bride. Two crisp red apples were held aloft for Poe's inspection.

"And me!" "And me." shouted Draculas, hunchbacks, little green men.

Spooks and wolfmen shouted too.

One apple left.

"Who hasn't tried yet?" cried Cleo, resplendent in witch's garb. She was a miniature Ms. Grinby. She leaned her broom against the tub, called for attention.

"Who hasn't tried?"

Raylee tried to sink into the shadows' protection but could not. A deeper darkness was what she needed; she was spotted.

"Raylee! Raylee!" shouted Cleo. "Come get your apple!" It was a singsong, as Raylee held her hands out, appleless, and stepped into the circle of ghouls.

She was terrified. She trembled so hard she could not hold her hands still on the side of the metal tub as she leaned over it. She wanted to bolt from the room, up the stairs, and out through the yellow doorway into the dark night.

"Dunk! Dunk!" the ghoul circle began to chant, impatient.

Raylee stared down into the water, saw her dark reflection and Poe's mingled by the ripples of the bobbing apple.

"Dunk! Dunk!" the circle chanted.

Raylee pushed herself from the reflection, stared at the faces surrounding her. "I don't want to!"

"Dunk! . . ." the chant faded.

Two dozen cool eyes surveyed her behind eyeholes; weighed her dispassionately in the sharp light of peer pressure. There were ghouls behind those ghoulish masks and eyes.

Someone hissed a laugh as the circle tightened around Raylee. Like a battered leaf with its stem caught under a rock in a high wind, she trembled.

Cleo, alone outside the circle, stepped quickly into it to protect her. She held out her hands. "Raylee—" she began soothingly.

The circle tightened still more, undaunted. Above them all, Poe's eyes in the low crimson light seemed to brighten with anticipation.

Desperate, Cleo suddenly said, "Raylee, tell us a story."

A moment of tension, and then a relaxed "Ah" from the circle.

Raylee shivered.

"Yes, tell us a story!"

This from someone in the suffocating circle, a wolf-man, or perhaps a vampire.

"No, please," Raylee begged. Her cat whiskers and cat tail shivered. "I don't want to!"

"Story! Story!" the circle began to chant.

"No, please!"

"Story, story . . ."

"Tell us the rest of the other story!"

This from Peter in the back of the circle. A low voice, a command.

Another "Ah."

"Yes, tell us!"

Raylee held her hands to her ears. "No!"

"Tell us!"

"No!"

"Tell us now!"

"I thought you were my friends!" Raylee threw her cat-paw hands out at them, her eyes begging.

"Tell us."

A stifled cry escaped Raylee's throat.

Instinctively, the circle widened. They knew she would tell now. They had commanded her. To be one of them, she would do what they told her to do.

Cleo stepped helplessly back into the circle, leaving Raylee under Poe's twisted grin.

Raylee stood alone shivering for a moment. Then, her

eyes on the floor, she ceased trembling, became very calm and still. There was a moment of silence. In the basement, all that could be heard was the snap of a candle in a far corner and the slapping of water against the lone apple in the tub behind her. When she looked up her eyes were dull, her voice quiet-calm.

She began to speak.

"They took Pumpkin Head away after that, and they put him in a place with crazy people in it. There was screaming all day and night. Someone was always screaming, or hitting his head against the wall, or crying all the time. Pumpkin Head was very lonely, and very scared.

"But Pumpkin Head's parents loved him more than he ever knew. They decided they couldn't let him stay in that place any longer. So they made a plan, a quiet plan.

"One day, when they went to visit him, they dressed him up in a disguise and carried him away. They carried him far away, where no one would ever look for him, all the way across the country. They hid him, and kept him disguised while they tried to find some way to help him. And after a long search, they found a doctor.

"And the doctor did magical things. He worked for two years on Pumpkin Head, on his face and on his body. He cut into Pumpkin Head's face, and changed it. With plastic, he made it into a real face. He changed the rest of Pumpkin Head's head too, and gave him real hair. And he changed Pumpkin Head's body.

"Pumpkin Head's parents paid the doctor a lot of money, and the doctor did the work of a genius.

"He changed Pumpkin Head completely."

Raylee paused, and a light came into her dull eyes. The circle, and Poe above them, waited with indrawn breath.

Waited to say "Ah."

"He changed Pumpkin Head into a little girl."

Breath was pulled back deeper, or let out in little gasps.

The light grew in Raylee's eyes.

"There were things that Pumpkin Head—now not Pumpkin Head anymore—had to do to be a girl. He had to be careful how he dressed, and how he acted. He had to be careful how he talked, and he always had to be calm. He was very frightened of what would happen if he didn't stay calm. For his face was really just a wonderful plastic one. The real Pumpkin Head was still inside, locked in, waiting to come out."

Raylee looked up at them, and her voice suddenly became something different. Hard and rasping.

Her eyes were stoked coals.

"All he ever wanted was friends."

Her cat mask fell away. Her little girl face became soft and bloated and began to grow as if someone were blowing up a balloon inside her. Her hair began to pull into the scalp, forming a circled knot at the top. Creases appeared up and down her face.

With a sickening, rubber-inflated sound, the sound of a melon breaking, Raylee's head burst open to its true shape. Her eyes, ears, and nose became soft orange triangles, her mouth a lazy, grinning crescent. She began to breathe with harsh effort, and her voice became a sharp, wheezing lisp.

"He only wanted friends."

Slowly, with care, Raylee reached down into her costume for what lay hidden there.

She drew it out.

In the black cellar, under Poe's approving glare, there were screams.

"My lunch and dinner," she said, "my dinner and breakfast."

Since the late 1980s, Manhattanite Lawrence Schimel has written scores of short fantasy, horror and science fiction stories that have been published in more than 100 anthologies, including The Random House Book of Science Fiction Stories, The Mammoth Book of Fairy Tales, Weird Tales from Shakespeare, *and* Phantoms of the Night. *A selection of his compact and often light-hearted fantasies can be found in* The Drag Queen of Elfland. *He is also an editor of distinction whose expertise on a wide variety of themes is evident in* Tarot Fantastic, The Mammoth Book of Gay Erotica, Blood Lines *and other volumes in "The American Vampire" series, and the cookbook* Food for Life and Other Dishes, *among others.*

You Say Potato, I Say . . . Trouble

Lawrence Schimel

I. A Recipe for trouble

Ingredients:

    1 woman, attractive
    2 men, both trying to get her
    1 potato with the evil eye

Directions:

    1. Pre-heat the romance to 450°.

2. Mix all the ingredients in a buttered apartment building.

3. Place one of the men to the side. He will be the landlord.

4. Place the other man and the woman side by side. They are neighbors.

5. Place the potato on the doorstep of the other man.

You now have plenty of trouble to go around.

Serves 3-4

II. Spud's Up, Doc?

There were three small, red potatoes and a yam on my doorstep when I came home for lunch. Affixed to the door was a green post-it note which read: *Love From Miss Potato Head.* My next door neighbor had joined Weight Watchers three days ago. Slowly, the various foods she couldn't eat were making their way into my kitchen. Why let them go to waste, especially when the act of giving them to me was part of our domestic flirtations?

I put the spuds in the cabinet and set a pot of water to boil. I'd just spent another morning job searching and didn't have the energy to make anything more complicated than spaghetti with Ragu right then. The doorbell rang as I idly stirred the pasta, watching the steam curl off the water. Must be Tina, I thought. It was a small building, and I didn't know anyone besides her, even though I'd been there for two months now. I guess you could say I also knew the landlord, but we didn't really get along too well. I had a feeling he was going to try stiff me for my security deposit when I moved out.

No one was there when I opened the door, but as I was closing it again something on the floor caught my attention. It was another potato. Smiling at Tina's games,

I brought the new spud inside and put it in the cabinet. I figured it must have gotten lost at the back of a cabinet or something and she only just noticed it now. It was smaller than the others, and more dried out, but I guessed it was still good enough to use in something. A stew, maybe. Or home fries.

As I poured Ragu onto my spaghetti I wished my food budget had allowed me to buy some grated Parmesan last week. But, I reflected as I slumped onto my futon, since the temp agencies hadn't found work for me all week, I couldn't afford not to eat it, no matter how much I would have preferred something more flavorful. I would be eating a lot of pasta and Ragu in the days to come.

Spiced with little gifts from Tina, of course.

III. Home Fries, Sweet Potato Home Fries, or, I Yam What I Yam

I spent the rest of the afternoon job searching again, and came home to an empty mailbox, save for a letter addressed to the previous tenant. As I stepped into the elevator the landlord walked by and asked, "Have you seen Claws?"

I stuck my foot out to hold the door for him and, smiling, answered, "No, but I'll keep my eyes peeled for her."

He continued down the corridor. Just before the door shut completely, he corrected me, "Him."

Him. OK. Nice talking with you, too.

There was a message from Tina on my answering machine: —So, are you going to cook my potatoes for dinner tonight? I can't have any more carbohydrates today. Miss Hawaii says "Hi." I'm making asparagus if you want some; I've got more than I'm allowed to eat."

There was also a cat in the apartment, which I discovered when I went into the kitchen to start dinner before I lost the edge of my hunger and ran out of inertia. "You must be Claws," I said, reaching out to scratch her under the chin. No, him. Him. "Now, how did you get in here?"

Claws took a swipe at my hand. I should have guessed how he had gotten his name, I mused, as I watched the blood bead along the red welts.

As I walked to the bathroom to pour peroxide on my hand I noticed the window over the fire escape was ajar. I didn't remember having left it open, but at least it explained how kitty got in.

I called the landlord, to come and retrieve his cat himself, not wishing another memento of the cat's name. No one was home. I went into the kitchen and stared at the cat, defiantly daring me to come within striking range. "Come on, kitty, why don't you go home now. Isn't it dinner time or something?"

Claws emitted a hiss.

I was resolved to get that cat out of my apartment. If I could at least get him out of the kitchen I could make myself something to eat; nourishment to battle the beast and all that. But Claws seemed just as resolute in his desire to dominate my kitchen. Finally I opened the door to the hallway, and taking the broom, tried to shoo the cat out. Claws began to yowl and hiss. I screamed back.

"What the hell is going on here," Ken (the landlord) asked.

I almost swatted him with the broom, I was so startled by his voice, suddenly booming out from right behind me. "Get it out of here," I hissed, indicating the beast with the end of the broom.

"Sure, you haven't seen my cat, and here you are trying to kill the poor thing with a broom. Come here, Clawsypoo, did he hurt you?" The cat docilely leapt into his arms, purring. Ken turned to me, "You bother him again, I'll have you thrown out of the apartment."

I was so surprised to see the transformation in Claws from hellcat to docile kitty that I could say nothing as the pair walked away. I winced as the door to the hallway slammed shut, a headache was well on its way. I let the broom drop to the floor, and sighed as I stepped into the kitchen—once again mine.

I opened the cabinet to get the potatoes and start dinner. They had all sprouted, except for the old, wrinkled one. And I don't just mean a little bud, there were two-inch stalks coming out of each eye. That takes care of my end of dinner, I thought, wondering if I should bring them over to Tina and let her cook the stalks with the asparagus. I had one potato left. Even the yam had sprouted, but not the old spud. I didn't know why it hadn't; could potatoes go bad? I wondered.

It didn't really matter, I thought, as I put the old potato back in the cabinet, and threw the rest out. I had run out of inertia. Hopefully, Tina had bought—a lot—of asparagus.

IV. See No Evil, Hear No Evil, Have No Fun

"Yes, it was hell, sheer hell, all day long."

Tina smiled at me as she measured vegetables with a scale. "So what you're saying is that you're not helping with dinner tonight?"

I grinned back. "I've only got one potato left. It won't go very far. It was tiny to begin with it, and its looks so old I don't know if it's still good. I mean, I'm probably more worried that its eyes—didn't—sprout, when all the others did."

"Potatoes can't go bad. Why don't you bring it over, and I'll throw it in the oven when I make these. I mean, if it's as old as you claim, you should eat it before it—does—go bad."

"You just said potatoes can't go bad."

"They can't."

"But then—"

"Just get it, will you?"

We both laughed, and I dragged myself out of my chair. There was a message from my mother on the answering machine and I figured it was easier to call her back now than put it off. I was still on the phone when I heard Tina at the door, "What's taking you so long?"

"It's open."

"I thought you'd fallen asleep, or something."

I held my hand over the mouthpiece. "My mother. The potato's in the cabinet with the beans."

Tina went into the kitchen, and screamed.

"Mom, I gotta go. I'll call you next week. Tina, what is it?" I rushed into the kitchen, imagining the worst.

"It—It—"

I looked into the cabinet where she pointed, expecting a roach, or maybe a mouse. It was an eyeball. And then another one rolled up to the edge of the shelf and pushed the first one off, onto the countertop.

This time it was me who screamed.

We decided to forget about collecting the potato and returned to Tina's apartment. "What were those things?" I asked. "And don't tell me they were eyeballs, because I know that. I mean, where did they come from."

"Could it be your potato?"

"Because its eyes didn't sprout before?"

"Because it has the evil eye."

"You believe in that kind of stuff?"

"You tell me why you've got eyeballs rolling around your cabinet."

I paused, taking a breath as I prepared to confront her. "But—why did you give me a potato with a curse on it?"

"I didn't give you that potato. I gave you three red bliss and a yam."

"Who then?"

Tina took the vegetables from the oven. "Who's been causing you hell today?"

"Ken?"

"Yeah."

"But why?"

"Who knows? He hates you. Probably because of me."

"What do you have to do with it?"

Tina placed a plate of steaming vegetables on the table between us and sat down. "Before you moved in he kept trying to ask me out on a date. But I'm not interested in him."

I took a heap of asparagus onto my plate. "Oh."

"I don't think it's safe for you to go back to your apartment tonight. Why don't you stay here. Tomorrow you can try and get rid of it, during the day, when the evil eye will be at its weakest."

Our eyes met for a moment, across the table. Then she looked away as she put an asparagus into her mouth.

V. *Epilogue: Monster Mashed*

I had to borrow Tina's silverware—the real silver stuff from her grandmother—to get rid of the potato. I mauled the stainless steel set I first attacked it with. But, after many hours of stabbing and a mess of peelings and chunks and eyeballs, it was finally gone.

The next morning I found a job.

Ken did not try anything else, at least as far as I knew. But even a week after I had killed the evil-eyed potato, I still felt uncomfortable in the apartment, feeling as if there were eyes all over me—sometimes literally, sometimes figuratively. So I moved out.

I'm still a bit skittish around potatoes, but so far Tina hasn't minded giving them up.

Elia W. Peattie (1862-1935) wrote ghost stories flavored with the country atmosphere of rural New England. Her short fiction was collected in 1898 in The Shape of Fear and Other Ghostly Tales, *and also appeared in the magazine* Outlook. *More recently, her work appeared in the anthology* Christmas Ghosts.

The Crime of Micah Rood

Elia W. Peattie

In the early part of the last century there lived in eastern Connecticut a man named Micah Rood. He was a solitary soul, and occupied a low, tumble-down house, in which he had seen his sisters and his brothers, his father and his mother, die. The mice used the bare floors for a play-ground; the swallows filled up the unused chimneys; in the cellar the gophers frolicked, and in the attic a hundred bats made their home. Micah Rood disturbed no living creature, unless now and then he killed a hare for his day's dinner, or cast bait for a glistening trout in the Shetucket. For the most part his food came from the garden and the orchard, which his father had planted and nurtured years before.

Into whatever disrepair the house had fallen, the garden bloomed and flourished like a western Eden. The brambles, with their luscious burden, clambered up the stone walls, sentineled by trim rows of English currants. The strawberry nestled among its wayward creepers, and on the trellises hung grapes of varied hues. In seemly rows, down the sunny expanse of the garden spot, grew every vegetable indigenous to the western world, or transplanted by colonial industry. Everything here took seed, and bore fruit with a prodigal exuberance. Beyond the garden lay the orchard, a labyrinth of flowers in the spring-time, a paradise of verdure in the summer, and in the season of fruition a miracle of plenty.

Often the master of the orchard stood by the gate in the crisp autumn mornings, with his hat filled with apples for the children as they passed to school. There was only one tree in the orchard of whose fruit he was chary. Consequently it was the bearings of this tree that the children most wanted.

"Prithee, Master Rood," they would say, "give us some of the gold apples?"

"I sell the gold apples for silver," he would say; "content ye with the red and green ones."

In all the region there grew no counterpart to this remarkable apple. Its skin was of the clearest amber, translucent and spotless, and the pulp was white as snow, mellow yet firm, and without a flaw from the glistening skin to the even brown seeds nestling like babies in their silken cradle. Its flavor was peculiar and piquant, with a suggestion of spiciness. The fame of Micah Rood's apple, as it was called, had extended far and wide, but all efforts to engraft it upon other trees failed utterly; and the envious farmers were fain to content themselves with the rare shoots.

If there dwelt any vanity in the heart of Micah Rood, it was in the possession of this apple tree, which took the prize at all the local fairs, and carried his name beyond the neighborhood where its owner lived. For the most part he was a modest man, averse to discussions of any sort, shrinking from men and their opinions. He talked more to his dog than to any human being. He fed his mind upon a few old books, and made Nature his religion. All things that made the woods their home were his friends. He possessed himself of their secrets, and insinuated himself into their confidences. But best

of all he loved the children. When they told him their
sorrows, the answering tears sprang to his eyes; when
they told him of their delights, his laugh woke the echoes
of the Shetucket as light and free as their own. He
laughed frequently when with the children, throwing
back his great head, while the tears of mirth ran from
his merry blue eyes.

His teeth were like pearls, and constituted his chief
charm. For the rest he was rugged and firmly knit. It
seemed to the children, after a time, that some cloud
was hanging over the serene spirit of their friend. After
he had laughed he sighed, and they saw, as he walked
down the green paths that led away from his place, that
he would look lovingly back at the old homestead and
shake his head again and again with a perplexed and
melancholy air. The merchants, too, observed that he
began to be closer in his bargains, and he barreled his
apples so greedily that the birds and the children were
quite robbed of their autumnal feast. A winter wore away
and left Micah in this changed mood. He sat through
the long dull days brooding over his fire and smoking.
He made his own simple meals of mush and bacon, kept
his own counsels, and neither visited nor received the
neighboring folk.

One day, in a heavy January rain, the boys noticed
a strange man who rode rapidly through the village, and
drew rein at Micah Rood's orchard gate. He passed
through the leafless orchard, and up the muddy garden
paths to the old dismantled house. The boys had time
to learn by heart every good point of the chestnut mare
fastened to the palings before the stranger emerged from
the house. Micah followed him to the gate. The stranger
swung himself upon the mare with a sort of jaunty
flourish, while Micah stood heavily and moodily by,
chewing the end of a straw.

"Well, Master Rood," the boys heard the stranger say,
"thou'st till the first of next May, but not a day of grace
more." He had a decisive, keen manner that took away

the breath of the boys used to men of slow action and slow speech. "Mind ye," he snapped, like an angry cur, "not another day's grace." Micah said not a word, but stolidly chewed on his straw while the stranger cut his animal briskly with the whip, and the mare and rider dashed away down the dreary road. The boys began to frisk about their old friend and pulled savagely at the tails of his coat, whooping and whistling to arouse him from his reverie. Micah looked up and roared:

"Off with ye! I'm in no mood for pranks."

As a pet dog slinks away in humiliation at a blow, so the boys, hurt and indignant, skulked down the road speechless at the cruelty of their old friend.

The April sunshine was bringing the dank odors from the earth when the village beauties were thrown into a flutter of excitement. Old Geoffry Peterkin, the peddler, came with such jewelry, such stuffs, and such laces as the maidens of Shetucket had never seen the like of before.

"You are getting rich, Geoffry," the men said to him.

"No, no!" and Geoffry shook his grizzled head with a flattered smile. "Not from your women-folk. There's no such bargain-drivers between here and Boston town."

"Thou'lt be a-setting up in Boston town, Geoffry," said another. "Thou'rt getting too fine to travel pack a-back amongst us simple country folk."

"Not a bit of it," protested Geoffry. "I couldn't let the pretty dears go without their beads and their ribbons. I come and go as reg'lar as the leaves, spring, summer, and autumn."

By twilight Geoffry had made his last visit, and with his pack somewhat lightened he tramped away in the raw dusk. He went straight down the road that led to the next village, until out of sight of the windows, then turned to his right and groped his way across the commons with his eye ever fixed on a deeper blackness in the gloom. This looming blackness was the orchard of Micah Rood. He found the gate, entered, and made

his way to the dismantled house. A bat swept its wing
against his face as he rapped his stick upon the door.

"What witchcraft's here?" he said, and pounded
harder.

There were no cracks in the heavy oaken door
through which a light might filter, and old Geoffry
Peterkin was blinded like any owl when the door was
flung open, and Micah Rood, with a forked candle-stick
in his hands, appeared, recognized him, and bade him
enter. The wind drove down the hallway, blew the flame
an inch from the wicks, where it burned blue a moment,
and then expired, leaving the men in darkness. Geoffry
stepped in, and Micah threw his weight against the door,
swung the bar into place, and led Geoffry into a large
bare room lit up by a blazing hickory fire. When the
candles were relit, Micah said:

"Hast thou supped this night, friend Peterkin?"

"That have I, and royally too, with Rogers the smith.
No more for me."

Micah Rood stirred up the fire and produced a bottle
of brandy from a cupboard. He filled a small glass and
offered it to his guest. It was greedily quaffed by the
peddler. Micah replaced the bottle, and took no liquor
himself. Pipes were then lit. Micah smoked moodily and
in silence. The peddler, too, was silent. He hugged his
knee, puffed vigorously at his pipe, and stared at the
blazing hickory. Micah spoke first.

"Thou hast prospered since thou sold milk-pans to
my mother."

"I've made a fortune with that old pack," said the
peddler, pointing to the corner where it lay. "Year after
year I have trudged this road, and year after year has
my pack been larger and my stops longer. My stuffs,
too, have changed. I carry no more milk-pans. I leave
that to others. I now have jewels and cloths. Why, man!
There's a fortune even now in that old pack."

He arose and unstrapped the leathern bands that
bound his burden. He drew from the pack a variety of

jewel-cases and handed them to Micah. "I did not show these at the village," he continued, pointing over his shoulder. "I sell those in towns."

Micah clumsily opened one or two, and looked at their contents with restless eyes. There were rubies as red as a serpent's tongue; silver, carved as daintily as hoar-frost, gleaming with icy diamonds; pearls that nestled like precious eggs in fairy golden nests; turquoise gleaming from beds of enamel, and bracelets of ebony capped with topaz balls.

"These," laughed Geoffry, dangling a translucent necklace of amber, "I keep to ward off ill-luck. She will be a witch indeed that gets me to sell these. But if thou'lt marry, good Master Rood, I'll give them to thy bride."

He chuckled, gasped, and gurgled mightily; but Micah checked his exuberance by looking up fiercely.

"There'll be never a bride for me," he said. "She'd be killed here with the rats and the damp rot. It takes gold to get a woman."

"Bah!" sneered Geoffry. "It takes youth, boy, blue eye, good laugh, and a strong leg. Why, if a bride could be had for gold, I've got that."

He unrolled a shimmering azure satin, and took from it two bags of soft, stout leather.

"There is where I keep my yellow boys shut up!" the old fellow cried in great glee; "and when I let them out, they'll bring me anything I want, Micah Rood, except a true heart. How have things prospered with thee?" he added, as he shot a shrewd glance at Micah from beneath his eyebrows.

"Bad," confessed Micah, "very bad. Everything has been against me of late."

"I say, boy," cried the peddler, suddenly, "I haven't been over this old house for years. Take the light and show us around."

"No," said Micah, shaking his head doggedly. "It is in bad shape and I would feel that I was showing a friend who was in rags."

"Nonsense!" cried the peddler, bursting into a hearty laugh. "Thou need'st not fear, I'll ne'er cut thy old friend."

He had replaced his stuffs, and now seized the branched candle-stick and waved his hand toward the door.

"Lead the way," he cried. "I want to see how things look," and Micah Rood sullenly obeyed.

From room to room they went in the miserable cold and the gloom. The candle threw a faint gleam though the unkept apartments, noxious with dust and decay. Not a flaw escaped the eye of the peddler. He ran his fingers into the cracks of the doors, he counted the panes of broken glass, he remarked the gaps in the plastering.

"The dry rot has got into the wainscoting," he said jauntily.

Micah Rood was burning with impotent anger. He tried to lead the peddler past one door, but the old man's keen eyes were too quick for him, and he kicked the door open with his foot.

"What have we here?" he cried.

It was the room where Micah and his brothers had slept when they were children. The little dismantled beds stood side by side. A work-bench with some miniature tools was by the curtainless window. Everything that met his gaze brought with it a flood of early recollections.

"Here's a rare lot of old truck," Geoffry cried. "The first thing I should do would be to pitch this out of doors."

Micah caught him by the arm and pushed him from the room.

"It happens that it is not thine to pitch," he said.

Geoffry Peterkin began to laugh a low, irritating chuckle. He laughed all the way back to the room where the fire was. He laughed still as Micah showed him his room—the room where he was to pass the night; chuckled and guffawed, and clapped Micah on the back as they finally bade each other good-night. The master of the house went back and stood before the dying fire alone.

"What can he mean, in God's name?" he asked himself. "Does he know of the mortgage?"

Micah knew that the peddler, who was well off, frequently negotiated and dealt in the commercial paper of farmers. Pride and anger tore at his heart like wild beasts. What would the neighbors say when they saw his father's son driven from the house that had belonged to the family for generations? How could he endure their surprise and contempt? What would the children say when they found a stranger in possession of the famous apple-tree? "I've got no more to pay it with," he cried in helpless anguish, "then I had the day the cursed lawyer came here with his threats."

He determined to find out what Peterkin knew of the matter. He spread a bear's skin before the fire and threw himself upon it and fell into a feverish sleep, which ended long before the purple dawn broke.

He cooked a breakfast of bacon and corn cake, made a cup of coffee, and aroused his guest. The peddler clean, keen, and alert, noted slyly the sullen heaviness of Micah. The meal was eaten in silence, and when it was finished, Geoffry put on his cloak, adjusted his pack, and prepared to leave. Micah put on his hat, took a pruning-knife from a shelf, remarking as he did so:

"I go early about my work in the orchard," and followed the peddler to the door. The trees in the orchard had begun to shimmer with young green. The perfume, so familiar to Micah, so suggestive of the place that he held dearer than all the rest of the world beside, wrought upon him till his curiosity got the better of his discretion.

"It is hard work for one man to keep up a place like this and make it pay," he remarked.

Geoffry smiled slyly, but said nothing.

"Bad luck has got the start of me of late," the master continued with an attempt at real candor.

The peddler knocked the tops off some gaunt, dead weeds that stood by the path.

"So I have heard," he said.

"What else didst thou hear?" cried Micah, quickly, his face burning, and shame and anger flashing from his blue eyes.

"Well," said the peddler, with a great show of caution. "I heard the mortgage was a good investment for any one who wanted to buy."

"Perhaps thou know'st more about it than that," sneered Micah.

Peterkin blew on his hands and rubbed them with a knowing air.

"Well," he said, "I know what I know."

"D— you," cried Micah, clinching his fist, "out with it."

The peddler was getting heated. He thrust his hand into his breast and drew out a paper.

"When May comes about, Master Rood, I'll ask thee to look at the face of this document."

"Thou art a sneak!" foamed Micah "A white-livered, cowardly sneak!"

"Rough words to call a man on his own property," said the peddler, with a malicious grin.

The insult was the deepest he could have offered to the man before him. A flood of ungovernable emotions rushed over Micah. The impulse latent in all angry animals to strike, to crush, to kill, came over him. He rushed forward madly, then the passion ebbed, and he saw the peddler on the ground. The pruning-knife in his own hand was red with blood. He gazed in cold horror, then tried in a weak, trembling way to heap leaves upon the body to hide it from his sight. He could gather only small handfuls, and they fluttered away in the wind.

The light was getting brighter. People would soon be passing down the road. He walked up and down aimlessly for a time, and then ran to the garden. He returned with a spade and began digging furiously. He made a trench between the dead man and the tree under which he had fallen; and when it was finished he pushed the body in with his foot, not daring to touch it with his hands.

Of the peddler's death there was no doubt. The rigid face and the blood-drenched garments over the heart attested the fact. So copiously had the blood gushed forth that all the soil, and the dead leaves about the body, and the exposed roots of the tree were stained with it. Involuntarily Micah looked up at the tree. He uttered an exclamation of dismay. It was the tree of the gold apples.

After a moment's silence he recommenced his work and tossed back the earth in mad haste. He smoothed the earth so carefully that when he had finished not even a mound appeared. He scattered dead leaves over the freshly turned earth, and then walked slowly back to the house.

For the first time the shadow that hung over it, the gloom deep as despair that looked from its vacant windows, struck him. The gloss of familiarity had hidden from his eyes what had long been patent to others—the decay, the ruin, the solitude. It swept over him as an icy breaker sweeps over a drowning man. The rats ran from him as he entered the hall. He held the arm on which the blood was rapidly drying far from him, as if he feared to let it touch his body with its confession of crime. The sleeve had stiffened to the arm, and inspired him with a nervous horror, as if a reptile was twined about it. He flung off his coat, and finally, trembling and sick, divested himself of a flannel under-garment, and still from fingertip to elbow there were blotches and smears on his arm. He realized at once the necessity of destroying the garments; and, naked to the waist, he stirred up the dying embers of the fire and threw the garments on. The heavy flannel of the coat refused to burn, and he threw it deeper and deeper in with a poker till he saw with dismay that he had quenched the fire.

"It's fate!" he cried. "I can not destroy them."

He lit a fire three times, but his haste and his confused horror made him throw on the heavy garments every time and strangle the infant blaze. At last he took them to the garret and locked them in an old chest. Starting at the shadows among the rafters, and the creaking of the boards, he crept back through the biting chill of the vacant rooms to the one that he occupied, and washed his arm again and again, until the deep glow on it seemed like another blood-stain.

After that for weeks he worked in his garden by day, and at night slept on the floor with the candles burning, and his hand on his flint-lock.

Meanwhile in the orchard the leaves budded and spread, and the perfumed blossoms came. The branches of the tree of the gold apples grew pink with swelling buds. Near that spot Micah never went. He felt as if his feet would be grasped by spectral hands.

One night a swelling wind arose, strong, steady, warm, seeming palpable to the touch like a fabric. In the morning the orchard had flung all its banners to the air. It dazzled Micah's eyes as he looked upon the tossing clouds of pink and white fragrance. But as his eye roamed about the waving splendor he caught sight of a thing that riveted him to the spot with awe.

The tree of the gold apples had blossomed blood-red.

That day he did no work. He sat from early morning till the light waned in the west, gazing at the tree flaunting its blossoms red as blood against the shifting sky. Few neighbors came that way; and as the tree stood in the heart of the orchard, fewer yet noticed its accursed beauty. To those that did Micah stammeringly gave a hint of some ingenious ingrafting, the secret of which was to make his fortune. But though the rest of the world wondered and wagged its head and doubted not that it was some witchcraft, the children were enraptured. They stole into the orchard and pilfered handfuls of the roseate flowers, and bore them away to school; the girls fastened them in their braids or wore them above their innocent hearts, and the boys trimmed their hat-bands and danced away in glee like youthful Corydons.

Spring-time passed and its promises of plenty were fulfilled. In the garden there grew a luxury of greenness; in the orchard the boughs lagged low. Micah Rood toiled day and night He visited no house, he sought no company. If a neighbor saw him in the field and came for a chat, before he had reached the spot Micah had hidden himself.

"He used to be as ready for the news as the rest of us," said they to themselves, "and he had a laugh like a horse. His sweetheart has jilted him, most like."

When the purple on the grapes began to grow through the amber, and the mellowed apples dropped from their stems, the children began to flock about the orchard gate like buzzards about a battle-field. But they found the gate padlocked and the board fence prickling with pointed sticks. Micah they saw but seldom, and his face, once so sunny, was as terrible to them as the angel's with the flaming sword that kept guard over the gates of Eden. So the sinless little Adams and Eves had no choice but to turn away with empty pockets.

However, one morning, accident took Micah to the bolted gate just as the children came trooping home in the early autumn sunset; for in those days they kept students of any age at work as many hours of the day as possible. A little fay, with curls as sunny as the tendrils of the grape, caught sight of him first. Her hat was wreathed with scarlet maple leaves; her dress was as ruddy as the cheeks of the apples. She seemed the sprite of autumn. She ran toward him, with arms outstretched, crying:

"Oh, Master Rood! Do come and play. Where hast thou been so long? We have wanted some apples, and the plaguy old gate was locked."

For the first time for months the pall of remembrance that hung over Micah's dead happiness was lifted, and the spirit of that time came back to him. He caught the little one in his brawny arms and threw her high, while she shrieked with terror and delight. After this the children gave no quarter. The breach begun, they sallied in and stormed the fortress. Like a dream of water to a man who is perishing of thirst who knows while he yet dreams that he must wake and find his bliss an agony, this hour of innocence was to Micah. He ran, and leaped, and frolicked with the children in the shade of the trees till the orchard rang with their shouts, while the sky changed from daffodil to crimson, from crimson to gray, and sank into a deep autumn twilight. Micah stuffed their little pockets with fruit and bade them run home. But they lingered dissatisfied.

"I wish he would give us of the golden apples," they whispered among themselves. At last one plucked up courage.

"Good Master Rood, give us of the gold apples, if thou please."

Micah shook his head sternly. They entreated him with eyes and tongues. They saw a chance for a frolic. They clung to him, climbed his back, and danced about him, shouting:

"The gold apples! The gold apples!"

A sudden change came over him; he marched to the tree with a look men wear when they go to battle.

"There is blood in them!" he cried hoarsely. "They are accursed—accursed!"

The children shrieked with delight at what they thought a jest.

"Blood in the apples. Ha! ha! ha!" and they rolled over one another on the grass, fighting for the windfalls.

"I tell ye 'tis so!" Micah continued. He took one of the apples and broke it into halves.

"Look," he cried, and in his eyes there came a look in which the light of reason was waning. The children pressed about him, peeping over each other at the apple. On the broken side of both halves, from the rind to the core, there was a blood-red streak the width of a child's little finger. An amazed silence fell on the little group.

"Home with ye now!" he cried huskily "Home with ye, and tell what ye have seen! Run, ye brats."

"Then let us take some of the apples with us," they persisted.

"Ha!" he cried. "Aye tale-bearers! I know the tricks ye'd play! Here then—"

He shook the tree like a giant. The apples rolled to the ground so fast that they looked like strands of amber beads. The children, laughing and shouting, gathered them as they fell. They began to compare the red spots. In some the drop of blood was found just under the skin, and a thin streak of carmine that penetrated to the core and colored the silvery pulp; in others it was an isolated clot, the size of a whortleberry, and on a few a narrow crescent of crimson reached half-way around the outside of the shining rind.

Suddenly a noise, not loud but agonizing, startled the little ones. They looked up at their friend. He had become horrible. His face was contorted until it was unrecognizable; his eyes were fixed on the ground as if he beheld a specter there. Shrieking, they ran from the orchard, nor cast one fearful glance behind.

The next day the smith, filled with curiosity by the tales of the children, found an odd hour in which to visit Micah Rood's house. He invited the tailor, a man thin with hunger for gossip, to go with him. The gate of the orchard stood open, flapping on its hinges as the children had left it. The visitors sauntered through, thinking to find Micah in the house, for it was the noon hour. They tasted of this fruit and that, tried a pear, now an apricot, now a pippin.

"The tree of the gold apples is right in the center," said the smith.

He pointed. The tailor looked; then his legs doubled

under him as naturally as they ever did on the bench. The smith looked; his arm dropped by his side. After a time the two men went on, clinging to each other like children in the dark.

Micah Rood, with his sunny hair tangled in the branches, his tongue black and protruding, his face purple, and his clinched hands stained with dirt, hung from the tree of the golden apples. Beneath him, in a trench, from which the ground had been clawed by human hands, lay a shapeless, discolored bundle of clothes. A skull lay at one end of the trench, and beneath it a moldy pack was found with precious stones amid the decaying contents.

Edward Wellen's short fiction appeared in Universe, Imagination, Infinity, *and numerous other science fiction and mystery magazines starting in the 1950s. His best known work, the comic "Galactic Origins" series, was a highlight in* Galaxy, *which between 1952 and 1962 published all nine of his pseudofactual examinations of the roots of future law, etiquette, medicine, philosophy, and other social doctrines. He is the also author of* Hijack, *a satirical novel of organized crime and space travel.*

Root of Evil

Edward Wellen

No one, it seems, can explain away the vanishing of Wilmer Kootz without dragging in the supernatural by its bedraggled tail. No one, that is, if you leave out me. And because I know you want to weigh the evidence for yourself, I'll give you the events leading up to the vanishing point—and let you take it from there. Here goes:

I was leaning out of the window to look down at the figure struggling across the campus under a heavy load. Dusk blurred everything in the scene into almost uniform grayness, but I got the feeling that poor Wilmer was cracking up. I pulled my head back into the room as he doggedly moved with his burden through the dormitory arch below. I returned to my seat and doodled sundry luscious curves on my chemistry notes while waiting for him to stagger upstairs and into the room we shared.

He elbowed the door open and gave me a perfunctory nod. Before he could set the bushel basket down it slipped from his weary grasp, tumbling out its contents as it crashed.

I clicked my pencil against my teeth. I examined my fingernails. I gazed at the ceiling. I cleared my throat. I said, "Turnips."

Wilmer busied himself wiping a film of sweat from his glasses. His naked eyes blinked rapidly. He said softly, "I hope you don't mind my bringing them here. I promise I'll keep them out of your way."

I was severely silent. Wilmer hurriedly replaced his glasses and peered at me. He evidently found reassurance because a smile kneaded his doughy face. He stowed his jacket in his locker. On the way back he looked over my shoulder at my notes. A puzzled frown crossed his countenance. "Hum," he said. "I must've dozed through part of today's lecture."

I watched him round up the turnips. Finally I said, "Wilmer, I can't hold out any longer. *Why* turnips? Or perhaps I'd better put it this way: why *turnips?*"

Wilmer's instinctive look of sheepishness gave way to one of holy fanaticism. He lifted up a maverick turnip and said, "You may not know that some vegetable tissue that grows at top speed radiates a kind of energy, energy that stimulates living tissue. For instance, if you place a turnip root at right angles to another root, with the tips one-fourth of an inch apart, the turnip will excite the growth of the other vegetable. Result, the number of cells on the vegetable's near side will increase as much as seventy percent. And I'm going to—" For no reason I could figure, he let his voice trail off.

I'd never thought of a turnip being particularly exciting—even to another turnip. But Wilmer Kootz seemed to be going overboard.

"Wilmer," I said kiddingly, "some day I'll tell my grandchildren, as the little tykes accumulate around lovable old gramps, that was the college chum of the great Kootz when he began his world-shaking turnip experiment."

So help me, his eyes gleamed moistly behind the thick lenses. And, as always, I was surprised. Wilmer so bordered on caricature of the bespectacled, befuddled, bookish type that I often had trouble thinking of him as a human being with human feelings. His pathetic gratitude shamed me.

To break a mood that was embarrassing both of us, I said heartily, "What say we cook up a mess of turnip greens, Wilmer?" He sprang protectingly in front of his turnips. Hastily I said, "After you're through with your experiment of course. Wouldn't harm them for the world, Wilmer." He relaxed. "What is your experiment? You didn't finish telling me."

But he was evasively vague, and I wasn't sufficiently rapt about turnips to press him. And because both of us were tired we soon hit the sack.

Wilmer was going through the motions of shaving his fledgling beard when I woke. I sat up in bed and stretched my arms. I froze in the middle of a yawn. On Wilmer's pillow, a fraction of an inch from the impression of his head, a turnip reposed.

I cut into Wilmer's cheery greeting. "Wilmer," I said, "are you part of the experiment?"

His eyes flashed to the turnip then back to me defiantly. "Yes!"

I suppose I gaped; for the first time since I'd known him, Wilmer had shown something like temper. "Sorry I flared," he said more calmly. "I guess you had to find out sooner or later. And now you may as well know it all." He paused, but not for dramatic effect; Wilmer was histrionically anemic. He visibly marshalled his thoughts, then said, "Just because I look the student, people think I'm brainy. But my IQ is nowhere near the genius mark. You've no idea how I've sweated to get good grades, all because my folks were always telling me what heights

I'd reach some day. It's a bitter thing to know your own limitations—and have others expect more of you than those limitations will allow."

I felt my face burn as I realized that what I'd taken for Wilmer's pathetic gratitude the night before could as easily have been an agony of humiliation if he had been aware that I was twitting him.

Wilmer was saying, "While I was in the library the other day I came across an old *Science*—the June 15, 1928 issue, I think. In it was an article called 'Emission of Rays by Plant Cells'; I've already told you the gist of it. Well, this thought hit me: here's this strange, untapped form of energy and here are the inadequate twelve billion nerve cells in my brain. . . .

"Now you know. I'm trying to increase my mental capacity so I can do things that are far beyond me now, maybe even surpass Einstein."

My first impulse was to laugh. Instead I said, and I meant every word, "Wilmer, I hope it works." And when a warm smile shined his face I found myself blinking hard.

In the following weeks the only noticeable change in Wilmer was the appearance of bags under his eyes, the effect of nights spent uncomfortably rigid. It had become a ritual: Wilmer would ease his head into a kind of clamp he'd rigged, then I'd strap his body to the bed, leaving his hands free, and he'd hold a mirror to watch anxiously while I placed a turnip root exactly one quarter of an inch from his right temple. Days and evenings Wilmer spent all his spare time testing fertilizers on the turnips growing in the pots that had whittled down our *lebensraum. Whew!* I still remember the reek.

I could see no visible reason for Wilmer's increasing cheerfulness, but one day he assured me that he had narrowed the field to a particular breed of turnip. He said he felt "in tune" with it.

It was about two months after the beginning of the

experiment. I was positioning a turnip when I noticed a slight swelling of Wilmer's temple. I asked the immobilized subject, "Bump yourself today?"

He sounded surprised. "Why, no."

I touched a finger gingerly to the spot. "Feel any soreness, Wilmer? Any pain?"

"No." He reached up and prodded the swelling. And suddenly his skinny frame trembled with emotion too big for it, and he said in a choked voice, "It's begun! It's begun!"

To forestall a lopsided development Wilmer decided to alternate the point of stimulus: one night the right temple got the benefit of turnip emanations, the next night the left. And Wilmer continued to respond. The swelling grew uniformly now, steadily but imperceptibly. You became aware of it only when normal objects proved inadequate, as when Wilmer could no longer hook his glasses over his ears. He held them in place with loops of string tied to the side-pieces, but he gave up wearing them altogether when the flesh of his bulging brow began to overhang his eyes. The most outsize of hats was soon unequal to the project of covering that shining dome. Shining, because Wilmer had lost hair rapidly as his scalp expanded. That acreage was an inverted dust bowl, at the end of the third month.

Wilmer had to give up going to classes. His gait was too unsteady and the great bulbous head bobbled dangerously on its pipestem support. I feared that his neck would snap, and I urged him to recline in bed. He agreed willing enough, because that meant he could undergo continuous turnip-excited cell development.

More than once I started to beg Wilmer to abandon the experiment, but always I fell silent when I looked into the depths of his eyes. Beady little things as they now appeared to be, the thought of the tremendous intelligence behind and almost enveloping them struck me dumb with awe and fear.

But it couldn't last.

The campus was a bee-hive of rumor, and one day the dean dropped in. He ignored the clutter of the room and directed his attention at the blank wall above Wilmer's recumbent form.

"Kootz," he said briskly, "I don't know what you're doing. I don't want to know. You'll have to pack up this—this equipment and leave. Whispers have begun to reach Senatorial ears that something queer is going on here. We want no investigations, Kootz." He whisked out.

He was a good old boy at heart, however, and he arranged for Wilmer to take sole charge of an agricultural experimental sub-station out in the middle of nowhere.

Although I was sorry to see Wilmer go, now I was able to attack my studies fully. For the rest of the semester I was busy making up for lost time, but as soon as exams were through I sped toward Wilmer's station. I felt both humble and exalted as I drove nearer to that mighty brain, for Wilmer might prove to be the hope of the world.

The custodian stopped his lawn-mower and scratched an armpit thoughtfully. "Nope," he said, "come to think of it I *ain't* seed that feller for couple-three weeks now. Always keeps to hisself. You can look around, if you want." He started his machine again.

In Wilmer's living quarters I found only strewn clothes and a few rotting turnips. I started a tour of the greenhouses, hoping to find him at work. I strolled through one given over to hydroponics experiments. Neatly aligned tanks, containing a variety of growing plants, stretched to the far end of the structure. As I passed, I glanced approvingly at the luxuriating vegetables. I paused before the huge tank at the end.

There, with a vestigial expression of contentment, was the *biggest turnip in the world.*

Best known as the author of "The Space Eaters" and "The Hounds of Tindalos," the first two tales of the Cthulhu Mythos drawn from the principles of H.P. Lovecraft's horror fiction, Frank Belknap Long (1903–1994) had a distinguished career as a writer of fantasy, mystery and science fiction. He began writing for Weird Tales *in 1924, and was a regular contributor to* Unknown, Astounding Science Fiction, *and numerous other science fiction magazines. The best of his weird fiction was collected in* The Hounds of Tindalos *and* Night Fears, *and many of his better science fiction tales were compiled as* The Rim of the Unknown. *He authored the poetry collection* In Mayan Splendor *and the memoir* Howard Phillips Lovecraft: Dreamer on the Nightside.

Step Into My Garden

Frank Belnap Long

Although Kendrick had walked home from the station with a golf bag slung across his back he looked and felt cool. It was a lovely June day, and up and down the neighborhood skewerwood trees were in full, luscious bloom. He had a feeling he might find this home-coming the best yet.

The garden would be blooming, and Anne—Anne would have a new hair-do. She was always surprising him by making little, adorable changes in herself.

He set his luggage down in the vestibule and fumbled in his pocket for his keys. In all the years he had known her she had never been the same woman twice. He was lucky to be married to a girl who knew how to rearrange the little intangibles which made a man feel that his home was an intimate part of himself.

Anne never failed to make changes in his absence, putting a new vase here, a floral innovation there, moving the piano a little, trimming down Scottie till he looked like a ludicrous old man, and even sprucing up his library by adding new titles, and dusting down the shelves.

Even in the winter months Anne made changes, so that when he returned from brief, frosty trips he'd find the logs in the fireplace crackling under a new and better updraft or a pair of fur-lined lounge slippers substituted for the leather ones he had left by his chair on his way out.

But now—now he felt in his bones that he was about to experience something which would make this particular home-coming unique. Spring was the season of changes, and he had been away three full weeks.

He was not disappointed. As soon as he threw open the front door a change came floating toward him which stopped him in his tracks.

It was an odor, a fragrance as of new-mown Paradise, gathered up in porous sacks and hung up in front of an electric fan which has wasted no time in wafting it around about.

For a moment Kendrick stood motionless, his nostrils quivering. Then he whipped out a handkerchief and mopped his forehead. He no longer felt cool. The house was humid, damp, and the perfume seemed to collect on his face, stifling him. It was the sweetest fragrance he had ever inhaled, but also the most cloying, so that he found himself struggling for breath.

He pulled himself together with a jerk. If his wife was alone in the house with that perfume, he'd better do something about it.

"Anne, I'm home," he called, and stood waiting for her voice to come downstairs to him. He waited in vain.

No human sound answered him, but he did hear little pattering footsteps descending the hall staircase.

Scottie, he thought, and flexed his knees to cushion the bounce of a little black friend against him. There was no bounce, because it wasn't a dog. It wasn't anything that he could see. It pattered down the high, dark stairway, swished around his legs, and went scampering "out in back."

The best part of Kendrick's home was "out in back." "Out in back" was a book-lined study where he spent his mornings reading, writing and listening to Anne moving about in the kitchen. From "out in back" there came the noon odors of cooking, snatches of bird song, and gentle clickings as Anne opened and closed the huge, new refrigerator which she had purchased impulsively back in February. Anne had made the down-payment out of her household savings, and left him only the installments to worry about.

He wasn't worrying about household expenses now, however. His heart was hammering against his ribs and a sickening dread had come into him. Something invisible that scampered was loose in his house, and—

He lifted his golf bag through the front door and wedged it into the umbrella rack at the foot of the stairs.

"Anne?" he called again, loudly.

Up above there was only silence. Striding through the long house to his study he kept checking and unclenching his hands and dampening his lips with his tongue.

Time seemed to stand still while he did this, and when he arrived "out in back" he felt as though an eternity had passed over him, filling his mouth with dust.

He tore through the study to the kitchen without stopping to search for changes in the big, sunlit room. The kitchen hadn't changed. Everything was drenched in sunlight and everything was in place. The electric clock above the stove was swinging its red minute hand around in a needlepoint crawl, the refrigerator was humming gently, and the radio by the window was dialed to McCabe's Food Hour, which was Anne's favorite kitchen program.

Kendrick turned his gaze about in a rotating scrutiny which was as reassuring as a tour of inspection could have been. All about him were Little-Boy-Blue-Things dutifully awaiting Anne's return.

He put up a hand to his face. His skin was clammy, cold. Well, that was just too bad, because he wasn't feeling that way now. He had gotten a grip on himself by pinning a half-nelson on the squirming part of his mind. He was sure he knew now why his neck hairs had risen out in the hall. He had stepped from bright sunlight into the house and the . . . the rat had scurried past him so rapidly that his eyes had drawn a blank.

Sun-dazzle and too much imagination had turned a big, frightened rat into an infinitely more terrifying *unthing*. It chilled him to realize that the house was infested, but rats could be gotten rid of easily enough. A little arsenic mixed with ground glass scattered around would do the trick.

The fragrance was overwhelming now. It filled the kitchen with an urgency which drew Kendrick irresistibly toward the garden.

It was coming from the garden, of course. The kitchen door was ajar and he could see a thin sliver of the garden which he and Anne had planned together.

It was a beautiful garden, filling the entire backyard and his neighbors with envy whenever he took them out and showed them what malt dustings, root prunings and night soil testings could do.

Anne had evidently introduced some new and odoriferous bloom which was flooding the house with a fragrance which was too cloying for comfort. This time she had made a change which was regrettable, a change which—

His brain became a cake of ice, freezing his thoughts

solid. He had thrown open the kitchen door and was staring out over—a garden in full bloom, a garden in which bright petalled plants cascaded over one another in such riotous profusion that the entire yard seemed a mass of purple, green and vermilion flowers.

Only—it wasn't *his* garden. It wasn't his garden at all. Gone were the yellow-pink moss roses, snapdragons, everlastings, red cardinal climbers and dwarf ageratums which he had set out back in May. Gone, too, were the bush fruit trees and cleft grafted shrubs which he had shortened back, and syringed with tobacco water earlier in the year.

There wasn't a flower in this new garden which was familiar, not a flower which he could name. The blooms were so bright they dazzled his pupils and made his throat ache.

Standing in the midst of the garden was a pot-bellied little figure scarcely three feet in height. His hands were locked around a long handled rake, and he was staring at Kendrick from beneath the brim of an old straw hat, his eyes squinting against the sun.

Kendrick experienced a sense of being not himself. It was as though someone who lived right at the intersection of Notreal Boulevard and Nowhere Avenue had stepped into his shoes and was using a wax impression of his brain to think with. The wax kept melting and running out of his ears, so that experiment was hardly a success.

He heard the someone say: "Who are *you*?" but he could only catch snatches of the little figure's petulant reply.

"—hired me. But, honest, mister, I never figured— the gnores. In a garden like this you gotta expect shants and digglies, but gnores are somethin' else again."

"Gnores?"

"Not often do they have gnores. They must've been here all along. You got 'em upstairs and down now, I bet, scamperin' through the house and makin' hay while the sun shines. Mister, look, with gnores chewin' at the roots how can I—"

Suddenly Kendrick was himself again. The change in his garden outraged something deep inside him which rose up with swinging fists and clouted the jeebies out of his brain. His eyes blazing, He strode down to the little figure, bent over and dug his fingers into—

Nothing at all. Where the dwarf's shoulders had been there yawned only empty air. Waist and legs faded out more slowly, but fade they did, leaving only a filmy face suspended in the air.

The face vanished with a swish, so quickly that the air about it quivered and backed up against Kendrick's vest. For a moment it seemed to blow over him, freezingly.

Kendrick's teeth were chattering when he went back into the kitchen and mixed himself a bracer—half rye, half ginger ale. He had never been able to take the stuff straight.

The liquor helped him. Upstairs and down it helped him, so that he didn't go off the deep end when he went from room to room and *found no trace of his wife*.

The house seemed more than deserted. There was a hollowness in the air as though even the memory-swish of Anne moving about had been sucked up in a vacuum-cleaner—right down to the last rustle.

He stood at the head of the staircase, mopping his brow and staring down into the darkness. There was a faint scampering down below and the perfume was still making him reel. "Oh, Anne, what am I going to do? There are gnores in the house, and I'm alone with them."

A surge of bitterness went through him. You'd think she'd have left a note for him somewhere in the house. A note—

It wasn't until he went into the upstairs bathroom for the second time that he found it, stuck in his shaving mug. With shaking fingers he pulled it out, and read:

> *Ted, darling,*
>
> *I'll put this in your shaving mug, where you'll be sure to find it when you wash up. If to-day I have vanished like a Rumpelstilskin away to-morrow I'll be coming home so fast I'll probably get a ticket.*
>
> *Ted, my neurotic little sister wants me to hold her hand and read to her out of a book—Thorne Smith, if I can find him in the library—while she is having her tonsils removed. So I'm taking the coupé, and driving over to East Andover.*
>
> *I'm taking Scottie with me. You'll find some cold roast beef and a bottle of half-and-half in the refrigerator.*
>
> *Did you sell Jackson the tractor?*
>
> *Your loving,*
>
> *Anne*

Kendrick moistened his lips. There wasn't anything in the note to cause alarm, even though it failed to dispel the feeling that something ghastly had taken place in his absence. There wasn't a word about hiring an ugly little dwarf to tear up his garden. Not one word about—

Something was crawling over the back of Kendrick's hand. It wasn't crawling rapidly, just making a slow snail track between his fingers. Something scratchy, moist.

But so what? There was no screen on the bathroom window and down below was a lush garden, alive with crawling things. Too, June was the month of beetles— of tumblebugs and lady-bugs, and weevils with spiny tail feelers.

Who would be alarmed? Not you, and you, and you perhaps, but Kendrick had never before encountered an invisible bug.

He leaped back with a startled cry, jarring a box of dusting powder off the bathroom shelf, and sending it crashing to the floor.

In little flakes the talcum settled down over the bugs.

There were several of them crawling up Kendrick's legs, and the white powder made them visible. Aside from the horns which sprouted from both sides of their conical heads they looked a little like silvery-textured carpet bugs grown fat and sluggish from feeding on stale plush.

"In a garden like this you gotta expect shants, and digglies."

Something was cruising around inside Kendrick's clothes. The bugs had evidently mistaken him for a flowering plant. The floor was slippery with them now, and they kept dropping down from the ceiling, and getting into his hair.

A man with courage and will power enough to look facts in the face would never have acted the way Kendrick did. Instead of letting dismay overwhelm him, such a man would have realized that a garden which had been hardened off by a vanishing dwarf would logically attract insects cut from the same cloth. But Kendrick was like everyone else rather than such a man. He choked, and started for the door, his temples pounding.

The door opened just as he reached it, swung in toward him, and almost knocked him down.

The man who had put his full weight on the door was quite the ugliest brute that Kendrick had ever seen. Heavy-jowled, sloe-eyed and pock-marked by acne he stood blinking at Kendrick in consternation, his shoulders blocking off the hallway and casting a bulky shadow on the bathtub and another fixture which might have justified his barging in so hastily had he not disclaimed all interest in it.

"My mistake, chum," he muttered. "I was lookin' for the little guy. I thought mebbe he'd be in here. He's supposed to have somethin' for me—a bowl of fruit I gotta eat, right outta the garden. Yur ain't seen him, have you, chum?"

"Well, I—"

"Right outta the garden, chum. Don't ask me what

kind of fruit. I wouldn't know, and I ain't curious, see? The judy says I should see the little guy. Apples, plums, peaches, what's the dif? To get outta this lousy clink I'd eat one of them there paddy-tailed rats."

Something was scampering up and down the hall, but Kendrick scarcely heard it.

"The judy is kind of pretty, but she won't stand for no just-you-and-me stuff. Not that dame. She acted like she owned the clink. 'He's my gardener,' she sez. 'When yur see him and eat yur'll see Scarpatti, on account of he has only been dead a week.'"

The big fellow had twisted his head sideways, perhaps unintentionally.

"Boy, that's a hot one. I'm gonna see Scarpatti. A week after I stick a shiv in him—"

Kendrick was staring at the little round black hole in the big fellows right temple. There was no blood, but the hole had unmistakably been made by a bullet working in.

"You—" Kendrick choked. His knees had turned to jelly, and there was a howling inside his skull. "You . . . you shouldn't be alive."

The big fellow frowned. "That's what the judy said. She steered me over to the mirra, and showed me this here rod crease. I gotta admit she had me scared for a minute, chum. But I'm still around, ain't I? It has to be a gag."

"Yes," Kendrick heard himself saying. "It has to be a gag."

"I gotta find the little guy. Yur sure you ain't seen 'im, chum?"

Chum, you sure you ain't seen him? Chum, *chum*, CHUM, I'm dead, but it has to be a gag. I've a bullet in my brain, but a living dead man is not one iota, jot, atom more shocking than a garden you didn't plant, and shants in your pants.

No more shocking, no more hideous, all things considered.

Kendrick sat staring out the window of a speeding taxi at skewerwood trees in full luscious bloom. It was still a bright June day, but there was no beauty coming out of it for him now.

He had brushed past the big fellow, torn down the stairs, rushed out hatless into the street and hailed a passing cab, one thought uppermost in his mind. I must see Ralph Middleton before anything more turned up to push him further along toward—he let his thoughts trail off.

"Where to, buddy?" asked the driver, twisting his head around.

"I told you. Didn't I—"

"No, buddy. You just said I should drive around."

"Oh. The . . . the number is 65 River Street."

"Okay."

Kendrick was shaking like a leaf when he descended in front of Middleton's three-story frame house, and paid the driver off. For one whirling instant he thought he had come to the wrong address. There was an air of desertion about the place which would have made itself felt even without such disheartening manifestations of non-tenancy as drawn blinds on all the windows, and the fact that someone had removed the little black sign which told the town in modest lettering that Middleton was a practicing psychiatrist—hours one to three, Sundays by appointment.

But that air, elusive, indefinable, had apparently started off for some other place, lost its way, and strayed into the wrong pew, for no sooner had the cab drawn away from the curb than Middleton appeared on the front lawn, his face gleaming with sweat.

He had come out from behind the porch, but so abruptly that Kendrick was taken aback. The illusion that Middleton had materialized out of thin air was so strong it wasn't dispelled until the psychiatrist reached his side and thumped him affectionately on the shoulder.

"Well, I'll be damned!" Middleton said. "I was just thinking about you—"

Kendrick gulped. "Ralph, I—"

"Say, this is really a break. I was afraid I'd have to leave without saying good-bye to my best and oldest friend."

"You mean you're breaking up?"

"Look, old man, come into the house and I'll tell you all about it. Funny thing, I was nailing down the cellar door over my garden hose, and that lawn mower your firm sold me last month and feeling sadder than hell. In a coupla months this place is going to look like the devil."

Silently Kendrick accompanied Middleton into the house and waited while he turned on the hall lamp, and brushed dust from his clothes.

"Mrs. Graham has just finished putting old-fashioned nightshirts on the furniture," he said. "The place looks like a morgue."

"That's all right, Ralph."

"Well, come into the library and we'll have a couple of whiskies and sodas."

In the library Middleton seated himself on a sheet-covered sofa, and motioned Kendrick to a chair that looked a little like a brokendown ghost.

"Ted, what would you say if I told you I'd grabbed off a job at the Riverdale Clinic in New York which will put me up in front. Of course, a man under thirty can't expect—"

"That's swell," Kendrick said, moistening his lips.

"Hey, just a minute. Give me a chance to tell you."

Kendrick leaned forward, clasping his hands over his knees, and trying hard to keep his face from breaking loose from its moorings, and floating up over his scalp.

"I'm in serious trouble," he said. "I'm afraid—I'm afraid it's in your department, Ralph."

Middleton raised quizzical blue eyes and stared at him levelly. "You mean you want to consult me *professionally*, Ted?"

Kendrick's eyes told him yes, yes, YES. He leaned still farther forward, clasping and unclasping his hands and shifting about in his seat.

"Well, let's have it," Middleton said.

Mostly while Kendrick talked Middleton remained in one position, but once while Kendrick was loosening his collar he uncrossed his legs and put the toes of his right fool behind his left ankle.

"So you see," Kendrick concluded, "I've got all the symptoms of—well, something I hoped you would assure me I haven't got. But while I've been talking to you I've been jockeying myself into a position which I'm not going to retreat from. It's the strong position of accepting the worst, and fighting back from there. Y'see what I mean?"

Middleton nodded approvingly. "I see perfectly. But you're taking all this much too seriously. If ever there was a clear-cut example of what Freud means when he speaks of the ingenuity of the Id—"

"I'm afraid I don't—"

Middleton rose, walked to the book-case behind him, removed a leather-bound volume and returned to where Kendrick was sitting. Without a word he put the book into Kendrick's hands.

It was Swinburne's *Poems and Ballads*.

"The last time you were over here you spent the whole evening chanting those Victorian limericks," he said. "Swinburne was a little boy who never grew up, an alliterative jackanapes with verbal-meningitis. I'd trade in a dozen of the likes of him for one Shelley, but every man to his taste."

"Well?"

"Well, turn to page eighty-six. 'The Garden of Proserpine.' You were reading that last month. Wait, don't turn. I'll quote from memory:

"Pale beyond porch and portal,
    Crowned with calm leaves she stands

Who gathers all things mortal,
With cold, immortal hands.

"You see, she has a garden. Proserpine has, daughter of Zeus and Demeter. What kind of garden? A garden of Death. When people die they are supposed to walk into that garden and never come out.

"From too much love of living,
From hope and fear set free
We thank with brief thanksgiving,
Whatever gods may be,
That no life lasts for ever,
That dead men rise up never,
That even the weariest river
Winds somewhere safe to sea."

"But I—"

"Get it? In your mind you have a clear, sparkling picture of Proserpine's garden and her bowl of fruit."

"Bowl of fruit?"

"All right, your conscious mind is a bit rusty on the uptake. But you've read the *Golden Bough,* and you're subconsciously aware that persons who have found their way into Hades can return to the upper world if they have not tasted the fruit from Proserpine's garden.

"It comes pretty close to being a universal human myth. If you don't believe me, ask a primitive black fellow from Australia or a Caledonian witch-doctor. The Greek variant is the most familiar, but to find the prototype of the grim little *vorstellung* you'd have to sit down to tea with Mr. and Mrs. Piltdown. You taste the fruit and you are altogether dead.

"She waits for each and other,
She waits for all men born.

"So what happens? You come back from a nerve-racking business trip with your head in a whirl. You've been trying to sell tractors to guys who are being paid by the government to plow under their farms. The trip has been a flop, but you've a mental picture of yourself relaxing in dressing-gown and slippers, with Anne smoothing the wrinkles out of your forehead with her cool, immortal hands.

"But—Anne isn't there. Old Lady Frustration is waiting for you instead, with a rolling-pin cradled in her arms. She swings at you, and you reel. You're so groggy your reading comes back to you, the verses from Swinburne, Frazer's *Golden Bough*.

"You go out into the garden and everything blurs. You see a garden that isn't there. Her garden, Proserpine's, with cold, immortal hands. You see a dwarf she's lured to do the menial work, seeding, pruning, bringing in the sheaves. Demonomania, you understand? Dwarfs, little devils with forked tails, leprechauns, blue-bottle imps are all symptomatic of demonomania. And sometimes you have an insect aura.

"You don't have to worry, though. It isn't a psychosis—just neuroticism raised to high C. A phobia. And you've got to remember that you can sometimes have the crawling things without a clear-cut symptomology."

"But how about the big ape with a bullet hole in his temple?" Kendrick asked. The horror was lifting now. Miraculously it was being dispelled by the astonishing psychiatric vistas which Middleton was unrolling with the deftness of a jinni warmed by wine.

"Why, don't you see? You brought Proserpine's garden into your home because you had a peg to hang it on. *He* was the peg. You imagined the garden growing up around him. When did the police notify you, by the way?"

Involuntarily Kendrick stiffened, his lips whitening as he returned the psychiatrist's stare. "Huh? The police? What are you talking about?"

It was Middleton's turn to evince agitation. "You mean to say you didn't know?"

Kendrick shook his head.

"Why, I thought . . . I thought, of course, the police

would get in touch with you. No reason to, I suppose, except that—well, it gave your wife a nasty jolt, and she may have to appear in court. I should think . . . but wait a minute. Of course. They took it for granted that Anne would wire you."

Kendrick was shaking now in every limb. The vista had stopped unrolling, was buckling into wormy folds. Something was crawling up his back, too—inching along his spine.

"What is it?" he demanded hoarsely.

"Ted, I'm your friend. You've got to remember that. You must have known, which suggests a case history going back for some time rather than, a momentary phobia brought on by strain. You must have known, and forgotten that you knew, subconsciously building up the garden to torture yourself *before* you arrived home. It's a little more serious than I thought—"

"In heaven's name, man, spit it out."

"Well, here is what you really know, Ted. Deep in your mind you know that the night before last a thug named Spike Malone held up a jewelry store on Elmhurst Boulevard, fled along Centre Street, and ducked into your backyard when the police closed in on him from three sides. He was shot twice, once in the right temple, once in the hip."

"You mean he died in my garden?" Kendrick choked.

"No, he didn't die. They rushed him to the Stonington Hospital, and for all I know he may be still alive. It can happen, you know. If the bullet passes down through the Gyrus Ling—"

Kendrick's face seemed all wrenched apart. "Anne did *not* wire me," he said.

"Oh, come now. You *must* have known."

"I tell you, she didn't. You've got to be careful not to contradict me."

Middleton turned pale. "Now look here, old man. There isn't a thing I wouldn't do for you. I'm your friend, the very best friend you have in the world. I'm postponing New York, because that's the very least I can do, and only the beginning of—"

"He came back to die," Kendrick groaned. "He was mortally wounded, and now—*he's eating the fruit!*"

"Oh, come now. I've explained all that."

"You've explained it too well." Stark anguish looked out of Kendrick's eyes. "I believe in that garden now, Middleton. I *believe* in it."

Middleton seemed not to hear him. He was squirming about in his seat and scratching himself, as though he had been suddenly assailed by a legion of ticks.

Abruptly, as Kendrick stared, the psychiatrist's jaw jiggled downward, and his lips began to jerk. Convulsively to squirm and jerk, as though all the words which he had uttered were rushing frantically back into his mouth.

Anne Kendrick drew in to the curb beneath skewer-wood trees in full luscious bloom. Humming "I'm Mad at the Moon, 'Cause the Moon Won't Talk," she silenced the car's throbbing motor, lifted an all-night bag over the back seat, and descended to the sidewalk with her skirts fluttering up about her knees.

She moved buoyantly across the sidewalk and into the shadow of the house. She glanced up, smiling, and for an instant thought of calling out: "Ted, darling, I'm back."

But no, better to slip quietly into the house and surprise him.

He'd probably be in the library "out in back," reading or making out his monthly sales report, and entirely oblivious to sounds from the street.

The fragrance surprised her even before she got the door open, filling the vestibule with a sweetness which made her choke.

"Hm-m-m," she thought, "lucky I'm not Katie with her tonsils wrapped in gauze. Katie wouldn't like all that fragrance, you can bet.

"Anne, girl," she thought, "you're home again, and in a moment you'll be in the arms of a pretty nice chap. All things considered, a husband to be proud of, and a worthwhile addition to *any* woman's house."

Her key clicked in the lock. Still humming, she stepped into the lower hallway, and set her bag down at the front of the stairs.

The fragrance was really something. It filled her with a vague uneasiness suddenly, so that she ceased to smile.

Now what had Ted done? Gone down to the dime store and bought a novelty plant—one of those yellow African air orchids that were supposed to bloom overnight? You put the orchid in a bowl, dry, and it was supposed to draw nourishment from the air and really blossom out. Would such a plant have an odor like that?

Down the hall she tiptoed, telling herself that she was not going to allow a mere odor to spoil her homecoming. The library was hushed and dark, but there was an air of recent occupancy in the room which dispelled her unreasoning dread until she heard someone say, not loudly, but with a menacing inflection that chilled her heart like ice: "You're gonna eat, see? Just because you find a shurm in this here apple ain't no reason for refusin' to put on the feed bag. You're keepin' these gentlemen waiting."

"To hell with them," said a second voice. "I ain't gonna eat no pink maggots."

A third voice interposed. "Very curious. He is compensating for a malignant inferiority complex *even* now. Blustering, putting on an act."

"You see? This gentleman is a sick-eye-atwist. He knows what you are. He's got you dead to rights."

"You may as well eat, Spike," said a fourth voice. "You're going out into the garden, and you're not coming back."

"That's what you think, chum."

"I don't think. I know. We're all in this together."

"I don't see why *you* have to eat, chum?"

"I don't either, Spike. But I do. I was having a quiet little talk with Dr. Middleton on the other side of town when we both realized we would have to eat, too. Spike, somehow, I feel very sorry for you. You're a social menace, but it wasn't your fault exactly. All your life something inside you has felt kicked around.

"Of every million lives how many a score are failures from their birth?"

"You'd better stick to Swinburne, Ted," the third voice said. "He wasn't as great as Shelley, but sometimes he hit the nail on the head.

"And all dead years draw hither,

And all disastrous things."

"So yur poits, eh? I gotta eat with a coupla rhyme-spoutin', wrist-slappin' poits."

"No, Spike, we're not poets. This gentleman is a psychiatrist, and I sell farm implements."

Anne had turned as pale as death. The voices were right in the room with her. Her husband's voice was the loudest; Dr. Middleton's fainter, but vibrant; the man called Spike gruff, but extremely faint.

Suddenly she heard a crunching sound, followed by an angry grunt.

"Yur call this an orange?"

"Sure it's an orange," said the first voice. "I grew it myself. A blue, bitter-rind orange. What you complainin' about?"

"Nothin' much. Just that this ain't my idea of an orange, yur little squirt. I oughtta cram it down yur throat."

"You better eat, fella. You put it off too long, and you'll be gaggin' on a funnel drip."

Crunch, crunch.

"Yur gotta lot tur learn about fruit growin', squirt. Ef I wasn't so set on gettin' outta this mangy clink—"

There was a scraping sound, as though a chair had been pushed back by someone getting up.

"He's gone," Ted's voice said.

"You mean he's goin'," the first voice amended. "You can't see him now, but he's walkin' out into the garden."

There was a momentary hush. Then Dr. Middleton's voice said: "Well, am I next?"

"You are, buddy," said the first voice. "What'll it be? For a gentleman like you I rekamend a bunch of very hollow grapes."

"I have never liked grapes," Middleton said. "I'll take a peach."

There was another crunch.

"He ate that like a man," the first voice said.

"Give me the bowl," Ted's voice groaned. "I'll take a—Oh, Anne, darling, if I could just—"

"If you could see her, buddy, you'd be sweatin' buckets."

"What do you mean?"

"Buddy, take a look at yourself. You want her to look like that?"

Ted's voice groaned.

"Buddy, givin' advice is out of my line, but if my wife didn't hafta eat I wouldn't ask to see her. No use givin' the three Spinning Sisters ideas. You see what I mean?"

"I see what you mean. The people I can see are going to die."

"Oh, don't." The first voice quivered as though in pain. "They just hafta eat, that's all. Don't use the word again, buddy."

"I drove over to Middleton's place in a cab," Ted's voice said. "I saw the driver."

"He's gonna eat, too, buddy, but he don't know it yet. His pump is missin' every second beat."

"I see. And Middleton was . . . Middleton was . . . the drawn blinds—"

"You're smart, buddy. Middleton was in New York drivin' around in your car. His house here is shut up tight."

"But I sat in his library and talked to him—not twenty minutes ago."

"Sure you did, buddy. You both came home to eat. Where could you find a better garden? I been workin' over it, just for you three guys. The big guy was shot here, and you—this is your home. She figured three together like that, all from the same town, oughtta sit down at the same table. Smart, eh? Saves time and trouble."

Suddenly a new voice spoke. Coldly, austerely, and as though from a great height. "Eat now. You have talked enough."

"Hi, goddess," Kendrick's voice said. It was taut with anguish but Kendrick had always vowed that he would go with a jest. It was something he had thrashed out with himself in his fourteenth year.

"I'll take a plum," he said. "Fortunately I can see the fruit. The bowl is a little misty around the edges, but it isn't invisible. I couldn't see the shants and digglies, but this plum—"

The first voice gasped. "You couldn't see the shants?"

"Not until I spilled some dusting powder on them," Kendrick said.

"Could you see the gnores?"

"No."

"Buddy, look. You walk out into that garden pulling a gag, and you'll wish you were never born."

"I didn't see the gnores," Kendrick reiterated. "Now if you don't mind, I'll—"

"Do not eat," said the high, austere voice.

"Mistress, its just a gag. The car turned over three times."

"He must not eat."

"Make up your mind," Kendrick almost screamed.

The austere voice said, "I can see him now. He is sitting up in bed. He is asking for his wife. There is a doctor and a nurse standing beside him. The nurse . . . the nurse is *smiling*, you little worm. I ought to have you thrashed."

"It wasn't my fault, mistress. I swear it wasn't my fault. He had a temperature of one hundred and six."

Two faces, a man's, a woman's, appeared simultaneously in the room—one on a level with Anne's eyes, and the other high up under the ceiling. The woman's face was thick-lipped, Negroid, and crowned with a circlet of gleaming flowers.

The man—Anne caught her breath—was regarding her tenderly. He was trying hard to smile, Ted was. She could see his body now, mistily, and the outlines of a table, and a pot-bellied little figure scarcely three feet tall with a bowl of fruit in his hands.

Down from the woman's face streamed a long, flowing robe. She was stooping a little now, and her eyes were wide, staring. Suddenly as Anne swayed, they seemed to fill the room. Two enormous orbs mirroring metal-gray skies, and a waste of tumbled sand that seemed to stretch out endlessly in all directions. In the depths of the sky vultures wheeled, and for an instant there was a carrion taint in the room.

Then—the eyes grew small again. There was a glimmer of purple light, and faces, table and bowl of fruit dwindled to luminous motes which darted about for an instant in the shadowed, quiet room and were suddenly gone.

"Long distance calling. Mrs. Kendrick? Mrs. Kendrick. K-e-n-d-r-i-c-k? This is long distance calling. Here is your party, sir."

"Hello, Ted? Ted? Oh, my darling, my poor dear—"

"Anne, hold on tight. I've had an accident, but I'm all right now, and you've got to stay steady. I wouldn't be 'phoning and talking in a calm, quiet way if I wasn't all right. You realize that, don't you?"

"I know, darling, I know—"

"I've been unconscious for twenty-six hours, but now they are going to give me something to eat. I'm sitting up, and the nurse on duty here is holding my hand, and I'm telling myself it's your hand I'm holding."

"I'm not jealous, darling."

"Dear, I . . . I tried to play the Good Samaritan.

Yesterday I dropped in at the Riverdale Clinic to see how Middleton was standing the gaff. He wasn't standing it so well. He said he felt like chucking the new job, and going back to Lynnbrook. He looked so played out I suggested eighteen holes of golf, and a spin on the Bronx River Parkway. We were leaving Grassy Sprain when a road skunk came out from behind a truck and pushed me off the road."

"Ted, I . . . please hold the wire. Just for a second. I don't feel so—"

"Anne, are you all right? Anne! Answer me."

"Gulpullul. Yes, I . . . I feel better now . . . Ted . . . darling."

"You sure? You want me to hold the wire while you get something?"

"No, dear. I've got something right here . . . a straight brandy."

"Anne, this may sound sort of screwy, but—is our garden all right?"

"Yes, it is, Ted. I was just out there."

"I must have been delirious all last night. I thought, I thought—"

"I know, Ted, darling. But we've got our own beautiful garden back now."

"Your time is up, sir."

"Operator, operator, listen. This is an emergency call."

"His time is *not* up, operator. He's going to live to be a hundred and six. I don't know what's in store for you, but he's going to grow old along with me. Park that with your gum, and step back from the line, young lady."

*Robert Sheckley vaulted to the front ranks of science
fiction writers in the 1950s with his prodigious output
of short, witty stories that explored the human condition
in a variety of earthly and unearthly settings. His best
tales have been collected in* Untouched by Human
Hands, Pilgrimage to Earth, *and the comprehensive*
Collected Short Stories of Robert Sheckley. *His novels
include the futuristic tales* The Status Civilization,
Mindswap, *and* Immortality Delivered, *which was filmed
as* Freejack. *He has also written the crime novels* Calibre
.50 *and* Time Limit. *Elio Petri's cult film* The Tenth
Victim *is based on his story "The Seventh Victim."*

Cordle to Onion to Carrot

Robert Sheckley

Surely, you remember that bully who kicked sand on
the 97-pound-weakling? Well, that puny man's problem
has never been solved despite Charles Atlas's claims to
the contrary. A genuine bully *likes* to kick sand on
people; for him, simple, there is gut-deep satisfaction
in a put-down. It wouldn't matter if you weighed 240
pounds—all of it rock-hard muscle and steely sinew—
and were as wise as Solomon or as witty as Voltaire;
you'd still end up with the sand of an insult in your eyes,
and probably you wouldn't do anything about it.

That was Howard Cordle viewed the situation. He
was a pleasant man who was forever being pushed
around by Fuller Brush men, fund solicitors, headwaiters and other imposing figures of authority. Cordle

hated it. He suffered in silence the countless numbers of manic-aggressives who shoved their way to the
heads of lines, took taxis he had hailed first and
sneeringly steered away girls to whom he was talking at parties.

What made it worse was that these people seemed
to welcome provocation, to go looking for it, all for the
sake of causing discomfort to others.

Cordle couldn't understand why this should be, until
one midsummer's day, when he was driving through the
northern regions of Spain while stoned out of his mind,
the god Thoth-Hermes granted him original enlightenment by murmuring "Uh, look, I groove with the problem, baby, but dig, we gotta put carrots in or it ain't
no stew."

"*Carrots?*" said Cordle, struggling for illumination.

"I'm talking about those types who get you uptight,"
Thoth-Hermes explained.

"They *gotta* act that way, baby, on account of they're
carrots, and that's how carrots are."

"If they are carrots," Cordle said, feeling his way,
"then I—"

"You, of course, are a little pearly-white onion."

"Yes! My God, yes!" Cordle cried, dazzled by the
blinding light of satori.

"And, naturally, you and the other pearly-white onions
think that carrots are just bad news, merely some kind
of misshapen orangey onion; whereas the carrots look
at you and rap *about freaky round white carrots, wow!*
I mean, you're just too much for each other, whereas,
in actuality—"

"Yes, go on!" cried Cordle.

"In actuality," Thoth-Hermes declared, "*everything's
got a place in The Stew!*"

"Of course! I see, I see, I see!"

"And *that* means that everybody who exists is necessary, and you *must* have long hateful orange carrots if
you're also going to have nice pleasant decent white

onions, or vice versa, because without all of the ingredients, it isn't a Stew, which is to say, life, it becomes, uh, let me see . . ."

"A soup!" cried ecstatic Cordle.

"You're coming in five by five," chanted Thoth-Hermes. "Lay down the word, deacon, and let the people know the divine formula. . . ."

"A *soup*!" said Cordle. "Yes, I see it now—creamy, pearl-white onion soup is our dream of heaven whereas fiery orange carrot broth is our notion of hell. It fits, it all fits together!"

"Om manipadme hum," intoned Thoth-Hermes.

"But where do the green peas go? What about the *meat*, for God's sake?"

"Don't pick at the metaphor," Thoth-Hermes advised him, "it leaves a nasty scab. Stick with the carrots and onions. And, here, let me offer you a drink—a house specialty."

"But the spices, where do you put the *spices*?" Cordle demanded, taking a long swig of burgundy-colored liquid from a rusted canteen.

"Baby, you're asking questions that can be revealed only to a thirteenth-degree Mason with piles, wearing sandals. Sorry about that. Just remember that everything goes into The Stew."

"Into The Stew," Cordle repeated, smacking his lips.

"And, especially, stick with the carrots and onions; you were really grooving there."

"Carrots and onions," Cordle repeated.

"That's your trip," Thoth-Hermes said. "Hey, we've gotten to Corunna; you can let me out anywhere around here."

Cordle pulled his rented car off the road. Thoth-Hermes took his knapsack from the back seat and got out.

"Thanks for the lift, baby."

"My pleasure. Thank you for the wine. What kind did you say it was?"

"*Vino de casa* mixed with a mere smidgen of old Dr. Hammerfinger's essence of instant powdered Power-Pack brand acid. Brewed by gnurrs in the secret laboratories of UCLA in preparation for the big all-Europe turn-on."

"Whatever it was, it surely *was*," Cordle said deeply. "Pure elixir to me. You could sell neckties to antelopes with that stuff; you could change the world from an oblate spheroid into a truncated trapezoid. . . .What did I say?"

"Never mind, it's all part of your trip. Maybe you better lie down for a while, huh?"

"Where gods command, mere mortals must obey," Cordle said iambically. He lay down on the front seat of the car. Thoth-Hermes bent over him, his beard burnished gold, his head wreathed in plane trees.

"You OK?"

"Never better in my life."

"Want me to stand by?"

"Unnecessary. You have helped me beyond potentiality."

"Glad to hear it, baby, you're making a fine sound. You really are OK? Well, then, ta."

Thoth-Hermes marched off into the sunset. Cordle closed his eyes and solved various problems that had perplexed the greatest philosophers of all age. He was mildly surprised at how simple complexity was.

At last he went to sleep. He awoke some six hours later. He had forgotten most of his brilliant insights, the lucid solutions. It was inconceivable. How can one misplace the keys of the universe? But he had, and there seemed no hope of reclaiming them. Paradise was lost for good.

He did remember about the onions and the carrots, though, and he remembered The Stew. It was not the sort of insight he might have chosen if he'd had any choice; but this was what had come to him and he did not reject it. Cordle knew, perhaps instinctively, that in the insight game, you take whatever you can get.

✧   ✧   ✧

The next day, he reached Santander in a driving rain. He decided to write amusing letters to all of his friends, perhaps even try his hand at a Travel sketch. That required a typewriter. The *conserje* at his hotel directed him to a store that rented typewriters. He went there and found a clerk who spoke perfect English.

"Do you rent typewriters by the day?" Cordle asked.

"Why not?" the clerk replied. He had oily black hair and a thin aristocratic nose.

"How much for that one?" Cordle asked, indicating a thirty-year-old Erika portable.

"Seventy pesetas a day, which is to say, one dollar. Usually."

"Isn't this usually?"

"Certainly not, since you are a foreigner in transit. For you, one hundred and eighty pesetas a day."

"All right," Cordle said, reaching for his wallet. "I'd like to have it for two days."

"I shall also require your passport and a deposit of fifty dollars."

Cordle attempted a mild joke. "Hey, I just want to type on it, not marry it."

The clerk shrugged.

"Look, the *conserje* has my passport at the hotel. How about taking my driver's license instead?"

"Certainly not. I must hold your passport, in case you decide to default."

"But why do you need my passport and the deposit?" Cordle asked, feeling bullied and ill at ease. "I mean, look, the machine's not worth twenty dollars."

"You are an expert, perhaps, in the Spanish market value of used typewriters?"

"No, but—"

"Then permit me sir, to conduct my business as I see fit. I will also need to know the use to which you plan to put the machine."

"The *use*?"

"Of course, the use."

It was one of these preposterous foreign situations that can happen to anyone. The clerk's request was incomprehensible and his manner was insulting. Cordle was about to give a curt little nod, turn on his heel and walk out.

Then he remembered about the onions and carrots. He saw The Stew. And suddenly, it occurred to Cordle that he could be whatever vegetable he wanted to be.

He turned to the clerk. He smiled winningly. He said, "You wish to know the use I will make of the typewriter?"

"Exactly."

"Well," Cordle said, "quite frankly, I had planned to stuff it up my nose."

The clerk gaped at him.

"It's quite a successful method of smuggling," Cordle went on. "I was also planning to give you a stolen passport and counterfeit pesetas. Once I got into Italy, I would have sold the typewriter for ten thousand dollars. Milan is undergoing a typewriter famine, you know; they're desperate, they'll buy anything."

"Sir," the clerk said, "you choose to be disagreeable."

"Nasty is the word you were looking for. I've changed my mind about the typewriter. But let me compliment you on your command of English."

"I have studied assiduously," the clerk admitted, with a hint of pride.

"That is evident. And, despite a certain weakness in the Rs, you succeed in sounding like a Venetian gondolier with a cleft palate. My best wishes to your esteemed family. I leave you now to pick your pimples in peace."

Reviewing the scene later, Cordle decided that he had performed quite well in his maiden appearance as a carrot. True, his closing lines had been a little forced and overintellectualized. But the undertone of viciousness had been convincing.

Most important was the simple resounding fact that he had done it. And now, in the quiet of his hotel room, instead of churning his guts in a frenzy of self-loathing, he had the tranquilizing knowledge of having put someone else in that position.

He had done it! Just like that, he had transformed himself from onion into carrot!

But was his position ethically defensible? Presumably, the clerk could not help being detestable; he was a product of his own genetic and social environment, a victim of his conditioning; he was naturally rather than intentionally hateful—

Cordle stopped himself. He saw that he was engaged in typical onionish thinking, which was an inability to conceive of carrots except as an aberration from oniondom.

But now he knew that both onions and carrots had to exist; otherwise, there would be no Stew.

And he also knew that a man was free and could choose whatever vegetable he wanted to be. He could even live as an amusing little green pea, or a gruff, forceful clove of garlic (though perhaps that was scratching at the metaphor). In any event, a man could take his pick between carrothood and oniondom.

There is much to think about here, Cordle thought. But he never got around to thinking about it. Instead he went sight-seeing, despite the rain, and then continued his travels.

The next incident occurred in Nice in a cozy little restaurant on the Avenue des Diables Bleus, with red-checkered tablecloths and incomprehensible menus written in longhand with purple ink. There were four waiters, one of whom looked like Jean-Paul Belmondo, down to the cigarette drooping from his long lower lip. The others looked like run-of-the-mill muggers. There were several Scandinavian customers quietly eating a *cassoulet*, one old Frenchman in a beret and three homely English girls.

Belmondo sauntered over. Cordle, who spoke a clear though idiomatic French, asked for the 10-franc menu he had seen hanging in the window.

The waiter gave him the sort of look one reserves for pretentious beggars. "Ah, that is all finished for today," he said and handed Cordle a 30-franc menu.

In his previous incarnation, Cordle would have bit down on the bullet and ordered. Or possibly he would have risen, trembling with outrage, and left the restaurant, blundering into a chair on the way.

But now—

"Perhaps you did not understand me," Cordle said. "It is a matter of French law that you must serve all of the fixed-price menus that you show in the window."

"*M'sieu* is a lawyer?" the waiter inquired, his hands insolently on his hips.

"No. *M'sieu* is a trouble-maker," Cordle said, giving what he considered to be fair warning.

"Then *m'sieu* must make what trouble he desires," the waiter said. His eyes were slits.

"OK," Cordle said. And just then, an elderly couple came into the restaurant. The man wore a double-breasted slate-blue suit with a half-inch white pin stripe. The woman wore a flowered organdy dress. Cordle called to them, "Excuse me, are you folks English?"

A bit startled, the man inclined his head in the barest intimation of a nod.

"Then I would advise you not to eat here. I am a inspector for UNESCO. The chef apparently has not washed his hands since D-Day. We haven't made a definitive test for typhoid yet, but we have our suspicions. As soon as my assistant arrives with the litmus paper. . . ."

A deathly hush had fallen over the restaurant.

"I suppose a boiled egg would be safe enough," Cordle said.

The elderly man probably didn't believe him. But it didn't matter, Cordle was obviously trouble.

"Come, Mildred," he said, and they hurried out.

"There goes sixty francs plus five percent tip," Cordle said, coolly.

"Leave here at once!" the waiter snarled.

"I like it here," Cordle said, folding his arms. "I like the *ambiance*, the sense of intimacy—"

"You are not permitted to stay without eating."

"I shall eat. From the ten-franc menu."

The waiters looked at one another, nodded in unison and began to advance in a threatening phalanx. Cordle called to the other diners, "I ask you all to bear witness! These men are going to attack me, four to one, contrary to French law and universal human ethics, simply because I want to order from the ten-franc menu, which they have falsely advertised."

It was a long speech, but this was clearly the time for grandiloquence. Cordle repeated it in English.

The English girls gasped. The old Frenchman went on eating his soup. The Scandinavians nodded grimly and began to take off their jackets.

The waiters held another conference. The one who looked like Belmondo said, "*M'sieu* you are forcing us to call the police."

"That will save me the trouble," Cordle said, "of calling them myself."

"Surely *m'sieu* does not want to spend his holiday in court?"

"That is how *m'sieu* spends most of his holidays," Cordle said.

The waiters conferred again. Then Belmondo stalked over with the 30-menu. "The cost of the *prix fixe* will be ten francs, since evidently that is all *m'sieu* can afford."

Cordle let that pass. "Bring me onion soup, green salad and the *boeuf bourguignon*."

The waiter went to put in the order. While he was waiting Cordle sang "Waltzing Matilda" in a moderately loud voice. He suspected it might speed up the service. He got his food by the time he reached "You'll never catch me alive, said he" for the second time. Cordle pulled the tureen of stew toward him and lifted a spoon.

It was a breathless moment. Not one diner had left the restaurant. And Cordle was prepared. He leaned forward, soup spoon in shoveling position, and sniffed delicately. A hush fell over the room.

"It lacks a certain something," Cordle said aloud. Frowning, he poured the onion soup into the *boeuf bourguignon*. He sniffed, shook his head and added a half loaf of bread, in slices. He sniffed again and added the salad and the contents of a saltcellar.

Cordle pursed his lips "No," he said, "it simply will not do."

He overturned the entire contents of the tureen onto the table. It was an act comparable perhaps, to throwing gentian violet on the *Mona Lisa*. All of France and most of western Switzerland went into a state of shock.

Unhurriedly, but keeping the frozen waiters under surveillance, Cordle rose and dropped ten francs into the mess. He walked to the door, turned and said, "My compliments to the chef, who might better be employed as a cement mixer. And this, *mon vieux*, is for you."

He threw his crumpled linen napkin onto the floor.

As the matador, after a fine series of passes, turns his back contemptuously on the bull and strolls away, so went Cordle. For some unknown reason, the waiters did not rush out after him, shoot him dead and hang his corpse from the nearest lamppost. So Cordle walked for ten or fifteen blocks, taking rights and lefts at random. He came to the Promenade des Anglais and sat down on a bench. He was trembling and his shirt was drenched with perspiration.

"But I did it," he said. "I did it! I! I was unspeakably vile and I got away with it!"

Now he really knew why carrots acted that way. Dear God in heaven, what joy, what delectable bliss!

Cordle then reverted to his mild-mannered self, smoothly and without regrets. He stayed that way until his second day in Rome.

He was in his rented car. He and seven other drivers were lined up at a traffic light on the Corso Vittorio Emanuele II. There were perhaps twenty cars behind them. All of the drivers were revving their engines, hunched over their steering wheels with slitted eyes, dreaming of Le Mans. All except Cordle, who was drinking in the cyclopean architecture of downtown Rome.

The checkered flag came down! The drivers floored their accelerators, trying to spin the wheels of their underpowered Fiats, wearing out their clutches and their nerves, but doing so with *éclat* and *brio*. All except Cordle, who seemed to be the only man in Rome who didn't have to win a race or keep an appointment.

Without undue haste or particular delay, Cordle depressed the clutch and engaged the gear. Already he had lost nearly two seconds—unthinkable at Monza or Monte Carlo.

The driver behind him blew his horn frantically.

Cordle smiled to himself, a secret, ugly expression. He put the gearshift into neutral, engaged the hand brake and stepped out of his car. He ambled over to the hornblower, who had turned pasty white and was fumbling under his seat, hoping to find a tire iron.

"Yes?" said Cordle, in French, "is something wrong?"

"No, no nothing," the driver replied in French—his first mistake. "I merely wanted you to go, to move."

"But I was just doing that," Cordle pointed out.

"Well, then! It is all right!"

"No, it is not all right," Cordle told him. "I think I

deserve a better explanation of why you blew your horn at me."

The hornblower—a Milanese businessman on holiday with his wife and four children—rashly replied, "My dear sir, you were slow, you were delaying us all."

"*Slow?*" said Cordle. "You blew your horn two seconds after the light changed. Do you call two seconds slow?"

"It was much longer than that," the man riposted feebly.

Traffic was now backed up as far south as Naples. A crowd of ten thousand had gathered. *Carabinieri* units in Viterbo and Genoa had been called into a state of alert.

"That is untrue," Cordle said. "I have witnesses." He gestured at the crowd, which gestured back. "I shall call my witnesses before the courts. You must know that you broke the law by blowing your horn within the city limits of Rome in what was clearly not an emergency."

The Milanese businessman looked at the crowd, now swollen to perhaps fifty thousand. Dear God, he thought, if only the Goths would descend again and exterminate these leering Romans! If only the ground would open up and swallow this insane Frenchman! If only he, Giancarlo Morelli, had a dull spoon with which to open up the veins of his wrists!

Jets from the Sixth Fleet thundered overhead, hoping to avert the long-expected *coup d'état*.

The Milanese businessman's own wife was shouting abuse at him: Tonight he would cut out her faithless heart and mail it back to her mother.

What was there to do? In Milan, he would have had this Frenchman's head on a platter. But this was Rome, a southern city, an unpredictable and dangerous place. And legalistically, he was possibly in the wrong, which left him at a further disadvantage in the argument.

"Very well," he said. "The blowing of the horn was perhaps truly unnecessary, despite the provocation."

"I insist on a genuine apology," insisted Cordle.

There was a thundering sound to the east: Thousands of Soviet tanks were moving into battle formation across the plains of Hungary, ready to resist the long-expected NATO thrust into Transylvania. The water supply was cut off in Foggia, Brindisi, Bari. The Swiss closed their frontiers and stood ready to dynamite the passes.

"All right, I apologize!" the Milanese businessman screamed. "I am sorry I provoked you and even sorrier that I was born! Again, I apologize! Now will you go away and let me have a heart attack in peace?"

"I accept your apology," Cordle said. "No hard feelings, eh." He strolled back to his car, humming "Blow the Man Down," and drove away as millions cheered.

War was once again averted by a hairbreadth.

Cordle drove to the Arch of Titus, parked his car and—to the sound of a thousand trumpets—passed through it. He deserved this as well as any Caesar.

God, he gloated, I was *loathsome!*

In England, Cordle stepped on a young lady's toe just inside the Traitors' Gate of the Tower of London. This should have served as an intimation of something. The young lady was named Mavis. She came from Short Hills, New Jersey, and she had long straight dark hair. She was slender, pretty, intelligent, energetic and she had a sense of humor. She had minor faults, as well, but they play no part in this story. She let Cordle buy her a cup of coffee. They were together constantly for the rest of the week.

"I think I am infatuated," Cordle said to himself on the seventh day. He realized at once that he had made a slight understatement. He was violently and hopelessly in love.

But what did Mavis feel? She seemed not unfond of him. It was even possible that she might, conceivably, reciprocate.

At that moment, Cordle had a flash of prescience.

He realized that one week ago, he had stepped on the toe of his future wife and mother of his two children, both of whom would be born and brought up in a split-level house with inflatable furniture in Summit, New Jersey, or possibly Millburn.

This may sound unattractive and provincial when stated baldly; but it was desirable to Cordle, who had no pretensions to cosmopolitanism. After all, not all of us can live at Cap Ferrat. Strangely enough, not all of us even want to.

That day, Cordle and Mavis went to the Marshall Gordon Residence in Belgravia to see the Byzantine miniatures. Mavis had a passion for Byzantine miniatures that seemed harmless enough at the time. The collection was private, but Mavis had secured invitations through a local Avis manager, who was trying very hard, indeed.

They came to the Gordon Residence, an awesome Regency building in Huddlestone Mews. They rang. A butler in full evening dress answered the door. They showed the invitations. The butler's glance and lifted eyebrow showed that they were carrying second-class invitations of the sort given to importunate art poseurs on 17-day all-expense economy flights, rather than the engraved first-class invitations given to Picasso, Jackie Onassis, Sugar Ray Robinson, Norman Mailer, Charles Goren and other movers and shakers of the world.

The butler said, "Oh, yes. . . ." Two words that spoke black volumes. His face twitched, he looked like a man who has received an unexpected visit from Tamerland and a regiment of his Golden Horde.

"The miniatures," Cordle reminded him.

"Yes, of course. . . . But I am afraid, sir, that no one is allowed into the Gordon Residence without a coat and necktie."

It was an oppressive August day. Cordle was wearing a sport shirt. He said, "Did I hear you correctly? Coat and necktie?"

The butler said, "That is the rule, sir."

Mavis asked, "Couldn't you make an exception this once?"

The butler shook his head. "We really must stick by the rules, miss. Otherwise . . ." He left the fear of vulgarity unsaid, but it hung in the air like a chrome-plated fart.

"Of course," Cordle said, pleasantly. "Otherwise. So it's a coat and tie, is it? I think we can arrange that."

Mavis put a hand on his arm and said, "Howard, let's go. We can come back some other time."

"Nonsense, my dear. If I may borrow your coat. . . ."

He lifted the white raincoat from her shoulders and put it on, ripping a seam. "There we go, mate!" he said briskly to the butler. "That should do it, *n'est-ce pas?*"

"I think *not*," the butler said, in a voice bleak enough to wither artichokes. "In any event, there is the matter of the necktie."

Cordle had been waiting for that. He whipped out his sweaty handkerchief and knotted it around his neck.

"Suiting you?" he leered, in an imitation of Peter Lorre as Mr. Moto which only he appreciated.

"Howard! Let's go!"

Cordle waited, smiling steadily at the butler, who was sweating for the first time in living memory.

"I'm afraid, sir, that that is not—"

"Not what?"

"Not precisely what was meant by coat and tie."

"Are you trying to tell me," Cordle said in a loud, unpleasant voice, "that you are an arbiter of men's clothing as well as a door opener?"

"Of course not! But this impromptu attire—"

"What has 'impromptu' got to do with it? Are people supposed to prepare three days in advance just to pass your inspection?"

"You are wearing a woman's water-proof and a soiled handkerchief," the butler stated stiffly. "I think there is no more to say."

He began to close the door. Cordle said, "You do that,

sweetheart, and I'll have you up for slander and defamation of character. Those are serious charges over here, buddy, and I've got witnesses."

Aside from Mavis, Cordle had collected a small, diffident but interested crowd.

"This is becoming entirely too ridiculous," the butler said, temporizing, the door half closed.

"You'll find a stretch at Wormwood Scrubs even more ridiculous." Cordle told him. "I intend to persecute— I mean prosecute."

"Howard!" cried Mavis.

He shook off her hand and fixed the butler with a piercing glance. He said, "I am Mexican, though perhaps my excellent grasp of English has deceived you. In my country, a man would cut his own throat before letting such an insult pass unavenged. A woman's coat, you say? *Hombre*, when I wear a coat, it becomes a *man's* coat. Or do you imply that I am a *maricón*, a—how do you say it?—homosexual?"

The crowd—becoming less modest—growled approval. Nobody except a lord loves a butler.

"I meant no such implication," the butler said weakly.

"Then is it a man's coat?"

"Just as you wish, sir."

"Unsatisfactory! The innuendo still exists. I go now to find an officer of the law."

"Wait, let's not be hasty," the butler said. His face was bloodless and his hands were shaking. "Your coat is a man's coat, sir."

"And what about my necktie?"

The butler made a final attempt at stopping Zapata and his blood-crazed peons.

"Well, sir, a handkerchief is demonstrably—"

"What I wear around my neck," Cordle said coldly, "becomes what it is intended to be. If I wore a piece of figured silk around my throat, would you call it ladies' underwear? Linen is a suitable material for a tie, *verdad?* Function defines terminology, don't you agree? If I ride to work on a cow, no one says that I am mounted on a steak. Or do you detect a flaw in my argument?"

"I'm afraid that I don't fully understand it. . . ."

"Then how can you presume to stand in judgment over it?"

The crowd, which had been growing restless, now murmured approval.

"Sir," cried the wretched butler. "I beg of you. . . ."

"*Otherwise*," Cordle said with satisfaction, "I have a coat, a necktie and an invitation. Perhaps you would be good enough to show us the Byzantine miniatures?"

The butler opened wide the door to Pancho Villa and his tattered hordes. The last bastion of civilization had been captured in less than an hour. Wolves howled along the banks of the Thames, Morelos' barefoot army stabled its horses in the British Museum, and Europe's long night had begun.

Cordle and Mavis viewed the collection in silence. They didn't exchange a word until they were alone and strolling through Regent's Park.

"Look, Mavis," Cordle began.

"No, you look," she said. "You were horrible! You were unbelievable! You were—I can't find a word rotten enough for what you were! I never dreamed that you were one of those sadistic bastards who get their kicks out of humiliating people!"

"But, Mavis, you heard what he said to me, you heard the way—"

"He was a stupid, bigoted old man," Mavis said. "I thought you were not."

"But he said—"

"It doesn't matter. The fact is, you were enjoying yourself!"

"Well, yes, maybe you're right," Cordle said. "Look, I can explain."

"Not to me, you can't. Ever. Please stay away from me, Howard. Permanently. I mean that."

The future mother of his two children began to walk away, out of his life. Cordle hurried after her.

"Mavis."

"I'll call a cop, Howard, so help me, I will! Just leave me alone!"

"Mavis, I love you!"

She must have heard him, but she kept on walking. She was a sweet and beautiful girl and definitely, unchangeably, an onion.

Cordle was never able to explain to Mavis about The Stew and about the necessity for experiencing behavior before condemning it. Moments of mystical illumination are seldom explicable. He *was* able to make her believe that he had undergone a brief psychotic episode, unique and unprecedented and—with her—never to be repeated.

They are married now, have one girl and one boy, live in a split-level house in Plainfield, New Jersey, and are quite content. Cordle is visibly pushed around by Fuller Brush men, fund solicitors, headwaiters and other imposing figures of authority. But there is a difference.

Cordle makes a point of taking regularly scheduled, solitary vacations. Last year, he made a small name for himself in Honolulu. This year, he is going to Buenos Aires.

In the 1980s, David J. Schow was the leading exponent
of splatterpunk, a hardboiled style of horror fiction
memorable for its graphic rendering of brutal contem-
porary horrors. His story collections Lost Angels, Seeing
Red *and* Black Leather Required *contain most of his*
exceptional short fiction, including the World Fantasy
Award-winning "Red Light." *He has written a number*
of pseudonymous novels, and under his own name The
Kill Riff *and* The Shaft. *An expert on film and television,*
he co-authored The Outer Limits: The Official Com-
panion, *and wrote the screenplays for* The Texas Chain-
saw Massacre III: Leatherface *and* The Crow.

Night Bloomer

David J. Schow

Steven Keller hated all the bitches at Calex.

When not weathering their stupidity as marginally
attractive cogs in Calex's corporate high-rise, he resented
the living foldout girls flaunting it in the commercials
for Calex Petroleum products that clogged up prime time
television. He had pulled far too few consummated dates
out of the female staff on the twenty-second floor to
suit him; sometimes he went more than a week without
getting laid, and that fouled his optimum performance
workwise. At home he was perpetually short on clean
socks. Most of his dress shirts did too much duty, and
had gained skid-tracks of grime on the inner collars.

This was not Steven Keller's idea of the joys of
upwardly mobile middle management.

That fat old bastard Bigelow had elevatored down this afternoon just to ramrod him. Business as usual. The cost estimates that had sputtered from Steve's printer had displeased Bigelow. That was the word the old lardball had used—*displeased*. As though he was not one vice president among many, but a demigod, an Academy Award on the hoof, fairytale king who demanded *per diem* groveling in exchange for meager boons.

Displeased. Steve had watched his manila folder slap the desktop and skid to a stop between his elbows. Before he could lift it or even react, Bigelow had wheeled his toad bulk a full one-eighty and repaired to his eyrie on the thirtieth floor. Steve's own office was illusory. A work area partitioned off from twenty others exactly like it by dividers covered in tasteful brown fabric. His MA in Business Administration hung on a wall that was not a wall, but a reminder that he was just one more rat dressed for success inside the Calex Skinner Box. *Displeased* meant his Thursday was history. The nine-to-five running lights on the twenty-second floor were dark now, and because of the change in illumination levels Steve could get a different perspective on his slanted reflection in the screen of his word processor. He laboriously reworked the quote sheets on his own time. He looked, he thought, ghostly and haggard. Used.

He punched a key and the revised lists rolled up. Bitches. Bastards. You could say those words on TV nowadays and nobody blinked. Their potency as invective had been bled away by time, and time scared the shit out of Steve. At thirty-five his time was running out. He had passed the point in his life where failure could be easily amortized.

He had spent his life living the introduction to his life. So far it had been all setup and no payoff. It had been a search that at times grew frantic; a dull joke with a foregone punchline. As he watched the printer razz and burp and spit up the new tabulated columnar lists—

pleasing, now—he reviewed his existence as a similar readout. As an index of significant events it ran depressingly thin.

Apart from his degree there had been two wives, one at twenty-one and another at twenty-nine. Both were a matter of record now. To Nikki, Steve had suggested what was now called a summary dissolution; the cut-rate legal beavers at Jacoby & Meyers had split them for about two hundred bucks plus tax. With Margaret, the roles had been reversed. She never suggested anything. She simply sought out more sophisticated counsel, and did for Steve's assets what Bigelow's nightly shots of Kaopectate did for the old fart's Sisyphian regularity.

Calex recruitment had been the goal of his entire college career. The dream had been first class; the reality, a budget tour, via steerage.

The face on the screen did not yet require glasses. He supposed that was something. Apart from beaning the class bully with a softball during Phys Ed, at twelve, he could recall no other little victories. He would always remember the sound the ball had made when it bounced off the bigger kid's anthropoid skull—*twock!* Like a rolling pin breaking a thick candle in half. Steve Kelowicz, school shrimp, did not suspect the full savor of this victory until a week later. The lunchtime poundings ceased. The berserker had shifted his tyranny to less reactive targets. No vengeance ever came.

Steve's growth was undistinguished, and while his objectives matured, his satisfactions remained childish. He sought those things expected of his station—corporate achievement, the accumulation of possessions, the company of the correct women. As soon as it became legally feasible he Americanized the mistake that had been his last name. A Kelowicz might be a fruit vendor. Keller was a name that begged imprintation on a door panel of plastic veneer, assuredly a proper name for a Calex executive.

As the printer shut down he realized that Bigelow

was just a grown-up version of the school bully—older, shrewder, more scarred, warier, like a veteran tomcat. Bigelow the Big just might need an unanticipated line drive to depose him from his nest on the thirtieth floor. A home run. It was a miracle that Steve could not force, though he felt entitled to a coup that would end Bigelow's taunts about his being an aging college punk.

Bigelow was just another threat, plumper, more streetwise. But still a bastard, and beatable. Steve's image on the video screen did not supply a very convincing affirmative, but at least he felt a bit better.

And what of all the bitches?

Once in Bigelow's extra-wide chair, Steve could order around the entire executive steno pool, and take his pick. His prime advantage over most of the denizens of the thirtieth floor was that he was a decade younger (and, he hoped, infinitely more potent) than the bulk of the veepee staff. The hierarchy inside the corporate headquarters of Calex was supremely feudal and caste-conscious. The peons working on the floors below you were more than literally beneath you. Steve's best sexual conquests so far had been career secretaries entrenched on his own level, women like Rachel Downey, captainess of the copy room, whom he had "dated" twice. He had discovered the hard way that Rachel the Red dyed her hair. Since their tryst had fizzled, he was finding it difficult to get Xerox work sent back to him on time . . . so thanks to her, he was yet again in the frypan with Bigelow through calculated, long-distance sabotage.

He shut down his machines and piled his work into his briefcase, the leather job with the blunt corners. On his way to the elevators he reviewed his mental checklist of local watering holes for "suits" like himself and came up with a few why-nots. Century City, alive with nightlight, blazed in through the windows of the twenty-second floor and tried to diminish him. Just as his finger touched the heat-sensitive button, he noticed the car was crawling downward on its own, and he counted along with the orange digits: 28, 27, 26 . . .

The brushed steel doors parted. Bigelow was not inside, lurking in ambush, as he had feared. The only passenger at this time of night was a woman.

He would remember her amber pendant until the moment of his death.

"You look like a man carrying a burden," she said, in the kind of throaty voice that might have conferred an amusing secret to a lover.

"Oh yeah," he said mechanically, stepping in. Then his eyes tarried.

She was barely inside of a clinging, silky-red dress featuring a pattern of black oval dots and scalloped, shortie sleeves. The front of the dress divided neatly over her breasts—not Body Shop silicone nightmares, but a warm swell that was the real, proportionate item. Broad, shiny black belt—real leather—black hose, black heels, large clunky bracelet in enameled ebony, matching the pendulant onyx drop earrings. The face between those earrings was cheeky and feline, with elliptical sea-green eyes, a sharp, patrician nose, and neat small teeth. Her weight was on one leg, the other inclined to an unconscious model's pose. Her hands held before her a large, flat-brimmed sunhat of woven black fibers and a petite clutch-brief of papers. Her hair was unbound, strong coffee black-brown, and lots of it. Her expression, which at first had been neutral, now seemed one of avid but cautious curiosity; she examined him with a quizzical, cocked-head attitude.

The doors guillotined shut behind Steve with slow, inexorable Nazi efficiency. *Thunk.*

"I'm working late again," he said with a shrug, and was suddenly astounded at the bilge his mouth was capable of spewing. He checked her out again, and regretted not spiffing up before quitting the twenty-second floor.

"I'm overtime on behalf of the great god Bigelow."
Her pendant, a rough-cut chunk of translucent yellow
stone, dallied on a foxtail chain of gold near the hollow
of her throat.

The orange floor digits winked from twenty-two to
twenty-one and Steve's gonads finally kicked into brain
override. *She spoke first*, the mechanism said. *You've got
twenty floors to fast-talk this muffin into having a
martini with you*. Chat footholds were already abundant—Bigelow, Calex, their mutual late oil-burning—but
he faltered in response, as though the sheer pheromone
outflow from this woman was stupefying him. "Uh,
Bigelow?" *Wake up, you moron!* Nineteen lit up as one
more floor of time ran out.

"Mm. You look like another of his bond-slaves." Her
eyes appraised him. "Nice to find a kindred spirit."

"Well, you know, we ought to be thankful that he
takes the burden of credit off our lowly shoulders."

Her melodic laugh was as pleasing as her voice.
She asked him his position, and he told her; she
fingered her pendant (it caught even the soft light in
the elevator, like a diamond sucking up the colors
of the spectrum) and asked point-blank why he did
not have Bigelow's job. He said something offhanded
and ironic in response, and instantly felt self-
consciously glib. She saved him again by speaking before he had time to think his unthinking words into
a real *gaffe*.

"You'd fit one of those thirtieth-floor suites just fine.
And I'd much prefer working under someone from my
own generation."

His brain was afloat with possibilities. "There aren't
many clean ways to erase a vice president." At once he
began to fear that this woman, who seemed all too eager
to be picked up, might be some sort of planted Bigelow
spy.

"Oh, I've got a way," she smiled. "What I've always
needed is a man willing to do it."

By now, there was no man in recorded history more willing to do it than Steven Keller.

Not too much later, when they were sweating and short of breath, Vivia told him about the seed.

"I can't see it." He disentangled himself from her hair.

"Just shy of the center." She broke the chain from around her neck and handed him the pendant. "Look at it while I go thrash out the ultimate martini, hm?" With that, she was up and striding across his bedroom, hips switching liquidly. Naked she was smooth of flank, balletically graceful; Steve's notice did not turn to the pendant until she was out of sight.

When he held it to the candle flame a tiny silhouette appeared, a dark bead trapped fast in the honey-colored amber. It was boring.

Vivia placed the martini shaker, frosty with condensation, on the nightstand within easy reach. The vermouth had given the ice the barest kiss; the drink was cold, and as she had promised, flawless, as perfect as her body was sleek, as her eyes were hypnotic.

Now Steve's brain was really rocking and rolling, and an imp voice said Vivia, Vivia *Keller*, not too shabby . . . but before he could polish off his drink she was tugging him down, wrapping her thoroughbred legs around him, engulfing him in her cascade of hair. Sometime before dawn she touched the empty shaker, and asked if he wanted more.

Not knowing what she was talking about, Steve nodded.

It seemed poetic that the perfect martini yielded what could only be called the perfect hangover—murderous, battering, as perfect as bamboo shoots or electroshock. The blatting of Steve's alarm did not penetrate his cognizance until 8:45, and the first thing he heard on the clock-radio was an advertisement for a perfume called Objet D'Art. Which, he knew, was manufactured by Michelle Dante Cosmetics, which had been co-opted by Calex Corporation in 1976. It was as though Calex itself had come home to invade his bedroom and whack him on the head with the guilt stick.

The revised cost estimate sheets waited in his briefcase while he attempted to shower, dress and drive to work with only five minutes available for each task. He finger-combed his hair in the blurry reflection afforded by the elevator doors and straightened his tie by touch, praying that the shitty coffee on the twenty-second floor would at least deaden his breath to neutral. His eyes itched. In his haste he had climbed into his trousers without underwear, and now felt vulnerably askew belowdecks. The trip up seemed unjustly quick in comparison to the deliciously slow descent he'd taken in the same car a scant thirteen hours previously. When the elevator disgorged him, he won few pitying looks. From the copy room, Rachel Downey saw him vanish into the brown-fabricked maze . . . and ignored him.

He found Bigelow seated on his desk, waiting. The bounceback of the ceiling fluorescents from the older man's harsh gold wire-rims gifted Steve with an instant migraine. No human pupils were to be seen behind those thick, blackhole lenses, merely multiple white rectangles of pain-giving light.

"It's nine fifteen and twenty seconds, Keller, did you know that? Your eyes are stubbornly red." Bigelow's voice was sepulchral and resonant, the bellows-basso of a vast, fat man.

Steve was weary beyond even snideness "Yes sir. I've brought the revised estimates you asked for on the—"

Upon seeing the proffered sheaf of pages, Bigelow's expression rivalled that of a man whose pet cat has proudly sauntered through the kitchen door with half an eviscerated snake in its jaws. He dropped the sheets into Steve's own roundfile. They fluttered helplessly on the way down. "When you did not deliver these figures to my desk at nine o'clock this morning, I had young

Cavanaugh revise them. Good morning, Keller." He slid off the desk, leaving a large buffed area, and trundled out without a backward glance.

Drained and hopeless, Steve just stood there. Cavanaugh did not drink. Cavanaugh was married. Cavanaugh had just neatly eroded another inch off Steve's toehold on the thirtieth floor. Should Bigelow die right this moment, he thought he might lock onto the vice presidency through simple corporate momentum . . . but not if Cavanaugh kept punching away, infiltrating his projects.

Vivia had been long gone by the time he opened his eyes, leaving neither last name nor current phone number. He stayed in a zombiatic funk through lunchtime, not eating, but his depression eased when he thought of accessing the Calex Building's personnel listings through one of the computer terminals on the twenty-second floor. With his eighth mug of silty company coffee in hand, he waded through the rollups searching for the first initial **V**.

Vinces and Valeries formed an entire platoon by themselves, with Victors, Vickies and Veras as the runners-up. Two Vondas, one Vianne, and no Vivia by the time he reached the last-name letter **M**.

God, what if her last name was Zamperini?

He'd risked all the computer time he dared, and decided to do **M** through **Z** on Monday, even though he'd hoped for a weekend tryst. As it turned out, Bigelow was not finished with him for this Friday, either.

No bulk blocked his doorway; this time Steve got his scorching over the phone: "It has just come to my attention, Keller, that you've been frittering valuable computer time in the pursuit of non-Calex—"

He squeezed his eyes shut as slivers of pain aligned themselves along his temples. Knowing full well that Rachel and some of the other bitches on the twenty-second floor were most likely eavesdropping, he held the receiver to his ear and went through the dance, not really giving a damn as Bigelow tiraded onward in his fat-cat drone, the sound of the axle of corporate doom pounding a few more dents into his sinecure at Calex. It had probably been a decade or more since the fat old bastard had last screwed his starched and reedy wife, and maybe sexual frustration was what gave Bigelow the stamina, at his age and with his rotten, cholesterol-gummed clock of a heart, to jump on Steve's head with both heels every time he made the slightest little . . .

Yes sir, he said robotically. *No sir. Yes sir.* And as with the best forms of torture, there at least came a hiatus.

The elevator doors slid back, revealing an empty car. Once again the twenty-second floor was mostly dark, and Steve stepped in, alone. Going down.

He felt like he was drowning.

"Your door was open."

His heart began to jitterbug with an accelerated thudding so sudden and intense he momentarily feared an internal fuckup. Vivia waited on his sofa, smothered inside of his brown plush bathrobe. The martini shaker waited on the glass-topped coffee table. It was very likely be had forgotten to lock his door while dashing out that morning; he locked it now, and as he did she stood up to greet him. The robe stayed on the couch.

Deep into the night, she mentioned the seed again, and Bigelow, and a solution to Steve's problem that sounded quite insane.

"It's simple, really, so it doesn't matter if what I say is crazy." She spoke past him, stroking his hair. "Just consider it a gesture. A contract, like marriage. If you'll do this tiny thing for me, I'm all yours. Desperate men have done crazier things for less return. You're shrewd, Steve—indulge me. I promise you it'll be worth it."

She demonstrated how. If he was not convinced, he was certainly intrigued.

Logy, he said, "So this is what you want me for," half-jokingly. Out of habit he'd been waiting for the catch

to the whole deal; the condition she'd put to him that
would render her down to the low rank of all the other
Calex women he'd known, the words that would make
her cease to be something special. Yes?

What came instead was a shiver of horror that he
might never become more special than she deemed him
at this moment, that *he* might never move up-market,
as they said in jolly old Great B. That fancy triggered
another, spurred by his notion that Vivia was of foreign
origin, (thus her trace accent, thus her exotic manner)—
not of Calex, not of L.A., but somewhere else. Somewhere else was where he needed to go; did he dare risk
losing her, after she'd explained her plan bluntly, just
because that plan didn't conform to linear corporate
logic? *This is what you must do to have me*, she had
said. No tricks.

That was when he decided to do what she asked, and
not fake it. This woman would know if her rules were
fudged.

He rose to begin dressing. When she rose on one
elbow in the bed to watch, and told him how she needed
him, he nodded, his blood hot and racing. He left to
perform his task, his gesture, before the sun could
announce Saturday morning.

Bigelow lived in a fashionably appointed ranch house
in Brentwood, on the far side of UCLA. The drive took
time even though traffic was sparse—cabbies, police,
battleship-sized garbage trucks, and the occasional rene-
gade night person.

Breaking Vivia's amber had proven simple; he'd used
a cocktail hammer, and the pendant scattered apart into
crushed-ice chips of see-through gold. The seed was tiny,
no larger than a watermelon pit, flat and glossy like a
legless bug. It was in his pants pocket, inside a plastic
box that had once held a mineral tie-tack.

Also in the pocket was his Swiss Army knife, and the
full moon was reflected in the car's windshield—two

more of Vivia's odd conditions fulfilled. It had to be done by the full moon, she'd said, so that they might both reap by the next full moon. Steve purposefully put her other instructions on hold while he drove; he wanted nothing to make him feel foolish enough to turn back. He thought of Vivia instead, of gaining her strange trust, of having her body for a long time. Longer than any of the bitches, since she could be many women for him—none of whom mucked about with excuses or mood-killing delays in the name of messy human givens like menstrual periods or birth control. She was admirably void of what to him was standard-issue female bellyaching. Instead she was very no-nonsense, a delicious riddle, perhaps beguiling. He judged her perfect for his needs, and wasted no time thinking of himself as selfish, or, as Rachel the Red had called him, a usurer. Rachel read too goddamned many gothic romances.

Bigelow's home occupied the terminus of a paved and winding drive that isolated it from the main road. Steve caught a flicker of a low-wattage all-nighter bulb glowing in a front kitchen window as he cruised the area. He parked around a corner a block and a half away and began his stealthy approach, thankful that the drive was not graveled.

The fat old bastard had once made bragging mention of his bedroom's western exposure, and Steve soon located the window above a precisely clipped hedge of rosebushes.

"You mustn't dig a hole," she had insisted. "You must uproot a *living plant*, and place the seed in the hole that results from the death of that plant." Luckily for Vivia's instructions, the Bigelow grounds had abundant flora.

He threaded into the tangle of sharp leaves and spiked branches and hefted gently, fighting not to stir up a commotion. A thorn sank into the palm of his hand and he grimaced, but the pain made the contest with the bush personal. For making him bleed, it would die.

He thought of Neanderthal men ripping each other's entrails out, of grappling with Bigelow and wrapping his fingers around his fat, wheezy windpipe. The bush rattled a bit but was no match for him. When it came up, clods of deep-brown dirt hung from its freed roots.

There was no reaction or notice from within the house. Of course, if Bigelow suspected a prowler he would take no direct action—for that function there was a little steel sign at the head of the driveway. Every home in Brentwood had one, and Bigelow's read CONROY SECURITY SYSTEMS / ARMED RESPONSE. The threat implied by that little hexagonal sign compelled Steve to finish up quickly.

There was no need for the pocket-knife, since his palm was already slathered with fresh blood. He dabbed the black seed; "consecrating it" was the term Vivia had used. Somewhere in the darkness right in front of him, beyond the window, the impotent Bigelow snored on, hoglike, lying in state next to his frigid cow of a wife. Maybe they lolled in separate beds, genuflecting to the grand old era of Beaver Cleaver, when sex equalled pornography, when nice girls didn't. Steve grinned. Then he groped his way back to the gout in the earth and tamped dirt over the seed with his fingers.

It was in. As Vivia had wanted.

He lugged the rousted bush out with him so that it might not be discovered and replanted by whatever minority Bigelow engaged to manicure his grounds. Walking heel-to-toe in burglar doubletime, palm stinging and wet, Steve felt absurdly victorious, as though he'd just bounced a homer off Bigelow's noggin instead of merely vandalizing a hedge. He had come through for Vivia, and thus gained a kind of control over her, too. In a single day he had galloped the gamut of rough emotions. By the time dawn began to tint the sky, he felt renewed—exhausted yet charged, back in the running, a success in the making, confirmed executive fodder. Definitely up-market.

He ditched the murdered rosebush in a supermarket trash dumpster on his way home.

According to the adage that defines *sanity* as the first twenty minutes following orgasm, what Casey (Steve's most recent non-Calex blonde) had told him not so long ago was sane, reasoned.

"I don't think you *like* women very much. Present company excluded, of course."

"Of course." He stroked her thigh, his lungs burning with immediate umbrage at her remark. Who in hell was this vacant twinkie to pass judgement? They had swapped climax for climax, shared a smoke, and now she was gearing up to pry into his psyche. It always began around the fourth fuck or so, these sloppy digressions into his private feelings. He'd given her a good technical orgasm and this was how she responded. They were past the stage where he could joke off such an accusation, as more tentatively acquainted people can. His fingers traced upward knowingly, commencing an automatic process guaranteed to shut her up.

Further, it was Casey's opinion that some woman had done vast damage to Steve in the past. That he had been avenging that hurt on every woman he'd touched since, trying to distill away the poison inside him. That things could change at last, now that she had arrived on the scene.

In that moment Steve's judgement on Casey banged down like a slamming cell door. Things did *change*, and quickly. He brought the prying bitch off hard, with some pain. While she was still moist he slammed into her as though driving nails. The next morning he subtracted her from his Rolodex, hoping she was sore for a long time.

That was lost in the past now.

Now, Steve lay next to Vivia, recalling Casey's words and wondering if they might have been true . . . and whether Vivia might not be the turnaround he didn't even know he had been seeking for most of his adult life.

The past four weeks had been a whirlwind of input for him. When not assimilating and processing the swelling workload dumping downward from Bigelow's office, he was wrapped up in Vivia, who had taken a fervently singleminded interest in his sexual wellbeing. Bigelow had called in sick in the middle of the first week, and Steve had marveled frankly and quietly. The fat old bastard finally lumbered into the office late on Thursday, and botched everything he touched. By Friday—exactly one week after Steve had been carpet-called for using the computer on the sly—Bigelow had mazed his way back to Steve's cubicle in person again . . . but this time, it had been to thank him.

Oh, how he had savored that moment!

"You've performed admirably, Keller," he'd croaked, red-faced and dappled with fever-sweat. "You've risen to the occasion and saved my calloused old butt; I was beginning to think you didn't have that kind of dedication. I appreciate all your help, and the extra hours you've put in during this . . . uh, time." Steve had said *yes sir* at the appropriate lulls in the rally-round-the company spiel, invoking his new prerogative as victor not to rub Bigelow's veiny nose in the events of the past.

When the old man finished, he had shuffled out, slump-shouldered. He didn't make another appearance in the office until the following Wednesday.

That was when the thought of just what might be growing, unobtrusively, amid the rosebushes in Brentwood, began to gnaw at Steve.

"Why my blood, anyway?" he asked Vivia. "Why not his? I mean, he's the object—the victim, right?"

Whenever he brought up the subject of the seed, she seemed to answer by rote. "Whose blood is used for the consecration isn't important. It's who the plant grows nearest to. It leaches away the life essence, thrives on it. As it grows larger, it needs more. Those asleep near it are especially susceptible. It reaches maturity in one month, from one full moon to the next." She draped on of her fine white legs over his. "Then it dies."

"The blood is just to prime the pump? Get it started?"

"Mm." Her hands were upon him. Getting him started.

"Just what is it you've got against Bigelow? You know, I tried to find your company employee index number on the computer and came up with zilch." She had long since given him a last name, but that had not dissipated the mystery.

"What is it *you* have against him?" she countered, with a trace of irritation. "And what does it matter? You're not the only person privileged to hate him for the things he's done!"

He thought she was sidestepping; then he caught on. Bigelow's blue-rinsed wife lent perspective to the supposition of a squirt of randiness somewhere in the boss's recent past. Promises, perhaps, traded for a bit of extra-marital hoop-de-doo with a Calex functionary who had just happened to be Vivia. Unfulfilled promises, naturally—the office rule was that verbal contracts weren't worth the paper they weren't written on. So Vivia had lain back and devised her retaliation. For Steve to bring this matter up in bed, he now saw, was deeply counterproductive.

She did not let him pursue it further, at any rate. "It'll be done soon now, darling, don't worry it." She poured them both another of her stinging-cold, perfect martinis. "And we'll both get what we want."

He was sure getting what *he* wanted. Vivia seemed satisfied, too. He had long since given her a door key; he usually found her awaiting his pleasure, and he liked that.

"Give me what I want," he said, and she rolled onto him. He thought he was happy.

During the final week, Bigelow did not appear in the

Calex Building at all. The scuttlebutt was that he'd suffered a minor stroke.

"I took a stack of escalation briefs out to his house, y'know?" It was Cavanaugh, Steve's former competitor, spreading the news. "Steve, he looked like *hell*; I mean, pallid, trembling. His eyes were yellow and bloodshot, the works. I was afraid to breathe air in the same room with him, y'know? It's like he got the plague or something!"

Steve nodded, appearing interested. He was learning the executive trait of letting subordinates do most of the talking. With open hands of sympathy he said, "Well, in the old man's absence I'm stuck with twice the work, and it's time I got back into it."

Cavanaugh was dismissed. That was something else new, and Steve was getting better at it. It made him feel peachy.

While he had made no effort to see what had blossomed at Bigelow's, his desire to know had germinated and grown at a healthy pace. Vivia had said the plant would die with the coming of the next full moon, its task complete. It all sounded like a shovelful of occult hoodoo, as vague as a syndicated horoscope. A thriving plant shouldn't keel over due to a timetable, he thought, horticultural genius that he was. Since the technique appeared to be working and producing results, simple Calex procedure dictated no need to scrutinize the hows and whys. You didn't have to know how a television worked to enjoy it; how Object D'Art functioned, to appreciate its scent on women.

Time was running short. Time for Bigelow, time to see what had sprung from the black seed.

"You don't really need to see it," Vivia had argued. "That would be . . . superficial."

Again he nodded. Her words were reassuring and correct. Once she drowsed off, he went out driving in the wee hours one more time.

He duplicated his original route and found the Brentwood streets unchanged. A blue and white Conroy security car hissed past in the opposite lane. That was the last Steve saw of the local minions of armed response.

Two curious sights awaited him at the bedroom window. The first was Bigelow, tossing about in his bed, sheets askew. He was in the grip of some nightmare, or spasm. His flesh shone greenly under a ghostly-soft nightlight, by which Steve saw the bedstand, littered with medications. The old man's movements were enfeebled and retarded by fitful sleep; the thrashing of a suffocating fish.

Then there was the plant. Against the all-weather white of the ranch house's siding, it was quite visible.

It was confused among the rosebush branches, and resembled a squat tangle of blacksnakes, diverging wildly as though the shoots wanted nothing to do with each other. Like the chitinous hardness of the seed, the branches were armored in a kind of exoskeleton of deep, lacquered black. The small leaves that had sprouted at the ends of each branch were dead ebony, dull and waxy to the touch, with spade shapes and serrated edges. He leaned closer, to touch, and felt a papercut pain in the tip of his finger that caused him to jerk back his hand and bite his lip in the dark.

Kneeling, he unclipped a penlight from his pocket, oblivious to the risk of being spotted, and saw that the skin of the plant was inlaid with downy white fibers, like extremely fine hair. They were patterned directionally, in the manner of scales on a viper; to stroke them one way would be to feel a humid softness, while the opposite direction would fill the finger with barbs like slivers of glass. Steve tried to tweezer the tiny quill out with his teeth.

The black plant exuded no odor whatever, he noticed. He found that to be the most unsettling aspect of all, since all plants smelled like something, from the whore's perfume of night-blooming jasmine to the clean-laundry scent of carnations. This had all the olfactory presence of a bowl of plastic grapes.

He heard a strangled cough through the window panes, and saw Bigelow stir weakly in his bed. The moon was ninety percent full. Tomorrow night it would be perfect.

Watching his superior whittled down in this way, Steve realized that it wasn't necessary that the old man actually die. Ever since his conjecture about Bigelow's dalliance with Vivia, he'd begun to feel an inexplicable fraternal sympathy for the old goat. Would Steve care to come to such a finish, merely because he'd chased a bit of tail in his declining years? Vivia sure was enthusiastic enough about jumping *his* bones to get her revenge on Bigelow. And Steve's future with Calex seemed locked without the nastiness of a death to blot it . . . didn't it?

Was he starting to feel sorry for the fat old bastard?

Inside the house, Bigelow let out a congested moan, and the sound put ice into Steve's lungs.

Impulsively he gathered the black plant into two fists and hoisted it upward, hoping to tear loose the roots. The rosebushes rattled furiously, shifting about like pedestrians witnessing an ugly car crash, but the plant remained solidly anchored, unnaturally so. Yanking a mailbox out of a concrete sidewalk would have been easier. Steve's hand skinned upward along the glossy stalks and collected splinter quills all the way up. This time he did scream.

Bigelow stopped flailing. Now he was awake, and staring at the window.

Tears doubling his vision, blood dripping freely from his tightly clenched fists, Steve fled into the night.

Shortly after lunch on Friday, Cavanaugh wandered into Steve's office wearing a hangdog H.P. Lovecraft face, broadcasting woe. His eyebrows arched at the sight of Steve's bandaged hands, but the younger man was determined to maintain the proper, respectful air of gloom and tragedy.

"I got the phone call ten minutes ago," he said, nearly whispering. "I don't know if you've heard. But, uh—"

"Bigelow?" Steve was mostly guessing.

Cavanaugh closed his eyes and nodded. "Sometime last night. His wife said he saw a prowler. He was reaching for the phone when his heart—"

"Stopped." Steve folded his hands on the desk. The old man had probably hit the deck like a sledge-hammered steer.

Cavanaugh stood fast, fidgeting. "Um, Blakely will probably be asking you up to his office on Monday for a meeting . . . you know." Blakely was Bigelow's superior.

Heavy on the *was*, Steve thought as his line buzzed. He excused himself to speak with Blakely's busty girl Friday, who was calling from the thirtieth floor regarding the meeting that Cavanaugh had just mentioned. And, incidentally, was Mr. Keller possibly free for cocktails after work? Was today too soon? Her name was Connie, and of course he already had her extension. Polite laugh.

At the flick of the wrist, Cavanaugh faded into the background. That was the last Steve ever saw of him.

Waiting for him at home were Vivia, the martini shaker—perfect—and a toast to success.

It took both his hands to navigate the first glass to his mouth, since both were immobilized into semi-functional scoops by the bandages. The more he drank, the more efficient he became at zeroing in on his face, and to his chagrin the anesthetizing effect of the alcohol permitted some of the last night's bitterness to peek out, and beeline for Vivia.

"Here's to us, to us," he said mostly to his glass. He was on the sofa, and Vivia sat cross-legged, sunk into a leather recliner across from him. His shoes were cockeyed on the floor between them. "Methnks I've just hooked and crooked my merry way into a higher tax bracket, thank you very much to my . . . odd little concubine . . . and her odd little plant. Perhaps we should consider incorporating Corporeally speaking, that is." His sight-line flew to the bedroom door and back.

Vivia raised her glass to him. She was wearing an Oriental print thing far too skimpy and diaphanous to qualify as a robe.

"So now, as—ahem!—partners in non-crime," he said as she refilled their glasses, "you have to fill me in on the plant. Where the hell did you come across something like that? You don't buy that sort of thing down at the Vigaro plant shop. How come people aren't using them to . . . Christ, to bump off everybody?"

She finished off her drink before he was halfway through his, and stretched languorously, purring. "This tastes like pure nectar," she said.

"Stick to the subject, wench."

She cocked her head in the peculiar way he'd become so familiar with, and mulled her story over before saying, "I had the only seed." That was it.

He remembered the amber, and nodded. So far, so logical. "Where'd you get it?"

"I've had it quite a long time. Since birth, in fact." She ran her tongue around the rim of her glass, then recharged it half from the shaker.

"An heirloom?"

"Mm."

She was preparing to lead him off to the track again; and he fully intended to bed her, but not before he could hurdle her coy non-replies and clear his conscience. "Tell me what happened between you and Bigelow." Instinct had told him to shift gears, and he expected a harsh look.

"I've never really seen the man."

The office coffee was starting to have an unlovely reaction to the quickly gulped booze, and he burped quietly. "Wait a minute." He waved his free hand to make her go back and explain. The surrender-flag whiteness of the bandages hurt his eyes in the room's dim light. "You two had some kind of . . . assignation; or something. You wanted vengeance on him."

"Hm." The corners of her generous mouth twitched upward, then dropped back to neutral, as though she was still learning how to make a smile. "In point of fact, Steven, I never said I wanted vengeance on anything. Perhaps you thought it."

Now this definitely registered sourly. For a crazed, out-of-sync moment he thought she was going to add, *no, I wanted vengeance on YOU!* like some daffy twist in a 1940s murder mystery. But she just sat there, hugging her knees to her chin, distracting him with her body. Waiting.

"Oh, I get it—you just help a total stranger, out of the blue, to do in his boss, whom you've never met, with the last special black plant seed in the entire universe." The sarcasm was back in his tone.

"I was interested in you, Steven. No other."

"Why?" *Urrrrp*, again, stronger this time.

"Except for one thing you've been perfect for me. You were . . . what is the word? Fertile. You were ripe."

"Where'd I slip up?" Now his head was throbbing, and he feared he might have to interrupt his fact-finding sortie by sicking up on the shag carpeting.

She gave him her quizzical little shrug. "You were supposed to go uproot the plant tonight, you sneak. During the full moon. Not last night, though I don't suppose it'll matter." She rose; her legs flashed in and out of the wispy garment as she approached. "Let me give you a refill. This is a celebration, you know, and I'm ahead of you."

"Ugh, no—wait," he muttered, his brains sloshing around in his skull-pan like dirty dishwater. "No more for me." He put out one of his mitts to arrest the progress of the shaker toward the glass and blundered it out of Vivia's grasp. He was reminded of the time he had tried to keep a coffeeshop waitress from freshening

up his cup by putting his hand over the cup to indicate
no more . . . and gotten his fingers scalded.

The shaker bounced on the rug without breaking. Its
lid rolled away and ice cubes tumbled out, clicking like
rolling dice. Mingled with the ice were several limp, wet,
dead-black leaves. Gin droplets glistened on them. They
were spade-shaped with serrated edges.

Steve gaped at them numbly. "Oh my god . . ."
Poisoned! Unable to grab, he swung at Vivia, who easily
danced out of range. He gasped, his voice dropping an
octave into huskiness as he felt a shot of pain in his
diaphragm. He understood that his body needed to
vomit and expel the toxin.

But he wanted to get Vivia first.

He launched himself off the sofa and succeeded only
in falling across the coffee table, cleaning it off and
landing in a drunken sprawl on non-responsive man-
nequin limbs. The feeling in his fingers and toes was
gone.

"Oh, Steven, not poison," he heard her say. "What
a silly thing to think, darling. I wouldn't do that. I need
you. Isn't that what you always wanted—a woman who
truly needed you? I mean *truly*? Not in all the petty
ways you so despise?"

His tongue went dead. His throat fought to contract
and seal off his airway. If he could force himself to throw
up, he might suffocate . . . or save his life. He was
incapable of snaring Vivia now, but he sure as hell could
use two fingers to chock down his tongue. He saw the
expression on her face as he did it.

She watched intently, almost lovingly, with that
unusual cocked-head attitude he remembered from their
first meeting in the elevator. It reminded him of a cocker
spaniel hearing a high-frequency whistle, or a hungry
insect inspecting food with its antennae. It was an
attitude characteristic of another species.

He heaved mightily. Nothing came up but bubbly
saliva.

A tiny, hard object shot up from gullet to click against the obverse of his front teeth. Its ejection eased his trachea open. While he spit and sucked wind, Vivia stepped eagerly forward with a cry of excitement identical to the sounds she had made in bed with him.

She picked up the wet black seed and held it between her thumb and forefinger. She tried to gain his attention while he retched. "This is the one I'll keep always, darling. You may not be aware, but amber takes *ages* to solidify properly."

He struggled to speak, to ask irrational questions, but could only continue what had begun. Another of the wicked little seeds chucked out with enough force to make a painful dent in the roof of his mouth. It bounced off his dry tongue and escaped. He did not feel it hit. It was chased by fifteen more . . . which were pushed forward and out by a torrent of several hundred.

The last thing Steve did was contract in a fetal ball, hugging his rippling stomach. His breath was totally dammed by the floodtide of beaded black shapes that had clogged up his system and now sought the quickest way out.

"I loved you, Steven, and needed you more than anyone ever has. How many people get that in their lifetimes?"

Then he could hear nothing beyond the rainstorm patter of the seeds, gushing forth by the thousands as his body caved in and evacuated everything, a full moon's worth. In the end, he was potent beyond his most grotesque sexual aspirations.

Vivia held the first seed of the harvest, and watched. The sight fulfilled her as a female.

A protégé of H.P. Lovercraft, Donald Wandrei (1908–1987) began publishing short fiction in Weird Tales *in 1927 and earned plaudits for his poetic evocations of supernatural horrors. His "Sonnets for the Midnight Hours" are among the masterpieces of weird poetry in the twentieth century and were eventually collected into* Poems for Midnight. *He contributed regularly to the detective pulps and to science fiction magazines such as* Astounding Stories, *where his novella "Colossus" was hailed as a landmark of early science fiction. His complete tales of fantasy and science fiction have been collected in* Colossus *and* Don't Dream. *He also co-founded Arkham House, the publishing company that sparked the fantasy and science fiction specialty press revolution.*

Strange Harvest

Donald Wandrei

The sun had scarcely risen when Al Meiers shoved himself away from the breakfast table and lumbered to his feet. A big, powerful man even for the Shawtuck County region of husky farmers, he had a face like tanned leather and arms whose hair lay swart over muscles like cables. He was all bone and solid flesh. Though past fifty, he strode with the ease of youth.

"That was a good breakfast, maw," he drawled to his almost spherical wife. She smiled out of eyes that had smiled through drought, storm, plague of locusts, and depression.

"Get along with you. Them apples'll never get picked with you aloafin' around here all day."

"Them apples'll be down by night. Hank!" he roared. The harvest hand, dripping of suds and rainwater on the doorstep, hastily smeared his face with a towel.

"There ought to be over two hundred bushel," said Al.

"Maybe more." Hank, a wiry drifter, slouched beside Al as they passed the chicken-coops. Roosters crowed, hens squawked out of their way, and the spring chickens beeped in alarm. Al made a splendid figure even in his dirty overalls, a bronzed giant of the soil.

They passed the pig-sty where sows and porkers squealed over a sour-smelling trough. The sun stood just above the horizon, and the warm air held that peculiar scent of late summer—smell of cattle and manure, of clover, hay, and wheat, of baked earth and ripening vegetation.

A wagon loaded with empty bushel baskets stood by the barn. Al hitched the horses and took the reins. The team of Belgian Grays ambled down a dirt road.

"It's been a good year for crops," said Al. He jammed tobacco in an old corncob pipe and lighted it without loosening the reins.

"Yeah. Only there's something funny about 'em this year."

"Yeah. They're bigger. Biggest ever."

Hank spat out a hunk of plug. "That ain't all. They kind of shake even if there ain't no wind. As I was sayin' yesterday, I got to feelin' pretty queer when the tomato patch kind of shook when I was hoen' it."

"Giddyap!" Al bellowed. The team clattered faster. He inhaled and blew out a cloud of fragrant smoke. "Uh-huh. I don't know what's got into things. Best weather and best crops we ever had but—something's wrong. Last fall the crops started growin' again about harvest-time. The damnedest thing. It wasn't till October we got all the spuds in and the corn-crib full."

Hank looked uneasy. "I don't like it. There been times when I, well, I just didn't feel right."

"Yeah?"

Hank lapsed into moody silence.

"Yeah?" Al prodded.

"There wasn't any wind yesterday but I swear the north clover patch flattened out when I started to mow."

"Yeah? You been seen' things." Al was noncommittal. Hank kept silent.

"I never saw corn grow like this year," said Al after awhile. The horses clopped along. "Ten foot high if it's an inch. Fred Altmiller was sayin' the other day that he figured on gettin' a hundred fifty bushel to the acre. Nary an ear less'n a foot long."

Hank moped. "Last time I went through your corn was the damnedest racket you ever heard. You'd of thought a storm come up. There wasn't a cloud nowhere. Wasn't any wind."

"Lay off the corn likker," Al jibed.

"Wasn't corn likker," Hank protested. "It's the crops are queer. I'd of bet there was somebody around when I weeded the melons last week. Sounded like voices."

"What did?"

"Why, just everything. Whispers, like the corn was talkin'."

Al snorted. "You're headed for the bug-house. I been farmin' here for thirty years an' I never hear tell of such a story."

It's so! It's been goin' on all summer!"

The wagon bumped through fields of ripe wheat and oats, lurched around an immense boulder, and rattled up a hill where the cows munched at grass strewn between.

Al agreed with Hank but he wouldn't admit it. The first principle of stolid people is to deny the existence of what can not be explained and does not harmonize with the run of experience. Ever since the phenomenal post-season growth of vegetables and fruit last fall, he

had been wondering. The spring planting, the perfect
weather, bumper crops, truly miraculous yields—these
blessings were offset by certain evidence that had made
him increasingly uneasy. There was the matter of waving
grass on still days. He hadn't yet gotten over the way
the trees hummed one hot afternoon when he was
spraying the apple and cherry orchards.

"Anyway, it's been a good year," he repeated. "Them
apples are prize winners. The trees are bustin' with 'em."

The wagon bumped across the hill-top and the horses
plodded down. "Just look at 'em, just look—well—uhh,"
his voice petered out.

Yesterday an orchard of Jonathans had occupied this
acre between two small hills.

Yesterday.

Today there was only torn soil and furrows stretching
toward the opposite hill.

Al gaped and his face turned a mottled red. Hank's
eyes popped. He opened his mouth and closed it. He
stared as if at a ghost. He ran a finger around his neck.
The sun slanted higher. The field lay bright and newly
ploughed. But there were no apple trees.

Al blasted the morning air with a howl. "Some dirty
thief has swiped my apples!" he yelled.

Hank looked dazed. "There ain't any trees, ain't any
apples, ain't nothing."

Al sobered. "Not even roots."

"No stumps," said Hank.

They stared at the bare ground and at each other.

"The orchard walked off," Hank suggested.

The horses whinnied. The red in Al's weathered face
died out. It became a study in anger and bewilderment.

"Come on!" he choked and flicked the horses' flanks
with a whip. They plunged down-hill, slewed onto the
field, and followed the furrows over the looted soil,
across undulating mounds, and straight through a field
of wheat. There was a swathe like the march of an
army.

"It can't be. I'm dreamin', we're both crazy," muttered Al.

Hank fidgeted. "Let's go back."

"Shut up! If someone's swiped my apples I'll break him in half! The best crop in thirty years!"

Hank pleaded, "Listen, Al, it ain't only the apples. The whole trees're gone, root an all. Nobody can do that in a night!"

Al drove grimly on. The horses galloped over a hill to the road and followed it as it wound down toward a small lake between terminal moraines. There they jerked to an abrupt halt under Al's powerful drag.

Al glared. Hank's eyes roved aimlessly around. He fumbled for a chew which he bit off and absently spit out. He tried to loosen an open shirt. He didn't want to see what he saw. "So help me God," he muttered, "so help me God," over and over, like a stuck phonograph record.

Here stood the orchard of Jonathan apples grouped around the pond; a half-mile from its accustomed place, but otherwise intact.

Al leaped out, a peculiar blank expression on his face. He walked with the attitude of a cat stalking prey.

The orchard of Jonathans wavered.

There was no wind.

The orchard looked for all the world like a group debating. Whispers and murmurs ascended, and the branches shook.

Hank leaned against the dash-board. Tobacco juice dribbled from his gaping mouth and watered his new crop of whiskers.

"Come on!" snarled Al. "Get them poles and nets. We're gonna pick apples!"

But he did not need to pick apples. He reached for a luscious red Jonathan hanging low on the nearest tree. The branch went back, then forward, like a catapult. Al ducked. The apple smacked the wagon. Both horses whinnied and raced off. As if that were a signal, the orchard launched into violent motion. A noise like a rushing wind rose. The tree-tops bent and lashed as in a gale. Apples showered the farmers, darkened the air, bounced and squashed painfully from faces and shins and bodies.

The ungodliest yell ever heard in Shawtuck County burst from the throat of a hired hand whose terrific speed carried him after the careening wagon out of the picture, and the county.

Lars Andersen was walking along a path with a scythe on his shoulder to mow some odd plots of hay, early that morning. His Scotch collie bounced beside him. The path went around a vegetable garden and then paralleled a wind-break of elms. Now it is a well-known fact that any intelligent dog will have nothing to do with grass or mere vegetables.

The collie, being a dog of rigidly conventional habits, made a bee-line for one of the trees, Whatever he intended to do was postponed. The lowest branch of the tree curved down and not only whipped his rear smartly but lifted him a good dozen feet away. He yelped and tore for home like mad.

Lars had a thoughtful expression on his face as he turned around and headed back. He guessed he didn't feel much like mowing today.

Old Emily Tawber fussed with her darning until midmorning before laying it aside. "Jed can wait for his socks," she muttered crossly. "I can't cook and sew and tend to the crops all at once, and them watermelons ripe for market."

She put her mending back in the big wicker basket, pulled a vast-brimmed straw hat over her head, and went out in an old rag dress that she used for chores.

She stomped across the yard and through her flower garden to the melon patch. There were about fifty big melons ready for picking. She would pile them up alongside the path for Jed to load and take to market in the morning.

"Land's sakes, I never see such melons in all my born days." Old Emily stuck her arms on her hips and surveyed the green ovals. These were giant watermelons, three and four feet long, weighing a hundred pounds or more. She had been surprised throughout the summer by their growth.

"Well, the bigger they be, the more they'll fetch," she decided and went after the first one.

It must have been on a slope for it rolled away as she approached.

"Well, I swan!" said old Emily. "Things is gettin' to a pretty pass when you can't get at your own seedin's."

She walked after the watermelon. It rolled farther. Old Emily became flustered. She increased her stride. The melon bumped unevenly in a wide circle around the vine-root. Old Emily panted after it and it wobbled crazily always just ahead of her.

Old Emily began to feel dizzy. She guessed the sun was too much for her. She wasn't as spry as she used to be. The world reeled around. The melon kept going, while she paused for breath, then it rolled all the way around, came toward her, and crashed into her ankles. The blow sent her sprawling. This was when peril first entered her thoughts. She staggered to her feet and from the patch.

"Watermelon won't get me," she crooned. "Watermelon run along but he won't get me. Don't let old watermelon get me." This was all that anyone heard her say during the rest of her earthly existence.

The harvester thundered as Gus Vogel gave it the gas and it clattered toward his wheat acreage.

Gus hollered, "With this weather we'll be done come night!"

"If the machines don't break down," bawled brother Ed above his machine's racket.

"Wheat is two dollar 'n' a quarter a bushel," Gus chortled. "I bet we get a hundred bushel to the acre this year."

The two machines rattled along a dirt road that was little more than weed-grown ruts until a sea of tawny appeared beyond the brook and cow pastures.

A full half-section in extent, the field of ripe grain rolled away in a yellow-brown flood shoulder high, the tallest wheat within memory, headed by two-inch spears with dozens of fat grains.

Gus and Ed jockeyed the harvesters into the near corner of the field. Those long rows erect as soldiers would soon go down in a wide swathe. The three hundred twenty acres of wheat were worth over seventy thousand dollars.

Gus roared lustily as his machine lurched ahead and the blades whirred to reap, "Let 'er go!"

As if struck by a mighty wind, the wheat flattened against the ground in a great area that widened as the harvester advanced.

Not a breath of wind stirred. The air hung warm and fragrant, the sunlight lay mellow on ripe grain, meadowlarks carolled morning-songs, and the black crows cawed harshly high overhead. But the wheat lay flat, mysteriously, in a large strip. Beyond this strip, the golden ranks rose tall again, but a myriad murmuring issued from them like voices of invisible hosts. The hair prickled on Gus's scalp. He looked behind him. Not a stem had been cut by the reaper, and the full ears were intact. In a sudden vicious, unreasoning rage, he drove the combine ahead at full speed, and the blades sang a song of shirring steel, and the wheat went down in a racing band farther ahead at a faster pace than he could achieve, and the slicing blades whirred idly over the prone grain.

Then Gus and Ed stopped the machines and climbed out. Gus knelt over and bent his face low to study this extraordinary field. A patch sprang upright like wires, lashing his face. Gus gaped, pop-eyed. The veins stood out on his temples in purple. Somewhere within him something happened and he pitched to the ground, his face livid, as Ed ran to his aid.

Not least among the remarkable events in Shawtuck County that morning was the saga of the fugitive potatoes.

The potatoes were only a small planting of an acre or so that Pieter Van Schluys had raised. They should have matured in early August but they didn't. They kept on growing and their tops got bigger and greener and lustier. Pieter was a stolid Dutchman who knew his potatoes as well as his schnapps.

"Dere iss someting wrong," he solemnly told his American frau. "Dey haff no business to grow furder. Already yet dey haff gone two veeks too late."

"Dig 'em up, then," said the bony Gertrude. "If they're ripe, they're ripe. If they aren't, you can tell quick enough by diggin' a couple out."

"Ja," Pieter agreed. "But it iss not right. Potatoes, dey should be in two veeks already."

"Maybe if you weren't so lazy you'd of dug 'em two weeks ago."

"Dat iss not so," Pieter began, but Gertrude tartly gathered dishes and pans with a great noise.

Pieter blinked and rose. It was hard to have such a shrewish frau. In this *verdaemmte* America, *frauen* were too independent. You could neither boss them, nor beat them.

He rolled to the door and waddled past a silo to the barn where he took a potato-digger from a mass of tools. He leisurely filled a well-stained meerschaum pipe which had a broken stem, and lighted it. A couple of geese honked sadly as he passed in a cloud of burley smoke.

Pieter paused by the potatoes to wipe his sweating face with a kerchief bigger than a napkin. "Gertrude," he muttered, "she iss no better as a potato."

Having expressed his rebellion, he dug and heaved.

The tubers did not come up. Pieter strained, struggled, perspired. The heap of earth grew larger, but no potato appeared.

"Dat iss some potato," Pieter muttered. "Himmel, vat a potato it must be."

Pieter looked at his planting. "Diss iss not right for a potato," he spoke in reproof, and shovelled more soil away.

Had his eyes deceived him? Or had the plant actually sunk? He looked at the vegetable tops with thoughtful disgust. It seemed beyond question that the leafy tops were considerably nearer ground level than when he arrived.

"So?" Pieter exclaimed. "Iss dat how it iss? So!"

He scooped again. He watched with a kind of bland interest at first, then a naive wonder, and finally anxiety. It did seem that the potato was getting away from him. No, that could not be. He must have taken too many schnapps last night. Or it was too hot. He wiped perspiration off his face with a sleeve of his blue denim shirt. The potato was as far below his digger as ever, and surely his eyes did not befool him when they registered that the potato's topmost leaf was now at ground level. Quite a heap of soil lay beside it. The rest of the potato patch stood as high as before. Only this one pesky tuber had sunk unaccountably.

Pieter dug deeper.

The mound of dirt increased. The hole grew larger. The elusive potato continued to slide below his digger. It was maddening. There must be a cave as big as the Zuyder Zee under this vegetable. He might fall into it with the plant!

His slow brain, obtaining this thought, brought him to a momentary halt. But no. Ten years he had farmed here, ten years had harvested. It was very strange. Pieter did not feel quite so chipper as after breakfast, and he certainly had not been jovial then. Pieter became stubborn. The devil himself was in this potato. The devil was leading him to hell. Or nature had gone crazy. Or he had.

Pieter shovelled and scooped, but the tuber dug down like a thing possessed, a mole, a creature hunted. The pile of dirt had spread far by now, and Pieter stood in a deep pit with the potato still below him. He had reached sandy, thin, base soil. He was angry and stubborn. He dug till his arms ached. He panted in Dutch and cursed in English. He muttered, he swore.

"Something iss crazy or I am," he decided and made a halfhearted plunge at the vanishing vegetable.

"You seem to be having some difficulty. Can I be of help?" inquired a polite voice.

A stranger stood on the rim of the hole. The stranger wore old corduroy trousers, a stained work-shirt, and a slouched hat. He had amused gray eyes. A briar pipe stuck out of his mouth. He twirled a golden key idly so that the chain wrapped round and round his forefinger. His face was full of angles, and a peculiar mark, not a scar, possibly a burn, made a patch on his left temple. By that mark, Pieter recognized him from hearsay as a comparative newcomer. He had bought the Hoffman farm a mile out of Shawtuck Center on County Road C somewhat over a year ago. He paid cash, and claimed the odd name Green Jones.

Pieter scowled. "Danks, but I vill manage. De potatoes iss hard to dig diss year."

The stranger's jaw fell open. "You don't mean to tell me you're digging potatoes! Way down there?"

Pieter felt acutely unhappy. "Ja."

"You sure plant 'em deep! Why don't you try for those nearer the surface?"

Pieter stared glumly at Green Jones, then back at the potato plant, now a good five feet below ground level, and still going down in the crater he had dug. Damn the potato! Damn the stranger! Damn all this business!

"Ja," said Pieter. "Be so kindly as to help me out."

Green Jones lent a willing hand, heaved while the

rosy Dutchman puffed, and helped him scramble up. "Dat vas very good of you," Pieter thanked him.

"Don't mention it."

Pieter marched to the next cluster of potato tops, spat on his hands, and made a ferocious jab at the ground. His digger sank a foot. The tuber sank a foot and a half. Pieter glowered.

"Haw!" exploded the onlooker. Pieter glared murder. Green Jones chuckled to himself and blew out a cloud of pungent smoke.

"How you did it beats me, but I never saw anyting like it." Green Jones walked off in great good humor, a lank figure striding down the road, leaving behind him the aroma of fine tobacco, the echo of his chuckles, and a wrathful Dutchman.

"Potatoes!" Pieter muttered. "Himmel, everyting iss crazy mit de heat."

Like the first, thus second group of fugitive potatoes seemed to be burrowing into the earth. The magical submersion was too much for him. He reeled toward his farmhouse to drown his troubles in a sea of schnapps.

The incident at Loring's farm was notable for its spectacular brevity. Mrs. Loring wanted to can corn. Lou Loring said he'd haul her in enough for the winter. Between other chores, he went to his sweet-corn field about ten o'clock with his daughter Marion.

Marion held a bushel basket and would have followed him down the rows if there had been any stripping.

Lou reached for an ear.

The ear moved around to the other side of the stalk. A weird caterwauling went up from the whole field and the stalks, standing ten feet high and more, seemed to shake.

Lou hesitantly pursued the ear. The cob returned to its original position. Lou batted his eyes. Marion gave a peculiar squawk and raced pell-mell for home.

Lou swore and reached for another ear. Did the

whole stalk revolve? Or did the ear slide away? Was he out of his head? The furious sounds of the cornfield alone were enough to make his flesh creep.

Between the rows of corn, pumpkins had been planted. A few weeds grew, and a sprinkling of wild groundcherries. Lou reached for a lower ear and in so doing almost stepped on one of the groundcherries. The plant leaped straight up and fell a foot away. The roots moved feebly, began to sink in the soil, and the groundcherry rose gradually erect.

What with revolving ears of corn and leaping groundcherries, Lou felt that he needed a day off, to have his eyes examined. And off he went.

The main hangout in Shawtuck Center was Andy's general store. On Saturday night, Andy usually did a whale of an illicit business in Minnesota Thirteen, a strain of corn that eager moonshiners quickly, and happily discovered made superior whisky. Weekdays were dead, especially the early days. But the way farmers began drifting in on this Tuesday was a caution. A dozen had collected before noon. Andy did not know what it was all about, but the corn liquor was flowing. There were rickety chairs, empty barrels up-ended, and nail-kegs aplenty to hold all comers.

The universal glumness was a puzzle to Andy. "How's tricks?" he asked when Al Meiers came in.

"So-so." Al twiddled a cracked tumbler, drained it, clanked it on the counter.

"Something wrong?"

"We-ell, no."

"Here, take a snifter of this."

"Don't mind if I do." Al gulped the drink.

"You ain't lookin' so well, Al."

Pieter Van Schluys waddled up.

"Hi, Pieter, why aren't you hauling in?"

Pieter glowered at the speaker. "Dose potatoes," he muttered, "dey iss full mit de devil!"

"So?" Andy perked his ears. An amazing interest developed among the rest of the group.

"Ja. I dig for vun potato and so fast as I dig, de potato dig deeper. Ja. I tink dere iss a hole so big as China under dose potatoes or de potatoes iss, how you say it, haunted, ja, else I am crazy mit de heat."

"I'll be damned," Al broke in, "and I thought I was seen' things. Listen!" he told of the orchard that walked away. Hesitantly at first, this big farmer almost pleaded for belief, and when he saw that the jeers he expected did not come, he warmed to his tale like a child reciting a fairy-story.

"That must of been your hired hand went by here like a blue-streak in that old jalopy a couple hours back," Andy guessed.

"Yeah. Hank lit out. I don't blame him much. I don't s'pose he ever will come back."

Ed Vogel had a grim face. "I just saw Doc Parker. He says Gus had a stroke when we was mowin' this mornin', but he'll pull through. Only there wasn't no mowin'. The wheat don't cut. It just lies down an' then springs up again. You'd of thought it was alive and knew just what I was gonna do."

"My apples ain't worth a dime a bushel now," said Al. "After they got through throwin' themselves around, they was so banged up they ain't even good for cider."

Ed wore a reflective air that turned to a scowl of apprehension. "Say, if things go on like this, we won't have no crops this year. We're ruined."

Until he spoke, not one of the farmers had fully realized the extent of the disaster that faced them. Each had been preoccupied with his own worry. The fantastic rebellion of nature was a mystery. Now Ed's remark drove home understanding of what they were up against. If this was not all a collective hallucination; if they were as sane as ever and had witnessed what they thought they saw; if they had no more success in harvesting than they had had so far—then they were bankrupt, ruined.

They could pay off neither mortgages nor debts. They would be unable to buy necessities. They would not even have food for themselves, or seed for next year's sowing.

"I wouldn't eat one of my leapin' apples for a million dollars," Al Meiers declared, and meant it.

"What are we gonna do?" Ed asked helplessly. "We can't all be batty. Somethin's wrong, but what? No crops, no food, no cash. Crops are bringin' high prices this year, but we're done for."

Andy peered over his shell-rimmed glasses. "Why don't you go see Dan Crowley? Maybe he could help you out."

"Good idea," Al agreed, lumbering to his feet. "How about it, boys?"

"Sure, let's see the county agent."

Gloom hung thick on the anxious group that faced Crowley.

"Take it easy, boys," Crowley advised genially. He was county agent for the Department of Agriculture. He was fat and bald. His nose stood out like the prow of a ship and stubble covered his jowls. He smoked black, twisted, foul stogies that smelled to heaven. His feet were on the desk of his office when the farmers came, and there his feet remained while he puffed poisonous clouds and listened. His muddy blue eyes were guileless. Dan Crowley looked harmless, hopeless, and dumb. They were deceptive traits. Dan had a good head. He just didn't believe in extending himself needlessly.

"So that's how it is," Al Meiers finished. "I'm ready to move out of the county now and burn the damn' wheat to the ground."

"Now, now, Al, don't be that way. You know I work for you all."

Pieter Van Schluys moped. "Ja. Vat good iss dat?"

"Plenty. Just leave it to me." Dan hooked his thumbs in his arm-pits and leaned farther back.

"You haff an idea?" Pieter asked hopefully.

"Sure thing. Now run along while I'm thinkin' about

this. I'll get it straightened out." Dan was vaguely definite. The farmers filed away.

Shawtuck Center grew more and more restless as the afternoon waned—and farmers arrived with newer and wilder accounts of the pranks that nature was playing. Andy's general store buzzed with anxious and angry voices. The population of Shawtuck County was made up almost exclusively of hard-headed Dutchmen, Scandinavians, and Germans who had settled through the mid-West during the great immigration waves of the late nineteenth century. They were a conservative, strong-working, sturdy lot. They clung to past customs, and some of the superstitions learned in the Old Country. The town simmered with tales of witchcraft and hauntings, of the Little People, of goblins and evil spirits.

What caused this strange revolt of the plant kingdom at Shawtuck Center? Nothing of the sort seemed to be afflicting the outside world. And what possible action could he take? He could at least make a field inspection for a special crop report.

Dan went out, climbed into his official car, and headed out of town on County Road A.

The land, under the warm, mellow light of the sun, gave testimony of abandonment, without the voice of any farmer. Harvesting ought to be in full swing, but not a figure tramped the fields, not a reaper moved. Here and there stood threshers, harvesters, wagons, farm implements, and combines, all untended.

Yet the fields, though deserted, were not wholly silent. This was a day of quiet, such a day of stillness and ripe maturity as often comes at harvest time; but ever and again, as Dan drove along, he saw strange ripplings cross wheat and hay fields, watched clover sway, heard a sound like innumerable murmurous faint voices sweep up from grains and grasses and vegetables; and one patch of woods was all an eerie wail, and infinite restless disturbances of flower and leaf and blade set the forest in motion; while the wild chokecherry and sumac nodded in no wind and shook for no visible reason alongside the dirt road.

Dan felt uneasy. All summer there had been little signs, increasing evidence, that a change had come over nature; and now the rapid and sinister character of that change became intensified with its completion. The trees, the plants, the vegetables had mysteriously developed a life and will-power of their own. And they had cast off the dominance of man.

Dan drove on through back roads, and twisted over cart paths, weaving in and out around Shawtuck Center during the afternoon. Everywhere he went, he found the same uncanny solitude, the constant whispers whose speakers remained invisible, alfalfa and barley and corn that quaked though no presence was near and rarely a breath of air stirred. The sun was sinking when Dan headed homeward, and it seemed to him that new and deeper murmurs issued from the bewitched fields and the enchanted woods. But he had learned one fact, and it puzzled him.

The phenomena were limited to the valley where Shawtuck Center lay in a bowl of low hills.

Returning to his office, Dan passed a group to whom Pieter Van Schluys was relating again the saga of the fugitive potatoes. "So dere I vass, fife feet down already, ja, and der man; de Jones person, he stand dere and laugh. Himmel, maype it vass funny as a funeral, nein?"

Dan wondered why anyone should be amused by such a strange occurrence. He went thoughtfully into his office and looked at the routine blanks and forms on his desk.

He could well imagine the results if he reported the facts to Washington. "Meiers's apple orchard walked away last night and the trees planted themselves around a pond on the Hagstrom farm because they liked it better there." And, "The Vogels' wheat refuses to be harvested. Kindly advise proper action to take." Or, "Emily Tawber's melons object to being picked. Does she lose her guarantees under the federal Watermelon Pickle Price Support Program?"

No, Dan decided, if he sent in these official messages, he would only be fired and replaced. His only course was to make a further investigation in search of a cause for the bizarre happenings.

He went to the wall and studied the large map of Shawtuck County. It showed the size and location of every farm, the variety and acreage of every crop. He drew a rough circle around the area of the phenomena. At the center of the circle lay the farm of Green Jones. Dan decided to pay Jones a visit.

As Dan turned in at the private road by the mailbox lettered G. Jones, he noticed immediately in the twilight that the land had not been tilled at all. Jones was no farmer. Only lank weeds grew in his fields.

Dan stopped at a gray old frame house guarded by elms and maples. Lights burned in the ground floor windows.

Dan heaved his bulk out with a sigh and lit the inevitable stogy. He rang the bell, and presently a tall, thin man with an angular face appeared at the screen door.

Dan said, "I'm the county agriculture agent. Mind if I drop in for a few minutes?"

Jones replied firmly, "Why, yes, I do mind. I've a lot of work to do and I'm pressed for time."

"So'm I." Dan blew a cloud of reeking smoke at Green Jones. "I have to get off a special crop report to Washington tonight."

"What have I got to do with that? I don't grow any crops," said Jones, frowning.

"Maybe not. Maybe you just help to make other people's crops grow."

A wary look came into Jones's eyes. "What do you mean by that?"

Dan said slowly, "It's like this. There's been queer things going on around here all summer. All year, in fact, ever since you moved in. Walkin' trees an' gallopin' potatoes and God knows what all."

Jones spoke with a tone of bored indifference, "I heard some of those wild rumors."

"They ain't rumors. I went out for a look-see this afternoon. Crops an' everything else that grows have gone crazy all around Shawtuck Center. There's a borderline maybe a quarter-mile wide where things are kind of uncertain, an' after that the trees an' such haven't anything wrong with 'em. So I looked at my map and saw that the center of that circle is right here."

Green Jones straightened up coldly. "Are you implying that I have some connection with these phenomena?"

"Implying? Hell, no, I'm tellin' you."

Jones regarded the county agent with a peculiar, shrewd appraisal. Finally, after appearing to weigh many matters, he shrugged and said, "You win. Nice crop detective work. I suppose I might as well take you into my confidence. I don't want a lifetime's work wrecked in a day." He stepped aside. "Come in."

The parlor was severely furnished. Besides a sofa, several chairs, and a desk, Dan noticed two prints on the walls: one of Burbank, and another of Darwin.

"Have a chair," his host suggested.

Dan sank into a wing-backed piece that promptly collapsed under his weight.

"Dear, dear," Jones protested. "That was a good chair."

Dan eased himself into the more substantial sofa and blew his nose violently to indicate that he was sorry but unembarrassed. Unfortunately, he dropped his stogy which left a scorch on the thick blue carpet amid a fine powder of ashes.

"My beautiful rug," mourned Jones.

"Sorry," mumbled Dan.

"Never mind. It's done."

"An' everybody hereabouts is done for the way things

are goin' now." Dan steered back to his original topic. "Jones, I don't know who you are or how you done it but you sure raised hell with the crops."

Jones slouched against a mantelpiece. From far away came an insidious drone that Dan could not quite identify. His host idly twirled a golden key on a chain. He looked cool, slightly detached, and yet there was a deep passion behind his features. "Right. My real name doesn't matter. I'm a botanist. Some years ago I got the idea that vegetation seemed to show a sort of rudimentary awareness. It couldn't be called intelligence. I noticed how tree roots turned off and travelled considerable distances straight to underground water pipes. Then there is the fly orchid that acts with almost human ingenuity. It attracts, traps, and devours insects.

"I became convinced that there was a kind of dormant awareness in the plant world. It would be a great achievement for science and a possible blessing to man if plants possessed instinct and science could develop it to reason or at least the power of free motion. Then food materials, like animals, could seek a water supply and largely do away with the harmful effects of drought. I worked on that line. I didn't get far until other scientists discovered that ultraviolet rays, even the ordinary illumination of electric lights, could be turned on plants all night long and they grew almost twice as fast as other plants. Physicists found that various cosmic radiations produced definite effects on vegetation and could cause radical changes.

"Two or three years ago, I found that a universal radiation isolated first by Diemann greatly accelerated all activity of plants. I built apparatus to capture and to concentrate that radiation. I turned the intensified radiation loose on some hothouse plants and they grew like mad. I decided to experiment on a larger scale, and bought this farm because it was in a secluded district. For the past year I've been bombarding vegetation around Shawtuck Center with Diemann's radiations. You know the results—abnormal growth, mobile powers, and apparently rational, rudimentary impulses. That's the whole story. Now I've laid my cards on the table."

Dan knitted his brows. "You say the ray makes plants *think*?"

"No, I don't know that it does. All I know is that Diemann's radiations have always been essential for the growth of plants. I proved that by trying to raise flowers in an insulated hothouse. Nothing I experimented with would grow at all without Diemann's radiations. I reasoned that a concentration of the rays, if strong enough, might cause abnormal developments and hasten the evolution of species. I'm only experimenting and recording data as I go along. There seems to be something more than instinct developing, but it's too early to call it reason."

Dan said, "Hmm. Why did everything happen today? That's kind of suddenlike if you've been usin' this ray for a year, ain't it?"

The stranger shrugged. "Yes, but remember, I too am almost as much in the dark as you are. I know the cause of the change but I don't know the how or why or what. I must observe for years to determine these factors. Possibly there was a dividing-line. On one side stood inanimate vegetation, constantly but feebly irradiated. Then my concentration of Diemann's ray built up the change until its influences reached their climax last night and inanimate plants crossed the line to animation."

Dan suggested, "You might be smart if you quit now."

Jones looked aghast. "But my experiment has hardly begun! Think of what mankind may learn as a result of my researches! The whole course of civilization may be affected!"

"Yeah," Dan answered grimly. "That's what I'm afraid of. If this goes far enough there won't be anybody left. Animals won't get no food except each other an' we won't have much except animals an' they won't last long.

If the crops lie down or walk off an' can't be harvested, how're we gonna live?"

Green Jones looked thunderstruck. Dan could not help having a half-liking for him. He was obviously sincere, and evidently had meant well when he began his experiment. It was not wholly his fault that it had worked out differently from the way he expected.

"I didn't realize the change had gone as far as that." The botanist twirled his key, but his mind was elsewhere.

Dan stood up. "Jones, you're in a tough spot."

"Yes?"

"Van Schluys is pretty dumb an' so are a lot of the boys but sooner or later they're gonna start thinkin' like I did about why you were so tickled when he was tryin' to dig spuds. Or they'll pin you down on the map. God help you when the boys come tearin' out here hell-bent for your hide. You ruined their crops an' they'll tear you limb from limb."

For the first time, the botanist came all the way down to earth from his remote dreams, speculations, and theories. His face paled a bit. "That was a bad mistake on my part, I'll admit." The ghost of a smile hovered in his expression. "Just the same, it was a sight for the gods to watch that Dutchman pursue his fleeing potatoes."

"Take my advice and move out while you can," Dan said gruffly.

The botanist seemed unnerved. "As bad as all that? But I can't leave my experiment unfinished!" he cried shakily. "Besides, how'll I get away? My car's broken down."

"If your experiment's worth more'n your hide to you don't blame me for what happens. But I guess this is official business, so I could use my official car to drive you to the next town if you wanted to leave tonight."

Mr. Jones carefully, moodily, replaced the gold key in his pocket. He seemed to be undergoing an inner struggle to make up his mind.

"Where is the machine?" Dan asked out of idle curiosity.

"Next room." The scientist's indecision and worry fell away. He snapped erect, "I've got myself into a jam all right but it's too late for regrets. I'll take your kind offer. If you'll give me an hour or two, say till ten o'clock, to collect my data and a few belongings I'll be ready to go."

"An' you'll turn off the rays?"

"Yes, I promise." His voice was eager, sincere. Dan knew men and knew that Jones would keep his word.

"I'll be back at ten sharp. Better not let anyone else in."

Dan left, jubilant over the success of his visit. He had discovered and he had eliminated the menace to Shawtuck County agriculture.

It was eerie driving through the woods. There was neither moon nor wind. The stirless air lay like a cool and weary sleep over the aging world; but the autumnal quiet that should have prevailed was missing. There were great rustlings abroad, and dark movements among the blacker masses of trees and crops, a continuous ghostly murmur issuing from the shapes of things possessed. The entire landscape seemed restlessly alive. There were voices without speakers, and slow creeping without breeze or visible agency; and Dan felt the impact of dimly remembered legends from childhood, about haunted woods and forests where witches resided, the Druids of the trees, the gnomes, and the Little People who lived under blades of grass and toadstools. It would be strange indeed if somewhere in the long ago, Diemann's radiations had been stronger when the world was younger, and all manner of growing things had then owned powers of life and motion that declined through the ages, leaving only ancestral memories for record until Jones brought back to nature its ancient gift. They were mysterious and disturbing activities that obsessed Dan as he drove toward town; and he was glad to leave behind him the soft and wailing wide whisper of inarticulate things, as the lights of the town drew near.

Back in his office, having firmly shut the door, Dan cocked his feet on the desk and smoked interminably. A small shaded lamp on the desk kept the room in semi-darkness. The air became stale and bluish with smoke. Through the half-curtained windows, he watched figures drift by; arguing farmers; worried old crones; harrassed and hopeless and blank faces, strong ones and weak ones, some dull and others furious, all showing the paralysis, the demoralization that the revolt of nature had produced. Beset by events alien to their lives, they were unable to cope with them, much less understand them. The only refuge lay in herding together and trying the forced gayety of town, with plenty of potent drink, as an antidote; as if the courage of the individual might return through combined strength and association with his neighbors. It was a night of fights, altercations, and bitter argument, and rowdy choruses from Andy's store.

Dan folded his hands on his lap. He had no desire to mingle with them until his task was finished. Tonight would see the end of the strange harvest, and tomorrow he could worry about the crop reports to Washington. The day's work had been strenuous, for him. He dozed, being one of those fortunate mortals who can snatch a cat-nap under almost any circumstances.

He could not have slept long. It was only just past nine when he blinked awake. He had a vague impression of some distant and receding roar, echoing through slumber to wakefulness; but all he now heard were the sounds of a few racing feet. The street outside his window was deserted.

Dan regarded the window and the empty sidewalk for perhaps a minute before a thought struck him with such force that he sent the chair spinning away as he crashed to his feet and pounded out.

The street was almost deserted. The tumult of less

than an hour ago had subsided. A few broken windows, a picket-door hanging askew, some smashed bottles, and a couple of overturned kegs in front of Andy's store were the only remaining evidence of the crowd. The one person in sight was an old woman with infinitely wrinkled face and slow steps passing the Church.

Dan called, "Where's everybody?"

Old Mrs. Tompkins peered out of ancient eyes. "Eh? They all went out to the Jones place."

"What!"

"Lordamercy, you don't need to yell so. I ain't stone-daft yet. They're gone and much good may it do. Pieter was telling his story and I don't know who it was decided Jones could say a-plenty about these goings-on. I'm a religious woman, Dan, but I tell you, if it's this Jones who's the cause of all this grief I'd—"

Whatever she thought was lost on Dan who jumped into his car and sped off toward the Jones farm.

Dan hoped to overtake the angry farmers. He didn't know exactly what he could say or do, but he thought they would at least listen to him. Dan sympathized with their feelings. They had been baffled, scared, and ruined by the perverse results of Jones's experiment. There was a certain justice to any punishment they might inflict on him. But Dan could see the scientist's side too; his passion for discovery in unknown fields; his willingness to experiment, whatever the cause; his primary purpose of aiding humanity and increasing the general good. The experiment had gotten beyond control. Vegetation given a new power, had responded in a far more willful and independent manner than Jones anticipated. He could scarcely be blamed for the curious developments which had occurred. He might have hoped to benefit mankind, but the character of Diemann's radiations had ruled otherwise and given the plant kingdom a new vitality that fought human control.

There were differences and changes in the farmlands through which Dan sped. He remembered well the

Hanson grapevines, but they had somehow vanished, leaving only torn earth. And the Ritter chestnut grove—of which no trace remained, save deep furrows.

As Dan approached the Jones place, he felt a sudden tightness in his chest. A crowd of farmers surrounded the house, milling around.

Beam of flashlights and glow of lanterns cast flickering lights and shadows on alarmed faces. The surging mob seemed checked. Then, to Dan's amazement, they all suddenly broke and fled to their autos. They raced away, leaving Dan alone in the moonlight.

An ominous chill came over Dan as he stopped his car. A vast, dark mass, a writhing mound, engulfed the house. Dan got out and stood paralyzed for an instant. Forest trees and cultivated fruit trees, flowers and climbing vines, vegetables of countless variety, bushes and brambles and berries, representatives of all the plant life of Shawtuck County had converged here and overflowed Jones's place. And Dan heard an indescribable sound, a strange, eerie, inarticulate murmur of vegetation.

Now he heard other sounds, the sharp crack and tinkle of broken glass, the splintering of wood, and he knew that the windows and the very frame of the house were giving way. Suddenly there came a cry, a scream for help from within, and he barely recognized the voice of Green Jones. A great shudder convulsed the tangle surrounding the house. There was nothing familiar in the now loud, incessant, and threshing roar of vegetation; a weird tumult such as the wildest gale had never produced.

With unaccustomed agility, Dan leaped to the rear of his car. He habitually carried a variety of new farming aids that he demonstrated as part of his duties, products such as weed-killers, insecticides, fertilizers, and implements. Among these was a portable flame-thrower designed for burning out infected fields and blighted trees that he had been showing off in recent weeks. He grabbed it and aimed the nozzle at the heaving mass. A burst of intense flame struck and clung to the tangled foliage of shrubbery and vines and trees. Briefly, then, a sad sound flared up, like a many-bodied, sub-human, voiceless thing crying for life.

Now a great rent appeared in the mass and even the front of the house began to burn. Dan shut off the stream of fire but carried the thrower with him as he ran inside the burning structure.

His bulk was unused to such exertion, but he gave a convulsive leap when he saw the dark branches and vines beating at the side windows of the parlor, and watched a pane smash. He hurled himself against the door to the next room with a force that burst it from its hinges. He looked at a dynamo that hummed a faint drone on the floor near the doorway, its brushes occasionally sparking, and connected with an object that occupied the whole center of the room. It looked like a huge metal box. Its plates glowed with a pulsing and ghostly radiance that shifted between soft silver and the crimson of fire. Near the ceiling above it and completing the circuit by thick cables that pierced the metallic concentration box to whatever mechanism lay within, hung a globe between anode and cathode. The globe swam with blinding mist, a purple, impalpable force that streamed out constantly and almost visibly in all directions. The giant globe had sound all its own, a peculiar, intense whine, at the upper range of audibility.

The rear window to the room had been burst, and a flowing tide of plant growths had already enveloped part of the machine. Jones lay on the floor, evidently knocked unconscious when the mass burst in. For an instant Dan used the thrower again. The vegetation burned into ashes, and suddenly the huge globe melted with a violent flame of purple and red and silver streaked with blue.

Dan dragged Jones from the burning house. The night air became filled with one loud, prolonged, and mournful wail that faded into an inchoate murmur, an inarticulate whisper, then silence. Gone were the eerie voices and the purposive movements.

Only the crackle of flames and pungent smoke came from the dying house and the dead mass.

Harvesting of crops proceeded normally around Shawtuck Center the following day. The destruction of the machine had also destroyed the newly acquired powers of the plants and fruits and vegetables.

Dan often wondered about that last night. Had the growing things, impelled by some dawning intelligence, converged to destroy their creator, or to encompass and protect him and his machine? He never knew. While Dan watched the burning house, Green Jones must have regained consciousness. He had walked away down the lonely roads of night.

Bill Pronzini's eclectic tastes have yielded a vast number of contributions to the mystery, western, horror, and science fiction genres. In addition to his critically acclaimed Nameless Detective series, he is the author of Masques: A Novel of Terror *and* Night Screams. *He has collaborated with Barry Malzberg on the science fiction novel* Prose Bowl, *and his wife Marcia Muller on the horror-mystery novel* Beyond the Grave. *His work as an anthologist includes his "chrestomathies"* Voodoo!, Mummy!, Creature!, *and* Spectre!, *and co-editing credentials on* The Arbor House Treasury of Mystery and Suspense, The Arbor House Treasury of Horror and the Supernatural, *and* Hard-Boiled: An Anthology of American Crime Stories. *A leading historian of popular fiction, he is the author of the indispensable guide to crime fiction* 1001 Midnights, *and the entertaining studies of bad mystery and western fiction* Gun in Cheek, Son of a Gun in Cheek, *and* Six-Gun in Cheek.

Pumpkin

Bill Pronzini

The pumpkin, the strange pumpkin, came into Amanda Sutter's life on a day in late September.

She had spent most of that morning and early afternoon shopping in Half Moon Bay, and it was almost two o'clock when she pointed the old Dodge pickup south on Highway One. She watched for the sign, as she always did; finally saw it begin to grow in the distance, until she could read, first, the bright orange letters that said SUTTER PUMPKIN FARM, and then the smaller black letters underneath: *The Biggest, The Tastiest, The Best— First Prize Winner, Half Moon Bay Pumpkin Festival, 1976.*

Amanda smiled as she turned past the sign, onto the farm's unpaved access road. The wording had been Harley's idea, which had surprised some people who didn't know him very well. Harley was a quiet, reserved man—too reserved, sometimes; she was forever trying to get him to let his hair down a little—and he never bragged. As far as he was concerned, though, the sign was simply a statement of fact. "Well, our pumpkins are the biggest, the tastiest, the best," he said when one of their neighbors asked him about it. "And we did win first prize in '76. If the sign said anything else, it'd be a lie."

That was Harley for you. In a nutshell.

The road climbed up a bare-backed hill, and when she reached the crest Amanda stopped the pickup to admire the view. She never tired of it, especially at this time of year and on this sort of crisp, clear day. The white farm buildings lay in the little pocket directly below, with the fields stretching out on three sides and the ocean vast and empty beyond. The pumpkins were ripe now, the same bright orange as the lettering on the sign—Connecticut Field for the most part, with a single parcel devoted to Small Sugar; hundreds of them dotting the brown and green earth like a bonanza of huge gold nuggets, gleaming in the afternoon sun. The sun-glare was caught on the ruffly blue surface of the Pacific, too, so that it likewise carried a sheen of orange-gold.

She sat for a time, watching the Mexican laborers Harley had hired to harvest the pumpkins—to first cut their stems and then, once they had had their two-to-three weeks of curing in the fields, load the bulk of the crop onto produce trucks for shipment to San Francisco and San Jose. It wouldn't be long now before Halloween. And on the weekend preceding it, the annual Pumpkin Festival.

The festival attracted thousands of people from all over the Bay Area and was the year's big doings in Half Moon Bay. There was a parade featuring the high school band and kids dressed up in Halloween costumes; there were booths selling crafts, whole pumpkins, and pumpkin delicacies—pies and cookies, soups and breads; and on Sunday the competition between growers in the area for the season's largest exhibition pumpkin was held. The year Sutter Farm had won the contest, 1976, the fruit Harley had carefully nurtured in a mixture of pure compost and spent-mushroom manure weighed in at 236 pounds. There had been no blue ribbons since, but the prospects seemed good for this season: one of Harley's new exhibition pumpkins had already grown to better than 240 pounds.

Amanda put the Dodge in gear and drove down the road to the farmyard. When she came in alongside the barn she saw Harley talking to one of the laborers, a middle-aged Mexican whose name, she remembered, was Manuel. No, not talking, she realized as she shut off the engine—arguing. She could hear Manuel's raised voice, see the tight, pinched look Harley always wore when he was annoyed or upset.

She went to where they stood. Manuel was saying, "I will not do it, Mr. Sutter. I am sorry, I will not."

"Won't do what?" Amanda asked.

Harley said, "Won't pick one of the pumpkins." His voice was pitched low but the strain of exasperation ran through it. "He says it's haunted."

"What!"

"Not haunted, Mr. Sutter," Manuel said. "No, not that." He turned appealing eyes to Amanda. "This pumpkin must not be picked, señora. No one must cut its stem or its flesh, no one must eat it."

"I don't understand, Manuel. Whyever not?"

"There is something . . . I cannot explain it. You must see this pumpkin for yourself. You must . . . feel it."

"Touch it, you mean?"

"No, Mrs. Sutter. *Feel* it."

Harley said, "You've been out in the sun too long, Manuel."

"This is not a joke, *señor*," Manuel said in grave tones. "The other men do not feel it as strongly as I, but they also will not pick this pumpkin. We will all leave if it is cut, and we will not come back."

Amanda felt a vague chill, as if someone had blown a cold breath against the back of her neck. She said, "Where is this pumpkin, Manuel?"

"The east field. Near the line fence."

"Have you seen it, Harley?" she asked her husband.

"Not yet. We might as well go out there, I guess."

"Yes," Manuel said. "Come with me, see for yourself. *Feel* for yourself."

Amanda and Harley got into the pickup; Manuel had driven in from the fields in one of the laborers' flatbed trucks, and he led the way in that. They clattered across the hilly terrain to the field farthest from the farm buildings, to its farthest section near the pole-and-barbed-wire line fence. From there, Manuel guided them on foot among the rows of big trailing vines with their heart-shaped leaves and their heavy ripe fruit. Eventually he stopped and pointed without speaking. Across a barren patch of soil, a single pumpkin grew by itself, on its own vine, no others within five yards of it.

At first Amanda noticed nothing out of the ordinary; it seemed to be just another Connecticut Field, larger than most, a little darker orange than most. But then she moved closer, and she saw that it was . . . different. She couldn't have said how it was different, but there was something . . .

"Well?" Harley said to Manuel. "What about it?"

"You don't feel it, *señor*?"

"No. Feel what?"

But Amanda felt it. She couldn't have explained that either; it was just . . . an aura, a sense of something emanating from the pumpkin that made her uneasy, brought primitive little stirrings of fear and disgust into her mind.

"I do, Harley," she said, and hugged herself. "I know what he means."

"You too? Well, I still say it's nonsense. I'm going to cut it and be done with it. Manuel, let me have your knife . . ."

Manuel backed away, putting his hand over the sharp harvesting knife at his belt. "No, Mr. Sutter. No. You must not!"

"Harley," Amanda said sharply, "he's right. Leave it be."

"Damn. Why should I?"

"It is evil," Manuel said, and looked away from the pumpkin and made the sign of the cross. "It is an evil thing."

"Oh for God's sake. How can a pumpkin be evil?"

Amanda remembered something her uncle, who had been a Presbyterian minister, had said to her when she was a child: *Evil takes many forms, Mandy. Evil shares our bed and eats at our own table. Evil is everywhere, great and small.*

She said, feeling chilled, "Harley, I don't know how, I don't know why, but that pumpkin is an evil thing. Leave it alone. Let it rot where it lies."

Manuel crossed himself again. "Yes, *señora!* We will cover it, hide it from the sun, and it will wither and die. It can do no harm it if lies here untouched."

Harley thought they were crazy; that was plain enough. But he let them have their way. He sat in the truck while Manuel went to get a piece of milky plastic rain sheeting and two other men to help him. Amanda stood near the front fender and watched the men cover the pumpkin, anchor the sheeting with wooden stakes and chunks of rock, until they were finished.

Harley had little to say during supper that night, and soon afterward he went out to his workshop in the barn.

He was annoyed at what he called her "foolishness," and Amanda couldn't really blame him. The incident with the pumpkin had already taken on a kind of surreal quality in her memory, so that she had begun to think that maybe she and Manuel and the other workers were a pack of superstitious fools.

She went out to sit on the porch, bundled up in her heavy wool sweater, as night came down and blacked out the last of the sunset colors over the ocean. An evil pumpkin, she thought. Good Lord, it was ridiculous—a Halloween joke, a sly fantasy tale for children like those that her father used to tell of ghosts and goblins, witches and warlocks, things that go bump in the dark Halloween night. How could a pumpkin be evil? Pumpkins were an utterly harmless fruit: you made pies and cookies from them, you carved them into grinning jack-o'-lanterns; they were a symbol of a grand old tradition, a happy children's rite of fall.

And yet . . .

When she concentrated she could picture the way the strange pumpkin had looked, feel again the vague aura of evil that radiated from it. A small shiver passed through her. Why hadn't Harley felt it too? Some people just weren't sensitive to auras and emanations, she supposed that was it. He was too practical, too logical, too much a skeptic—a true son of Missouri, the "Show Me" state. He simply couldn't understand.

Understand what? she thought then. I don't understand it either. I don't even know what it is that I'm afraid of.

How did the damned thing get there? Where did it come from?

What *is* it?

She found herself looking out toward the east field, as if the pumpkin might somehow be pulsing and glowing under its plastic covering, lighting up the night. There was nothing to see but darkness, of course. Silly. Ridiculous. But if it were picked . . . she did not want to think

about what might happen if that woody, furrowed stem
were cut, that thick dark orange rind cracked open.

The days passed, and October came, and soon most
of the crop had been shipped, the balance put away in
the storage shed, and Manuel and the other laborers
were gone. All that remained in the fields were the
dwarfs and the damaged and withered fruit that had
been left to decay into natural fertilizer for the spring
planting. And the strange pumpkin near the east fence,
hidden under its thick plastic shroud.

Amanda was too busy, as always at harvesttime, to
think much about the pumpkin. But she did go up there
twice, once with Harley and once alone. The first time,
Harley wanted to take off the sheeting and look at the
thing; she wouldn't let him. The second time, alone, she
had stood in a cold sea wind and felt again the emanation
of evil, the responsive stirrings of terror and disgust. It
was as if the pumpkin were trying to exert some telepathic
force upon her, as if it were saying, "Cut my stem . . .
open me up . . . eat me . . ." She pulled away finally,
almost with a sense of having wrenched loose from grasping hands, and drove away determined to do something
drastic: take a can of gasoline up there and set fire to the
thing, burn it to a cinder, get rid of it once and for all.

But she didn't do it. When she got back to the house
she had calmed down and her fears again seemed silly,
childish. A telepathic pumpkin, for heaven's sake! A
telepathic evil pumpkin! She didn't even tell Harley of
the incident.

More days passed, most of October fell away like dry
leaves, and the weekend before Halloween arrived—the
weekend of the Pumpkin Festival. The crowds were thick
on both Saturday and Sunday; Amanda, working the tra-
ditional Sutter Farm booth, sold dozens of pumpkins,
mainly to families with children who wanted them for
Halloween jack-o'-lanterns. She enjoyed herself the first
day, but not the second. Harley entered his prize

exhibition pumpkin in the annual contest—it had weighed out finally at 248 pounds—and fully expected to win his long-awaited second blue ribbon. And didn't. Aaron Douglas, who owned a farm up near Princeton, won first prize with a 260-pound Connecticut Field giant.

Harley took the loss hard. He wouldn't eat his supper Sunday night and moped around on Monday and Halloween Tuesday, spending most of both days at the stand they always set up near Highway One to catch any last-minute shoppers. There were several this year: everyone, it seemed, wanted a nice fat pumpkin for Halloween.

All Hallows' Eve.

Amanda stood at the kitchen window, looking out toward the fields. It was just after five o'clock, with night settling rapidly; a low wispy fog had come in off the Pacific and was curling around the outbuildings, hiding most of the land beyond. She could barely see the barn, where Harley had gone to his workshop. She wished he would come back, even if he was still broody over the results of the contest. It was quiet here in the house, a little too quiet to suit her, and she felt oddly restless.

Behind her on the stove, hard cider flavored with cinnamon bubbled in a big iron pot. Harley loved hot cider at this time of year; he'd had three cups before going out and it had flushed his face, put a faint slur in his voice—he never had been much of a drinking man. But she didn't mind. Alcohol loosened him up a bit, stripped away some of his reserve. Usually it made him laugh, too, but not tonight.

The fog seemed to be thickening; the lights at the barn had been reduced to smeary yellow blobs on the gray backdrop. A fine night for Halloween, she thought. And she smiled a wistful smile as a pang of nostalgia seized her.

Halloween had been a special night when she was a child, a night of exciting ritual. First, the carving of the jack-o'-lantern—how she'd loved that! Her father always brought home the biggest, roundest pumpkin he could find, and they would scoop it out together, and cut out its eyes and nose and jagged gap-toothed grin, and light the candle inside, and then set it grinning and glowing on the porch for all the neighbors to see. Then the dressing up in the costume her mother had made for her: a witch with a blacked-out front tooth and a tall-crowned hat, an old broom tucked under one arm; a ghost dressed in a sewn white sheet, her face smeared with cold cream; a lady pirate in a crimson tunic and an eye patch, carrying a wooden sword covered in tinfoil. Then the trick-or-treating, and the bags full of candy and gum and fruit and popcorn balls and caramel apples, and the harmless pranks like soaping old Mrs. Collier's windows because she never answered her doorbell, or tying bells to the tail of Mr. Dawson's cat. Then the party afterward, with all her friends from school—cake with Halloween icing and pumpkin pie, blindfold games and bobbing for apples, and afterward, with the lights turned out and the curtains open so they could see the jack-o'-lantern grinning and glowing on the porch, the ghost and goblin stories, and the delicious thrill of terror when her father described the fearful things that prowled and hunted on Hallowmas Eve.

Amanda's smile faded as she remembered that part of the ritual. Her father telling her that Halloween had originated among the ancient Druids, who believed that on this night, legions of evil spirits were called forth by the Lord of the Dead. Saying that the only way to ward them off was to light great fires, and even then . . . even then . . . Saying that on All Hallows' Eve, according to the ancient beliefs, evil was at its strongest and most profound.

Evil like that pumpkin out there?

She shuddered involuntarily and tried to peer past the shimmery outlines of the barn. But the east field was invisible now, clamped inside the bony grasp of the fog. That damned pumpkin! she thought. I *should* have taken some gasoline out there and set fire to it. Exorcism by fire.

Then she thought: Come on, Mandy, that's superstitious nonsense, just like Harley says. The pumpkin is just a pumpkin. Nothing is going to happen here tonight.

But it was so quiet . . .

Abruptly she turned from the window, went to the stove, and picked up her spoon; stirred the hot cider. If Harley didn't come back soon, she'd put on her coat and go out to the workshop and fetch him. She just didn't like being here alone, not tonight of all nights.

So quiet . . .

The back door burst open.

She had no warning; the door flew inward, the knob thudding into the kitchen wall, and she cried out the instant she saw him standing there. "Harley! For God's sake, you half scared me to death! What's the idea of—"

Then she saw his face. And what he held dripping in his hand.

She screamed.

He came toward her, and she tried to run, and he caught her and threw her to the floor, pinned her there with his weight. His face loomed above her, stained with stringy pulp and seeds, and she knew what the cider and his brooding had led him to do tonight—knew what was about to happen even before the thing that had been Harley opened its goblin's mouth and the words came out in a drooling litany of evil.

"You're next . . . you're next . . . you're next . . ."

The handful of dripping rind and pulp mashed against her mouth as she tried again to scream, forcing some of the bitter juice past her lips. She gagged, fought wildly for a few seconds . . . and then stopped struggling, lay still.

She smiled up at him, a wet dark orange smile.

Now there were two of them, the first two—two to sow the seeds for next year's Halloween harvest.

John D. MacDonald is best known for his 21 colorful novels of Travis McGee, the philosophically-inclined detective whose adventures began with The Deep Blue Good-By *in 1964 and extend from the hardboiled crime milieu of the early postwar years to the age of contemporary global politics and espionage. Prior to his career as a writer of crime and mystery paperback originals in the 1950s, he published fantasy and science fiction in* Weird Tales, Astounding Science Fiction, *and other pulp magazines. The best of these stories have been collected in* Other Times, Other Worlds. *His three science fiction novels,* Wine of the Dreamers, Ballroom of the Skies, *and* The Girl, The Gold Watch, & Everything, *can be found in the omnibus volume* Time and Tomorrow.

The White Fruit of Banaldar

John D. MacDonald

The auctioning of the five planets took place in the quiet main lounge of the Transgalactic Development in the corporation's new and glistening building at the corner of Reforma and Insurgentes in Mexico City, capital of the world.

For Timothy Trench, ex-employee of Transgalactic, siting tense and expectant in a back row seat waiting for the auction to begin, it was the end of one part of his life, the beginning of a new. He touched his pocket and felt the reassuring bulge of the wallet.

In the wallet, crisp as a celery kiss, was the cashier's

check. It was the hour that marked the end of five long years of planning. That check for two thousand mil-pesos was the result of pleading, begging, demanding—arguing the others down.

Five years before Timothy Trench had been a member of the habilitation crew which Transgalactic had put on the surface of the third of the five planets. At that time it had been known by a number. Now its name was Banaldar. In the hot harsh winds, in the drifting sand, in the salt-crusted seas, Timothy saw what he had been looking for.

Only a visionary's mind could have worked that way. Through the long months of building the power source, of starting the long slow process of oxygenation that would bring to Banaldar a cycle of seasons, a climate fit for man, Timothy had pictured the rolling hills clad in green, the river beds filled once more, the breezes gentle and full of the smell of growing things.

During the last month, after all the soil tests were in, they had brought down the torrential rains and then, low and fleeting, the aircraft had spread billions of seeds in thousands of varieties in the long-dead soil of Banaldar. The small animals were released and the habilitation crew left, taking Timothy along—leaving his dreams behind.

The lounge was filling up. He looked around, saw the agents of overpopulated areas, the buying agents of the industrial combines, the agents of the speculators who clawed into the crust of far places. They would be due for a surprise.

He remembered the look of Banaldar when he had last seen it. The only trace of the life that had once been there were the enormous trees—long dead. They dwarfed the redwoods of Earth and their bark was like wrought iron, so grooved and striated that a bold man could climb three hundred feet to the lowest limbs. Timothy had climbed and looked out over the world that he vowed would once be his.

It had taken five years to make certain that it would

be his. He knew that one day Transgalactic would put the five planets up for auction. Two thousand young people were behind the crisp check in Timothy's billfold. Slowly and relentlessly he had sold them his dreams.

A world to call your own—a beautiful Earth-size planet with rolling seas and gentle green hills—a place to become home, to raise children in, to set up the sort of society that Earth had long lacked and sadly needed. Maybe—maybe—it was the chance mankind had been waiting for. A thousand years would tell.

Some of those who had pleaded to join the group Timothy had turned down, regretfully but firmly. Others had been so desirable that, even though they could contribute next to nothing, he had spent months convincing them they should come.

It is no small thing to ask a man to move across space to a new world. But some dreams cannot be denied.

The auctioneer moved quietly to the front of the lounge and all conversation stopped,.

Even with the amplifiers his voice was so low as to be difficult to hear. "Today, gentlemen, we are auctioning off the five planets of Epsilon Aurigae, a convenient fifty-two light years from Earth.

"Those of you who have attended other auctions are familiar with our system. All bidding must open at our stated figure, which is just sufficient to cover our development expense plus a reasonable profit percentage. These five planets are the most desirable offered in recent months, all of them close enough to Earth-size to obviate gravitational difficulties, all of them quickly adjusting to our habitational procedures.

"There are three other planets circling the sun in question, two of them too close to be made livable and one too far out. The five will be offered for sale in the order of their distance from the sun. You have all had an opportunity to look over the charts, specifications and space photographs.

"The first planet has been named, in our literature,

Caenaral. The minimum bid is eight hundred and eight mil-pesos. I am bid nine hundred. Nine hundred is the bid. Nine twenty-five is the bid.

"World for sale, gentlemen. You will make no mistake on any one of the planets. Mineral concentrations are high. Nine hundred and fifty, fifty, fifty, seventy, one thousand. I hear one thousand. . . ."

The bidding went on. Timothy Trench slouched in his chair and the auctioneer's voice faded from his consciousness. He thought of other things. The first city, not really a city, must be where the great river emptied into the largest sea. They must not permit ugliness. For a long time the ship they traveled in must be their base.

The first planet was knocked down for one thousand seven hundred and sixty mil-pesos. The second one, less desirable, went for thirteen hundred mil-pesos. Timothy came quickly out of his dreams as he heard the man speak of Banaldar.

His strategy was firm in his mind. Leave the bidding alone—let it climb to where the bidding began to slow down—wait until the last moment and then put in a bid a full hundred mil-pesos higher.

He sat with his fingernails biting his palms. He was a tall man of thirty with coarse ginger-colored hair, with eyes used to probing vast distances. The bidding soared quickly to thirteen hundred and fifty, then began to slow down. As he was getting ready to put in his bid it gathered new momentum and went rapidly up to sixteen hundred and twenty-five. One of the chemical outfits made it sixteen thirty.

"I have been bid sixteen hundred and thirty. Do I hear forty? Sixteen hundred and thirty. Going for sixteen hundred and thirty. Going for—

"Seventeen hundred and fifty!" Timothy shouted.

The auctioneer peered at Timothy, recovered his aplomb. "The young man has made a bid of seventeen hundred and fifty. Going for—

"I bid nineteen hundred," a thick voice said. Timothy gasped and turned quickly. A heavily bearded man had bid the new figure. His clothes were rumpled and soiled.

"Two thousand!" Timothy said with a thin note of panic in his voice.

"Twenty-one hundred," the man said, his voice the slow and measured note of doom.

"Going for twenty-one hundred. Going, going, GONE to Mr.—uh—"

"I am Leader Morgan of the Free Lives," the rumpled heavy man said proudly.

"Oh? Yes, of course—the Free Lives," the auctioneer said. "You have the funds with you, of course."

"Hah!" Morgan said. "I notice you don't ask these others. But you ask me. Ruth! Harriet! Take him the money."

Two women came from the back. They staggered under the weight of heavy suitcases. They were drab worn-looking females with tight thin-lipped mouths, narrow eyes, long gray tubular dresses of a style utterly outmoded.

The auctioneer laughed in an embarrassed way. "It will take a long time to count all this."

Morgan stood up. "Count it when you have time. There are twenty-five hundred mil-pesos there. Count it and send me my change." He walked out.

Timothy caught the man in the main lobby. The man would have continued on if Timothy hadn't planted himself squarely in front of him. Morgan had a heavy animal smell about him. His small eyes were red-rimmed.

"Well?" he said.

"You bought Banaldar!"

"I seem to remember doing something of the sort, young fellow."

"This is serious to me. I—"

"Serious to you? Twenty-one hundred mil-pesos isn't a joke, my young friend."

"For five years I've been working and planning to buy Banaldar."

"So?"

"You can't take it this way. Look, give me some time. I'll see that you make a profit. Let me have some time and I'll buy it from you. I promise."

Morgan sucked at his teeth. He laughed. "No. We want it. It is a good place for the Free Lives. We go there now. We live there from now on. Not for five thousand mil-pesos can you have it. You know our group. We do not buy or sell for profit."

"You're some sort of sect, aren't you?"

"Sect? No. We are men and women. We live the way men and women were meant to live."

He pushed by Timothy and walked toward the door, the two women followed him meekly. "What are you going to do on Banaldar?" Timothy asked hopelessly.

Morgan turned. "Do? We live naked and eat berries and hunt with stones and clubs. What do you think men are meant to do? Live like this?" He included in an expressive gesture all of the glitter and bustle of the capital. "No. We live in caves and we fill our bellies and breed our children and sleep well at night. Good day to you. I have a lot to do. We all leave soon, seven hundred of us."

When the auction was over Timothy sought out the representative of Transgalactic Development. The man said, "That was quite a surprise, wasn't it? I mean that bunch of crazy-heads buying themselves a planet. They've been chased out of most respectable areas. Nudity and inability to accept moral codes have made them undesirable."

"How did they get that much money?"

The auctioneer shrugged. "I understand they've taken wealthy widows into the tribe with the understanding that they sign everything over to the Leader. There have been lawsuits but the Free Lives seem to be able to afford pretty good legal talent."

"I want to ask about something," Timothy said. "I've gone over the laws pretty carefully. If, for any reason, at the end of three years, the purchased planet has not been developed in any way and is not populated the sale can revert to the second highest bidder. Is that right?"

"Yes," the man said dubiously. "but only if the second bid money is left on deposit with Transgalactic as a guarantee of good faith. And I frankly don't see much point in such a move. Those Free Lives aren't going to vacate in a hurry. We have a lot of attractive planets in various stages of preparation for sale. Wouldn't it be better . . ."

Timothy Trench wrapped his big hand in the front of the auctioneer's jacket and shook him gently. "I want Banaldar," he said.

The man, who had started to be friendly, pushed Timothy's hand away coldly. "Suit yourself. The auction seems overcrowded with crazy people today. Come with me and we'll prepare the papers."

The two thousand, infected by Timothy's dream, had impatiently awaited word of the purchase. Many of them had burned bridges behind them. Their immediate disappointment at losing out on the legendary Banaldar was submerged in a mighty and towering anger when they found that Timothy, in a moment of amazingly poor judgment, had put the fund out of their reach for a three-year period.

They cursed themselves for fools, cursed Timothy for a charlatan. Eyes which had looked to the stars turned regretfully back to Earth and to the construction of bridges to replace the burned ones.

Timothy, after getting word to all his followers, haunted the Free Lives. He could not believe that they would actually embark for Banaldar. But at last, one cool morning, he stood on Take-off Mesa in the state of Hidalgo and watched the unwashed sleazy women, the whining brawling children, the heavy-bodied men, all carrying bundles of personal effects, file aboard the chartered converted freighter. Leader Morgan stood off to one side and watched them file aboard, scratching himself ruminatively.

Then there was the ballooning anti-grav lift, the straightening by means of the gyroscopes. At the warning gun, Timothy, the only spectator, turned away as did the port crews. The flash lit the countryside like a vast photo-bulb. When he looked again the freighter was gone. Timothy took the shuttle back to Mexico City and got thoroughly and completely drunk on a combination of mescal and pulque.

Two weeks later he awoke in a rancid hotel room in Rio, broke, dirty and with a bad case of the shakes. He presented himself at the nearest Reclaim Office, signed the agreement and was forthwith cleaned, fed and given employment. He worked mechanically and well and did not permit himself to think. To think meant Banaldar and thoughts of Banaldar hurt. It wasn't good to think of his virgin world infested with the Free Lives.

He could picture them, hunkered around their fires in the evening, strong teeth ripping meat from small animal bones, chanting gutturally for their crude dances— a scene from the dawn of man—whereas Timothy had planned that Banaldar would be the high noon of mankind. To think of Banaldar given over to brute orgy was like thinking of a lovely mistress assaulted in the dark alleys of an evil city.

And so Timothy Trench avoided thought as much as possible.

At the end of a full year he found that he had saved a respectable sum, two cien-pesos. For a time the money meant nothing to him. He was too far sunk in gloom. And then he began to wonder how Banaldar looked at the end of a year. It was, he guessed, a form of masochism.

He wondered and slowly wonder turned to determination. Maybe Leader Morgan didn't like Banaldar any more. Maybe he could be talked into leaving or selling. Determination strengthened into iron resolve. Timothy began to haunt the spaceports, to read the classified advertising.

And at last he found the two-man launch he wanted. It was six years old but the hull was sound. It had lodged only thirty-one months and the agency man said that it had belonged to an elderly couple who always brought it in like a feather.

Finally the agency man said, "Okay, okay. So we take a loss on it. I'll let you have it for two and a half cienpesos. Nobody ever made a better buy. You'll never regret it, fella."

Within two weeks, Timothy had got his license renewal, his space permit and his astrogation pattern. He took off for Banaldar.

As the launch bucked and shuddered and trembled its way out of hyper-flight, Timothy gagged and retched and shook his head until his vision cleared. It took a half hour to pick up his point of manual reference and plot his position. And then, with deep excitement in him, he saw the pin-head of light slowly growing larger, centered on the cross-hairs of the landing screen.

Within two hours continental land masses appeared, cloud formations like tiny white scatter rugs against them. He set the launch in orbit, braking it into concentric circles, watching the skin gauges as he hit the atmosphere. At ten thousand feet he nullified his own gravity to the equivalent of a five pound mass, peeled back the direct vision port and cruised slowly across the smiling sunlit face of the planet.

It was as he had imagined it would be. Around the tropical waist of Banaldar the vegetation was lush. Vast temperate plains were covered with grasses and he could see the waves that went across them as the winds blew. The seas were deep blue, rimmed with white surf. He found a desert and frowned, making plans as to how to correct it, then remembered with empty heart that this planet was not his.

He felt no need of sleep. He cruised on the edge of night, adjusting his speed to the planet rotation so that for many hours he was in perpetual dawn, the sun behind him.

At last he remembered that he was looking for the Free Lives. He had seen no sign of habitation but then he hadn't been searching diligently. Remembering their penchant for nudity he limited his search to the semi-tropical regions. The dense tropics would be too alive with the insects which had been released, the more temperate regions would be too cool.

He dropped to two thousand feet for his search. Exhaustion came before success. He fell asleep at his task and the launch settled slowly, landing with a gentle jar that did not awaken him.

After many hours he awoke refreshed, ate with new hunger and continued the search. And at last he found them. It angered him to see where they had settled. Right on the spot that he had once picked at potentially the finest on the planet. His judgment had proved to be right. The wide green-tinted river emptied down into the blue sea. The grasses were high. Dotted here and there were the scars of their fires and a haphazard arrangement of several hundred brush huts.

Timothy set the launch in the middle of the crude village. The little motor chattered busily as it unwound the port. He restored full gravity and felt the launch sink a few inches into the ground.

Timothy took a deep breath and stepped out onto the planet, stepped out onto his broken dream, stepped out to feel the sun warmth on his face, to smell growing things, to taste the spiced breeze against his lips. He turned quickly toward the launch and for a few moments he wept. Then, squaring his shoulders, he turned back and walked toward the nearest hut.

"Hallo!" he called. "*Hallo* there!"

No answer. He frowned and walked to the hut, noting that the grasses seemed to be recapturing the paths that wound through them. The crude doorway was low and the hut was windowless but tiny spots of sunshine slipped through holes in the brush and made yellow coins on the packed dirt floor.

Grass was beginning to sprout from the floor itself. A wide bed of grasses in the corner was parched and dry.

He called again and again, going from hut to hut, his voice loud in the great silence. At last he admitted to himself that the village, for some reason, was deserted. He found eight crude graves, a hundred small piles of sun-whitened animal bones, a listless attempt at the cultivation of wild grains, a broken bow.

In four days he had covered all of the rest of the planet and a new wild hope began to fill him. The Free Lives seemed to have disappeared from the surface of Banaldar. The impossible and improbable had happened. He whistled and sang as he searched. He made little poems about the personal habits of the Free Lives, admiring himself when they scanned.

And, finding nothing, he returned to the village to look for clues as to what might have happened.

Trees have leaves. That is a normal thing and thus a thing which is not noticed. Timothy had not noticed the leaves during his first look at the village. He noticed them the second time He looked casually at the trees and looked away, then swiveled back. The trees had leaves! Those five hundred foot monsters had leafed!

He realized at once what had happened. Throughout the long dead years before Transgalactic had arrived to give the planet life again a thin germ of life had remained in those monster trees, the root system reaching far enough down to tap the limited moisture. And now, with the new atmosphere and the warmth it brought, with the rains started again, with the whole planet stirring with life, the trees had come back.

It made him feel humble to think of the remarkable tenacity those aged giants had displayed. The mere idea of computing their age dizzied him.

For a little time his thoughts of the Free Lives were forgotten. Timothy walked through the waist-high grass toward the row of trees. Of twenty-one huge trees, only three had failed to come back.

They had leafed densely, making blots of shadow so dark that the grass was failing around the trunks. The wind had torn a leaf loose. He picked it up by the edge. It was a full yard across, colored a deep satin green. The stem of the leaf was as big around as his thumb.

He stood in the tree shadows and a curious feeling of peace came over him. It made him feel as though he had come home after a long, wearying journey.

He stood and tilted his head back and his glance ran up the trunk, up to the dark and secret places under the umbrella of overlapping leaves. Up there was rest and surcease and the soft happy end of striving and wanting and trying. In the gloom he could make out the clusters of fruit, pale fruit, swaying heavily, and he heard a warm sighing that was pleasant to his ears.

He yawned so deeply that he shuddered and, without conscious thought, he walked to the trunk of the tree, found the places to put his hands and feet and began climbing methodically up the trunk, not looking back, his eyes on the heavy darknesses above him. There was a happy song in him.

Not much longer now. This is where I belong. This place has been waiting in the back of my heart. Climb a bit faster and then it will come sooner. Climb faster. It's been waiting a long time. There's the first limb, just overhead. Move over to the side now and climb up even with it, beyond it, up and up and into the darkness and the beauty and the perfection. . . .

He went higher, climbing as though with long practice, his hands finding the holds before his eyes saw them. He realized he was waiting for something.

When he saw it he seemed to recognize it, it was a long flexible green-ribbed stalk, as big around as his wrist, the blunt end of it cupped and damp. He stopped climbing and clung to the bark. He smiled at the stalk. It brushed his shoulder, nuzzled like a puppy at his neck. He saw the pale fruit.

They hung in clusters, the Free Lives. They hung white and fat and soft, the green stalks entering the backs of their necks. They swayed a little in the breeze as they hung there. Their eyes were almost closed and their faces wore a look of utter and ineffable content.

Their fat-ringed arms and legs hung limp and their pallor was of a whiteness faintly tinged with green. From their parted lips came the soft minor-key sighing that he had heard from the ground, a sighing of ecstasy. Somehow the children were the worst. And all of them were incredibly bloated.

Horror broke the spell. The thing that nuzzled at the back of his neck had begun to nibble with a million little needle-teeth. Clinging with one hand Timothy struck it away, felt the tearing pain, felt the wetness run down between his shoulder blades. In his haste he nearly fell as he clambered down. The stalk reached down and hit him a bruising blow across the shoulders.

Timothy, gasping and sweating in panic, climbed down and down. He had lost the ease with which he had climbed up. When he was well out of the reach of the stalk, the feeling of peace and well-being suddenly became intensified. It was a siren song. He clung motionless, wanting to climb back up. But he looked at the white fruit, shut his teeth hard, continued descending.

Fifteen feet from the ground his hold slipped. He fell heavily, rolled to his feet and ran in panic away from the trees. A hundred yards away he dropped and lay panting, half-sobbing.

Back in the launch he dressed the circular wound in his neck and then stretched out on the bunk.

It would be so easy. Return to Transgalactic and claim that the planet had been vacated and demand the right to take possession. They might not give immediate approval but within a year and four months the three year period would be up and they would have to approve. Transgalactic might insist on a search of the planet but the odds were against their finding the Free Lives. Then he could warn the two thousand about the trees. "What do I owe those Free Lives?" he thought. "Dirty, primitive little bunch of misfits!"

But he thought of the children. The trees emitted some sort of hypnotic control. The specialists could find out what band the waves were on and shield themselves against it. Then the Free Lives could be cut down. Maybe the physiological changes had been so severe that to cut them down would mean killing them. Why take the chance? But he realized that he was rationalizing. The chance had to be taken. Humans deserved better than to be enlisted into the life cycle of a plant.

His mind made up, the loss of the planet a sickness within him, Timothy took off and drifted outside the atmospheric envelope that insulated space casts. With a fifty-two-minute transmission time he made his emergency report to Central Communications on Earth's moon. He waited and at last the answer came, promising a rescue ship within fourteen days.

When the rescue mission arrived the neuro-surgeons immediately took charge of Timothy Trench and it took them eleven days to bring him back from the brink of nearly hopeless insanity.

They found then that, during the fourteen days of waiting, the fruit had ripened, fallen, burst and its seed had taken root in the damp soil under the trees. Great care was taken to eliminate all the pale green shoots as well as the massive trees.

Transgalactic decided to make an exception to the waiting time in Timothy's case.